Emile Gaboriau

The Intrigues of a Poisoner, and Captain Coutanceau

Emile Gaboriau

The Intrigues of a Poisoner, and Captain Coutanceau

ISBN/EAN: 9783337091170

Printed in Europe, USA, Canada, Australia, Japan

Cover: Foto ©Andreas Hilbeck / pixelio.de

More available books at **www.hansebooks.com**

GABORIAU'S SENSATIONAL NOVELS.

XII.

THE

INTRIGUES OF A POISONER,

AND

CAPTAIN COUTANCEAU.

By ÉMILE GABORIAU

TWENTIETH THOUSAND.

LONDON:

VIZETELLY & CO., 42 CATHERINE STREET, STRAND.

1886.

THE INTRIGUES OF A POISONER.

I.

IT was Wednesday, November 15th, 1665, and there was a supper that night, and a numerous assemblage at the establishment kept in the Rue Vieille-du-Temple, by La Vienne, the fashionable bather and *étuviste*, and most renowned barber of the time.

The Parisians of the present day, who fancy they have reached the acme of civilisation and comfort, because they have erected taverns and other convivial resorts, will, no doubt, require us to explain to them what was understood by the terms barber, bather and *étuviste*, during the earlier years of the reign of Louis XIV. In the seventeenth century Paris numbered far more establishments where warm baths or *étuvies* were provided for the middle and lower classes, than there now-a-days exist. And scattered through the city there was a large number of taverns and inns for folks of all degrees, with a few magnificently furnished hotels. The latter were frequented by such members of the higher nobility who did not belong to the court and possessed no mansions in Paris.

For the members of the aristocracy having houses of their own, for the noblemen attached to the royal household, there were one or two establishments of a particular class, which it is extremely difficult to define, as none of the kind now-a-days exist. These establishments were generally kept by men expert in everything pertaining to the toilet, and renowned for their dexterity in dressing the hair of noblemen and ladies.

Barbers and bath-keepers followed the same profession in those days—forming a corporation known as that of the *barbiers-étuvistes ;* but the owner of the establishment we speak of, and who enjoyed a higher reputation than his fellows, was not bound by the rules of this corporation. He plied his calling by a special licence, which emanated either from one of the princes or from one of the great dignitaries of the state.

People repaired to his establishment for different reasons. First of all, from motives of health and cleanliness ; and indeed, the best baths could be had here, for instance, depilatory baths, and others mingled with perfumes and cosmetics, which imparted increased strength to the body, additional softness to the skin, and greater flexibility to the limbs.

The establishment was provided with discreet, reserved, and skilful servants. People shut themselves up there on the eve of a departure, or on the day of an arrival, so as to prepare themselves for the fatigue they would

have to endure, or to recover from that which they had just undergone.
Did any one wish to disappear from society for a moment, avoid duns and
bores, or escape from the inquisitive eyes of servants—he had simply to repair to the bath-keeper's, where he found himself duly attended to, feasted
and pampered.   All the pleasures akin to luxury or depravity could indeed
be found there.

The landlord and his retainers guessed by your signs or looks whether
you wished to remain *incognito*, and every one around you, though they
knew you well, appeared ignorant even of your name.   Your arrival, and
your sojourn in this mysterious place, were indeed like a secret never revealed.

And thus to the bath-keeper's went women who could not otherwise escape
from jealous supervision.   They repaired there, disguised, with their faces
hidden by masks, and alone or accompanied by their lovers.   Moreover,
youthful lords, the friends of unrestrained pleasure and free love, often
met at these places and indulged in wine and gambling, in the society of
those courtesans who through all ages have known how to entice the ama-
teurs of seasoned pleasure.

However, La Vienne's establishment was so extensive and so skilfully arranged, that the presence of these noisy or guilty guests could not be suspected from outside.   Everything was quiet and orderly in the neighbourhood.   In fact this Babel of aristocratic and refined vice had every appearance of being the abode of virtue.   At the time of his earlier passions, Louis
XIV. himself had several times visited La Vienne's, and he was subsequently
pleased to make him one of his grooms of the bed-chamber.

At the moment we introduce the reader to La Vienne's, supper was just
over, innumerable flagons had been drained, and gambling was at its height.
Round the table, on which glittered piles of gold mingling a tawny light
with the illumination of the pink tapers in the girandoles, there crowded a
number of individuals, who although extremely different in appearance,
did not scruple to jostle one another in the fraternity of inebriation; among
them were officers whose only fortune was their sword, libertine abbés,
clerical financiers, titled blacklegs and courtesans from the court, the city
and the stage.

M. de Sainte-Croix, a captain in the regiment of Tracy-Cavalerie, was
playing against Maître Hanyvel, lord of Saint-Laurent and receiver-general
of the French clergy.   The Chevalier Gaudin de Sainte-Croix had given
proof of his courage in the army, and his wit and liveliness had long been
appreciated in the drawing-rooms of the capital.

Little was known of his family, which some asserted to be an humble
one of Montauban, and even less was known respecting his fortune ; but he
maintained that he was a bastard of a great family, and his mien supported
his assertion.   Money slipped as easily through his fingers as his sword
from its scabbard.   In other respects he was a man of five-and-thirty, good-
looking, and of pleasant address, lettered and polished, prodigal, ever ready
to fall in love, jealous to madness, and embarking in a charitable undertaking with the same zest as he would engage in a pleasure party.   He was
noted for the elegance of his attire, his feathers were always irreproachable,
and the invariable freshness of his ruffles spoke greatly in his favour.
More was not asked of him in a society which had seen Philippe d'Orleans,
the king's brother, pick citizens' pockets on the Pont Neuf, and which was
destined to see the Comte de Horn drawn and quartered on the Place de
Grève, for having murdered a money-monger of the Rue de Venise.

For the moment M. de Sainte-Croix was in luck. The money of Hanyvel the financier was passing to his side of the table, and the pile was constantly growing larger. So the actresses from the Hôtel de Bourgogne, the "demoiselles" from the Comédie-Italicune, the chance marchionesses and *incognito* countesses, who formed the usual company at La Vienne's suppers, favoured him with killing glances and engaging smiles. But the chevalier remained as stoical in presence of gain as in presence of loss.

It was not the same with his adversary, the treasurer of the French clergy, who had lost three hundred pistoles, and bewailed them as much as if he had lost a million.

"Shall I take your place, Hanyvel?" asked the young Marquis de Rubentel, suddenly.

"No, indeed," replied the financier. "Had I to empty all the coffers of their lordships, the bishops of Languedoc, I must find out how long the chevalier's luck will last."

"Oh," carelessly rejoined M. de Sainte-Croix, "I required a few thousand crowns for my charities, and I could not do better than apply to the clergy's banker."

"Chevalier," said the Marquise de Soubiran, "lend me fifty pistoles to play against you."

"Here they are, marquise; but be careful, they will come back to me."

"If they return to you I will follow them," resolutely replied the young woman.

"Do we double the stakes?" asked Hanyvel.

"Willingly, only I beg to give you notice that it is ten o'clock, and in an hour's time I must cease playing, as I have an appointment elsewhere."

"An appointment!" exclaimed Marietta Zambolini of the Comédie-Italienne. "I'll bet it is with one of those shrews from the Hôtel de Bourgogne!"

"Unless it is with one of those grasshoppers from the Théâtre de la Foire," rejoined Mademoiselle Aurore de Boisrosé, tragedian in ordinary to the king.

Hereupon La Zambolini flung a glass at the head of Mademoiselle de Boisrosé, but Sainte-Croix caught it as it passed before him.

"Softly, my darlings," he said, "you make such a noise that one cannot hear M. de Hanyvel lose."

"Has he lost again?" exclaimed the fair Aurore.

"Of course!" muttered the financier with some show of temper, "the chevalier is so lucky he must carry about him a piece of the rope which he will one day be hanged with."

Mademoiselle Aurore slipped on to the chevalier's knees. "Give me my share," said she.

"Did we go halves?"

"Certainly, as you have won."

The Marquise de Soubiran, who defrayed the expenses of a young lieutenant of musketeers, now whispered to the Présidente d'Embermesnil, who was ruining a tax receiver: "These actresses move me to compassion. They would sell themselves for a crown."

"We pity you still more," retorted La Zambolini, who had overheard her. "You would give yourself for nothing."

This remark caused a perfect uproar. The aristocratic belles rose up to protest both with tongue and nails. The actresses prepared to charge them;

but Rubentel and others darted between the conflicting parties, while Sainte-Croix threw two or three handfuls of pistoles on to the floor. Thereupon ladies and actresses alike forgot their quarrel in their eagerness to appropriate these spoils.

"All this," said the Abbé de Sourdry, "does not tell us, chevalier, who you expect to-night at your quarters in the Rue des Bernadins."

"Is it my cousin, De Flavigny?" asked Rubentel.

"Or my sister-in-law, De Chastellny?" continued the abbé.

"Or La Champmeslée?" queried another.

"Or the lovely draper from the Rue des Gravilliers?" added a third.

"Or the Duchesse de Chaulnes?"

"Or little Florimonde of the mountebank troupe on the Pont Neuf?"

"Or I?" asked Madame de Soubiran.

"Or us?" asked La Zambolini and La Boisrosé.

"You are all singularly mistaken," replied Sainte-Croix. "I shall receive two persons this evening : one of them my confessor, and the other a professor of chemistry."

"You believe in God, then, chevalier?" exclaimed the abbé.

"As I am not in orders I can answer, yes."

"And in the evil one?" asked Aurore.

"You once made me believe in him for an hour."

However, the game continued. The men drank and the women laughed. Whilst playing with unequalled skill, Sainte-Croix remarked, "My confessor, a very eloquent and learned Jesuit, has called my attention to several points of the new doctrines. I have given these points a serious and thoughtful examination ; and the result of my researches is a book which I intend to publish shortly. I am pious, gentlemen, and I glory in the fact ; but my piety has nothing that censures or embarrasses about it, and the deity I revere is too reasonable to wish to thwart the passions with which he has endowed me. I believe, besides, that there are several ways of serving the State ; and after having served it with my sword, I am trying to benefit it with my knowledge. This is why I think when I don't play, why I seek when I am not fighting, why I find when I do not love. At present science is my only mistress."

"And what kind of science, chevalier?"

"Toxicology."

"What is that?" asked the women.

"It is the knowledge of poisons," quietly answered Sainte-Croix.

The play had not ceased. Gold was still rolling over the table, and luck was decidedly against the financier, for the captain won unceasingly. Suddenly, however, he paused, and looking successively at his watch and the cards, he said, "You have again lost, Hanyvel, and now I must go."

"Double," urged the financier.

"Double," repeated Sainte-Croix, although this was interverting the parts.

Once more the chevalier won.

"Double," again urged Hanyvel in a querulous tone.

"Double or quits, if you like," replied his adversary. "I assure you I must go."

"There's a fine player," muttered the men.

The women said nothing ; but the chevalier and his crowns had to stand a fire of killing glances. Madame de Soubiran even threw the key of her boudoir into the midst of the stakes.

"If I win," said Sainte-Croix, "I shall return it to Guébriac." But this time luck turned ; the chevalier lost. "Good-night, gentlemen," he said, coldly. And pushing towards Hanyvel the piles of gold which had not ceased to accumulate in front of him throughout the evening, he rose up and ordered a valet to bring him his hat and his sword.

The financier jubilantly wallowed among his crowns. "I knew very well," he said, "that the proverb couldn't be false."

"What proverb?" asked Sainte-Croix, while he buckled on his belt.

"You know it as well as I do. 'Lucky at cards—'"

"'Unlucky in love,' isn't that it? But I'm not married, Monsieur Hanyvel."

"It's true your friends are married for you."

The chevalier, who was on his way to the door, turned round abruptly. "What do you mean by that?" he asked, haughtily.

"I'm merely repeating what everybody says."

"And what does everybody say?"

"Don't be too modest, my good fellow. Everyone knows that Monsieur de Brinvilliers is one of your intimate friends, and that the excellent marquis possesses a very attractive wife, who must have sought in you what she did not find in him. Besides—"

But the financier did not finish ; for Sainte-Croix, drawing his sword, rushed impetuously towards him.

"What are you doing? what are you doing?" exclaimed everyone in the room.

"Can you not see?" answered the chevalier in a furious passion. "This man is a knave, and, by heavens ! he sha'n't utter his calumnies elsewhere."

Meanwhile Hanyvel endeavoured to draw his sword ; he was paler than a corpse. Several men attempted to restrain the chevalier and disarm him, which was no easy matter, while the scared women sought refuge in the corners of the room.

However, at this moment, the door opened ; one of Sainte-Croix's lackeys entered, and making his way through the excited throng, he succeeded in reaching his master and whispered these words in his ear : "You are awaited, monsieur."

The chevalier already had his hand on Hanyvel, but on hearing his servant's words, he took two steps backwards. The tempest of wrath gathered on his brow was suddenly dispelled, and he burst into a loud laugh. Then sheathing his sword again, he exclaimed, "Come, monsieur, the treasurer of the clergy, collect yourself. Your hide is no longer wanted ; and you are so ugly when you tremble that you have actually terrified these ladies. But thank La Chaussée, who checked me in time ; for had it not been for him, as truly as the Marquise de Brinvilliers is the chastest woman in the world, I intended to cut your ears off."

With these words he bowed to the company with a proud bearing and left the room.

Hanyvel proceeded to pocket his money. Mademoiselle Aurore de Bois-rosé and the Signorina Marietta Zambolini hastened to assist him in this task and to sympathise with him for his mishap.

Affrays of this kind were frequent at that time between those who carried swords in public resorts such as La Vienne's establishment. So after the departure of the chevalier, the others returned to their pleasure as though nothing whatever had happened.

One of the gentlemen present had to all appearance evinced the greatest

interest in this dispute, though he had taken no part in it. His name was
Reich de Penautier, and he was the treasurer of the States of Languedoc.
A friend of Hanyvel's, he had not even moved when Sainte-Croix threatened
the financier with his sword; but with his elbow resting on the marble
chimney-piece, against the whiteness of which his black velvet cloak, trimmed
with jet, stood out in bold, fantastical relief, he had surveyed the whole
scene with an impassive face. However, when the quarrel ceased—almost
as suddenly as it had begun—and when the chevalier had sheathed his
sword again, a gleam of vexation shot from M. de Penautier's eyes, and his
thin, pale lips parted to give utterance to this one word, "Blockhead!"
Sainte-Croix, having gone, M. de Penautier at once ordered his carriage.

II.

FATHER AND HUSBAND.

WHILE the scene we have described was taking place at La Vienne's establishment, a plain coach, draped according to the fashion then in vogue,
drew up in front of the richly carved door of the Hôtel de Brinvilliers, one
of the most magnificent houses of the Rue des Lions-Saint-Paul, in the district of the Marais, which was the aristocratic quarter during the seventeenth
century.
Almost immediately, and before the footman had time to lower the heavy
step, three people alighted from the vehicle—two young men and an old
one.
The old man, dressed in the costume of the previous century, was M.
Dreux d'Aubray, a lieutenant of police, who had been one of the councillors of
Anne of Austria during the Fronde. He was the father of the Marquise de
Brinvilliers, and the two young fellows who accompanied him were his
sons.
The trio paused and held council under the archway, and after a few
minutes had elapsed one of them made a sign to the coachman, who, whip-
ping up his horses, went off at a brisk trot in the direction of the Place Royale. The young men then turned up the collars of their cloaks, lowered the
brims of their large felt hats, and posted themselves at some distance in
a recess formed by a wall.
As for M. d'Aubray, he raised the heavy knocker which fell back noisily,
arousing the echoes of the deserted street. The door swung on its hinges
with a loud clanking of chains and bolts; the porter bowed respectfully on
recognising the marquise's father, and at his order a valet, carrying two
candles and walking backwards, preceded the lieutenant of police up the
stairs leading to Monsieur de Brinvilliers' room.
He was a very worthy man, the Marquis de Brinvilliers, colonel of the
regiment of Normandy. War left him but little leisure, but he put it out
at interest, and was considered a good player and generous lover in the
pleasure-seeking society of officers and yielding women. He had all but
exhausted his fortune in trying to gain this reputation; but he cared very
little about that, and his mind was at ease since he had placed his wife's
dowry out of the reach of his creditors. He had settled her property upon
her, not that he might have it to fall back upon, he was too much of a nobleman to entertain such middle-class ideas, but so as to prevent her from suffering on account of his extravagance.

M. de Brinvilliers had at first been deeply in love with his wife, but time had greatly cooled his passion. There now remained but a sweet and confiding intimacy between them, and according to the custom of the age, the marquis troubled himself very little about his wife's conduct, gallantly leaving her as much liberty as he claimed for himself.

That evening the marquis was reclining in a large arm-chair by the fireside in his study. He was half asleep, having sat up late at supper the night before, and having gambled with persistent ill-luck throughout the day. So he was disagreeably surprised when a footman timidly opened the door and announced M. Dreux d'Aubray.

However, the marquis was too well bred to show his annoyance at being awakened in this manner. He rose with apparent eagerness, and went to meet his father-in-law. After the usual embraces and compliments, he ventured to inquire, " Dear me, monsieur, has anything vexatious happened to you, to bring a person of your quiet habits to my house at this hour ? I should be almost pleased if such were the case, in order to place myself and all belonging to me at your disposal."

The lieutenant of police did not immediately answer. He slowly seated himself opposite the marquis, and after a pause of a few seconds, during which he appeared to be reflecting, he said :

" Believe me, monsieur, when I tell you that it is extremely painful to me to have to speak to you on a subject which I consider a disgrace to my family. I have come to speak to you about my daughter."

" About my wife ? "

" Unfortunately, yes ! And also about the Chevalier de Sainte-Croix."

The marquis assumed the doleful air of a man threatened with a tedious sermon, and who regretfully realises that he cannot escape it. He heaved a deep sigh. " Well, what has the poor chevalier done now ? " he asked.

" What has he done ? " replied M. d'Aubray. " Look here, marquis, there are none so blind as those who won't see, and I believe you belong to the class. The Chevalier de Sainte-Croix abuses your confidence shamefully, and my daughter, your wife, is his accomplice."

" You are mistaken, monsieur."

" I am positive of it."

" Well, what can I do in the matter ? " asked the marquis, impatiently. " The Chevalier de Sainte-Croix is my friend, the most upright man that ever breathed. After knowing him for a long time in the army, I brought him to my house and introduced him to my wife. At first she seemed to feel an unaccountable aversion for him, but by degrees she appeared interested in his conversation, which is always very witty ; and upon my word, between my wife and my friend, I considered myself the happiest man living."

" That is to say they were plotting to deceive you."

" You told me so, or rather you told me that this friendship caused scandal, and so I reluctantly closed my door to the chevalier, whom I miss more than you can imagine. Does not that suffice ? "

" No, you must still watch your wife ! "

" For shame, monsieur ! would you wrong me to the extent of believing me jealous of the marquise ? Understand that I trust her implicitly."

" She deceives you."

" Allow me to doubt it ; I only believe what I see."

The lieutenant of police angrily struck the arm of his chair. " And supposing I proved it to you," he said, rising. " If I showed you—"

"You would certainly cause me great grief and it would be but a sorry service you would render me. But I am at rest on that score," concluded the marquis, laughing.

"And you are wrong," sternly replied M. d'Aubray, "you are wrong; for in this instance I, the father, have fulfilled the duty appertaining to you, the husband, and I am able to give you proofs."

"Come," objected the marquis, "let us admit for a moment that your suppositions are correct, in what way can the matter affect me? Did not the marquise bare me heirs to my name during the early years of our marriage?"

"What!" cried the indignant lieutenant of police, "is this the value you set on the honour of families and the virtue of women? Yes, I know what you are about to say—you are going to mention the example of some of the noblest families in the kingdom, so as to show me that it is in good taste to act as an indulgent husband and close one's eyes to the errors of an unworthy wife. But I do not belong to the court, monsieur, and I do not consider my name above dishonour. You are free to abdicate the sacred rights with which God and men have fortified you, but I shall know how to uphold the privileges of my forefathers. It is now for you to decide whether you will follow me and join my sons who await us outside."

"At this time of night and in this weather?"

"Honour requires it, monsieur, the honour of two noble houses whose escutcheons have been stainless until now This scandal must be put a stop to."

"Very well, I am at your service," answered the marquis. "I will follow you, though I really don't see what will be gained by all this."

Taking his hat and cloak from a valet, the Marquis de Brinvilliers thereupon followed M. d'Aubray.

When the heavy door had closed behind them, the lieutenant of police uttered a peculiar cry which had doubtless been agreed upon with his sons, for the two young men left their post of observation and approached immediately.

"Well?" asked M. d'Aubray.

"Nothing as yet," replied the young men.

"Let us wait, then ; she cannot be much longer."

"Now, monsieur," impatiently exclaimed the marquis, "will you kindly tell me what we are doing here?"

"Certainly, since you refuse to understand anything," replied M. d'Aubray in a husky voice. "We are waiting for your wife, who leaves your house every evening in order to keep an appointment with her lover."

"Ah!" said the marquis. "So she leaves the house every evening? Really, I did not suspect it."

"We are going to follow her," added the lieutenant of police, "and when you have surprised the culprits you will be convinced."

"Let us wait, then," answered the marquis.

"Not here," observed one of the young men, "we should not see her ; she uses the garden gate when she goes out at night."

"So she knows of the little gate," said the marquis. "I was under the impression that I alone had its key. Really, it is very considerate of her to take such precautions, for she could easily leave by the front door."

"Rest assured, it is not from us that your wife conceals herself," rejoined M. d'Aubray. "She knows us too well to do that."

The four crossed the street and concealed themselves in the recess where the two young men had awaited their father during his conversation with the marquis. M. de la Reynie had not yet introduced street lamps into Paris, and the moon, to which the lighting of the capital was exclusively intrusted, fulfilled its duty very badly on this occasion. The night was extremely dark, and one of those fine and penetrating rains, peculiar to the capital of beautiful France, was steadily falling.

Still, from where they stood the four watchers could see the gateway of the mansion distinctly enough, for it was dimly lighted by a small lamp glimmering dismally in a niche below a little statue of the Virgin. For about half an hour none of the watchers spoke, save that from time to time the marquis interrupted the stillness of the night with a muttered oath. At length, unable to restrain himself any longer, he observed to his father-in-law : " Don't you consider, monsieur, that we are plying a nasty calling here and fruitlessly besides ? "

" Hush ! " replied M. d'Aubray.

" It is abominable weather," continued the marquis, " and all I can fore-see from this is an attack of rheumatism."

Neither M. d'Aubray nor his sons answered him.

" By the fiend's horns," continued the marquis, whose ill temper was momentarily increasing, " we should be infinitely better off in our beds. As regards myself, I am beginning to be inconvenienced by several wounds I received in Flanders."

" For heaven's sake, marquis, a truce to recriminations," whispered the elder of the two young men.

By way of reply the marquis stifled an oath, and then silence reigned once more.

At last the clock in the belfry of the chapel of the Célestine monastery mournfully struck ten, and the dismal sounds died away in the fog.

" She won't come to-night," said M. d'Aubray, impatiently.

But, almost at the same moment, the little garden gate was partly opened, and a woman stealthily popped out her head ; she seemed to be peering into the darkness, and trying to penetrate its depths as though she suspected that some danger lurked there.

" Here she is, father," whispered the youngest M. d'Aubray.

" Upon my word, it is really she," said the marquis.

The marquise, for she it was, reassured, no doubt, by the quiet of the street, decided to sally forth ; she glided gently through the gateway, and closed the gate after her, making visible efforts to deaden the grating of the key in the lock. For a moment she seemed to hesitate as to which road she should take ; but soon making up her mind, she went off rapidly through the by-streets leading to the Place de Grève.

When she had almost disappeared from view, the lieutenant of police turned to his sons and said : " Follow her ; two men will alarm her less than one ; the marquis and I will remain behind."

The two brothers hastened to follow in the steps of their sister.

" Well ! " sadly remarked M. d'Aubray.

" In truth," replied the marquis, " you see me as astonished as one can well be. What strength of purpose ! Who would have believed that the marquise, who seems so timid and nervous, would dare to venture out alone at such a time of night in the streets which are, now-a-days, far from safe. It is really too imprudent."

" You would, doubtless, have advised her to take a footman," mockingly remarked the lieutenant of police.

"Certainly," replied the marquis in perfect good faith, "and it would have been more worthy of her position and mine if she had taken a coach."

The lieutenant was unable to stifle an expression of anger ; but not considering it an opportune moment for a discussion, he did not give vent to the scornful words that were on the tip of his tongue. The father and the husband continued on their course in silence, without losing sight of the young men who preceded them in the wake of the marquise.

She was walking along with a quick and determined step, keeping close to the houses as if to conceal herself in the shadows they threw, and invariably turning from her path, and crossing the street whenever she espied one of the few lamps which devout citizens lighted in front of some holy image ; she feared, no doubt, that its feeble flickering light might betray her. On she went, regardlessof the puddles and open drains which in those days transformed Paris into a perfect quagmire, so that in rainy weather only those who were willing to sacrifice their clothing, ventured forth on foot for any distance.

On reaching the Place de Grêve, she waited for a minute in order to let a patrol pass by. At that time folks hardly knew which they ought to fear the most—night-guards or thieves. Gliding round the Place, still keeping close to the houses, the marquise now walked towards the Louvre, along narrow and almost impassable alleys which crossed and intertwined one with another in a maze-like manner round about the palace of the burgesses.*

She walked thus as far as the church of St. Germain L'Auxerrois, which doubtless served her as a beacon ; for once there, she appeared to collect herself for a moment, secured her velvet mask, drew forward her hood, which the wind had raised, and rapidly retraced her steps.

M. d'Aubray and his sons were, no doubt, prepared for this change of tactics, for they had joined one another, and dragging the marquis with them, had concealed themselves between two buttresses of the old church. The marquise passed close to them without perceiving their presence. She then turned into the Rue de l'Arbre-Sec, and the four men emerging from their hiding place overtook her in time to see her enter a hostelry of equivocal appearance, over the door of which there swung, creaking in a most lugubrious fashion, a sign which represented a swarthy white turbaned Moor, who was blowing with all his lungs in a huge trumpet. It was the well-known sign of the *More-qui-trompe.*

With one accord M. d'Aubray, his sons, and the marquis peered through the grimy windows of the hostelry, and were able to see the marquise take a key from the landlord, who bowed respectfully, and then spring up the stairs like a woman familiar with the people and the ways of the house.

"What a disgrace !" sadly exclaimed the lieutenant of police ; and he added in a lower key, "To think that my daughter dares to frequent such a hole."

"At least it shows discretion," said one of the brothers. "Look, father, at the men who are drinking in this room ; not one of them would suspect that the woman who had just gone upstairs is our sister, the Marquise de Brinvilliers."

At this moment two drunkards came out of the hostelry singing boisterously, and the four watchers were compelled to draw aside.

"What a hole !" reiterated M. d'Aubray.

* The Hôtel de Ville of now-a-days.—*Trans.*

"Oh ! stop a minute," answered the marquis. " Don't judge the place by its appearance ; it is a thoroughly respectable house, I assure you."

" You know it?" asked M. d'Aubray.

"Certainly, I have often supped there with my friend Penautier, the treasurer of the States of Languedoc—a very gallant fellow, I assure you."

" Then you know something about the arrangements of the apartments, marquis ?"

" No one better, by the fiend's horns ! The first floor is very different to this ; there are some rooms there as richly furnished as those in my house, and the cooking of Master Hugonnet, the landlord of the *More-qui-trompe* is not to be despised by any means."

The marquis, led away by his recollections would, no doubt, have continued in this strain if the lieutenant of police had not cut him short.

" Well, are you convinced ?" the latter asked.

" Of what ?"

" Why—of your wife's infidelity ?"

" Not at all. My wife is very pious. How do you know she is not here on some errand of charity ? Moreover, she is passing credulous and may have come to consult a sorceress. Sorceresses are all the fashion just now. They have taken the place of the flounced dresses à la Montespan. Besides, it doesn't follow that the Chevalier de Sainte-Croix is in the house."

"That is what we shall now ascertain," said the youngest of the Messieurs d'Aubray, and thereupon he whistled in a peculiar manner.

Immediately afterwards a man, who had hitherto been crouching so closely against the wall on the opposite side of the way that he could not be perceived, stepped forward and reached the party.

" Desgrais," asked the lieutenant of police in a whisper, " has M. de Sainte-Croix arrived ?"

" Not yet, monsieur," answered the new-comer, " but he will not be much longer, for his valet, La Chaussée, has gone to fetch him from La Vieune's where he was supping. But listen, I fancy—"

One could indeed hear the step of a cavalier at the farther end of the street.

"It is he," continued Desgrais with that quick scent which the police agents of those days have bequeathed to the detectives of the present time. " We mustn't stir ; the chevalier cannot see us where we are."

The group remained motionless, and thanks to the fog it was so difficult to distinguish it amid the surrounding objects that the Chevalier de Sainte-Croix, for he it really was, did not even suspect the presence of his foes.

He entered the hostelry, followed by his lackey, spoke a few words to the landlord, and disappeared up the same stairs that the marquise had previously ascended, whilst La Chaussée sat down in front of a flagon of sufficient capacity to beget patience.

For the third time that evening the lieutenant of police addressed the marquis with the manner of a judge.

" Well, monsieur," he asked, " are you at length convinced?"

"I own," replied the marquis, "that a jealous husband might entertain some doubts."

" Well, what do you contemplate doing, Monsieur le Marquis de Brinvilliers ?"

"I am very embarrassed. Between noblemen these differences are generally settled on the field of honour."

"You cannot think of it, marquis? A man does not fight with a fellow who has robbed him of his honour."

"Well, monsieur, see to the matter yourself. I know many husbands would not scruple to use a lettre-de-cachet in such a case; but apart from the means being distasteful to me, I must admit that I have none with me."

"I have one, monsieur, and the man you see there has been placed at my disposal to execute the order which I personally solicited of his Majesty."

"What! you wish—"

For sole answer the lieutenant of police turned towards Desgrais. "Are all your precautions taken?" he asked.

"Be easy, monsieur," answered the agent, "the Chevalier de Sainte-Croix won't play us false; for though only a beginner in the business, I have prepared everything and provided for all emergencies, and it is such an honour for me to work for your family, that I shall feel disgraced if within two hours from now the man you have named to me is not between four walls behind the bolts of the Bastille."

"What are we waiting for then?"

"A coach which one of my sergeants has gone for."

"The poor chevalier will be grateful to you for this attention," exclaimed the marquis; "but is my presence here really necessary?"

"What! do you wish to leave us, monsieur?" asked the lieutenant of police.

"Between ourselves, an arrest has always been a painful sight to me. The fate of the chevalier distresses me more than you imagine, and although he has wronged me, according to your showing at least, still if he were to appeal to our former friendship I believe, God forgive me, that I would draw my sword on these rascals in order to set him free."

"Then farewell, monsieur; it is I who will avenge your honour."

M. de Brinvilliers took a couple of steps forward, and then turning to his father-in-law he said, "Above all, mind you tell the chevalier that I have taken no part in this absurd affair."

III.

THE HOSTELRY OF THE MORE-QUI-TROMPE.

THE Marquis de Brinvilliers had spoken truly when he mentioned the sumptuous character of the apartments on the first floor of the *More-qui-trompe*.

Host Hugonnet, like a man acquainted with the requirements of the times, had accumulated in this part of his house all the superfluities of refined luxury; and if he continued keeping a common drinking den downstairs, frequented by the worst characters, it was because he knew that the more disreputable his establishment appeared the greater would be the security of the noblemen or titled dames who sought out his house as a safe shelter for their intrigues.

And we may here remark that host Hugonnet did not lack customers, and good ones too, so that his neighbours, although they censured his trade, could not help envying him the comfortable fortune they imagined he possessed.

Certainly, on entering the common room the most attentive observer would never have suspected the mysteries of the upper floors. The beams of the ceiling were black and damp, the walls were stained, the tables rickety and dirty, and the floor almost as sodden as the street outside. The rude staircase, the first steps of which were to be seen at the rear, could, to all appearance, only conduct to some wretched garret.

But at the tenth step the aspect of this staircase suddenly changed. A treble door carefully padded, and covered with rags on the side facing the pot-room, shut it off ; but once this door was opened the wonders began. The bannisters were of precious wood, thick carpets covered the steps, and high tapestry hangings draped the walls.

The marquise, as we have already said, rapidly ascended this staircase, and opening a small door at the end of a narrow passage, entered a sumptuous apartment where host Hugonnet, with commendable foresight, had prepared everything for her reception. Perfumed tapers burned in the candelabra, a large fire blazed cheerily in the hearth, and in a corner of the room a dainty collation was spread out on a small rosewood table.

Having carefully closed the door, the marquise took off her cloak, removed her mask, and rapidly exchanged her wet and mud-stained clothes for a coquettish négligé, laid out for her in an adjoining dressing-room.

She then breathed more freely ; plainly enough she felt at home after her transformation. She wheeled a spacious arm-chair to the fireside, languidly stretched herself out in it, and presented her tiny feet, encased in dainty velvet slippers, to the gentle warmth of the fire.

Madame la Marquise Marie Madeleine de Brinvilliers was then in the full pride of her beauty : she was short, but admirably formed and harmoniously proportioned ; her oval face had all the childlike grace and enchanting delicacy with which Largillière has endowed several of the feminine portraits he painted. Her calm, deep blue eyes were at times softly caressing, while at others their beams were tempered by an expression of gentle melancholy. Betwixt the purple of her slightly disdainful lips there gleamed a double row of pearls.

No expression of fear or emotion ever disturbed the calm of her open ingenuous countenance. Such was the command that the marquise possessed over herself, that her features never betrayed the horrible agonies and piercing emotions that tortured her soul. Although subsequently implicated in the darkest tragedies and the most frightful crimes, she maintained, even before her judges and in the torture room, the same cold and smiling impassiveness. No one ever saw her blush or look disturbed. You might have taken her for a lovely statue—a chef-d'œuvre—chiselled out of a block of ice from the Polar seas. She was, as it were, Galatea ere Pygmalion, anxious to endow his creation with life, purloined for her the vital spark.

For about a quarter of an hour or so Madame de Brinvilliers had been dosing by the fireside, when the sonorous sound of a large clock placed between two windows startled her.

"He doesn't come," she murmured, "and I was afraid I should keep him waiting !"

She rose as she spoke and took several steps across the room with evident impatience. "Has anything happened to him ?" she continued.

But at the same moment the door opened, and Sainte-Croix stood smiling on the threshold.

"At last!" exclaimed the marquise, pointing to the hands of the clock which now marked half past eleven.

"Yes, I know," said the chevalier. "I have to beg your forgiveness." And sinking on to his knees at the marquise's feet, he covered the lovely hands she extended to him with kisses.

"However, I can assure you," he said, as he rose again, "that these few moments cost me dear. To come here more quickly, I have allowed a handsome pile of pistoles to pass into Maître Hanyvel's pockets."

"So you always gamble, chevalier?"

"Well!" said Sainte-Croix lovingly, "what would you have me do when I am far from your lovely eyes? Yes, I gamble for lack of anything better to do; but, dear heart, don't let us talk of such trifles, our time is too short and too precious for us to think of anything save our love."

"Alas!" sighed the marquise, "the hours we spend together each evening, and which constitute my only happiness, will perhaps be taken from us."

"What do you mean, Madeleine?"

"I do not know, dear, but I feel vaguely anxious as though some great danger threatened us. M. Dreux d'Aubray—"

"What, your father again!" exclaimed Sainte-Croix. "Let him beware! I have not forgotten that he was the cause of the greatest misfortune that ever befell me; that, thanks to him, I was ignominiously forbidden your house."

"He is my father, chevalier!"

"Yes, Madeleine; but I love you and you love me. I would gladly shed the last drop of my blood for you, and my claims upon you are more sacred than his. I repeat it, let him beware."

Sainte-Croix had risen whilst uttering these words; his lips quivered with anger, his eyes sparkled, and his hands were clenched as though the enemy on whom he wished himself to revenge himself were present.

The marquise, still calm and smiling, looked at him lovingly. This temper, shown at the thought of losing her, was it not a proof of love?

"Calm yourself, chevalier," she said at last, "no serious danger threatens us yet awhile."

"Then why did you speak like that, my dear beloved Madeleine? Can I be calm when I think of the possibility of losing you? Never to see you more! why, at the very thought of it I feel beside myself, for nothing more terrible could befall me, no nothing, not even death itself."

"Come, drive away these disagreeable thoughts," rejoined the marquise, "and tell me if you have any news of our little one."

Sainte-Croix remained silent.

"What!" continued the marquise, "nothing yet?"

"Nothing."

"And you tell me that away from me the hours seem intolerably long, and that you pass your time wearily and aimlessly! And yet somewhere in the world we have a child, a son, and you cannot tell his mother what has become of him. I don't know whether I ought to bewail his death or his existence. Oh! if I were only a man!"

"Madeleine, pray do not reproach me thus. Have I not done all I possibly could do?"

"All? you say you have tried everything. Well, do you know what I should do if I were free? I would go from town to town, from village to village, I would knock at every door and enter every house, I would

question every mother, and I should find out his whereabouts and take him to my heart, unless, indeed, I found his tomb and went to weep beside it."
"You are torturing me, Madeleine ! What have I done that you should treat me so cruelly ? "
"Ah ! " continued the marquise, "you do not love this child whose birth was a disgrace ! Do you ever think of what he may be doing now ? Does it never strike you that without parents, friendless and penniless, he may perhaps be struggling against the world ; it must be very hard."
"Yes, it is very hard," answered Sainte-Croix sorrowfully, "I know it, for has not that been my fate? I have but one friend in the world, and she forsakes me. You are my life, my happiness, and you treat me more cruelly than my bitterest foe." And hiding his face in his hands, the chevalier sank back in an arm-chair ; he was weeping bitterly—he, the soldier, the gambler, the adventurer, was weeping.
At the sight of these tears which she had caused to flow, the marquise fell on her lover's neck. "Pardon ! forgive me !" she said, resting her lovely head on his shoulder. "Yes, I have been cruel, unjust, pitiless. Punish me as I deserve, cease to love me if you can, since I have been so unfortunate as to pain you."
A smile of joy, a ray of the sun of love, lit up Sainte-Croix's handsome countenance ; he drew the marquise to him, and pressed her to his heart.
"Cease to love you," he whispered in her ear, "cease to love you ! Do you think it is in my power to do so ? Who could separate us ? We are young, we love each other, the future is ours ; and the future is felicity."
At this moment a loud knock at the street door of the hostelry disturbed the quiet of the neighbourhood.
Springing from the arms of Sainte-Croix, the marquise darted to the window.
"Open in the king's name !" cried a voice in the street, and the door was shaken by repeated knocks.
"Good heavens !" exclaimed Sainte-Croix, "who are they after ? "
"Hush ! listen," answered the marquise, placing her hand on her lover's lips.
The voice of the landlord of the *More-qui-trompe*, could now be heard ; he had opened a little casement and was parleying with the folks outside. "Who are you ?" he asked.
"Open in the king's name," was the answer.
"Oh !" continued host Hugonnet, "I know you, I'm not to be taken in like that, you are a parcel of drunkards who want to come and tipple here. Well, I have no wine at this time of night, so be off to bed. Good-night."
"Open, you dog of an innkeeper," continued some one from without.
"In the king's name, will you open ?" said another voice. "This delay may cost you dear."
"Very well," rejoined Hugonnet, "I'll come down and draw the bolts ; only have a little patience. But if you are joking, I swear by St. Luke, my patron saint, that I shall summon the watch. Just wait a moment and don't beat down the door of a respectable house."
The anxiety of the two lovers was terrible, during this short parley. Sainte-Croix, mad with rage, turned round the room like a captive tiger ; it seemed as though he were seeking for an outlet, as if the fire burning in his eyes could cause the wall to melt and give him egress. The marquise had remained standing by the window. With her forehead pressed against the window-pane, she was trying to see who was besieging the inn.

At this moment, host Hugonnet appeared at the door of the room followed by La Chaussée, who seemed quite scared. "The king's men are below, monsieur le chevalier; " said the landlord, "what am I to do?"

"I forbid your opening the door," exclaimed Sainte-Croix.

"They will force it," remonstrated La Chaussée.

"I am afraid they will," said Hugonnet. "Ah! what a scandal for a respectable house like mine!"

"Sure enough they are after monsieur le chevalier," muttered La Chaussée.

"You scamp of an innkeeper," exclaimed Sainte-Croix, "haven't you any other door by which we can escape?"

"Alas, no," sorrowfully answered Hugonnet. And as the knocking continued he resumed: "I must go and open the door, or some misfortune will befall me." Thereupon he prepared to leave the room.

"Go, my friend," said the marquise, "leave us."

Hugonnet retired, followed by La Chaussée. Downstairs the knocking still continued.

"If you do not open," resumed some one, "we shall force the door of this infamous hole."

On hearing this voice, the marquise stood as though petrified.

"Do you hear?" she said to Sainte-Croix.

"We will defend ourselves," answered the chevalier, and at the same time he began to move the furniture the room contained towards the door.

"It is useless, my friend; the voice I have just heard is my father's; we are lost."

"Not yet," replied Sainte-Croix, carried away by his fury.

"Quite lost," continued the marquis, with strange and terrible calmness, "lost! This means exposure, disgrace, and the convent. It is our parting. Oh, my friend, it is my death!"

"Curse them!" yelled Sainte-Croix, "there is no one to protect us, no one to save us!"

"You are mistaken, chevalier," replied a voice which appeared to emanate from the wall.

Sainte-Croix and the marquise turned round in amazement. One of the panels of the wood-work had turned on a pivot, disclosing a secret passage, and in its place stood Reich de Penautier.

"Wretch," exclaimed Sainte-Croix, "it is you who betrayed us!"

Blinded by passion he had swiftly drawn his sword and thrown himself on the financier. But by a swift retreat Penautier evaded the thrust. "By the plague!" he said quietly, "you are over prompt, chevalier."

"How is it that you are here, monsieur?" asked the marquise.

"That is my secret, madame, but it cannot concern you as I am here to save you."

"Is it possible!" exclaimed Sainte-Croix.

Penautier's only answer was to draw aside and offer his hand to the marquise. Then, with the quiet politeness he would have shown in a ball room, "Pass, madame la marquise," he said.

"What will become of him?" asked Madeleine, pointing to the chevalier.

"He will remain here to protect our retreat."

"But supposing anything were to happen to him."

"The worst that can happen to him would be arrest," replied Penautier.

"Arrested!" repeated the marquise in a fright.

"Do not trouble yourself about me, Madeleine. As this way of escape is open to you leave me ; for pity's sake leave me."

"The chevalier is right," continued the financier. "time is precious ; come, madame."

The young woman fell on her lover's neck. "But how shall I know—"

"A single knot tied in this handkerchief, which La Chaussée will bring you, will show that I am at the Bastille, two will signify that I have left Paris, and three, that I am out of France."

"Once more let us be off," exclaimed Penautier. "They are coming up." And tearing the marquise away from her lover's embrace, he almost dragged her to the secret passage.

The panel turned again, and all traces of egress disappeared. It was time ; for some one was already knocking at the door of the room.

Sainte-Croix did not wait for the summons to be repeated ; wrapping his cloak round him, pulling his felt hat over his eyes, and making sure that his sword worked properly in the scabbard, he went straight to the door and opened it.

He found himself face to face with Desgrais. Four sergeants followed their chief. The lieutenant of police and his two sons remained in the background ; while on the last steps of the staircase stood two agents who were watching La Chaussée.

Sainte-Croix assumed the offensive. "What do you want, monsieur?" he asked Desgrais, in a haughty and imperative tone.

"In the first place," answered the police officer, who did not allow himself to be intimidated, "have the goodness to reply to my questions."

"I am all attention," replied the young man, making obvious efforts to keep cool.

"Are you the Chevalier Gaudin de Sainte-Croix?"

"I am he."

"Captain in the Tracy regiment?"

"Yes."

"Then make way for us; there is some one in this room whom we require."

The chevalier shrugged his shoulders. "You are mistaken," said he, "there is no one here."

"He lies," said a voice in the passage. The voice was that of M. Dreux d'Aubray. "He lies," continued the old man, "but his lies will not save his accomplice. So enter, gentlemen, and do your duty."

A gleam of hatred flashed from Sainte-Croix's eyes, and singled out the lieutenant standing between his two sons. "I don't know what the person who is hiding over there means when he accuses me of lying," said the chevalier, with marvellous coolness. "At any other time, or in any other place, I should know how to make him retract his rash words. But one owes respect to the king's orders, and you hold one I believe, monsieur?"

"Here it is, monsieur," answered Desgrais, exhibiting a parchment.

Sainte-Croix who remained in the doorway, barring the officer's passage, minutely examined the document.

"Come, what are you waiting for?" exclaimed the lieutenant of police. "Enter ; enter !"

Sainte-Croix felt comparatively sure that the marquise and Penautier were safe by now, and that the secret panel might be forced with impunity even were it discovered ; so he took two steps backwards, and said ironically to the sergeants : "Obey your orders, gentlemen ; enter."

Desgrais went in the first. In a moment all the corners and recesses of the room were explored, searched, and probed by the officer and his men.

"The bird has flown !" exclaimed Desgrais, "but I could swear she was in the nest ; here are her feathers." And he thereupon exhibited to the lieutenant and his two sons, who had now entered, the cloak and damp clothes which the marquise had left in the dressing-room.

"She cannot escape us !" exclaimed M. d'Aubray ; "this inn possesses but one door."

"Oh, as for that," rejoined Desgrais, "it is hard to tell much about these two sided establishments, inns below, and boudoirs above. They are built for intrigues, and are full of trap doors and secret passages."

"Search everywhere, probe the walls, don't leave a stone unturned."

"It would be useless, I know my business, the person we seek is out of our reach by now."

"This one has remained, however," said M. d'Aubray, pointing towards Sainte-Croix.

"Of course—he was covering her escape. But, no matter, I will have my revenge."

During this dialogue the chevalier had remained standing by the fire, his elbow resting on the mantelpiece. The lieutenant of police turned towards him. "Let us put an end to this," he said.

Desgrais immediately approached the captain, and touching him on the shoulder, said : "I arrest you in the king's name ; follow me."

"Let us go," quietly answered Sainte-Croix. And he began to descend the stairs, preceded by two sergeants.

When he had reached the door, in front of which a coach was waiting, he asked : "May I know where you are taking me ?"

"To the Bastille," answered M. d'Aubray.

Sainte-Croix bowed without a word, while one of the sergeants stepped on in advance to open the door of the vehicle, and meantime the chevalier had time to tie a knot in the corner of his handkerchief ; then, drawing back an instant, he jostled La Chaussée, who was standing between two of Desgrais' assistants, and slipped the handkerchief into his hands, whisper-ing these words :

"For the marquise."

"Come, get in, sir," said M. d'Aubray, impatiently ; "we have lost too much time already."

"This is too much," cried Sainte-Croix, allowing the storm of fury he had so long controlled to burst forth at last ; and repulsing the guards who surrounded him, he drew his sword, which they had forgotten to take from him.

"Now for it !" he cried, "now for it ; cowards who call yourselves noblemen, but who forget your swords, and have only a *lettre-de-cachet* and some police hirelings at the service of a lady's honour." Then with a roar of rage more like that of a wild beast than a human being, he rushed upon the two young d'Aubrays.

But Desgrais' assistants had already recovered from their surprise. They threw themselves upon him, hemming him in, so that he could not use his sword.

"I surrender," he said, at last dropping his weapon.

They then pushed him into the coach, and Desgrais and two of the ser-geants entered it after him.

M. d'Aubray himself closed the door, and stepping back, motioned the coachman to drive on as he gave this sinister order : "To the Bastille !"

*　　*　　*　　*　　*　　*

A secret staircase had enabled Madame de Brinvilliers and her preserver to speedily reach a coach which was awaiting them in a small street running parallel with the Rue de l'Arbre Sec, and in a few moments they were being borne swiftly along towards the Rue des Lions Saint-Paul.

Every trace of past danger and anxiety had vanished from the face of the marquise. She seemed to be marble. But for all that she was a prey to the most intense anxiety. What would become of Sainte-Croix? Would he perish by the sword of her father or her brothers in an unequal struggle ? or were the doors of an eternal prison about to close upon him ?

Madame de Brinvilliers' passion for her lover was one of those intense infatuations which nothing can master ; the very fact that it was unlawful had increased its vehemence, and she only thought of giving it full rein. For Sainte-Croix she had sacrificed and repudiated everything ; to save him, she would have hesitated at nothing, even the most atrocious crimes ; and she was already asking herself in what way she could free herself from the surveillance of a parent whom she considered far too solicitous in regard to the preservation of his family honour.

Still, this woman, who was destined to play a prominent rôle in the criminal records of the world, possessed such strength of character that she had already learned to assume that insolent indifference which so effectually conceals mental anxiety. So it was in a tranquil voice that she addressed Penautier, who, though he pretended to respect her meditations, had not ceased watching her, but in a furtive manner.

"May I ask, monsieur," she inquired, "where you are taking me, and to whom I am indebted for so great a service ? "

"To a friend of the chevalier's, madame—to a friend who craves the honour of becoming yours—Reich de Penautier, whom you may have heard spoken of as the treasurer of the States of Languedoc. I have ordered my coachman to drive to your house ; but it will be advisable, I think, not to take the shortest route. I fear some unfortunate encounter."

"And will you not tell me how you happened to come to our aid in such a miraculous fashion?" inquired the marquise, with winning grace of manner.

"It would be easy, madame, for me to impute it all to chance ; but, in my opinion, chance is merely the providence of fools, and I am not accustomed to attach much importance to it ; so I will frankly confess that I found myself on the topmost step of that staircase at such an opportune moment merely because I foresaw what was going to happen."

"What ! you know? But who—"

"Oh, madame," replied Penautier, bowing, "I am slightly connected with the church, you know, and when I have an interest in discovering anything—"

"Well?"

"I always discover it. A secret is a commodity which naturally seeks a purchaser."

The marquise looked intently at her companion. "And you had an interest in discovering ours?" she said, slowly.

Penautier bowed in sign of acquiescence. "Everything connected with the chevalier interests me deeply, madame. It makes me miserable to see a man of his merit in such a precarious and ambiguous position, when the affection he has succeeded in inspiring should certainly elevate him to the highest rank. Monsieur de Sainte-Croix has never asked any favours of me, nor has it ever been in my power to do anything for him. You may even have noticed that it was a little against his will, almost under compulsion, that he accepted my offer of assistance just now. Still, I have always hoped that the chevalier would some day be indebted to me for an elevated position in the world."

"And what would you ask in exchange?" inquired the marquise.

"Oh, a mere trifle. Only an offensive and defensive alliance between you, him, and myself."

The marquise offered both of her lovely hands to her companion. "We will sign it, then," she said, smiling. "Monsieur de Sainte-Croix will not oppose me."

Penautier gallantly kissed the lady's tapering fingers.

Just at that moment the coach paused before the residence of the Marquis de Brinvilliers. A man was standing under the porch. He was still out of breath and covered with mud from a long run.

The marquise recognised him. "La Chaussée!" she exclaimed.

The valet, without a word, handed her a handkerchief.

Madame de Brinvilliers seized hold of it with an eager hand.

"Sainte-Croix is in the Bastille!" she cried.

"Have no fears, madame, we will soon obtain his release," said Penautier, encouragingly.

The marquise alighted, and the door opened to admit her. But on the threshold she paused, and turning to Penautier said : "One word more. You, who know everything, can also tell me who sold the secret of our meetings, and of our place of meeting, to my father."

"It was Hanyvel de Saint-Laurent," was the response.

"Thank you," rejoined the marquise. "I shall not forget either the name or the man."

IV.

IN THE BASTILLE.

ALL the clocks of Paris were striking the hour of midnight, when the sentinel stationed at the outer drawbridge of the Bastille espied the coach which conveyed Sainte-Croix under the custody of two sergeants. In response to the sentinel's call, a subordinate officer emerged from the guard-house, accompanied by a soldier carrying a lantern.

After a short conference with Desgrais, the coach entered the fortress. Another soldier was sent to summon the governor's lieutenant, who made his appearance yawning, half asleep, and secretly cursing the blockhead fool enough to be sent to prison at such an hour of the night. M. de Baise-meaux de Montlezun, at that time governor of the royal fortress, only disturbed himself for prisoners of importance.

Sainte-Croix was ordered to alight; and Desgrais displayed his *lettre-de-cachet*. "Bah!" exclaimed the lieutenant, after perusing the document, "a mere captain, a prisoner of the fourth class. We have more than enough of these already."

Thereupon, he took a pen and wrote upon the prison record : "At midnight on the 15th of November, 1665, Gaudin de Sainte-Croix entered this prison by order of the king, and at the request of Monsieur Dreux d'Aubray. The said Sainte-Croix had upon his person—"

"How much have you on your person?" the officer inquired, turning to the prisoner.

"Two hours ago I had several thousand pistoles; now this is all I have left," replied Sainte-Croix, depositing about a dozen gold coins on the table.

"Have you any jewellery?" continued the officer.

"These two rings and my watch."

"Give them to me."

Then the officer proceeded to fill in the regular formula: "The said Gaudin de Sainte-Croix hereby certifies that he had no other property in his possession on the aforesaid day of his entrance."

While Sainte-Croix was signing this document, the officer was saying to himself: "Where can I possibly put this new-comer? All our cells are occupied, and I can't give to a low-grade, penniless officer one of the apartments reserved for prisoners of rank."

He summoned one of the warders, and inquired in a low tone: "What have we unoccupied just now that we can give to this new-comer?'

"Nothing, monsieur."

"Then put him with some other prisoner; he will be glad of company."

The warder ordered Sainte-Croix to follow him, and after a long walk through cold and damp passages and up gloomy staircases, he opened a door, the wood-work of which was all but entirely hidden by massive iron bars and bolts. Sainte-Croix was pushed inside, then the hinges creaked noisily and the door closed.

For an instant he stood motionless, listening with a terrible sinking of heart to the jailer's heavy footsteps as they died away in the distance. He was stunned by the terrible misfortune which had overtaken him, and inexpressible anguish filled his heart. What fate awaited him? What would be the duration of his imprisonment? Was he destined to see his hair grow white in this stronghold of tyranny? Entering it a young man, would he leave it only when he became old, or would he ever leave it at all? At the doors of the Bastille, as at the doors of Dante's "Inferno," those who entered there were doomed to leave all hope behind.

When every sound had died away and Sainte-Croix had reason to suppose himself alone and forever separated from the rest of mankind, the thought of examining his prison occurred to him. To aid him, he had no other light than that of a pale moonbeam, which filtered through a narrow window at least six feet from the floor, and protected by a heavy iron grating. This light fell upon a miserable pallet in one corner of the room, and left all the rest of the cell in utter darkness.

Sainte-Croix staggered towards this couch like a man under the influence of drink, and threw himself upon it in a paroxysm of despair, which found vent in cries and sobs. In one of those sudden revulsions of feeling which are almost sure to follow great catastrophes, his entire life passed before him as in a faithful mirror. All the pleasant episodes of his past career crowded upon his memory, making him feel his present misfortunes all the more keenly. He found himself recalling the minutest details of the evening just spent with the marquise, and he still seemed to hear her silvery voice murmuring words of love in his ear.

Fanned by these memories, his anger became more and more intense, and he cursed the men who had torn him from his free and joyous life to bury him alive in this dungeon cell; he cursed the God who knew and permitted such a crime; and finally he entreated some power either of heaven or hell to come to his relief, offering his life and his soul in exchange for one day, or even one hour, of liberty and vengeance.

"I accept your offer," suddenly said a strange voice, close by.

Pale, with haggard eyes, and hair bristling with terror, the chevalier raised himself from his reclining posture. In the luminous circle described by the window, stood a man clad in a tattered, black doublet.

He slowly approached the pallet. His face was wan and emaciated; his long hair streamed upon his shoulders; his untrimmed beard bristled round his prominent cheek bones, a phosphorescent light shone from beneath his heavy eyebrows, and the moonbeams-formed a sort of aureole around his furrowed brow.

On beholding this strange apparition, the chevalier involuntarily made the sign of the cross. The ashes of the sorcerers, burned for having invoked the aid of the evil one, were still smoking at that period; and their names were inscribed upon the walls of more than one cell in the Bastille. People believed in the fiend, and the chevalier was not far from fancying himself in the presence of a denizen of the spirit-land.

But whether the apparition was man or phantom, it was still advancing, and Sainte-Croix felt a cold sweat rising to the roots of his hair, and his teeth chattered with fear. His hand instinctively sought his sword in its accustomed place, but the weapon had been taken from him.

At last, he felt that the strange being was about to touch him. "What do you desire of me, demon?" he asked, in a voice husky with terror.

"Did you not ask succour of any power whatsoever?" inquired the apparition. "You called, here I am."

"Who are you?"

"If you desire it, young man, I will be an avenger."

"Of course I desire it, even at the price of life and eternal damnation; but still, I must know who it is that speaks to me thus."

"Ah, well, I, like yourself, am a prisoner in the Bastille, your companion in captivity. It is ten years since I began to count the hours in this cell which you entered for the first time only a few moments ago."

On hearing these words, Sainte-Croix made a gesture of profound discouragement. He was no longer afraid; he blushed now, at the recollection of his own cowardice, but the absurd hope which had made his heart throb wildly for a moment had forsaken him. "In that case," said he, "what use is it to talk of vengeance? How can a person who is unable to do anything for himself aid me?"

"You are impatient," said the stranger; "you have not yet allowed me to tell you my name."

"Because I do not believe it would matter much to me to know it."

The old man smiled faintly. "Perhaps it might," he said, quietly. "I am Exili, the Italian."

More frightened even than when he had imagined himself to be in the presence of the fiend, Sainte-Croix sank back on his couch. His fancies had given place to a still more frightful reality.

This name, Exili, was terribly notorious in Italy and in France. To all, it was the synonym of murder and poison. For twenty-five years it had been written in letters of blood in all the courts of Europe. A disciple of René the Florentine and La Tophana, the inheritor of the deadly secrets of the Medicis and of the Borgias, Exili had long surpassed those celebrated and implacable murderers in the atrocity of his crimes. When only a youth he had been a concocter of poison in Florence. Was a person kept waiting too long for an inheritance, did some one desire a secret and cowardly revenge for an injury, it was to Exili he applied. To some, he sold the death of their parents ; to others, the death of their enemies.

Later, at Rome, he had placed his skill at the service of Olympia Mancini, the famous Comtesse de Soissons, and for several years he had spread terror and death through the Eternal City, striking as blindly and relentlessly as destiny itself when it was a question of obedience to his terrible protectress. People said he had caused the death of at least one hundred and fifty persons connected with the noblest families ; and there were few who did not make the sign of the cross when they whispered Exili's name.

Driven from Italy, rather by the hatred of the people than by the government, Exili had come to France for the purpose of taking up his abode there, but his terrible fame had preceded him. He was not allowed time to exercise his skill, but disappeared one fine day without any one being able to say what had become of him. The fact is, he had been arrested and thrown into the Bastille, undoubtedly for life.

Sainte-Croix knew all this, and consequently the name of Exili sent a shudder through his veins. He knew only too well with how terrible a weapon he might be provided by the man who had been the instrument of Olympia Mancini's vengeance. But intense as was his hatred, he had not yet arrived at the frame of mind in which a man can calmly contemplate the greatest of crimes. It was with genuine anger, therefore, that he raised himself upon his pallet, and extending both hands as if to ward off a danger, exclaimed, "Leave me, demon, leave me ! "

"And yet you say that you crave vengeance," murmured Exili, scornfully. "Poor fool ! the day will come when you will be weary of suffering, and will long for liberty and for weapons to enable you once more to mingle in the conflicts of life. Then you will come to me and entreat me upon your knees to assist you and offer you my hand."

"Never ! never ! " replied the chevalier, recoiling in terror.

Exili retired as noiselessly as he had come, making his way back through the darkness to his own bed, and leaving the young man a prey to the deepest despondency.

It was with unspeakable terror that Sainte-Croix found himself still in the presence of this terrible companion when day dawned the next morning. He entreated the jailer to change his quarters, but that official replied that the Bastille was very much crowded just then, and besides, they were not in the habit of submitting to all the caprices of their prisoners.

So Sainte-Croix was obliged to submit to his fate. Besides, his aversion to his companion in captivity was not destined to be of long duration, for the great master had found a pupil worthy of him. Sainte-Croix, with his fatal temperament, a strange compound of good and evil, virtue and vice, was not long in conceiving an admiration for the strange man whom his evil genius had placed in his path.

And this admiration can be easily explained. Exili was not one of those common-place poisoners who kill suddenly and brutally. He was a gifted man in every sense of the word ; and if he had applied the rare genius with which the Creator had endowed him to good works, he would undoubtedly have taken his place among the benefactors of mankind, and have connected his name with some of those discoveries that shed lustre upon a century. A profound thinker, philosopher and investigator, he had seen and studied everything, and his wonderful memory was a vast encyclopædia which Sainte-Croix could constantly consult on all subjects, and which he never found in fault.

But above all and before all, Exili was an expert in poisons. He had made murder an art. The possessor of terrible secrets, he had endeavoured to discover new ones, and had pursued his studies and his experiments without cessation. He had ended by imparting fixed positive rules to death ; so that interest no longer guided him, but rather an uncontrollable desire to experiment. Whenever he happened to talk of his fatal science, Sainte-Croix listened with superstitious terror.

"How many," exclaimed Exili with a radiant face and inspired voice, "how many wear themselves out in striving to discover the secret of life which will ever evade them—but I have discovered the secret of death !"

"Alas !" murmured Sainte-Croix, "to what has it brought you ?"

"To an equality with the Divinity," replied the gloomy alchemist. "He has preserved for Himself the divine power of creating or imparting life ; to mankind He has left destruction and death. Do you not then understand that in the power to punish and destroy I equal the Deity ?" And as the chevalier made a gesture that implied doubt, Exili continued, "Am I not all-powerful, besides? I who hold the lives of all in my hand, and can strike like the thunderbolt. What king is possessed of a power that equals mine ?"

A day at last came when Sainte-Croix ventured to admit to Exili, that he, too, had devoted some attention to the science of toxicology, and he began to describe some of his experiments.

His companion smiled. "You are still studying the mere rudiments of the art," he remarked. "Twenty years of assiduous work will barely admit you into the realm of true science, of that science only transmitted by the great alchemists of Italy ; for their secrets, you see, are never divulged, but secretly bequeathed by each master to a favourite and long-tried pupil."

"Do you wish me to be *your* pupil?" exclaimed Sainte-Croix.

The Italian shook his head with an air of doubt. "We do not know each other sufficiently for me to feel certain that you are worthy of becoming the recipient of my knowledge."

"I am still young, but I have already suffered much."

"But I do not see what you can have lacked. You are young, rich, handsome ; you must be loved."

"A name has been wanting," interrupted Sainte-Croix, "and heaven created me proud."

A gleam of Satanic satisfaction illumined Exili's face. "Pride," he murmured, "very good. We shall make something of you yet, chevalier ; but go on, pray, for it is from the past that I read the future."

"Every one supposes me to be the illegitimate son of a noble house," continued Sainte-Croix. "My sword and my valour have at least won me this much. But I really belong to one of those humble families whose obscurity but imperfectly conceals their poverty. My father was a mechanic, and he would undoubtedly have made me one also, had I not been too proud and ambitious. Even in my childhood, I longed for money, amusement and fine clothes. The sight of a ribbon, the clinking of glasses, the rattle of dice, the smile of a great lady, all filled my precocious mind with a thousand vague aspirations ; so at an age when the children of poor parents are usually in the workshop or on the forms of a schoolroom, I had deserted both for the wine-shop, the fencing-school, and the gambling den. There, in company with the bullies and sharpers of Montauban, I acquired that keenness of vision, that adroitness of hand, and that skill in play which have rarely failed me. But my father died of grief, and I mourned for him."

"A man is not perfect at such a tender age," interrupted Exili.

"I was seventeen," resumed the chevalier, "when an unfortunate affair, the killing of a man, or the ruin of a young girl—I have forgotten exactly which—compelled me to leave Languedoc. Paris is the sun around which all satellites of my stamp congregate : so I came to Paris. But to open the doors of the fashionable circle to which I desired admittance, a name and title, as well as money were needed, so I called myself the Chevalier Gaudin de Sainte-Croix, and the pockets of simpletons furnished me with the money I required. However, I fought several duels. A man cannot call himself the Chevalier de Sainte-Croix with impunity. A nobleman of Beauvais one day came to the conclusion that his pistoles passed too readily from his pockets to mine. He told me so in rather impolite language, and even went so far as to express some doubts in regard to the authenticity of my title. I requested him to measure swords with me—and he doubted no longer."

"Then you convinced him ?" inquired Exili.

"I killed him. Unfortunately, the affair created a stir. The family made quite an ado ; and as I did not want to get into trouble, I fled to Compiègne, where the principal love adventure of my life happened to me."

"And what lady figured in this adventure ?" inquired Exili.

"A young girl called Marie-Madeleine d'Aubray. I was eighteen, she sixteen—a lovely child who has since become a wonderfully beautiful woman. We met by chance in the forest surrounding the château of Offemont, where her father, a lieutenant of police, had come in search of rest and recreation after his arduous labours. Madeleine's heart contained that wealth of tenderness which a woman consecrates to God when she does not meet a man who steals it from the Creator. We met and loved each other. This is one of those memories which the most reckless adventurer tenderly cherishes, so delightfully does it contrast with the rest of an agitated feverish existence. To meet her, I each night scaled the walls of the park, and effected a furtive entrance into the old château, which the presence of my beloved transformed in my eyes into a Paradise. Monsieur d'Aubray had returned to Paris, where the duties of his office called him, leaving his daughter in charge of an aged nurse, as her health seemed to require the fresh, exhilarating air of the forest.

"But our bliss was of short duration. Monsieur d'Aubray returned, and Madeleine was *enceinte*. You will understand the prudence and courage this young girl needed to conceal from the vigilant eyes of her father, a fault he would have punished as a crime ; but I may tell you that she possesses the same indomitable will as I did prior to my prison-life. She was confined at night-time, without help or attendance, but a few steps from the spot where her father Monsieur d'Aubray reposed. I was wandering about the park that night, and suddenly, Madeleine, overcome with sorrow, fear and remorse, dragged herself to me through the trees, and placed a child in my arms. The watch-dogs barked, and the servants began moving about the château; so I fled through the fields with my burden. At daybreak, I rapped at the door of a lonely farm-house on the road to Beauvais, and the farmer's wife consented to nurse my son—for I had a son."

"On the road to Beauvais, did you say?" interrupted Exili, who had been paying the closest possible attention to the chevalier's story.

Absorbed in his reminiscences, Sainte-Croix did not notice the Italian's question. "I stood there watching the child and thinking of the mother, when suddenly the clanking of weapons and the sound of horses' hoofs resounded on the road, and turning, I saw several mounted horsemen approaching the farm-house. Had Monsieur Dreux d'Aubray discovered our secret and his dishonour, or had the authorities been informed of my presence? I did not know. At all events, overcome by present terror, as well as by all the excitement and anxiety of the past night, I flung all the gold I had about me upon the table, and, opening the window, jumped out into the little garden at the back of the house, whence a moment after I reached the woods, where I found shelter. Two days later, Monsieur d'Aubray had taken his daughter to Paris, and I had joined the army!"

Exili bestowed a searching glance on his companion. "Did you never return to the farm-house?" he asked, "and don't you know what became of your son?"

"Martial life gained as complete an ascendancy over me as love had done. For ten years I fought in Spain, in Piedmont, and in Flanders, in every country where there was any fighting to be done, and I defy any one to say that the Chevalier de Sainte-Croix has not faithfully performed his duty as a soldier. When I returned to France, I was a captain. Of my youthful escapades there remained only a vague desire to know what had become of the child. I visited the farm-house on the road to Beauvais, and there I learned that the child left by a stranger ten years before had been kept at the farm-house as long as the gold left by its supposed father had lasted. These people were not rich; the child was a burden which they wished to rid themselves of, and they had begun to think of placing it in some foundling asylum, when one day a traveller, whose name and station could not be ascertained, offered to take charge of it. The child was given to him, and he departed with it.

"But though I was not fated to find my son, I was destined to find myself face to face with his mother but a few months later.

"During the campaign in Flanders I had made the acquaintance of a nobleman of ancient lineage and most agreeable character. After the signing of peace, we met again in Paris. I was poor and he was rich. He offered me his purse and his services. There was no reason why I should refuse them. My companion in arms was married, and he proposed to introduce me to his young wife. I accepted the offer, and judge of my surprise to find that Marie Madeleine d'Aubray had become the Marquise de Brinvilliers. The marquis lived in grand style, and he insisted upon my residing with him, at least for a time. Passion was only slumbering within me, and the sight of the marquise sufficed to awaken it in a stronger and more impetuous manner than ever. Madeleine did not love her husband, and that gentleman, being of an easy and yielding disposition, allowed the marquise the same liberty which he himself desired to enjoy. What more need I say? Madeleine was beautiful, and time had not extinguished the passion inherent in my nature. Our years of separation were forgotten in a kiss."

Relinquishing the *rôle* of an attentive listener, Exili assumed that of an almost suspicious questioner.

"Hasn't the marquise ever received any news of her son," he asked, "any information that might put her on his track, or that would aid her in her search? For she must have made some effort to discover him, chevalier. A mother cannot forget her child."

"Madeleine," replied the chevalier, not without some embarrassment, "was fully persuaded that I had taken the child with me, and that he had been reared under my charge. Her despair was terrible when she learned the truth; and the loss of this child is the only cloud upon our love to-day."

"Have you told her the truth, then?"

"Wholly and without reserve."

"Why, artful as you appear to be, did you not try to assuage her regret by assuring her, for example, that her son died in your arms a few moments after his birth?"

"I could not lie to Madeleine," replied Sainte-Croix gravely.

His companion seemed to fall into another profound reverie as the cheva lier continued his narrative, which was now fast approaching conclusion. "We abandoned ourselves without constraint to the rapture of a passion which nothing seemed likely to disturb. The Marquis de Brinvilliers paid no attention to us, and being a guest in the house, I could enjoy Madeleine's society at all hours without danger, protected by the careless indifference of her husband. Such was the condition of affairs when suspicion entered our abode with Monsieur d'Aubray. He is a dangerous man, and we shall have more than one account to settle with each other, one of these days. The marquis had closed his eyes; but Monsieur d'Aubray made him open them. On account of this surveillance and tyrannical interference, even violence, I was compelled to leave the house. But we did not abandon the idea of seeing each other—Madeleine and I—and I finally succeeded in discovering a safe place for our meetings. Aided by some demon I know not, Monsieur d'Aubray managed to discover our retreat. He had two sons both of an age to wield a sword; but for all that, he provided himself with a *lettre-de-cachet*, and protected by the minions of the law, he surprised us together, and the doors of this prison closed upon me in consequence. But I will leave it some day, even if I am compelled to sacrifice my life to the work of deliverance; and when I have returned to the land of the living, I will compel that man and his sons to leave it. They would not make use of the sword to punish me, and I will not resort to it to gain my revenge. That is why, Exili, I have decided to give myself to you; that is why re- flection has armed me against foolish fears and absurd scruples, and made me the disciple of your death-dealing art. Take me either as your pupil or accomplice; neither will be wanting in the hour of need."

The Italian's only response was to rise and walk straight to the wall against which his pallet stood. A large stone yielded to the pressure of his hand, and turned round revealing to the astonished eyes of Sainte-Croix a deep cavity, in which stood several retorts and crucibles, vessels of glass and earthenware, jars containing strange compounds, vials filled with my- sterious liquids, and a little pile of charcoal and a chafing-dish. He took out the chafing-dish, silently placed it in the middle of the cell, and then lighted the charcoal. Next, in response to his companion's look of in- quiry, he said: "Those who have need of me, and there are some close to the throne, have never allowed me to lack anything here. It is through them, and for them, that I have improvised this laboratory, which con- tains the means of satisfying every ambition and gratifying any revenge. Until now I have had with me mere companions—they are all dead—I needed a disciple."

Sainte-Croix looked Exili searchingly in the eyes.

"Yes," continued the Italian, "they are all dead. The air of this cell seems fatal. The physician of the Bastille was unable to relieve their agony, and found it difficult to give a name to the strange maladies they died of. But for you there is no danger. The demon of pride sent you here. I could not have found a better disciple. Be the inheritor of my secrets, the minister of my hatred. My fatal science shall be yours. If we leave this place together, we will reign together ; if you leave it alone, you shall avenge me. And now to work, my pupil !"

V

THE ALCHEMIST.

THEY toiled long and arduously, those gloomy alchemists. An entire year was spent in bending over the crucible in which the great art of poisoning was being perfected.

Sainte-Croix, now completely under the influence of the Italian, devoted himself body and soul to the science of crime, impelled to do so even more by the violence of his resentment, than by the strange paradoxes and infamous arguments of his companion. He devoted himself to these experiments with the same ardour he had always displayed, even in the most trivial acts of his life, and this impassioned earnestness was increased in the present instance by the intensity of his hatred against those who had torn him from his life of love, pleasure, and adventure, and subjected him to the miseries of a captivity which seemed likely to last for life.

The doors of the Bastille had closed upon a somewhat dangerous man ; but they would give passage to a veritable scourge of mankind whenever they opened to set him at liberty. Moreover, the mysteries of toxicology had always possessed a mysterious charm for the chevalier. Without any definite object, but merely from caprice and curiosity, he had endeavoured to fathom the secrets of this art which engrossed the attention of so many people during this part of the seventeenth century. So it may be imagined what ardour he displayed, and what progress he made under such a master as Exili, and with the thought of associating the result of his labours with his schemes of vengeance !

The Italian was marvellously gifted as a teacher. His words had a brilliancy which seemed borrowed from the flames of the infernal regions, and, in some remarkable and unanswerable way, he always succeeded in excusing assassination by making it appear a simple act of justice.

We feel no hesitation in asserting—and history has already recorded it—that Exili possessed genius, that is if such a term can be applied to anything that does not emanate from on high, and that is not exercised for the benefit of mankind. He was one of those strange and terrible anomalies of which the criminal records furnish so many examples from Cardellac to Papavoine. Endowed with a mania for destruction like the Thugs of India, who believe that their crimes give satisfaction to their gods, he had devoted his entire life to the compounding of different poisons, and had reduced them to a form of frightful simplicity.

"I have only one poison," he often remarked to Sainte-Croix, "but it is a compound of all the others, and I have been working thirty years to perfect it. Its effects are certain. They only vary according to the dose and to the subject. Administered in certain mathematical proportions, it will be months or years in acting. A few grains more or an additional drop or two, and death ensues as instantaneously as if a dagger had been thrust into the victim's breast, or a bullet had penetrated his heart. It will then act like a thunderbolt, and it assumes all forms, attacks each organ, and eludes all investigation. A post-mortem examination of the bodies of its victims fails to reveal its presence, and often some imaginary malady will become its accomplice.

"The Borgias, those great experts in the art, bequeathed to those who preceded me certain secrets, which would undoubtedly be lost in the future if you were not here to learn and make use of them.

"But the Borgias were only children in comparison with what I hope to become. You and I are destined, I am certain, to fathom the deepest mysteries in the domain of toxicology. To impart mortal effects to a fruit, a liquid, a glove, or a flower, whatever is partaken of, touched or inhaled, that were a petty accomplishment worthy at the utmost of René the Florentine, Queen Catherine de Medici's chemist. I must attain to the ideal. I have already discovered a narcotic which is the image of death : I wish to find a poison which is the image of life, an invisible and impalpable poison which will corrupt the air, kill from a distance, and destroy a nation as easily as it does a man—that is my ambition. The most complete gratification of all the passions which devour mankind lies in the discovery of this poison, my son, and we need not seek elsewhere for the philosopher's stone, or the art of making gold, in which pursuits former generations exhausted their strength and lost their souls."

The chevalier listened eagerly to these mad, feverish remarks. Still, day followed day without bringing any change in his life. No message from without reached him ; there was nothing to indicate that the hour of his release was approaching, or that Madeleine and other friends were exerting themselves in his behalf. Friends ! what friends had he save the companions of his pleasures, as indifferent to him as he had always been to them ; and the mistress, who had been obliged to deceive father and husband for the sake of meeting him, was scarcely likely to remain faithful to his memory for any length of time.

When Sainte-Croix thought of all this, there was a terrible outburst of grief, anger and despair in the cell. The names of Madeleine and her father were uttered amid sobs and imprecations. Sometimes the prisoner fairly writhed in his paroxysms of anger ; his hair bristled, foam gathered on his lips ; he struck the bars with his clenched fists, and threatened to dash his brains out against the wall. Then he would fall upon his pallet, utterly exhausted, and weep. Yes, he, the adventurer, formerly steeled against emotion of every kind, he who had abandoned his child to chance without remorse, and who had contemplated its mother's tears with dry eyes !

However, Exili would calmly remark : "In order that poisoning may become an art, and a legitimate art, impunity is an absolute necessity. I do not mean by that the impunity which is the result of the weakness of mankind, or its inability or neglect to punish. René, the Florentine, died quietly in his bed, but what does this prove except that Henri IV. had forgiven him for Jeanne d'Albret's apple, and Madame de Sauvès' perfumed gloves? René's guilt was known, and the people cursed his memory. Nor did Pope Alexander VI. enjoy impunity. The old rascal allowed himself to be caught in his own trap ; he died with the cardinals he had invited to supper ; and moreover, Olympia Mancini has been threatened in Rome. And even I am in the Bastille—Why ?

B

"Because there was still something left for us to learn. Do you suppose, for example, that if they had possessed the secret I am in search of, René would have needed the apple and gloves which proclaimed his crimes, and Borgia the Orvieto wine, which sent him into the other world? Do you suppose the Roman populace would hurl mud and stones at the coach of my protectress, and that the name of your companion would be the symbol of horror and dismay throughout Europe? Oh, my pupil! Oh, my son! the impunity I desire for us is that which endures even beyond the grave, and which, after it has made us powerful, rich, beloved, and honoured in life, will leave us publicly esteemed after our deplored demise. This will be an achievement worthy of us; one which will make us the masters of the vulgar herd we deceive, at whom we shall be able to laugh from the depths of the grave."

Under the influence of words like these, Sainte-Croix rose and resumed his work with increased ardour.

The two companions were seldom or never disturbed in their studies and experiments. Exili was considered an inoffensive, rather crack-brained prisoner, with no inclination to make his escape or to rebel. Moreover, certain friends in high places, who had formerly called his services into requisition, had given orders that, though he was to be carefully guarded, he should be allowed to occupy himself as he liked; and the jailer, to whom he very willingly relinquished his ration of wine, and whose good will he had also won by curing him of a fever, allowed him to work in what he styled his devil's kitchen unhindered. As for Sainte-Croix, he was of too little importance to attract much attention.

At last the chevalier began to relinquish all hope of regaining his liberty, and proposed an attempt to escape. But the Italian replied: "By-and-bye. We have not yet succeeded."

"But we will fly together!" exclaimed Sainte-Croix.

"When I have nothing more to teach you."

Eventually one morning the jailer entered the cell, and said to the chevalier: "Here is a visitor to see you." And, ushering in a gentleman, he added: "You have a quarter of an hour to talk. I will make it twenty minutes in consideration of the double pistole I have just received, so go ahead. I will come for you when your time is up."

The jailer went out, and M. Reich de Penautier almost smothered Sainte-Croix in his enthusiastic embrace.

"Do you come to restore me to liberty?" asked the chevalier.

The visitor's gloomy look was too profound to be entirely genuine. "Alas! my poor chevalier," he replied, "you have powerful enemies, and all my solicitations have been in vain." The most abject despair succeeded the hope which had beamed on the prisoner's face an instant before. Then his anger regained the ascendancy. "So the wretches have sworn to make me end my days in this granite tomb!" he hissed. "What terrible crime have I committed that the entire world should unite against me?"

"A fault that a father never forgives," replied Penautier, with a despondent air; "one that violates both the laws of morality, and those of our holy religion. Think of it, chevalier, the peace of a family destroyed, dishonour brought upon a household; a husband separated from his wife, and a daughter from her father—these are crimes which the world only pardons on condition that they remain shrouded in the most profound secrecy, and are committed by persons of the same rank in life. But your passion, so unfortunately shared by the Marquise de Brinvilliers, is quite a different matter. If I may believe the malicious reports which are in circulation, Captain Gaudin de Sainte-Croix is not the equal of those he has wronged."

The visitor ceased speaking, and anxiously awaited the effects of his words.

But Sainte-Croix had lent them but slight attention. "And Madeleine," he murmured, "Madeleine whom I believed bound to me for ever, Madeleine who had sworn to consecrate her entire existence to me, to live and to die with me—Madeleine to whom the past and the present alike bound me, has she too deserted me? For more than a year I have been immured within the walls of this dungeon—more than a year, each long and dreary day of which has brought me despair. And she who might have consoled me, she who might still prevent me from ruining myself irremediably, she who can alone rise between me and my revenge in the future—she has not deigned to bestow a single word of remembrance on the man who was torn from her arms to be buried here, with his lips still moist with her kisses."

"You are mistaken, chevalier," replied Penautier softly. "Your accusations are unjust, but your misfortunes lead me to forgive them, as the marquise herself will forgive them. Have you forgotten the *convenances* that fetter a woman of rank in spite of herself?"

"True passion scorns the conventionalities known as the requirements of position," interrupted Sainte-Croix.

"She would have done what you desire had it been possible. Believe me, my friend, the Marquise de Brinvilliers has not ceased to love you. She has mourned your absence from the moment of your parting, and her tears are her only resource. Under constant espionage, and struggling incessantly against parental severity and the calumnies of your enemies—"

"And who besides the D'Aubrays have any cause to dislike me?"

"I will mention no names, but question your own memory, chevalier. It cannot fail to respond."

"Question my memory?"

"A man like yourself, who has had so many adventures, met with so much success, and who is endowed with your charms of person, must have made many enemies. Don't you recollect, on the very evening of your arrest, of having offended a certain person by forcing him to cringe before your sword, and display his cowardice in the eyes of everyone?"

The chevalier buried his face in his hand and began to reflect.

"Try to think," insisted Penautier.

Sainte-Croix at last lifted his head and looked at his visitor. "If you tell me to think, monsieur, you must know the person."

"Charity compels me to come to your aid, in spite of the grief I must naturally feel in presence of such a display of weakness on the part of one of my colleagues; but don't you recollect how that evening at La Vienne's, Hanyvel—"

"He!—impossible!" exclaimed Sainte-Croix.

"It is said that he too is in love with the marquise," replied Penautier, hypocritically. "Was it not on account of a rash remark on his part that you drew your sword?"

"That is true. I remember now."

"This remark, which he so inconsiderately made in the presence of everyone, he had undoubtedly whispered in the ear of Monsieur Dreux d'Aubray. *He* knew your place of meeting, and there were but few who knew your secret."

"Ah, if I were sure of it!" hissed the chevalier through his set teeth.

"Take notice that I do not affirm anything; nevertheless, I believe I hold the clue to this mystery, and appearances are certainly very much against Hanyvel."

"That is true," interrupted Sainte-Croix; "the man's doom is sealed."

The same flash of joy which had sparkled in Penautier's eyes when Sainte-Croix threatened Hanyvel with his sword at La Vienne's establishment, again transfigured his face, and he cried impulsively, "Satisfy me of that, and your liberty is assured."

A third person now advanced to take part in the conversation. It was Exili, who had been lying on his couch pretending to be asleep, but who had, nevertheless, not lost a word. "Monsieur de Sainte-Croix is not obliged to leave the Bastille to reach his enemies," he said, in a slow, impressive manner.

At the sight of the Italian's fantastic head and tall form emerging from the shadow, M. Reich de Penautier recoiled.

"Have no fear," said Sainte-Croix, "this is my companion, my friend and instructor."

"I am called Exili," said the Italian, "and as you can plainly see, we understand each other."

"Really I do not know," faltered Penautier, making a desperate effort to recover his composure.

"The matter is scarcely susceptible of any misunderstanding. If Monsieur de Sainte-Croix were not naturally so violent and impulsive, he would have already realised that mutual hatred unites you both against Hanyvel."

"You are mistaken, sir."

"I am never mistaken. Is not the man you speak of the Receiver-General of the Clergy? A fine position, truly, worth a hundred and fifty thousand livres a year. And have I not heard that you, being the treasurer of the States of Languedoc, would be quite competent to take Hanyvel's place if any misfortune happened to him?"

"Well?"

"Ah well, the misfortune will happen to him."

"Sir, I request you to explain," exclaimed Penautier, breathless with emotion.

But just then the footsteps of the warder resounded in the corridor outside.

"We have not time," was the Italian's reply. But going straight to the cavity in the wall, he took from it a small phial which he handed to Penautier, who had become deathly pale, and who was wiping away, with his lace handkerchief, the perspiration that bathed his forehead.

"Take this," said Exili; "two drops will suffice to relieve our friend Sainte-Croix of a painful memory, and to relieve the Marquise de Brinvilliers of any further fear of the indiscretion of a malicious person, not to mention the treasurership of the clergy, which might certainly fall to you if that man Hanyvel died."

The warder was at the door. "Take it, take it!" urged Sainte-Croix, in a low tone.

The visitor seized the phial with a trembling hand, and secreted it in his richly embroidered ruffle.

"Come, monsieur, you must go now," said the warder.

Penautier staggered to the door, and was about to disappear, when Exili sent him a sneering farewell in the shape of: "My compliments, Monsieur Receiver-General of the Clergy!"

When the door had closed upon the prisoners again, and the sound of their visitor's footsteps had died away in the distance, Exili approached Sainte-Croix, and taking him by the hand, said : "Chevalier, do you know the traitor whom you will have to call to account? Do you know the man who, with the patience of a Jesuit and the ferocity of a Tartuffe, devised the infamous conspiracy that threw you into the Bastille? That man, my son, I tell you, is the hypocrite who has just left us—Monsieur Reich de Penautier."

"I know it," replied Sainte-Croix quietly.

The Italian gazed at his companion in profound astonishment.

"Yes," continued Sainte-Croix, "I suspected it at the beginning of the conversation, and the conclusion of the interview converted my doubts into a certainty."

"And yet you gave no sign?"

"No, for it is upon this man that I rely for my fortune in the future."

"Good, very good!" exclaimed the Italian, shaking his companion's hands enthusiastically. "Now I recognize in you my beloved son and worthy disciple in very truth."

VI.

THE LEAGUE OF DEATH.

AFTER Penautier's visit there seemed to be a complete change in the character of Sainte-Croix. There were no more outbursts of gaiety or paroxysms of passion, on his part; on the contrary, he seemed to be constantly absorbed in a gloomy reverie.

His fellow-prisoner often noticed him sitting with fixed and dilated eyes, so deeply engrossed in thought that he did not even hear his companion when he spoke to him.

"Will you not tell me, chevalier," the Italian asked one day, when Sainte-Croix had seemed even more taciturn than usual, "will you not tell me the thoughts that thus cloud your brow, and draw an occasional muttered oath from you?"

Sainte-Croix hesitated a moment. "Ah, well," he replied at last, almost angrily, "I will confess it. I am afraid."

"You, chevalier? Fie! you do yourself injustice. Your heart is, I am sure, above the senseless anxiety and foolish terror that torment the vulgar herd."

"Yes; but for all that, I repeat that I am afraid."

"But of what?"

"Of the terrible weapon you have rashly placed in Penautier's hands."

"Remorse—remorse! Is it possible?" exclaimed the Italian, in real or well-feigned astonishment.

The chevalier shrugged his shoulders. "Are you really sure of your poison, Exili?" he inquired.

"Ah, so that is it! Well, you need have no fears."

"It is in Penautier that I have placed all my hopes. What if he should fail us? What if he should be detected, tried, put to torture, and then place the blame upon us? Then all hope of regaining my liberty would be lost forever."

"Fool! the poisons I distill have never betrayed me."

"Would that I could believe you!"

"Have I ever deceived you?"

"How can I tell?" replied the chevalier. "Have I not always been obliged to accept your work without proof? You have said to me, 'This is a poison.' I have believed you. You have said to me, 'This substance produces such and such effects.' That, too, I have believed; but I have never had any *proof* that you were right, and that is why I am beset with doubts which I cannot overcome. Now that the test is near at hand, will the fatal elixir do its work, and will not Hanyvel's corpse reveal the secret of my revenge and Penautier's cupidity?"

The Italian reflected a moment. "What you say is true, chevalier," he said at last. "You desire proofs—that is only right—and you shall have them; for the experiments on the few rats we have succeeded in capturing cannot have been particularly convincing. A man is needed, and here is one at your service."

"What do you mean?"

"Listen, oh, thou of little faith, and thou wilt believe, like the apostle after having seen and touched, and no longer question thy master's word."

The Italian drew a tiny phial from his bosom, and uncorked it with the greatest care. Then, inserting a needle into the liquid it contained, he shook the point twice over one of the goblets which the prisoners used at their meals. Two almost invisible drops fell into the cup.

Just at that moment the jailer entered, bringing the prisoners' dinner. "Good news, gentlemen," he said, depositing two bottles of wine upon the table; "this is the birthday of Monseigneur de Baisemeaux de Montlezun, and our worthy governor desires his guests to celebrate it by drinking to the health of the King. Taste this, and you will tell me what you think of it." And he smacked his lips with a gusto that testified to the exalted esteem in which the governor's gala wine was held in the Bastille.

Exili cast a meaning glance at Sainte-Croix; and, pointing to one of the bottles, he said: "Pour some out, my good fellow, and let us enjoy the bounty of Monsieur de Baisemeaux together."

The jailer quickly uncorked the bottle and filled the goblets.

"Will you have some, chevalier?" inquired the Italian, addressing Sainte-Croix. The chevalier shook his head. "You are wrong, upon my word! Wine is a prisoner's only sunshine. When you have spent ten years in our company you will not thus scorn the great consoler."

And offering the jailer the goblet in which he had let fall two drops from the tiny phial, he took up the other, chinked it lightly against the jailer's, and drained it, after crying: "God grant long life to His Majesty Louis XIV."

The jailer also lifted the glass to his mouth. But the liquid had scarcely touched his lips when he fell to the ground as if struck by lightning.

Sainte-Croix stood watching the scene in a state of stupefaction. "Is the man dead?" he exclaimed at last.

"Yes, if I so choose," replied Exili, quietly. "But just now I am content that he shall fall asleep rather suddenly. Still if I did not arouse him from this terrible slumber which, as you see, has all the appearance of death, he would never awake again."

Sainte-Croix bent over the apparently lifeless body of the jailer.

"Yes, that is right," exclaimed the Italian; "look at him, examine him closely, lift his rigid arms, lay your hand upon his heart which has ceased to throb, and tell me if it is not a corpse that lies before you."

The chevalier obeyed the directions of his master, and soon began to perceive that the jailer's hands were growing cold. Then he rose, and in a terrified voice, exclaimed : " You are mistaken, Exili, this man is really dead. You have killed him."

" I can allow him to remain in this condition for thirty hours with perfect safety," responded the impassable Italian. "Yes, I have made this experiment several times, and have even caused a suspension of life for two days, and then resuscitated those who were to all appearance dead. To delay longer than that, however, is imprudent, as I have satisfied myself by numerous experiments."

" Is it in this way that Hanyvel will die ? "

" Yes, but more quickly. Two minutes after he falls to the ground he will cease to live, for his dose will be infinitely stronger, and all my art cannot restore life when the spark has been entirely extinguished."

"But what if the physicians had any suspicion of the truth, or if the family demanded an autopsy ? "

" The physicians would discover that he died from a rupture of one of the lobes of the heart. "

" But what if they analyzed the wine left in the glass ? "

" Have I not told you a hundred times that my elixirs defy all detection ? Have I not told you a hundred times that the most skilful chemists in Italy attempted in vain to analyze the wines that Madame Olympia Mancini served to her guests, those exquisite wines that produced such swift and certain death ? "

" And they found nothing ? "

" Nothing."

There was a long silence between the two accomplices. A fiendish pride beamed on the face of the Italian ; while Sainte-Croix was overcome with wonder and awe.

" As for that man lying there," continued Exili, " I alone can draw him from the trance into which he has fallen. The surgeon's scalpel could mutilate his flesh, but would not awaken him."

Exili then turned to the secret cavity in the wall, and took from it a bottle about three quarters full of a crimson liquid. "Now watch closely, chevalier," was all he said.

The Italian lifted the head of the unfortunate jailer and placed it upon his knee ; then with the aid of a knife he unlocked his set teeth, and allowed five or six drops of the liquid to drop into his mouth. The jailer made a slight movement. Exili allowed some moments to pass, and then repeated the operation. This time the man opened his eyes.

"What has happened to me ? " he asked after a moment.

"Nothing of much consequence," replied the Italian ; and turning to Sainte-Croix he added : "Lend a hand here, and help me to set this poor fellow on his feet again."

Sainte-Croix complied, and his companion, having poured some water into a goblet, and added to it about half that remained of the crimson liquid, presented it to the jailer, saying : " Drink, my good fellow, this will set you right again."

"Thank you, my masters," replied the warder, after he had drained the glass. " I feel much better now, though my head seems a little heavy and there seems to be a fire raging in my breast."

"That will amount to nothing," replied Exili, " you only need to be bled a little."

" Do you really think so, monsieur ? "

"I am sure of it. But you have cause to congratulate yourself on your good fortune, for if such a thing had happened to you in any other cell, you would certainly have died."

"That's true," answered the jailer, shuddering at the idea. "The prison doctor lives at Versailles, and I should have had time to die a dozen times before he could have got here."

"That is very reassuring for us prisoners," remarked Sainte-Croix.

"Oh, you have nothing to fear, monsieur; isn't your friend with you? He would save you as he just saved me." Then taking Elixi's hand, and raising it to his lips, the jailer continued: "God bless you, monsieur. I was already indebted to you for the life of my wife, now I owe you mine. Whatever you may ask of me, rest assured it shall be done. Everything except helping you to make your escape, for I could be of no assistance to you in that, and any effort of the kind would certainly cost me my place."

"Thanks, thanks, my friend," said the Italian; "but now go, for your absence may be misinterpreted."

"I am going, monsieur, but allow me to thank you once more. Ah! when I think that there are men who say that you are a poisoner! How can people be so wicked?"

And the jailer departed, leaving Exili triumphant, and Sainte-Croix positively confounded.

The next day, the same warder took Exili aside. "Monsieur," he said, "I think I have found a way to be of service to you."

"How?"

"By taking charge of a note for your friend Monsieur de Sainte-Croix."

"Who gave it to you?"

"A man I don't know. At the same time he handed me ten pistoles. I accepted them, but I will return them to him if you say so."

"You may keep them, my worthy fellow, but now the note."

The jailer looked cautiously around, as if fearing that the walls had eyes; then reassured, he drew from his pocket a tiny note rolled into the smallest possible compass, placed it in the hands of the man he called his preserver, and hurried away as fast as his legs could carry him.

"News from Penautier, chevalier," exclaimed Exili, "and good news, I'll be bound!"

"Give it to me! give it to me!' cried Sainte-Croix, frantic with excitement. He unrolled the paper and found written upon it, these words: "Our lovely friend deigned to fill the festal cup. He drained it to the last drop. All goes well. We hope to see our dear prisoner soon again."

"Curses upon him!" cried Sainte-Croix. "The infamous wretch compelled the marquise to poison Hanyvel. He was afraid, the coward! And she—it was from love for me that she consented to do the deed."

"Where is the harm?" inquired Exili gently. "You are unreasonable, my friend. Will you not need her aid on the day you attack Monsieur Dreux d'Aubray and his sons?"

"So be it then. There are now four of us united in this terrible league of blood. You are in my power, Penautier, and this note which in your delight you have been imprudent enough to send to me, after being mad enough to indite it with your own hand, makes you doubly mine, so henceforth my will must be yours. I shall maintain my hold even if I am obliged to ruin myself to do so."

"I thought Penautier a shrewder man," said Exili, shaking his head.

"For a person to commit himself in writing, under such circumstances, is an unpardonable blunder. But this decides me. Once out of prison now, the means of leaving France will not be lacking."

"What do you mean?"

"Nothing, except that I believe the hour of freedom has come at last."

On hearing the word freedom, which had so long been the subject of his thoughts and aspirations, Sainte-Croix could not repress an eager exclamation. "Can we make our escape?" he cried.

"I think so."

"But you have told me a hundred times that you had renounced all hope of regaining your liberty."

"No; I told you that the hour had not yet come; now it is different. I have taught you all that I can teach you here; and now your knowledge is sufficiently great to enable you to pursue alone the studies we began together. I have revealed to you the secrets I reverently received from my master, and if anything remains to be told, it is only because I must see you at work in prosperity, after having been tried in adversity. Do you think this year of toil and privation has been lost to you?"

Sainte-Croix replied by silently pressing the old alchemist's hand.

"I hope not, for the sake of humanity," continued Exili; "for you are the pupil I have been vainly seeking for years."

A diabolical smile played upon the thin lips of the terrible poisoner, as he uttered these words, and the chevalier could not repress a shudder in spite of the firmness of his will.

"No. I have never renounced the idea of regaining my liberty," Exili resumed, after a pause; "but my devotion to science enabled me to wait in patience. In past times I hoped for the intervention of those who had availed themselves of my skill since I had been an inmate of this prison, they were certainly sufficiently powerful to open my dungeon doors for me—"

"And now?"

"Now they probably feel able to dispense with my services, and perhaps even desire my death. We will do without their aid."

"Then you propose an attempt at escape?"

"You have said it, chevalier."

Sainte-Croix remained thoughtful and motionless; but upon his brow and in his eyes, Exili could read his every thought as from an open book. The chevalier was silently enumerating all the obstacles to be overcome. One by one he counted all the precautions taken to prevent the escape of prisoners from the Bastille, the innumerable guards and sentinels and the lofty walls; and he asked himself what two poor captives could accomplish against such fearful odds. He had made this recapitulation again and again before, and each time he had said to himself: "Impossible." This time, he arrived at the same discouraging conclusion, so it was with an air of profound dejection, and in answer to his own thoughts rather than to the words of the Italian, that he cried: "Ah! it would be madness to make the attempt even."

"No," replied Exili, firmly, "not when a prisoner has one chance out of a hundred."

"But have we even that solitary chance?"

"Yes, we have."

"Then God grant that we may succeed!" murmured the chevalier.

"Perhaps you are wrong to invoke God's aid in this matter, my dear pupil," said the Italian. "It would certainly be greatly to His advantage if we never emerged from this prison."

Exili uttered these words in a tone of intense scorn and sarcasm, and although Sainte-Croix took a strange pride in proving himself his master's equal in all that was vile, he blushed deeply. "I see that it has pleased you to test my strength of character," he said sullenly. "It was an unpleasant experiment to make."

"Have I ever deceived you?" asked Exili, sternly. "Do you suppose I have lost sight of my liberty for a single instant during my imprisonment? My plan was made while you were still free. Its very impossibility is an element of success; and that is why I say to you: 'Hope;' that is why I repeat : 'We have a chance of success.'"

"Speak, I entreat you," exclaimed the chevalier, breathless with excitement—"speak, tell me your plans, or rather your hopes !"

The Italian answered not a word, but taking up a rude chisel made from an iron kitchen utensil stolen from the jailer, he knelt down near the wall against which stood the pallet of Sainte-Croix. He examined this wall carefully for an instant, then having evidently found what he sought, he began to pick at the cement which united the blocks of stone.

Sainte-Croix noticed that this cement, instead of being pulverized by the instrument, was removed in long narrow strips; and on stooping in his turn to discover the cause of this phenomenon, he saw that what he had supposed to be mortar, was merely bread crumbs. "Our task seems to have been strangely simplified," he exclaimed joyfully.

The Italian gave no sign of having heard his companion's words, but worked on with feverish haste. He had already loosened five or six large stones which he removed with the greatest caution, and a brick wall had become visible. After removing some of these bricks which had also been previously loosened, an opening large enough for a man to pass through was revealed. With an agility certainly not to be expected in one of his years, he glided through this opening, motioning his companion to follow him. They then found themselves in a kind of loft between the floor of their cell and the ceiling of the room below, and large enough for a man to stand in, by stooping a little.

"The deuce," said Sainte-Croix. "How is it that Monsieur de Baisemeaux, who is so embarrassed where to lodge his guests, has not thought of utilizing this spot by installing two or three prisoners here?"

"He is probably ignorant of the existence of this loft, which was doubtless constructed some time ago to diminish the height of the ceiling in the room below, which was probably occupied by some prisoner of distinction. But look, chevalier."

Exili had just cautiously removed a large stone, blackened with smoke.

"Yes," said the chevalier, "in that way, it would be easy to make one's way through the chimney, but this would simply lead us into another cell, would it not?"

"You need feel no anxiety on that account; but let us go back. At this time of day we are liable to interruption and a surprise, but I can now explain my plan."

As he spoke, he replaced the stone. They made their way back to their cell with very little difficulty. The bricks were restored to their places, the stones were carefully re-adjusted, and the interstices between them again filled up with crumbs of bread. Exili satisfied himself that no one could detect the work in which he had just been engaged, and made assurance doubly sure by sprinkling a handful of dust over the place. Not till then did he show himself disposed to resume his revelations.

" I am listening, master," said Sainte-Croix, devoured by impatience.

" You are perhaps aware," said the Italian, " that the room in which the prisoners are tortured is situated on the first floor of the tower which we occupy."

" I was not aware of it."

" Fortunately for us, I made this discovery on the day following my entrance into the Bastille, for they concluded to torture me a little in order to extort a confession from me."

" What, my friend, is it possible you were put to torture ? "

" Yes, but in a very gentle manner, I assure you. They desired a confession, and I seemed very willing to make it. Never did a prisoner display a more ready tongue."

Sainte-Croix looked at Exili with an intensely astonished air. " What !" he exclaimed, " is it possible that you, who always evince such wonderful strength of will, were daunted by the prospect of physical suffering ? "

The Italian smiled. " The judges, seeing me so willing to speak, were suddenly overcome by a truly extraordinary terror."

" But what could they have been afraid of ? "

" Of a mere trifle. Merely of hearing my replies."

" But what did they ask you to divulge ? "

"The names of the persons who had visited me, since my arrival in France."

" Yes. I understand."

" The anxiety and alarm of the poor creatures actually excited my pity. Their lips questioned me, but their eyes entreated me to be silent. Perhaps you will some day be favoured with the sight of a tribunal examining a prisoner with fear and trembling, and dreading his answers far more than he dreads their questions. This was the case with me, and thus it is with all those who have been in any way connected with the intrigues of the court. As a rule, princes are by no means fond of the men who have been made conversant with their peccadilloes, either by chance or curiosity, and I myself am well acquainted with a good many secrets dangerous to their possessors."

" I can very readily understand then why they like to feel that you are in a safe place. The Bastille guards secrets very effectually."

" That was the opinion of my judges ; but they preferred not to share my secrets for fear they might be obliged to share my prison as well ; and as I succeeded in convincing them that I would reveal everything as soon as I was put to torture, they acted with infinite caution."

" Ah ! " exclaimed Sainte-Croix, " everything is explained now ! "

" What, pray ? "

"The length of my captivity and the obstacles my friends encounter when they plead for my release."

" What do you mean ? "

" Yes, that explains it," continued the chevalier, involuntarily recoiling from his companion in a sort of horror. " It is known that I share your cell, and people probably imagine that you have confided your secrets to me. Consequently your friendship dooms *me* to eternal imprisonment as well as yourself."

" Child," replied the Italian compassionately, " the matters of which I speak are far above the comprehension of the governor of the Bastille. In his eyes, I am only an inoffensive simpleton. No : your prolonged imprisonment is not due to that cause, but rather to Penautier, who, if he is shrewd, must be extremely anxious for you to remain in your present quarters."

"Ah ! if I really thought that ! "

"Still, this matters little as we shall soon both be free. Now listen to me. While they were torturing me with all the gentleness imaginable, I had an opportunity of examining the apartment at my leisure. At the end of the room I noticed a sort of furnace or forge at which the irons were heated. A large fire is made there sometimes, so I said to myself that the chimney must be large and go straight up to the roof. I afterwards satisfied myself that the wall against which this furnace stood must correspond with one of the walls of my cell."

"Then this was the chimney we have just seen ? "

"Precisely; but as you may suppose, I had considerable difficulty in finding it. For more than a week I vainly sounded all the stones in the wall ; but the fact is, the chimney makes a sudden turn, and if it had not been for the loft between the ceiling of the room below and the floor of our cell, all my hopes would have been destroyed, for I had already in thought devised a plan for making my escape by way of this chimney."

"But what revealed the existence of this loft to you ? "

"Chance. Summoned to the office one day, I noticed that the door of the cell below ours was open, and I caught a glimpse of the ceiling. I measured its height with my eyes, then, after counting the steps on my way up here again, I arrived at the conclusion that there must be a large vacant space. So the same night I set to work and soon discovered what I sought."

"But in what way shall we be any better off when we have reached the torture-chamber ? "

"Wait a moment." rejoined the Italian. "It had originally been decided to subject me to the water ordeal, but the judges abandoned the idea. When they gave orders that I should be taken back to my cell, I could see the executioner pour the water which had been prepared in advance into a large circular orifice not far from the furnace. I listened attentively, and a dull, prolonged sound convinced me that this water must fall a great depth, so I concluded that the receptacle must be some unused cistern communicating with the moat of the Bastille. It was necessary to make sure of this fact, however. As soon as I had discovered the loft and found the chimney I did not hesitate to enter it. On reaching the torture-chamber I succeeded without much difficulty in lifting the cover of the cistern. I entered this, too, without the slightest hesitation."

"And you found you were mistaken, were you not?" interrupted Sainte-Croix, who was listening to his companion's narrative with terrible anxiety.

"No, I was not mistaken. Reaching the bottom of the cistern, not without considerable danger, I found there a sort of narrow canal, in which about half a foot of sluggish, muddy water flowed slowly along. I already considered myself saved, and was fancying myself free when, after proceeding about fifteen feet, my progress was suddenly arrested by an unexpected obstacle. An enormous block of stone obstructed the channel at this point, only a tiny opening underneath it giving passage to the water. Alas ! all my efforts to move this mass of stone were useless : I only bruised my hands in vain. At last, I realised that I could remain there no longer. Morning was approaching, so I went back to my cell, resolved to excavate a passage for myself under the stone ; but, unfortunately, the next day I had a companion."

Sainte-Croix shuddered at these words. He remembered the mysterious death of those who had previously shared the cell of the terrible poisoner. "The new-comer might have been a most valuable assistant," resumed Exili, after a moment's silence, "but before confiding my hopes to him I wished to know if he were worthy of my confidence, for an imprudent disclosure might cost me my life."

"But why should you feel any such suspicions? His desire to be free would be a sufficient guarantee, it seems to me."

"An act of treachery might also insure him his freedom. To test him, I told him some harmless secret. The very next day he sent for the commandant and disclosed what I had confided to him."

"And that sealed his fate!"

"You have said it."

"Poor wretch!" murmured Sainte-Croix.

"Yes," said Exili bitterly, "poor wretch, who unscrupulously betrayed the confidence of a companion in misery. Ah! his death does not weigh very heavily upon my conscience. Had I not a right to protect myself? Several times I repeated my perilous expedition, but I was obliged to abandon the idea of digging a passage under the stone. The channel was carefully paved, and the block of sandstone resisted all my efforts to displace it. Then I tried to remove the stone—a gigantic task which would have appeared impossible to any one but a prisoner—destitute as I was of every sort of implement, and obliged to labour in the most profound darkness. But time and patience are two forces which nothing can withstand. Give me time enough, and I will tear down the Bastille with a pin. An imperceptible drop of water constantly falling eventually wears away a solid rock; hence I hoped to win a final victory over this stone, which was all that separated me from freedom. Every night for two long years I repeated my perilous expedition; then another companion was given me, but he, too, died. I wished to be free. I had succeeded in manufacturing several tools—a file, a rude chisel and a lever—and at last, one night after unheard-of efforts, I felt that the stone was beginning to loosen slightly. I went almost wild with joy, but my exultation suddenly abated, alas! for I realised for the first time that I should never succeed unaided in pushing the stone far enough on one side to allow me a passage."

"Oh, but now I will join my strength to yours," exclaimed Sainte-Croix, "and we will overcome this obstacle. Come, Exili, don't let us delay a moment. I feel that I am endowed with sufficient strength to move the world!"

Exili smiled. "You are impatient, chevalier," he said quietly.

"Impatient! when I see that liberty, the most precious thing on earth, is within my grasp. Oh, my friend, why have you allowed me to suffer such untold agony by your side for more than a year in this dreary dungeon, when you could have opened its doors for me? The day you decided that I was worthy to become your pupil, why did you not say to me: 'Come, let us depart—freedom is ours?' Don't you understand that by conferring such a boon upon me, you would have bound me to you more indissolubly than by associating me in your researches—"

"But I have not yet told you all the obstacles," interrupted Exili. "There is one which time only could remove."

"And that?"

"While I devoted my time at night in toiling to perfect my work of deliverance, I employed my mental faculties during the day time in an attempt to obtain a correct plan of this part of the Bastille, for it was of the utmost importance that I should discover the outlet of this subterranean canal. It would take too long to recount the thousand and one stratagems to which I resorted to achieve this end, but at last I ascertained that the canal was not connected with the moat of the fortress, but with another cistern in the governor's garden."

"And did not despair seize you then?" inquired the chevalier, astounded at so much patience and at such a display of indomitable will.

"A true man never yields to despair. He makes his way around the difficulties which he cannot surmount. Only fools fling themselves down before the obstacle that impedes their progress. By feigning illness, I managed to obtain permission to visit the governor's garden. There I saw the cistern. To scale its walls would be an easy matter, and this achieved, only one serious difficulty remained to be overcome—the rampart. It would be necessary to descend to the moat, and the height is immense.

"'A ladder is indispensable,' I said to myself, 'and that ladder I must have.' And to accumulate the necessary material now became my only aim. The linen you have heard me ask for so often for you and for myself was intended for that purpose; the bandages I have obtained from the surgeon on the plea of a rheumatic limb, which I have never had, have all been devoted to the same object. But such is your inexperience and thoughtlessness that you have never even noticed this fact."

"That is true!" exclaimed Sainte-Croix. "I recollect now. How many times I have seen you tear strips from the sheets on your bed, and then hem them again! But escape seemed such an utter impossibility that I did not even think of asking you what you intended to do with the strips. Why did you not tell me sooner?"

Exili smilingly shook his head. "By acquainting you with my plans, I should have made your captivity a thousand times more painful. By my instructions and our experiments, I have been able to shorten the time a little."

"But could I not have assisted you?"

"In no way. The only thing that could be done was to wait, and you do not know how to do that."

"Still—"

"Look at yourself now. Your hands are trembling; your face is on fire; your eyes are as wild as those of a lunatic. I know you better than you know yourself; and I have acted wisely. But now—now everything is in readiness: we have the necessary material. We only need a little time to manufacture a strong ladder. I know where to find a safe refuge on leaving this place, and in a month, chevalier, we shall be free."

Frantic with joy, Sainte-Croix folded Exili in a convulsive embrace. "Oh, my friend, my instructor, my benefactor!" he exclaimed; "why can I not, at this very hour, pour out all my blood for you—for you, who after arming me against all mankind, treat me as a father treats his son, and allow me to share the fruit of your patience and courage! Ah, thanks! a thousand thanks! Madeleine, my beloved Madeleine, I shall soon see you again! I shall soon be doubly blessed, through my love and my revenge."

"Do not forget that the stone has still to be moved," interrupted the aged alchemist, smiling at his pupil's exultation.

"Can you doubt our ability to do it, Exili? I don't, I."

In the meantime Exili had removed the coverings from his bed and opened his mattress. It was filled with strips of linen of all kinds, accumulated during the past two years. "Here are our treasures," he said.

They began their task without delay. It seemed to Sainte-Croix that time passed with marvellous rapidity now—the nights only seemed intolerably long. He could not sleep. As soon as he closed his eyes, frightful phantoms disturbed his slumbers, and his dreams always ended in a terrible fit of nightmare. He imagined himself in the subterranean canal, exhausting himself in fruitless efforts to move the stone. It resisted his efforts, then finally fell upon his breast, crushing him with its ponderous weight.

Sometimes he fancied himself upon the ramparts of the Bastille; all obstacles had been successfully overcome; he had even passed the sentinels in the governor's garden, unobserved. He fastened his ladder securely, and made the perilous descent in safety. He had reached the ground; he was free! But the soldiers suddenly surrounded him; and he was again a prisoner! Then he woke up with a start, his forehead thickly covered with great drops of cold perspiration.

He was less fortunate than his companion. The impassible Italian slept, or pretended to sleep soundly. Seated upon his couch, Sainte-Croix awaited the dawn of day with feverish impatience, so intense was his longing to resume his labours. He ate almost nothing, and seemed to be scarcely conscious of what he was doing.

"You are killing yourself," Exili often said to him. "You are exhausting your strength by your foolish impatience. When the decisive moment comes, your strength will fail you."

"Never! This fever won't leave me until after I have made my escape from this place."

Formerly, Sainte-Croix had looked forward with genuine pleasure to the daily visits of the jailer who brought them their rations. He was a sort of link with the world from which the prisoners had been so long separated, a link between the realm of the living and of the dead. But now, these visits seemed unendurable to him. Each of them was at least a half-hour lost. Formerly, too, he had liked to chat with the jailer, and had detained him as long as possible, questioning him about the fortress, M. de Baisemeaux and his fellow prisoners; but now that his mind was engrossed with thoughts of liberty, he pretended to sleep in order to avoid talking or even replying.

Even the obtuse jailer observed the change and was alarmed by it. "The chevalier must certainly be ill," he remarked to Exili.

"It is the effect of prison life," replied the Italian.

"You must be right. Still, he seemed to have grown accustomed to it."

"It really did appear so."

"Ah! he is very wrong to mope like that and make himself ill. It does no good. Besides, what does he lack except freedom? Absolutely nothing. Why doesn't he resign himself to his fate? I don't know what makes our prisoners long so passionately for liberty. As if it were not easy enough to do without it!"

"That is what I tell the chevalier."

"You are very sensible, mousieur. Persuade him to ask the governor to increase his ration of wine, and he will become more cheerful."

"I will endeavour to do so."

"Besides, he is with you," said the jailer in conclusion, "which is certainly very fortunate for him, for in case he fell dangerously ill, you would be able to cure him." Thereupon the jailer left the cell.

"That man and his stupid conversation bore me to death!" exclaimed Sainte-Croix.

"That does not prevent him from being tolerably clear-sighted; and if such is the case, he will soon discover our plans."

"Woe to him if he does so! I am your pupil, Exili, and, like you, I know how to defend my liberty. If I suspected that the slightest suspicion of the truth had entered his stupid brain, I would close his lips not only speedily but effectually."

Their work progressed slowly, but without any interruption. According to Exili's calculation, the ladder must now be of about the required length. The prisoners had tested its strength with great care, and found that it would support a weight ten times greater than that of each of them. Large knots had been made at regular intervals in order to facilitate the fugitives' descent. Finally, two pieces of iron, of which they had secured possession, were bent in such a manner as to form two strong hooks.

Sainte-Croix and his companion could now count not the days but the hours that intervened between them and liberty. Everything was settled and arranged, and at the last moment they meant to break up one of their beds to obtain a lever to aid them in moving the stone.

While the two prisoners were completing their final arrangements on the afternoon preceding the evening appointed for their flight, they heard the bolts of their door creak, whereupon they hastily concealed everything likely to compromise them. "A visit at this hour," whispered Sainte-Croix. "What can it mean?"

"No good, certainly," replied Exili in the same tone.

The jailer entered. "Good and bad news, gentlemen," said he; "good for you chevalier, but bad for your friend."

"Are they going to separate us?" inquired Exili, anxiously.

"Alas! that such partings must be," continued the jailer. "I have orders to conduct the chevalier to the office. This evening he will be free."

"Free!" exclaimed Sainte-Croix, pale with emotion. "Free!" He staggered, flung up his arms, and fell heavily upon his pallet.

"Goor heavens! he is dying!" cried the jailer. "And I expected to cause him so much joy. I ought to have broken the great news to him more cautiously."

Exili, overcome with very different emotion, made no reply.

"Thanks, my friend, it is nothing," said Sainte-Croix, after a moment. "I feel better now. It was only an attack of dizziness which has passed off entirely. Lead on; I will follow you." And he tried to rise.

"What!" murmured Exili, "not a word for me?"

Sainte-Croix did not seem to hear him. "I will follow you, I will follow you," he repeated to the jailer. "Let us go at once."

"I beg your pardon, monsieur," responded the jailer, "but I must first visit one of my other prisoners. I thought I would come and give you warning a few moments in advance, so that you might have time to bid your friend farewell."

"But you will not be long," insisted Sainte-Croix. "I seem to be suffocating here."

" Have no fear, chevalier, I will soon return." And the jailer left the cell, closing the door behind him.

Sainte-Croix, who seemed to have entirely forgotten his friend's presence, placed his ear at the keyhole. " His footsteps are receding in the distance," he murmured. " I hear them now on the staircase; he is going down. Good God ! what if he should not return ! "

" He will return, be assured of that," said Exili, gloomily.

The Italian's voice seemed to arouse the chevalier from a dream, and he turned and looked at the companion he had styled his preserver and saviour only a moment before. " Pardon me, pardon me. I am ashamed of my joy, Exili," he exclaimed ; " but I am not master of myself. Think how little I was prepared for this event ! And now I am going to be free at last."

" Yes, and your release condemns me to eternal imprisonment. You forget that."

" I can only repeat what I have already said. Forgive me ; but rest assured—"

" Why should I not forgive you ? " rejoined Exili, exercising visible con- straint over himself ; " your selfishness is only natural. It is that of all happy and fortunate persons. The prison doors are to open for you ; what do you care for the one who will be left behind ? "

" You are cruel."

" Not so ; I only know the nature of mankind. I do not even complain of the fate that awaits me."

" But you exaggerate your misfortunes. Everything is ready for your flight. I was to aid you, but some other prisoner will be glad to do so. You will soon have another companion, without any doubt."

" I have had only too many already."

Sainte-Croix made an impatient movement which was almost instantly repressed, but Exili perceived it. " I understand the annoyance I cause you," he continued.

" My friend," interrupted the chevalier, "you know how devotedly I love you, tell me how I can serve you. By making an effort to secure your release as soon as I am at liberty ? "

" That would be useless."

" Then how can I aid you ? "

" Listen to me and do not let us waste the short space of time allowed us by the jailer. You can do everything for me."

" You probably exaggerate."

" No ; but have no fears. What I ask will not compromise you in the least."

" What ! can you suppose—"

" That you would do nothing that would bring you back here ? Certainly not ; and that is very natural." Sainte-Croix attempted to protest, but the Italian checked him. " Let us make haste," he said, in that stern, hard voice which peril and a desperate resolve give to even the most composed men—"let us make haste ; we have no time to lose. Remember every word I am going to say to you. I am tired of the Bastille, and your de- parture will make my prison life a hundred times more intolerable. I can- not reconcile myself to the thought of remaining here, and I will not do so. To-morrow I shall be free or dead."

As he uttered these words, the Italian fixed his eyes searchingly on Sainte-Croix, as if desiring to read his most secret thoughts. " You are familiar with my poisons," he continued. "Do you recollect the experiment we made together upon our unfortunate jailer?"

"What do you mean?"

"I mean that I shall make the same experiment upon myself this very evening."

"You intend to poison yourself, Exili?"

"It is the only resource that remains. This poison, you know, is the most powerful of narcotics. Did I not prove this to you? Thanks to it, I can, without danger, suspend life in my body for twenty-four hours. This evening, my death will be reported: to-morrow, two jailers will carry my body to the cemetery without much ceremony. A prisoner who has been so long forgotten will not be buried very deeply. They will dig a trench, throw in the body, and spread a few shovelfuls of earth over it; then the jailers will pay a visit to the wine-shop, and that will be the end of it."

"Are you sure that this is the custom?"

"Our jailer has told me so a hundred times. Now, if there happened to be at the cemetery a friend who was the possessor of that same liquid, a few drops of which restored the jailer, whom you believed dead, to life again, what would be the result?"

"Ah, I fear I understand you," exclaimed Sainte-Croix.

"This friend would remove my body from its grave, and, by pouring a few drops of the blessed antidote into my throat, restore me to life."

"But it is a frightful method."

"It is the only one, and I am determined to be free. Now, chevalier, will you consent to be this friend?"

"No, never, never! Allow the man I love above all others to risk his life like that! I refuse."

"So be it. It matters little if I am left in my grave to die. At all events, my body will not be in the Bastille to-morrow."

"I will obey you," said Sainte-Croix at last, terribly agitated. "I will be at the cemetery to-morrow."

"And I will not fail to keep my appointment, chevalier, rest assured of that. But, above all, lose no time: as soon as the grave-diggers have retired, begin your work, and remember the manner in which I administered the antidote to the jailer."

He then confided to his companion's keeping a small phial which he had taken from the secret cupboard. "Here is my life," he said, solemnly. "My life is now in your hands. This evening Exili will cease to live."

The Italian had just finished giving his final instructions to his pupil, when the jailer reappeared. "Are you ready, chevalier?" he inquired.

Sainte-Croix threw himself into Exili's arms.

"Farewell, my friend, farewell," he said; and then in a whisper he added: "until to-morrow."

"Until to-morrow," murmured the Italian. And the door closed with a dreary clanking of chains and creaking of bolts.

Left alone, the alchemist paced to and fro in a terrible state of agitation. Brought face to face with death, he no longer thought of maintaining his composure, and the frightful anxiety that tortured him could be plainly read on his usually impassive face. "It is madness to subject oneself to such a hazardous experiment," he said to himself, pausing in his agitated promenade. "It is defying God to act in such a way with death. But what does it matter after all?" he exclaimed, resuming his soliloquy. "Is not a quick and violent death preferable to a long struggle with agony?

Who knows? Prostrated by suffering, weakened by despair, I should, perhaps, be a ridiculous sight to those who surrounded my death-bed. I might even be afraid, perhaps—I, who have never been known to tremble or turn pale. Who can vouch for his courage when the final hour comes? Who knows? I might perhaps ask for a priest—a priest! Exili, the poisoner, the right hand of Olympia Mancini, asking for a priest! Who knows? His pious curiosity might induce him to wrest my secrets from me. He might, perhaps, threaten me with the flames of hell, torture my troubled soul, and bewilder my failing intellect, until I humbly confessed everything. What an absurd farce it would be!"

A sneering laugh, which re-echoed dismally through the cell, imparted additional bitterness to these last words.

"No, no," continued the poisoner, "no more hesitation, no more weakness! Even if I die, I shall only solve the great mystery the sooner. This gratification of curiosity is worth no slight sacrifice. So the die is cast. My poisons, which have never disappointed me in their effects upon others, will not fail me when my own existence is at stake."

Hastening to the place in which his treasures were concealed, he broke all the bottles and phials, poured the deadly liquids into the ashes, and scattered the powders to the winds. Then he removed the stones that concealed the loft, and threw the *débris* into it. He also hid the now completed ladder in the same place.

As he concluded his task, he said to himself: "It would be cruel to deprive the poor wretch who may succeed me here of the means of making his escape. I will warn him."

He thereupon wrote a hasty account of the cunning scheme he had devised, added a plan of that part of the Bastille, and fastened the whole to one end of the ladder. Then, mounting on a stool, he scratched high up on the wall with a nail the one word, "Search," from the last letter of which he drew a line, extending to the stones he had loosened.

"Now for my own affairs!" he exclaimed.

He had already taken up the cup into which he had poured a portion of the narcotic, when a new thought suddenly flashed through his mind and made him pause.

"What if Sainte-Croix should not keep his promise!" he exclaimed.

He reflected for a long time. This keen observer passed in review each trifling circumstance that had occurred during the long months of captivity he had spent with the chevalier. He recalled every word and act of his former companion, analyzed the hidden meaning of them all, and finally arrived at this appalling conclusion: "No, he will not come; or, if he does, it will only be to make sure of my death. Who can tell? He will, perhaps, stamp down the earth over my grave, in the fear of seeing me rise from it sooner or later like an avenging phantom. Yes," he continued, unconsciously speaking aloud, so strong was his emotion—"yes, he will betray me—he will certainly betray me. Reason would not be reason, nor logic, logic, if he did not hate me; for he owes everything to me. I have provided him with weapons, so he will turn them against me. Intoxicated with the little I have taught him, he believes himself all-powerful—the master of the world. In me he rather sees a rival than a friend; and this thought is galling to his pride. He fancies he is able to do without me, so he is anxious to have me out of the way. Free, what should I be to this man? An accomplice. Now a man always rids himself of accomplices when he can do so without danger; that is a well-established fact. So my former friend has become my bitterest enemy. What meaning can the word friendship have to a man who basely deserted his own child? Besides, should I not do exactly as he will do if I were in his place? He is my pupil—what more need I say? But take care, chevalier, sooner or later I will have my revenge. I am not yet in the grave, and when a man like myself apprehends danger he always guards against it. I have still another resource!"

Exili then seated himself at the small table, in one corner of the cell, and taking up a pen, covered two pages of a sheet of paper with fine, close handwriting. In this sheet of paper, the contents of which he perused carefully several times, he wrapped a small phial, similar to that he had given to Sainte-Croix, and after tying both up in a handkerchief he seemed more tranquil in mind. The ironical smile of a man who has just averted a dire calamity by his shrewdness again appeared upon his lips. The paper he had written was addressed, " *To my son Olivier.*"

When the jailer entered the cell at the accustomed hour, bringing the prisoner's dinner, he found the Italian reclining upon his bed. "Are you ill, monsieur?" he inquired with genuine solicitude.

"I feel very badly," was the reply.

"You must not give way to your feelings in this manner. You have lost your friend, it is true; but Monsieur de Baisemeaux will soon send you another companion."

"The new prisoner will find the cell empty."

"Don't talk in that way, monsieur," pleaded the jailer, approaching the couch where the man he so often called his preserver was lying. "You don't know how bad you make me feel. Come, come, cheer up; your day of release will come by-and-bye, and if a bottle of good wine—"

"Thank you, my friend, for your interest; but I feel that my time has come. I am old, you know, very old, and I have suffered a great deal during my long life. My mind is still strong and healthy, but the earthly tabernacle is worn out, and my life is now only a flickering light which the slightest breath of air may extinguish at any moment. The sorrow of this unexpected separation will prove fatal."

Exili uttered these words in a faint, almost inaudible, voice. The jailer, deeply affected, wiped big tears of compassion from his eyes. "Tell me, at least, if I cannot do anything for you, monsieur," he said.

"Alas, my friend, one can do little for me now; and yet—if you still remember any of the services I have been fortunate enough to render you—"

"Well?"

"You might, indeed, greatly soothe my last moments."

"In what way?"

"But the attempt might cost you your place and your liberty. It is too much to ask."

The jailer straightened himself up, as if indignant at the thought that the prisoner could doubt his gratitude and devotion. "I owe my wife's life to you, monsieur," he said, "as well as my own. Mine is at your service; make use of it."

"The favour that I would ask," rejoined Exili, slowly, "is, that this very day, this package here may be sent to the address indicated on it, and that I should know before evening whether it has reached the person for whom it is intended. The happiness, the future, and, indeed, the very life of the being I love best in the world depend upon this. Can you do it?"

The jailer scratched his head, in accordance with his habit when he was deeply engaged in thought. "It is a very difficult job," he said at last. "You know we jailers are almost as much prisoners as yourselves, and that we never leave the Bastille. But wait a moment ; I think I can manage it. I will send a soldier to inform my wife that I wish to speak to her. I can see her in the office. I will slip your package into her hand, and in less than an hour she will give me the desired assurance of its delivery."

"Thank you, my friend," said the Italian, visibly affected by this proof of devotion on the part of his humble friend. "You will have soothed the last hours of a dying man—"

"Alas, monsieur, I am ashamed that I can do nothing more to prove my gratitude ; but I, too, am unfortunate."

"What ! are you not content with your position here in a royal fortress?"

"Ah ! if it were not for my wife and children, I should have thrown away this bunch of keys long ago."

"And what would you do instead ? "

"That is a hard question to answer. Who would employ a man who was formerly a jailer in the Bastille ? Ah, if I only had some influential friend !"

"You are ambitious, then ? "

"Alas, yes ! I would like to be a jailer at the Châtelet. That is a good position. It pays well, and there are a good many perquisites, to say nothing of the fact that a fellow is not a prisoner there. He can come and go as he likes, and spend part of his earnings with his friends."

"Ah, well ! my worthy fellow, I am not only a physician, but something of a prophet, and I predict that in less than three months your ambition will be realized."

"Heaven grant it, sir ! In the meantime, I am going to execute your commission."

The Italian awaited the return of his messenger with feverish impatience. At last, just as the clock was striking six, the door of the cell opened, and the honest jailer popped in his head. "My wife found the gentleman, sir," he said ; and then he fled, fearing detection.

A gleam of intense relief spread over Exili's face. "You will rue it, chevalier, rue it deeply, if you break your promise," he murmured. And seating himself on the bed, he raised the terrible narcotic to his lips with a firm hand, and fell back as if struck by lightning.

That same night, the guard, on making its first round, discovered the death of the Italian prisoner and reported it to the surgeon. The commandant gave orders that he should be buried on the following day. Only one man wept—the kind-hearted jailer. He purchased a taper and reverently placed it near the dead man's pallet.

VII.

OLIVIER'S HISTORY.

THE magnificent mansion and splendid grounds of Hanyvel de Saint-Laurent, the rich financier and Penautier's hated rival, were situated near the Place des Victoires, close to the Hôtel des Fermes. The district enclosed between the Rue Saint Honoré and the Rue Jean-Jacques-Rousseau was then the chosen abode of those who lived by finance. They congregated around the Hôtel des Fermes—the temple of Mammon at the time—

like devotees congregated in the shadow of a parish church; and their luxurious homes imparted the animation and stir of wealth to the streets which now appear so narrow and gloomy. One of the richest of these splendid abodes renowned for their artistic treasures was undeniably that of Messire Hanyvel, Lord of Saint-Laurent, and Receiver-General of the Clergy of France.

His immense wealth had enabled him to purchase a large expanse of ground occupied by squalid dwellings, and suddenly, as if by the power of a magician's wand, lovely gardens shaded by lofty trees had appeared, with luxuriant lawns, choice shrubbery, bowers, fountains, and statues. Nothing disturbed the delightful solitude of this terrestrial paradise, revealed only by the tall trees that towered above the walls. By the power of money, the financier had closed all the windows in the neighbouring houses that commanded a view of his grounds, and had become sole and undisputed monarch of his domain.

But one tiny attic-window, high up under the eaves of an adjacent house, now looked down upon the Receiver-General's oasis. This tiny window had escaped his notice, and even if he had observed it, he certainly would not have troubled himself about it; for people so poorly lodged had no existence in the eyes of such a wealthy personage.

But about the same time that the Chevalier de Sainte-Croix was arrested in the hostelry known as the *More-qui-trompe*, a young man, unusually grave and even gloomy in appearance, took possession of the little suite of rooms to which the chamber lighted by the tiny window belonged. The sight of the garden, with its luxurious lawns and beautiful trees, had decided him in his choice, and to secure undisputed possession of the rooms, he paid a year's rent in advance, though that was not then a custom established by landlords. He lost no time in taking possession of his new apartments, and never had he been so well pleased. It was then early spring-time : the sun rays were again full of beneficent warmth, and trees, flowers, and grass were waking to fresh life under the caresses of the soft April breeze. Leaning out of his narrow window, the young man thanked God for the boon of wealth which had been conferred upon his neighbour; for was he not a sharer in the rich man's good fortune? Did he not enjoy the garden as much as if he had been the owner of it? Gradually he became accustomed to look upon all these beauties as his own, at least in some degree, and he jestingly said : "*My* trees, *my* lawn, *my* statues, *my* flowers."

He secretly scolded the idle gardener, who fell asleep over his weeding; his wrath was excited by the awkward fellow who uprooted a plant ; and at the end of a month he was much better acquainted with all the beauties of the garden than Hanyvel himself.

But soon there was another and far more powerful attraction than those which had at first drawn him to the window. One morning he perceived the daughter of the rich financier walking in the garden. She was a remarkably beautiful young girl, a blonde, extremely graceful in bearing, with an exquisitely-moulded throat of pearly whiteness ; her thick, golden hair formed an aureole around her pure forehead ; her small, delicate mouth was most bewitching in expression, and when her rosy lips parted, they disclosed the loveliest chaplet of pearls an Eastern emperor ever dreamed of ; as for her dark, blue eyes they sparkled like the stars of a beautiful May night.

Dazzled by her wondrous beauty, the young man closed his eyes. When he opened them again, the radiant vision had disappeared, vanished, like one of those enchanting dreams that delight the imagination of youth.

It was not a dream, however, for this celestial vision again appeared to him. But the tranquil happiness he had formerly enjoyed was at an end. Half concealed behind the folds of the curtains, he spent whole days in watching for the young girl's coming ; and, in order to see her better, he would gladly have hewn down all the trees which he had so greatly admired a few days before, and the leaves of which occasionally concealed her from his view.

Every morning, at about the same hour, she came into the garden to visit a magnificent aviary, constructed in the centre of a clump of choice shrubbery, and this was the most blissful hour of the day for the young man. He loved her. And already his love was so great, so intense, that he speedily realised that one of those passions which prove fatal when they are hopeless, had taken possession of his heart. Alas ! this young girl was probably already promised to some wealthy financier or to some nobleman desirous of regilding his escutcheon. And he who had ventured to lift his eyes to her, and who loved her with all the strength of his being—why was he so audacious ? Who was he ?

His name was Olivier, and he had neither relative nor parent, nor any one whom he could call by the endearing name of friend. Indeed, he scarcely knew his age, and was even ignorant of the exact place of his birth. He had often endeavoured to collect the fleeting memories of his early years, but they were extremely shadowy and indistinct, and resembled those dreams when the mind is on the border-land between slumber and wakefulness.

He vaguely remembered having been reared in the country, in a peasant home. When he closed his eyes, he fancied he could still see a little thatch-covered cottage, built on the edge of a highway, and only a few steps from an immense forest. Sometimes, too, he remembered, or fancied he remembered, three or four dirty, shabbily-clad peasant lads, the companions of his childish sports, with whom he rolled upon the grass, or threw stones into a small limpid stream that flowed through the end of a large garden.

There ended all the recollections of his childhood prior to the day when he had left the farm-house never to return to it. That eventful day stood out with wonderful distinctness in his mind. It was the first real episode in his life, and, undoubtedly, the most important.

One morning a carriage, which seemed magnificent to his unsophisticated eyes—for it was drawn by four horses, ridden by postilions—drew up in front of the farm-house. An elderly nobleman, whom two attendants treated with the most profound respect, alighted, and asked for some refreshment, and the privilege of resting a few moments. Of course, the request was readily granted, and all the inmates of the farm-house, delighted at the presence of such a great lord in their humble dwelling, and probably expecting a munificent reward, crowded around the stranger, and endeavoured to anticipate his every wish.

The nobleman allowed them to do so, without appearing even conscious of their efforts, accepting their attentions with that supreme indifference peculiar to persons who are convinced that homage is only their due ; and from all the rural dainties which had been spread on a rustic table in the shade of an arbour, in front of the cottage door, he deigned to partake only of a few strawberries and a bowl of milk. Then he condescended to look at the group of children who were standing a short distance off, overcome with fear and admiration, and not a little dazzled by the richness of his garments. After a silent scrutiny which lasted nearly a quarter of an hour, he entered into a low-toned conversation with the farmer and his wife.

The proposal made by the traveller must have been extremely pleasing to the poor inmates of the farm-house, for both the husband and wife uttered an exclamation of joy, and began a long rigmarole of thanks and protestations of gratitude.

But the nobleman interrupted them by throwing upon the table a heavy purse, which the farmer eagerly pocketed.

The farmer's wife then took the hand of little Olivier, who called her mother, like the others, and, leading him to the stranger, said : " Look at this kind nobleman, who, Heaven be praised ! my son, wishes to insure your happiness. We are too poor to rear and educate you, and he is going to take you away with him. He will give you fine clothes, and good things to eat—so thank him gratefully, and try to be good, and to love him as if you were his own son."

These words had made such a deep impression on the child's mind that, even after he became a young man, he fancied he could still hear them ringing in his ears. But at the moment they were uttered, they seemed a dreadful and terrible decree. He understood nothing, save that he was to leave the farm-house, and those whom he called father, mother, and brothers—that he would never see them again, and that he would be obliged to follow this stern, severe-looking, old man, whom he saw now for the first time. He uttered heart-breaking cries, and clung with all his might to the farmer's wife, struggling valiantly, and defending himself as well as he could from the stranger, who wished to take him away.

But his puny efforts were fruitless. The two lackeys seized hold of him, and carried him to the carriage, which the gentleman had already entered ; the door was closed with a bang, the driver cracked his whip, and the horses started off at a gallop. The child wept a long time, with his face buried in the carriage cushions ; but the greatest of sorrows are soon forgotten at that age—his tears ceased to flow, and he gained sufficient courage to peep through his parted fingers at the nobleman who had so rudely torn him from his friends.

The stranger, who had not ceased to watch him, drew him closer, took him upon his knee, and, parting his curly hair, kissed him gently on the forehead. "Don't weep any more, my little friend," he said to him, in a caressing voice. "Don't you see that I shall love you very dearly ? You will be much happier with me than with the poor people we have just left, for I am rich, very rich, and henceforth you will be my son. You have only to speak, and your every desire shall be gratified. Come, won't you accept me as your father ? "

The recollection of the farm-house, and of the kind woman he had called mother, flashed through the poor little fellow's mind, and he again began to sob and struggle, crying : " Mother ! mother ! I want to go back to mother ! "

"Ah ! " murmured the nobleman, " at this happy age, all the evil in-stincts are still dormant in the heart of a child ; but the germs are there, and I shall know how to awaken them when it becomes necessary to do so."

He again tried to soothe his little companion. "What is your name, my child?" he inquired, in a voice which he endeavoured to make as winning as possible.

"Olivier."

"Ah! well, my little Olivier, as a beginning of your new life, we are going to purchase you some pretty clothes, for here we are in a large town —so dry your tears."

The carriage, in fact, was just entering Compiègne. It drew up before the principal hostelry, and a courier had, undoubtedly, preceded it, for the host stood waiting upon the threshold, cap in hand, bowing obsequiously as he offered to conduct his customer to the apartments which had been prepared for him. In a few hours—thanks to the ease with which gold slipped from his fingers—the old nobleman had procured some new and handsome garments for his *protégé*. The lad was bathed in perfumed water, and placed in the hands of a hair-dresser; and by evening he looked like the heir of some great nobleman of the Court, for silk, velvet, and lace had not been spared on his attire.

When this transformation was effected, the nobleman said : "Look at yourself, my child. Do you still long for your humble home, and the ragged garments that covered you? I hope that if you chanced to meet any of those little peasants whom you were playing with this morning, you will not even look at them."

"Oh! I love them so much, I long to return to them," replied the poor little fellow.

His benefactor's only response was a grimace, which made it impossible to doubt of the dissatisfaction this answer caused him. "Can it be that I have come across a really good nature?" he said to himself; "one of those naturally superior minds for which vice has no attractions, and which pass through life untainted by sin? It would be a rare and strange experience for me, truly. But, nonsense! even if this should be the case, I should still find it an interesting study, a welcome relief, after my previous experience. To see an honest man grow up under my guidance—would not that be miraculous? Upon my word! I will do nothing to change this child's nature; he shall be free to follow his natural instincts, whether they be good or bad."

That same evening, after an excellent supper—to which Olivier did but scanty justice, so sorrowful was his heart—the nobleman ordered the horses to be put to. This order seemed to strike dismay to the heart of the landlord, for, delighted with the generosity his lodger had displayed, he had hoped to keep him several days. In vain he expatiated on the charms of the surrounding country, the comforts of his establishment, the softness of his beds, and the skill of his cook; the traveller did not even seem to hear him. The carriage was brought round, and the nobleman was driven swiftly away by the liberally-paid postilions.

Olivier could distinctly recall each event of his life from that memorable day, the slightest detail of which was indelibly engraved upon his memory. Still, he had never been able to explain the strange atmosphere of mystery, of which he was vaguely conscious, around him, and which disturbed him not a little.

So far as he was able to judge, his benefactor was an immensely wealthy Italian nobleman, known as the Marquis de Florenzi. He was a man of impassible physiognomy—one of those persons over whose features of bronze time exerts no perceptible influence, and who, though they appear old when they are comparatively young, seem to remain all the rest of

their lives on the furthermost limits of a green old age that never becomes
decrepitude.   The possessor of a mild, equable, and even affectionate disposition, the marquis seemed really desirous of acting a father's part to
the child.   The lad was the object of his constant care and solicitude, and
was not left exclusively to the charge of hirelings, like many children belonging to the nobility.   Olivier soon became attached to his friend, with
all the fervour of his loving heart, and, when only a few months had
elapsed, the farm-house was almost forgotten.

For him, existence dated from the moment he was borne from childhood's
home, in the stranger's carriage.   In proportion as his mind matured, the
impressions of infancy faded away, and he almost forgot he had ever called
any other person than his benefactor by the endearing name of father.

In company with the marquis, Olivier travelled through France and
Italy.   For several months they sojourned at Florence ; but after a winter
spent in Venice, the marquis returned to Rome, and took possession of his
palace there.   This abode in the Eternal City justified its owner's reputation for almost boundless wealth.   It was one of those magnificent palaces
in which ten successive generations of owners have accumulated all the
treasures of luxury and art peculiar to each historical epoch.   Pictures,
tapestries, curious weapons, richly-carved caskets, superbly-wrought plate,
statues, and jewels aroused the well-deserved admiration of all connoisseurs.
But the owner of all these treasures had, undoubtedly, long since become
indifferent to their possession, for he seemed to set no value whatever upon
them ; and the wonder and ecstatic admiration of a few favoured visitors
alone revealed to Olivier the beauty and value of the objects that surrounded him.

The marquis entertained but little company.   He lived mostly in
seclusion, and went out only at night.   He spent entire days in a spacious
library, crowded with manuscripts and dusty, old books, and communicating, by a small door, with a sort of laboratory, from which strange
odours and a pungent smoke sometimes escaped.   It was to this library
that Olivier went every morning, to kiss the benefactor he called father,
and sometimes, in the afternoon, he lingered there to play.

The countless servants in the palace were always at the child's orders,
and endeavoured to anticipate his every wish.   If he desired to go out, a
carriage was immediately made ready ; if he wished to play, the large
garden, and rooms full of new toys, were at his disposal.   Masters of all
kinds—the best that Italy could furnish—were charged with his education ; and their task was an easy one, for the child acquired knowledge
with wonderful facility, his mind being one of those fertile fields which
return a hundred-fold the seed which the hand of the sower scatters there.
He remained in Rome until his eleventh year, and every one around him
could not help admiring the wonderful development of his intellectual
powers, and the precocious maturity of his reason.

He was living thus happy and contented, when one night the marquis
appeared by his bedside.   "My child," he said to him, "you must rise,
and depart with me.   Bid adieu to the lovely skies of our dear Italy, to
this palace, this treasure-house of art, and to everything which now sur-
rounds you, which you love, and which you will, perhaps, never see again.
We must depart."

The features of the marquis worked convulsively as he uttered these
words ; his voice was husky and broken, and a tear trembled on his eye-
lid.

The child replied at first only by throwing his arm around his benefactor's neck. "I shall regret nothing, provided I am not obliged to leave you, father," he exclaimed, embracing him.

"Poor child !" murmured the marquis, pressing him fondly to his heart. "Heaven knows, you are the only being I have ever loved on earth. Your gentle voice and innocent caresses move me to the depths of my inmost soul. Oh ! would that I had only been able earlier to lavish upon you the wealth of affection which I feel in my heart—this heart which has never loved before !"

But when Olivier, surprised and alarmed by his benefactor's agitation, and the suppressed passion of these words—the meaning of which he did not understand—began to weep, the marquis continued, in a calmer tone : "Have no fears, my child. Whatever it may cost me, I am resolved to protect your life from the terrible vicissitudes to which mine is a prey. The pestilential breath of sin and corruption which has parched my soul shall not blight yours. I will always protect you, whether I am by your side, or widely separated from you. I will be your shield. My entire life shall be devoted to insuring your happiness. I owe you this, and far more."

Then the servants entered the room. Olivier was hastily dressed. The most valuable articles were thrown pell-mell into caskets and boxes. The frightened lackeys rushed wildly about, scarcely conscious of what they were doing. It was not a departure, but a flight.

When all the preparations for leaving the palace were completed, and the moment of departure had come, the marquis summoned an old confidential servant who had been specially charged with the care of Olivier from the first. He ordered him to close the doors of the apartment.

"Cosimo," he said, when he was satisfied that they were secure from any possible intrusion, "I am surrounded by dangers. Madame Olympia can no longer protect me, and to-morrow the populace will sack this palace. I have decided to fly before the storm bursts forth ; but I may be captured, killed, or imprisoned. They have, perhaps, already armed the hand that is to slay me."

"Oh ! my master, do not speak thus !" faltered the valet, deeply affected.

"Cosimo, you are devoted to me—is not this so ? You have proved it a hundred times."

"If my blood could but save you—"

"I know it," continued the marquis in that curt voice which imminent danger imparts to resolute men, "so I have depended upon you. I intrust to you this child, who is a thousand times dearer to me than my own life. You, too, love him, for you have told me so a hundred times. If I do not succeed in making my escape, regard him as your son and your master. Protect him from every one, even from my memory, if the truth should ever be divulged—and let not a hair of his head be harmed as long as breath is left to you."

The old servant raised his hand to an ivory crucifix standing out against a black velvet setting on the wall of the apartment. "I swear to live only for the child," he said, solemnly.

"Thank you, my old friend," replied the marquis ; "and now take this portfolio. It is to be opened should I fail to make provision for the wants of our son."

The marquis then flung a long, dark cloak about his shoulders, took

Olivier by the hand, and leaving the palace by one of the side doors, succeeded in reaching the gates of the city in safety, followed by a few distressed servants. Here a modest vehicle was awaiting the fugitives; they seated themselves in it, the articles saved from the wreck were packed in and upon it, and they started on their journey.

But the apprehensions of the marquis were not realised, and the fugitives reached Naples without being molested.

They remained concealed in that city for five days, at the expiration of which time Cosimo announced that he had effected an arrangement with the captain of an English vessel, who had agreed to convey them to any port in France they might designate. But at the same time he brought bad news. He had seen four or five suspicious-looking persons prowling around the house which served as an asylum for the fugitives. These could be none other than spies; so an immediate departure was imperative. But how should they gain the friendly vessel?

Here a generous quarrel arose between the marquis and his servant. They could not think of leaving their retreat together, for any chance suspicions would be changed into certainty if those who were watching saw two men and a child leave the house together; so Cosimo wished his master to start first, since he alone was in danger; but this the marquis refused to do, declaring that he would not leave the house until he knew that Cosimo and Olivier were in a place of safety. At last, after a prolonged discussion, it was decided that as soon as it became dark, the marquis should venture out and make an attempt to reach a spot, where a boat from the English vessel would be in waiting to take him on board.

Olivier and Cosimo were to start half-an-hour later, and to await the result of this attempt. If the plan succeeded, the marquis was to hang out a lighted lantern on the vessel which had received him, and his adopted son and faithful servant were to embark at once and join him.

The plan was duly carried out. The marquis left his hiding-place, and Olivier and Cosimo started some moments afterwards, taking an entirely different route. For a long time they waited on the shore, both eagerly watching for the signal which was to announce the safety of the fugitive who was so dear to them. They waited in vain for two long hours, anxiously questioning the mute horizon.

"Some misfortune must have befallen him," murmured Cosimo. "Perhaps he is dead by this time, who knows? Perhaps the boat was not at the appointed place."

He was already talking of retracing his steps and going in search of the marquis, when he was interrupted by a joyful cry from his young companion. "See!" said the child; "see! there is the signal. He is saved!"

A light had indeed just appeared on the poop of a craft which was gliding silently over the waves. Without losing a moment, Cosimo and Olivier sprang into another boat which was moored near by, and hastened to the vessel. All immediate danger was over.

Two months later the fugitives were installed in Paris, in a small house but a few steps from the Jardin du Roi, and they lived there during several months in apparent security. The marquis had resumed his studies and his experiments, and Olivier, as happy as in the sumptuous palace at Rome, had entirely regained his spirits and gaiety.

One morning, however, M. de Florenzi sent for his adopted son. "Olivier," he said to him, "I shall undoubtedly be obliged to leave you for a long time. Reasons, which you will learn later on, imperatively require this separation. I leave you Cosimo; he will take my place. I have made provision for your future ; without being rich, you will be placed far above the reach of want. Study, obey the dictates of your con· science, and try to be a man."

"No, no, father," exclaimed Olivier, bursting into tears, "I will never, never consent to be separated from you."

"It is a necessity, my child," continued the marquis, gravely and sadly. "I am glad to know that you will never forget your old friend. So long as it is possible, you shall receive news of me ; Cosimo will also take the necessary steps to insure my having tidings of you. And now, we must part. This house would not be free from danger for you, and so Cosimo has secured some fresh apartments in another part of the city. You will take possession of them this evening."

After several more words of loving counsel, which conclusively proved the Marquis de Florenzi's affection and the interest he took in his adopted son, the hour of parting came.

Olivier never forgot the final words of the marquis : they were an allusion to the mystery that enshrouded his life. "My child, fondly as I love you," he said to him, "I am not your father ; nor were the persons who confided you to my care, your parents. Even your family name was unknown to them. One day a stranger left you at their house, promising to return for you, which promise he failed to keep, so the worthy people brought you up for charity's sake. If the day ever comes when we can meet again without danger, in case my love does not suffice you, we will search together for your relatives, and we will find them."

Olivier had not seen his benefactor since that memorable day. At long intervals, Cosimo brought his young master a note from the marquis, and requested him to answer it. Olivier obeyed, intrusting his letters in turn to the old servant. Did they reach the marquis ? He was unable to say. Again and again he had persecuted Cosimo with questions, begged him to tell him what had become of the marquis, the place of his retreat, how he received news, and how in turn he managed to forward his own letters. But Cosimo returned no answer to these eager questions, or replied only in such evasive terms as these : "I cannot tell," or, "I am sworn to secrecy."

So Olivier, finding resignation a necessity, and seeing the grief he caused his faithful servant, finally ceased to interrogate him on these subjects.

Several years passed peacefully and uneventfully after the parting be· tween the marquis and his adopted son. Matured by experience and suffering, Olivier became a man at an age when most of his sex are still youths. With no other friend than Cosimo, he lived only in the past or in the future ; the present seemed hard to bear. Debarred from the affection which is the source of earth's truest happiness, he had learned to depend upon himself ; but his rather cold and austere manner concealed an enthusiastic nature, and a heart formed to love with absolute and unswerving devotion. An almost unconquerable timidity, self-respect, and a certain feeling of shame at his isolation prevented him from seeking companions of his own age. He feared he might bestow his friendship upon those who were either too much above, or too far beneath him. Too far beneath him for his pride and self-respect, or too much above him for his position and his fortune.

Having decided to live an isolated life, ambition became the sole passion of his ardent nature ; not that gloomy, fatal ambition which makes a man an atrocious criminal, but the generous ambition which prompts one to raise one's head erect and gaze firmly into the future. Work, the divine consoler, filled to a very considerable extent the void of which Olivier was conscious in his life. He worked to succeed. He wished to make himself a name, he who had no name; to secure a position, he who had no position, nor even a friend to whom he could confide his sorrows and his hopes.

When he attained the age of seventeen, he wished to enter the army. "With my courage and acquirements," he said to himself, "I should either be killed or win a fine position before I had been through three campaigns. Cordons, epaulets, and titles of nobility are plentiful on the battlefield; I will win mine there."

But Cosimo opposed this resolve. He assured his young master that the marquis would not approve of such a step, and he might return to them any day. What consolation would he have in his old age if his beloved child were killed? Olivier yielded to these objections, and attempted to cut out for himself a judicial career; but here, influential friends became almost a necessity.

However, Cosimo smoothed away these difficulties. Thanks to mysterious connections, and letters of recommendation which were in some way or other obtained by the old servant, Olivier succeeded in obtaining the position of secretary to M. de Mondeluit, a councillor at the Châtelet, a member of the Parliament of Paris, and one of the most highly respected magistrates of the time.

Convinced of the necessity of instructing himself—and instructing himself as expeditiously as possible—Olivier devoted every moment to his new profession. Nothing daunted him; undismayed by the dryness of the science of law and the tedious labour its acquirement involves, he devoted all the energy of his being to the task. Not unfrequently, Cosimo, frightened by the intense ardour with which his young master applied himself to his studies, regretted that he had helped him in obtaining this position with M. de Mondeluit, and entreated him to take some recreation. "You are killing yourself," he said to him. "Is it sensible to work as you do, even to the extent of endangering your health? Why don't you indulge in some of the amusements suited to young men of your age? Nothing could certainly be easier."

"Do you really think so, my old friend?"

"Certainly; why not? You are rich; at least, moderately so. We do not spend one-fourth of the income the marquis allows you. We are living, that is to say, you are living, like a beggar. Excuse me, I mean like a younger son or some unfortunate clerk. Were it not for the liberality you display in relieving all the poor that come in your way, I should almost believe that you were miserly, and that is a bad failing in a handsome young nobleman like yourself."

Olivier smiled at his faithful servant's remonstrances. "You call me a nobleman," he remarked, "and yet you do not even know my name. Is it with the name of Olivier that I can present myself in society? Would you have me appropriate a title to which I have no right? For you know as well as I that the marquis is not my father. He found me among some peasants who did not even know my origin. This fortune, which I owe to the marquis, is merely a fund intrusted to me; I can use it for my necessities, but not for my pleasures. As for the name which I don't possess, let me win it with a fortune. It is a fine thing to be the founder of a noble line. I will be the first of mine."

Cosimo sadly shook his head and indulged in no further remonstrances for several days. Not that he was convinced, but being accustomed to obey his young master's slightest wish, he thought it wrong to argue with him, and certainly his protests would have had little effect on the young man's firm determination.

But Olivier was soon to be rewarded for his arduous labours. Loved and esteemed by the councillor, he speedily became his friend and confidant rather than his secretary. The young man's progress had been so rapid as to actually astound the stern magistrate, who every day expressed fresh surprise on finding so much knowledge and soundness of judgment allied with such extreme youth. Three years had not elapsed before M. de Mondeluit undertook nothing without asking his secretary's advice; nor did he hesitate to intrust the most complicated and difficult cases to his charge. The worthy man was constantly boasting of the wonderful talent, industry and patience of his young secretary. "The day is not far distant," he often remarked to his colleagues, "when this young man will be one of the brightest ornaments of the French magistracy."

This was Olivier's exact position when he beheld the daughter of the financier Hanyvel for the first time. At first, there seemed to be no possible danger in this love. "I shall adore her afar off, like some divinity placed high above the reach of unfortunate humanity," he said to himself. "She will be the star to light my dreary pathway; it is to her that I will appeal in my hours of discouragement. She will never be aware of my existence, but I shall be here to watch for her, though I shall never trouble her with my presence unless she has need of my devotion."

He did not know that each day of solitude increases a passion, until it becomes the sovereign mistress of a man's nature, taking entire possession of his heart, his mind, and his entire being. But in less than a fortnight he was obliged to acknowledge the intensity of his love, and to confess that his life henceforth would be one of intolerable misery. He felt that he was utterly incapable of tearing his idol from his heart.

Then he began to try to devise means of approaching her, of breathing the same air as she breathed, and of hearing the sound of her voice. "But what good would that do me, unfortunate fellow that I am?" he exclaimed, angrily. "Should I not be covered with contumely if any one learned that I had ventured to raise my eyes to her? There are but two magic wands that will open a financier's door and win the hand of his daughter—gold or rank. And I am not only poor but a foundling. Even if the Marquis de Florenzi were still with me, what could he do? Do I even know who this mysterious man is who scatters gold with such a lavish hand, who owns a palace such as none of our princes possess; a man who, though he seems all-powerful, is nevertheless obliged to fly and conceal himself like some criminal. But, wretch that I am, in my madness I insult my benefactor! Pardon me, pardon me, my only friend, my second father: pardon me, I am a wretch and an idiot; I must have lost my senses!"

Overcome with grief, he sunk down into an arm-chair and shed bitter tears. Then he thought of suicide, of the eternal repose of the grave. "But I should never see her any more," he pondered, and at that idea his courage failed him.

All his plans for the future were upset. What did he care now for a profession that would bring him no nearer to the object of his adoration? He neglected his law studies, and ceased to visit M. de Mondeluit's house. He really lived but during one hour of the day, that which Mademoiselle Hanyvel spent walking in the garden. The rest of the time he wandered about like a soul in distress. Hoping to find in physical fatigue some relief from the sorrowful thoughts that haunted him, he rode from morning until night about the environs of Paris ; and when he returned exhausted, and scarcely able to stand, there was only another discomfort added to his other sufferings, for the nights that followed were still sleepless.

Surprised and alarmed by the sudden disappearance of his secretary, the councillor came in person to inquire the cause of his prolonged absence from the office. Olivier replied that he was ill, and when his employer questioned him, he answered in such a strange and confused manner that M. de Mondeluit, really alarmed, gave Cosimo all sorts of warnings before his departure.

To tell the truth, these were perfectly unnecessary, for the old servant was in a state of intense anxiety. He had endeavoured to expostulate with his young master ; but Olivier, for the first time in his life, had spoken to him harshly, ordering him not to meddle with matters that did not concern him. "So I really do not know what to do, monsieur," said poor Cosimo ; "and I see that you are unable to relieve my anxiety."

"I do not know what to advise," replied the magistrate ; "but I should think it would be as well to get your master out of Paris, if ouly for a few days."

Cosimo attempted to follow this advice, but his efforts were fruitless.

One morning, after a restless and sleepless night, in which he had again and again been tempted to put an end to the life which had become such a burden to him, Olivier said to himself : "How foolish I am to allow my-self to be reduced to such a state of wretchedness merely by my passion for a young girl to whom I have never addressed a word, who is not even aware of my existence, and who, perhaps, loves another ! And to think that I do not even know her name !"

Then, as a new idea suddenly flashed through his brain, he added : "But I can learn her name. I have ouly to go down into the street and ask." And without even waiting to put on a coat, he rushed downstairs.

"Monsieur !" cried Cosimo, beseechingly ; "monsieur !"

Receiving no reply, the faithful servant hastened after his young master, but age had impaired his agility, and when he reached the gate, no one was in sight. So after searching in vain through the neighbouring streets, he returned home with a heavy heart. "I am a poor guardian," he said to himself. "How shall I ever dare to face the marquis ? He confided a sacred trust to me, and I have not known how to guard it."

Meanwhile, Olivier was hanging about the gate of the Hanyvel mansion, waiting for some servant to emerge, in order that he might enter into con versation with him. At last, a valet appeared at the gateway ; but just as Olivier was about to address the man, his courage failed him, and, after advancing a few steps, he turned back. Soon the doors and windows in the neighbouring houses began to open. Paris was awaking from its slumbers ; the few shopkeepers in this aristocratic quarter were taking down their shutters, and lackeys were hastening to and fro. People began to look inquisitively at the pale and haggard young man without a hat, who was leaning against one of the posts in front of the magnificent mansion.

"Enough of such cowardice !" Olivier said to himself at last. "It is time to act."

Thereupon, he resolutely approached a servant in gorgeous livery, who had just emerged from the mansion. This flunkey, judging him by his clothes, fancied he was a servant from some neighbouring house, and readily accepted the glass of wine which Olivier invited him to partake of, so they repaired to a neighbouring lodge, for at that time nearly all the house-porters, even in the wealthiest abodes, kept a little shop where they sold wine.

After a common place conversation in which Olivier engaged in order to avert suspicion, he ventured to ask the servant in the most indifferent manner he could assume, the name of the young lady of the family. The lackey replied that it was Henriette. This was all that Olivier desired to know, and having obtained the information he was strongly inclined to fly, but prudence deterred him. So he continued chatting some moments longer, first on one subject, then on another ; but at last, concluding that he had talked as long as was necessary, he paid the score and hastened back to his lodgings, happier than he had been for a long time.

On beholding him, Cosimo raised an exclamation of joy. Olivier ran to the old fellow, and embracing him cried : "My faithful friend, her name is Henriette, and I am the happiest of men."

"Then, sir, you will perhaps make up your mind to take a little breakfast, in order to gain strength to bear your happiness."

"As you like, my friend." Then speaking to himself : "Henriette," he murmured, "was there ever a sweeter name !"

"Evidently my poor young master is a trifle insane," thought Cosimo. "Ah ! I have seen plenty of young lordlings in love in my time, but not after this fashion. They did not lose their desire to eat, much less to drink."

For two or three days it was sufficient happiness to Olivier to be able to repeat to himself the dear name of the girl he loved ; but soon he desired even more. "I must see her near," he thought, "so that I may do homage to her wondrous beauty."

Accordingly, one morning he again stationed himself near the gate of the Hanyvel mansion, firmly resolved not to desert his post until he had seen Henriette pass out. Was the young girl ill ? Was she away from home ? It was impossible for him to learn, and for three whole days he waited in vain. However, on the fourth day, which was a Sunday, just as he was beginning to despair, the heavy gate turned upon its hinges, and his divinity appeared, even more beautiful and radiant than Olivier had pictured her in his dreams. Behind her walked a servant carrying a prayer-book and a velvet cushion. After some hesitation, the young man decided to follow her. She was evidently on her way to some neighbouring church.

"Why did I not think of this before ?" muttered Olivier. "Did ever man have a better chance of contemplating and adoring his idol at his leisure, than in church ?"

He could not take his eyes off the lovely girl, who was praying so devoutly a short distance from him. He speedily discovered, moreover, that Henriette was in the habit of attending mass at this hour every morning. He now felt that his happiness was assured, and he did not even ask himself if she had noticed him.

Such had been the case, however ; and Mademoiselle Henriette felt a strange but profound emotion on beholding the young man leaning against one of the pillars of the church every morning. Her heart had involuntarily gone towards him. We must admit that Olivier was well worthy of this sympathy. His was one of those faces which are not robbed of spirit and determination by sorrow. A dark downy moustache graced his upper lip; his pallor, and an expression of subdued melancholy imparted a peculiar charm to his physiognomy; and his large and expressive eyes, sad and impassioned by turns, seemed the mirror of a generous and noble soul. Nor was there any mistaking the meaning of the glances that made Henriette tremble with emotion.

That his personal attractions had excited her admiration, there could be no doubt, for, when her eyes first met those of Olivier, they beamed with all the radiant softness of chaste and innocent love. Under this look the young man tottered as if about to fall. Never in his wildest dreams had he ventured to picture such happiness. He returned home, telling himself that he had nothing more to wish for on earth.

But this did not prevent him from repairing to the church at the accustomed hour the next morning. This time he left the building a little in advance of his divinity, but paused under the portico to see her pass. Henriette perceived him; and either from emotion, chance, or a sudden impulse, she dropped her prayer-book. Olivier sprang forward, picked it up and presented it to her. She turned pale with emotion; then recovering herself, thanked him in a silvery voice that plunged him into another fit of ecstacy.

After this important episode in the history of his love affairs, Olivier walked out in advance of Henriette, every morning at the conclusion of the service, and pausing at the door, respectfully offered her the holy water. They had never talked together, but they knew beyond a doubt that they loved each other. They were as certain of this as if they had exchanged all the pledges upon earth.

At last Olivier wrote a little note, which he folded carefully, and reduced to the smallest possible dimensions. During the service, taking advantage of a moment when Henriette's eyes met his, he showed her the paper which he had kept in his hand. She blushed, and averted her eyes as if indignant; perhaps she really was so, but on going out of church, she let her book fall a second time. Olivier again picked it up, but before he returned it to her he had time to slip the note between the leaves.

She thanked him coldly, and passed by almost without looking at him this time.

Olivier felt chilled to the heart by this icy demeanour. "Fool that I was," he exclaimed. "What have I done? I was happy, and now I have endangered my happiness. Ah! I richly deserve to be punished for my folly."

The note was nothing more or less than a request for an interview. At one end of the garden, in a shady and secluded spot, Olivier had noticed a breach in the stone wall, which M. Hanyvel had neglected to repair, though to shut out any trespassers and marauders, a substantial barricade of boards had been erected. Still these planks were in some few places sufficiently far apart for one to be able to slip one's hand through the opening. Two lovers would have nothing to fear from within, nor, indeed, from without, for this part of the garden was next to some unoccupied ground. It was to this spot that Olivier had entreated Henriette to repair at twilight that same evening, for he was sufficiently acquainted with the habits of the inmates of the Hanyvel mansion to know that the girl would be free at that hour.

On his return home, he locked himself up in his own room and waited for the appointed time with the most intense anxiety. Indeed, his fears were so deeply aroused that he no longer had sufficient courage to look the situation in the face.

In the afternoon, Henriette made her appearance in the garden. Usually, her first glance was bestowed on the little attic window, but to-day she pretended not to raise her eyes to it. Leaning far out of the casement, at the risk of breaking his neck, Olivier watched her through the winding walks of the garden until she disappeared under the trees. This little incident restored the poor lover's courage, for he fancied she might be going to pay a visit to the spot which he had spoken of in his letter.

At last evening came, and long before the appointed time, Olivier had seated himself upon a block of stone not far from the fence. It was still daylight, and he was calculating how much longer he would be obliged to wait, when a rustling sound in the garden announced Henriette's approach. He sprang to his feet and tried to speak, but the violent beating of his heart suffocated him, and his words died away, unuttered in his parched throat.

A calm, calculating love has always plenty of presence of mind, and seizes skilfully on every propitious opportunity. Possibly this is the reason why women so often love those who do not love them. True love is always awkward, but its awkwardness is often sublime. Unable to speak, Olivier could only fall upon his knees and stretch out his clasped hands imploringly. "To-morrow," murmured a silvery voice. And a little hand appeared through one of the interstices of the fence.

Olivier caught hold of it and covered it with kisses, but it was quickly withdrawn again. For several hours he remained in the same spot, lost in a sort of ecstatic trance, and utterly oblivious of everything around him.

VIII.

THE APPROACH OF MISFORTUNE.

THE morrow that followed was succeeded by many others, for the lovers fell into the habit of treating themselves to one of those delightful meetings every evening. Never did chaster love animate two hearts more worthy of each other.

Gradually, but without the slightest misrepresentation or reserve, Olivier related his history to Henriette. "Alas, my dearest, I am unworthy of you!" he exclaimed one day.

"No," replied the girl, "not since my heart has chosen you."

"Will your father ever consent to our union?"

"Why not? He was not always rich."

"That is true, my sweet Henriette; but, in spite of my limited experience in worldly matters, I know very well that successful men do not like to be reminded of the point from which they started."

"My father is not a man of that kind."

"Heaven grant it."

"Besides, have you lost all your courage? Is it so very difficult to win fame and fortune when the woman one loves is to be the reward? And you love me, do you not, my friend?"

"Oh, a thousand times more than I can ever tell you, or than you can imagine." And for the hundredth time Olivier related the tortures he had endured before the day when his hand had for the first time touched that of his Henriette.

He now resumed working more enthusiastically than ever, and with such success, that the councillor informed him that he was about to take the necessary steps to procure him an official appointment—the first step on the road to judicial eminence.

Thus hope had been beaming for some time on the two lovers, when one evening, on arriving at the trysting place, Olivier found Henriette already awaiting him, though he himself was considerably in advance of the hour.

" We are lost ! " she exclaimed, bursting into tears.

" Good heavens ! what has happened ? "

" My father has chosen a husband for me."

" He wishes you to marry ? "

" Yes, and before the end of the month."

" And you have consented ? "

" Oh, Olivier, how can you be so unjust and ungrateful. Can you thus doubt my affection ? I did everything. Alas, I entreated him to spare me. I wept. I fell at his feet—"

" And he could resist your tears ! "

"I even told him I loved another. 'And what of that?' was his response."

" Oh, misery ! " exclaimed Olivier. " Henriette, what is the name of this man who has been chosen for you ? His name, tell me his name."

" My friend, your anger frightens me. I will not tell you his name, but believe me, you are cruel to blame me. I *have* resisted, and I shall continue to resist. Even though they drag me to the altar, they shall never wring from me the fatal ' yes ' that will bind me to another."

"Thank you, thank you a thousand times ; but what will become of us?"

" I am only a woman, Olivier ; it is for you to decide. Whatever you advise I will do without hesitation, even if it costs me my life. Do you still doubt my love ? But farewell ; my absence will, perhaps, be noticed. Adieu—until to-morrow." And she hastened away, leaving Olivier overwhelmed with despair.

" It is for me to judge and advise, she says," he repeated again and again to himself. " What course is it best to pursue ? What can I do, weak, isolated, and friendless as I am ? "

In his perplexity he resolved to consult Cosimo. After making him swear to keep the matter a profound secret, he told him the history of his love. The old servant smiled ; for a long time past he had known this great secret quite as well as his young master.

" And now what would you advise me to do ? " asked Olivier, when his narrative was concluded.

" Upon my word, monsieur, it does not require much reflection to be able to answer that question."

" Why so ? "

" We have plenty of money, have we not? A very considerable amount, if I am not mistaken. In fact, I am often afraid at keeping so much money in the house. Ah, well ! send old Cosimo to purchase a good coach, put the gold in your pocket, your pistols in your belt, a trusty blade at your side, and—"

" Carry her off ? "

" You have said it, monsieur."

" But where shall I take her ? "

"The world is wide."

"No!" exclaimed Olivier, passionately, "no; you counsel an unworthy act. I will never be guilty of such a want of respect towards the woman I love."

"Then let her marry another, monsieur."

"Silence! silence!" roared Olivier.

He next hastened to the residence of M. de Mondeluit, hoping to find good advice there. The magistrate was at work in his private room when the young man entered. "I am going to ask you to listen to me and give me your valuable counsel," Olivier began in a solemn tone. "I desire to consult you in a matter that is destined to have an important influence over my whole life, and I should bitterly reproach myself if I came to a decision without first asking your advice."

M. de Mondeluit seemed greatly surprised by this solemn exordium, and pushing away the pile of papers before him, and drawing an arm-chair to the fire, he asked his visitor to be seated. "Proceed," he said, "I am listening."

The unhappy lover began an account of his romance and his misfortunes; but as he proceeded with his story, his listener's expression became more and more stern and severe, and occasionally he even indulged in a significant shrug of the shoulders. In fact, the worthy magistrate did not understand the first word of the narrative. He was certainly the best and most honourable of men, but the word "love" had always been utterly void of meaning to him. Indeed, he was strongly inclined to believe that this passion, of which he had heard so much, was merely an invention of the poets.

When he had reached the age of twenty-five, his father, who had an income of fourteen thousand francs, had introduced him to the daughter of one of his colleagues, who enjoyed a revenue of eighteen thousand. The young lady was neither pretty nor ugly. She was said to be a capital manager; the young man, on his side, had an excellent reputation; and the preliminaries were speedily arranged. The pair were conducted to church and there made man and wife. There was a grand banquet in the evening, and that was the end of it.

The only thing connected with his marriage-day of which M. de Mondeluit retained a vivid recollection, was the tightness of the shoes he had then worn for the first time; they had gorgeous gold buckles, and had hurt his feet frightfully all day. With what impatience he awaited the coming of evening, that he might take them off! He had been strictly faithful to his wife ever since, he was the father of two children, and he fancied that no one could love any differently.

The story his secretary told him consequently seemed to him the most foolish and absurd matter in the world. In his secret heart he thought the young man slightly demented. Olivier might as well have attempted to translate the Koran for his edification.

"My dear child," he said, when the narrative was concluded, "have you bestowed any attention on the case I intrusted to you last evening?"

"But, monsieur," entreated Olivier, "in pity give me your advice—"

"I consider the case a rather remarkable one."

"Oh, monsieur, how can you thus jest at my misfortunes?"

"What misfortunes?"

"Will you not tell me what course to pursue?"

"I should advise the young lady to marry the man her father has chosen

for her, by all means.   I do not think you have any right whatever to aspire to her hand."

"But, monsieur—"

"If you have, go to Messire Hanyvel de St. Laurent, and ask for his
daughter in marriage.   He will show you the door, I imagine, and he will
be quite right in doing so."

"But I love her, monsieur," exclaimed poor Olivier; "I love her to
desperation, and at any cost—"

"Take care," continued the magistrate, impressively, "do not be guilty
of any imprudence.   It would be very painful to me," he added, "to he
reduced to the necessity of paying you a visit in prison.   The path you are
now pursuing does not lead to the bench, by any means.   And now, good-
bye, I must get to work, and you do not seem to be in any condition to
assist me.   Above all, don't forget the case I spoke of."

Olivier left the house in a state of mind verging on despair.   He was
thinking of adopting the plan suggested by Cosimo, when he suddenly recollected a young lieutenant in the Guards, the Chevalier de Tancarvel,
with whom he had played more than one game of tennis, and whose character pleased him.   "He, at least, won't jest at my misfortunes like this
unfeeling magistrate," he said to himself.   So he hastened towards the
Louvre to ascertain his friend's address from the soldiers stationed there,
but on the way, just as he reached the church of Saint Germain-l'Auxerrois,
he was fortunate enough to meet him.

The chevalier, who recognised him the first, advanced with open
arms.   "Ah, my dear friend, what a lucky meeting!" he exclaimed.
"You have been a great stranger for several months past.   I have made
fruitless efforts to learn your whereabouts—"

"Thanks, chevalier," interrupted Olivier, "believe me—"

"But, my dear fellow, the longer I look at you the more firmly I am
convinced that really you have a most disconsolate face.   What misfortune
has befallen you?"

"A great misfortune truly; and it was for this reason that I was going
in search of you."

"And I am delighted to see that you have so much confidence in me.
What can I offer you?   My purse?   my sword?"

"Alas, no!"

"What then?" inquired the chevalier, surprised that one could desire
anything else.

"I should like your advice—"

"That is fortunate, for my stock of that commodity is larger than my
supply of money just now.   Speak up."

And the chevalier took an easy posture like a man who is preparing himself to listen attentively for some time.

For the third time since the beginning of the evening, Olivier repeated
the story of his love, taking care, however, to omit certain details, and
change the names of the people he had to deal with.

However, the chevalier did not allow him to finish his narrative; and
the first sentence he uttered bore a strange resemblance to Cosimo's.
"Have you plenty of money, my dear fellow?" he asked, "if so, send your
friend Tancarvel to purchase a carriage—"

"I do not desire an elopement," said Olivier.   "I do not wish to taint
the name of the woman I love with dishonour; and it was in the hope of discovering some other mode of escape from this difficulty that I applied to you."

"Very well ; we will discover one, my dear friend," said the chevalier. "But don't you think we can do so just as well in a cosy little tavern, only a few steps from here? It is astonishing how much the wine of Anjou brightens up my ideas."

"Let us go then," sighed Olivier. He had found the magistrate too austere ; and he now feared that his new adviser took things too lightly.

When the young men had seated themselves at the table, and a bottle of wine had been nearly emptied, the chevalier remarked : "I think, my dear friend, that I have discovered a way out of the difficulty."

"Oh, speak, speak, I entreat you."

"You object to the elopement only on account of the scandal, I imagine."

"I confess it."

"But you would not be sorry to withdraw your sweetheart from her father's authority."

"That is the exact situation."

"Ah well, my dear friend, then it is not necessary to elope with the girl, but simply to help her in leaving her father's house."

"But that seems to me much the same thing."

"Not by any means, as you will soon perceive. Can your lady-love go out whenever she chooses?"

"Not through the gateway ; but there is a gap in the wall which has been boarded up. An opening can easily be made there."

"Very well ; suppose that to-morrow your beauty reasons somewhat in this way : 'My father's house is very worldly ; I am endangering my soul and my salvation by remaining in it. So to linger there any longer would be a sin ; and it is my duty to retire to a convent. But if I ask my father's permission, he, in his blind love, will refuse it : so I am going to dispense with it.'"

"What an idea !"

"Wait a moment. What will your sweetheart do then? She will make up a little bundle containing whatever she desires to take with her ; she will repair to this opening in the wall you speak of, and through which, you say, she can easily effect a passage. Once outside, as if by chance, she will find a carriage belonging to two gentlemen, you and me, for instance. They have given the coachman orders to wait for them. The young lady will go straight to this coachman and request him to take her to such and such a convent. He will refuse ; she will give him a louis, but he will still refuse ; then she will give him two, three, four, ten, twenty, until he finally consents. On reaching the convent, she will ask for the Lady Superior, tell her that she is rich, and that she has fled from the paternal home to enter upon a religious life in that sisterhood, which she desires to enrich with her virtues and her fortune. She will be received with open arms. And her father, even though a prince of royal blood, could not force her to leave this refuge unless she chose to do so. But her father is not a prince, I fancy."

"Not in the least," replied Olivier, whose drooping courage was beginning to revive.

"Then she can remain in the convent as long as she chooses. She will perhaps find life rather dull there, but if the siege of the father is well conducted, his consent to your union will be quickly obtained."

"My friend, you have saved my life," exclaimed Olivier, throwing his arms round M. de Tancarvel's neck. "Your plan shall be carried into execution to-morrow. I count upon your assistance."

"In life and in death ! By the way, are you a nobleman ? "

'Alas! murmured Olivier, blushing and disconcerted, "I am only a foundling."

"A foundling, so much the better ! Why, you may be the son of His August Majesty Louis XIV. But, tell me, sha'n't we have some supper ? "

Olivier could not do less than invite his confidential friend and preserver to join him at table, so he rattled the gold which he happened to have in his pocket.

"You are a charming friend," said the chevalier. "Come with me and make up your mind to spend a jolly night while waiting for the adventure of to-morrow ; an adventure which is not altogether to my liking, however."

"In what respect, my dear chevalier ? "

"Because, in spite of all my efforts, I can discover no possible chance of giving or receiving a sword thrust. That is all that is needed to make the adventure complete."

IX.

THE CATASTROPHE

It was not long before Olivier heartily repented of having followed his new adviser. From the moment, indeed, when the chevalier placed his hand in that of the young lover and said : " Let us leave serious matters until to-morrow," he seemed to have but one thought—to kill time in the most pleasant manner while awaiting the decisive hour. The chevalier conducted his young friend first to a fashionable restaurant, then to a gaming-house ; and Olivier, sick at heart, allowed himself to be led about becoming more and more gloomy and uncomfortable in proportion as the chevalier's gaiety and hilarity increased.

M. de Tancarvel seemed to be in the best of spirits. The viands at supper had suited his taste exactly, and he had drunk immoderately. Chance favoured him, too, at play, and each deal of the cards increased the winnings piled up before him.

"You bring me good luck, my dear fellow," he remarked to Olivier, "and I declare that I shall never leave you in future. This good fortune is a favourable omen for to-morrow, so lay aside that lugubrious countenance.'

But Olivier was not reassured : day was breaking, making the light of the candles appear pale, but for all that, M. de Tancarvel did not seem at all inclined to leave the card-table.

"Chevalier," said the young man at last, tired of waiting, "I will retire. You seem to have entirely forgotten the service you were to render me to-day."

"What ! my dear fellow," replied M. de Tancarvel, with an air of surprise. "You think of leaving already? Our expedition is to come off this evening, and now it is scarcely daybreak. Recollect that we still have twelve hours before us, an entire day. Do you know where we can spend the time more agreeably than here? However we will stop playing if you like. I consent to that, but only to go to breakfast ; I am the entertainer, and who loves me must follow me."

As he spoke, the chevalier pocketed the gold piled up before him, and buckling his sword, went away, taking part of the company with him.

The young lover resigned himself to his fate, and four o'clock in the afternoon found him still seated at table, beside the chevalier. The day had seemed intolerably long to him, and he had secretly accused time of standing still.

But if Olivier's gloom and anxiety had increased, the gaiety of his adviser knew no bounds; indeed, he appeared considerably intoxicated, and utterly unconscious of his condition. Olivier already began to curse his folly, and to bitterly repent that he had not acted alone.

"What need had I of this fool's assistance?" he said to himself. "Was any aid necessary to carry out the plan he indicated? I have spent a wretched night and an equally wretched day, and what good has it done? Here is my adviser and pretended friend scarcely able to stand. In less than half an hour, he will be under the table unless some one puts him to bed. I will hesitate no longer, but go at once."

But as he rose from table the chevalier followed his example, and taking up a bottle of wine, he filled his glass, exclaiming: "This toast is the last. I drink to the successful termination of my young friend's love affair. Who will refuse to join me?"

No one declined. Every glass was filled and enthusiastically drained.

"And now, *au revoir*, gentlemen, and may we soon meet again," said the chevalier, and calling the host, he settled the bill with the greatest composure. He afterwards asked for some water, bathed his face and hands, adjusted his lace ruffles and curled his moustache; then turning to his companion, he remarked, in the most careless tone imaginable: "Now, my friend, I am entirely at your service. Let us make haste, if we wish to be there in time."

M. de Mondeluit's secretary could not conceal his astonishment. This sudden transformation was entirely beyond his comprehension; and his amazement could be so plainly read in his eyes that the chevalier could not refrain from saying as they descended the stairs: "So you really supposed I was drunk and that I had forgotten you?"

"I must confess that you have guessed the truth."

"Ah, my dear friend, you are still young. Learn, then, that we soldiers are well versed in the art of preventing any conflict between duty and pleasure. I said to myself: 'I can drink and forget everything until four o'clock without the slightest inconvenience or danger.' It is four o'clock; I have regained my calmness, and am now ready to serve you."

In less than a couple of hours the two friends had procured a coach, which they stationed at a short distance from the palisade edging the grounds of Hanyvel's mansion. They then once more came to an agreement. Olivier wished to take the driver into their confidence, and tell him that in a few moments a young lady would undoubtedly ask for the use of his coach, but the chevalier demurred to this proposal.

"The coachman might betray us," he said, "if there were an investigation; and since we are quite sure that money will triumph over all his his scruples sooner or later, what is the use of exposing ourselves to any risk of detection through his stupidity or indiscretion?"

Olivier was obliged to admit that his friend was right; and after simply ordering the coachman to wait for them, the pair approached the appointed spot.

"An escape is the easiest thing in the world," the chevalier remarked, after an examination of the surroundings; "and if you are sure of your sweetheart's affection—"

"She told me that she would consent to anything to escape from a marriage that she regarded with such abhorrence."

"Then we need apprehend no trouble. But as she must not be exposed to the danger of losing a moment, we ought to prepare everything for her immediate flight. You have brought a saw, I presume?"

"Here it is."

"Very well. Now keep watch to prevent me from being surprised while I saw these planks in such a manner that we shall only be obliged to give them a kick to open a passage."

Olivier complied, and in a few moments his companion recalled him. "It is done," he remarked.

Then it was agreed that when the young lady made her appearance the chevalier should retire a short distance off in order not to increase her confusion. He was even to conceal himself, and not to make his appearance unless any imminent danger threatened the fugitive. The two friends then seated themselves on a large block of stone close to the wall and waited. But the hours went by, and Henriette gave no sign of life. It had been dark for a long while ; indeed, it was almost time for the vesper bell to toll.

During this protracted waiting, the chevalier did not give the least sign of impatience ; on the contrary he did his best to calm the terrible anxiety of his friend. "There is no hope, chevalier," said poor Olivier, wringing his hands despairingly. "By this time she, perhaps, belongs to another. At the last moment she did not have strength to resist."

"Don't despair," replied the chevalier. "People don't marry at this hour ; she is probably detained at home by some cause or other, and is no less anxious and miserable than yourself. Let us wait a little while longer."

At last, unable to bear the suspense any further, Olivier exclaimed : "I must know the worst." And without listening to his friend's remonstrances, and at the risk of wounding himself with the broken glass that strewed the top of the wall, he sprang into the garden.

The chevalier in his turn climbed the wall in order to be ready, if necessary, to go to his friend's assistance. Olivier had probably hastened towards the house, the lighted windows of which could be plainly seen through the trees, but though M. de Tancarvel listened attentively, he heard no sound. He, too, was about to jump into the garden when suddenly the young lover reappeared. Without uttering a word, he leaped with feverish agility over the wall, and offered his hand to the chevalier to aid him in his descent, saying : "Make haste, my friend, something strange is going on here."

"What is the matter ? You are pale and agitated—"

"I have *seen* nothing calculated to justify my fears, but I am sure that my presentiments don't deceive me. I meant to have entered the house, but unfortunately the doors and windows communicating with the garden were all fastened. But I listened, and suddenly I heard a great commotion inside—shrieks sobs, and frightful shouts. Some terrible misfortune has occurred, believe me."

"Come, you must be mistaken," said Tancarvel.

"No, no ; I looked, too, at the upper windows, and could see lights moving to and fro. Persons were running from room to room, and up and down the stairs. She must have resisted her father, and finding him determined to compel her to accede to his wishes, and even to resort to violent measures if necessary, she has attempted to put an end to her life. Perhaps even now, my poor Henriette is no more."

As he spoke, Olivier dragged his friend towards the street which the mansion faced, and the chevalier, who had never witnessed such despair, found it exceedingly difficult to keep pace with him.

He made no attempt at consolation, for he realized that he was in the presence of one of those terrible sorrows which time alone can soothe, and in some case prove fatal. Without explaining it, so great is the contagious influence of any sincere and profound feeling, the chevalier finally began to share his friend's fears. He was certainly much more alarmed than he had ever been on his own account.

They found the door of the house wide open; but in the hall, which was brilliantly lighted, as if for a *fête*, not a single valet was to be seen.

"You see I was not mistaken," exclaimed Olivier, in a voice husky with emotion.

"There seems to be no one that we can question."

"What would be the use? I know only too well the answer I should receive."

"Go in, at all events," advised M. de Tancarvel. "Perhaps you will find some one on the staircase; I will wait for you here."

"Even if I am compelled to effect an entrance into Hanyvel's private room by force, I will know the truth," said Olivier, and he rushed into the hall and up the staircase.

But he had not ascended a dozen steps when he met a lady, who tottered and almost fell close beside him.

Olivier involuntarily opened his arms to catch her. She had almost fainted, and as he glanced at her he saw that she was some thirty-five years of age, short of build, and still very pretty, her very elegant, low cut dress, revealing a pair of lovely shoulders. She murmured some incoherent words, as if she were still haunted by the horrors of some frightful scene she had witnessed. "What a catastrophe!" she said. "Oh, how horrible—to die like that!"

Olivier was scarcely less agitated than the unknown lady, for the words he heard corresponded only too well with the terrible presentiments that were torturing his soul. He would have given his life to draw a word of explanation from her.

At last she seemed to regain consciousness. She raised her startled eyes to Olivier's face, apparently made a violent effort to collect her thoughts, and then suddenly asked:

"Who are you, monsieur, and how do you happen to be here supporting me?"

Olivier told her what had occurred as briefly as possible.

"Ah, yes, it is true," she said; "I had forgotten. Oh, it is terrible! Be kind enough, monsieur, to help me to my coach, which must be awaiting me at the corner of the street."

"Madame, for Heaven's sake, tell me what has happened," entreated Olivier.

"A most frightful catastrophe!" replied the lady, and she would say no more.

On reaching the vestibule, Olivier found the chevalier leaning against the door-post; he went rapidly towards him, and letting go his hold on the strange lady's arm, he said: "My friend, let me intrust this lady to your care."

He turned away, but not without seeing M. de Tancarvel bow deferentially to the lady, address her as if she were a person of his acquaintance, and
offer her his arm.

Olivier again ascended the staircase and found all the doors open, and
the apartments brilliantly lighted; but not a guest nor a servant was visible.
A silence like that of death pervaded the spacious mansion—a silence
strange and oppressive indeed, in comparison with the tumult which the
young man had heard when he entered the garden. And yet there must
have been a *fête*, and one attended by numerous guests. There were a thousand things to prove that, beyond the shadow of a doubt.

Olivier paused in an antechamber, and held his breath to listen; but he
heard nothing save the violent throbbings of his own heart. He passed
hastily through another room, and then paused in inexpressible horror on
the threshold of the apartment that adjoined it. It was the dining-room,
and there was here startling and frightful evidence of some terrible accident.
The greatest confusion reigned all around, chairs were overturned, and the
curtains were torn and disarranged. Upon the table, in the centre of the
room, the disorder was even greater and more eloquent. The valuable china
and cut-glass were heaped up pell-mell upon it; the candelabra had been
overturned; some candles were still burning, and one of them had set fire
to the table-cloth, which was being slowly consumed; while the floor was
strewn with fragments of porcelain and broken flagons.

While Olivier was surveying this strange scene, overcome with anxiety and
terror, he heard hurried steps approaching him. He turned aside so as to
allow the person to pass, but it proved to be a valet, who rushed up to him,
exclaiming: "Oh, for God's sake, monsieur, make haste!"

"What, me? Do you know whom you are addressing?"

"Why, are you not the physician?"

Olivier shook his head. "Why did you not tell me so at once?" exclaimed the servant, disappearing on the run.

The last words the young man caught, were: "He will be too late."

The unhappy lover's despair was at its height, but the very intensity of
his grief imparted to him some slight degree of courage and determination.
"My fate is now decided; she is dead," he said to himself. "Dead, and
my love has been the cause of her death. I, too, may say with the lackey,
too late! too late! Still I will at least see her once more and for the last
time. But then her relatives will ask me who I am, and inquire what
right I have to intrude upon their sorrow and mingle my tears with
theirs; perhaps they will even have me forcibly expelled from the house."
This thought made him hesitate for a moment, but after a little sorrowful
reflection, he added: "I must see her, all the same. Besides, what have
I to fear? Is my life of any value now? Yes, I am resolved to kneel beside her to bid her a last farewell, and then put an end to my own wretched
existence; and woe to him who attempts to hinder me!"

Catching up a knife from the table, he advanced slowly and automatically
towards the door leading into the adjoining apartment. He was frightful to
behold, but so great was the excitement prevailing at that moment, that
three or four lackeys who hastily passed by did not even notice him.

He traversed room after room until the appalling silence which had so
terrified him was at last broken. He could now distinctly hear the sound
of low voices, occasional moans, and high above the confused murmur some
heart-rending sobs. The same servant who had addressed him in the antechamber now reappeared, followed by some gentlemen whom Olivier recog-

nized as physicians. He was about to follow them, when the heavy tapestry curtain that concealed the door was again lifted, and the one he had
supposed dead appeared. Yes, it was indeed Henriette. Her face was
very pale, her hair dishevelled, and her clothing disordered; but it was she!
He attempted to spring towards her, and fall on his knees at her feet, but
his strength failed him. The revulsion was too intense for human endurance. He staggered like a man shot at the heart; the knife he had seized
fell from his nerveless hand; he flung up his arms; a smothered groan
escaped his breast, and he fell, apparently lifeless, almost at Henriette's
feet.

But soon the gentle pressure of the hand that had caught hold of his, and
the warm breath from the lips so close to his own recalled him to life again.
He opened his eyes. Was not this one of those divine but deceitful illusions which sometimes temporarily assuage human despair? Henriette
was there close by him, her face close to his. With one hand she supported her lover's head; with the other she felt for the heart which beat
only for herself.

After so much poignant anguish and such abject terror, this was a most
rapturous moment for Olivier. He was able to speak now, but he felt no
inclination to do so. A word might dispel the dream, or if it was not a
dream put an end to this scene so sweet to his heart, and he closed his eyes
again thanking God and entreating Him to allow this happiness to last
forever.

But while lost in ecstasy he felt big, burning, silent tears, tears of despair, fall upon his forehead. Half raising himself, and carrying Henriette's
hand to his lips, he murmured : " Forgive the selfishness of my love, my
dearest. Alas ! I believed you lost to me forever, and when I was reassured on seeing you I forgot all in my happiness, and did not think of asking
what cruel misfortune had caused your tears to flow."

The young girl rose, and hiding her face in her hands exclaimed :
" Olivier, my friend and brother, I am very miserable, oh, very miserable ! "

Sobs choked her utterance. A prey to fresh anxiety, Olivier sprang to
his feet.

" Have I not a right to share your sorrow? " he asked. " Speak, tell
me what has happened ? "

" Oh, my father, my poor father ! Olivier, I am alone in the world ! "
And forgetting everything in the intensity of her grief she let her lovely
head fall on her lover's shoulder. As she clung to him, sobbing wildly,
Olivier bitterly reproached himself. He certainly sympathized with this
sorrow on the part of the woman he so fondly loved ; and yet, he was overcome with joy in spite of himself. He had believed her dead ; but she was
still alive, and for the first time, he could press his lips upon her lovely
golden hair, and hold her close to his wildly throbbing heart. So he dared
not speak, for fear that his voice might betray him.

He was still standing there motionless, without daring to make the
slightest movement, when Henriette suddenly repulsed him violently, and
exclaimed : " Wretch that I am ! my father is lying upon his death-bed,
only a few steps from me, and I abandon myself to the happiness of weeping in the arms of the one I love. Fly, Olivier, fly from this house ; our
love has been a sin and your presence here is almost a crime."

Frantic excitement blazed in her eyes, and her manner and gestures
betokened positive insanity. Olivier was frightened. " You repulse me,

and drive me away, Henriette!" he rejoined. "I am very miserable: you love me no longer."

"I love you no longer?" she repeated in a calmer tone. "Is it in my power to cease to love you, even if I wished to do so? But are not such words uttered here, beside a death-bed, positively impious? My poor father! to think that I wished to leave him! Oh, the thought fills me with remorse. If this had happened on the day following my flight, I should have been obliged to say to myself: "I was the cause of his death."

Olivier tried to utter a few words of consolation.

"Go, my friend, I beseech you," continued Henriette, "and do not attempt to see me again. Your heart will suffer, but remember that I shall be equally wretched. This terrible affliction has opened my eyes, and revealed the awful abyss upon the verge of which we were standing; and if I am ever united to you, Olivier, it will only be with my mother's consent. Perhaps she will listen to me when I tell her that you will be a true son to her; but, however she may decide, I shall obey her. So let us part, my friend and brother. We will hope for the best, but come what may, we must accept our fate with resignation."

She raised her forehead to her lover's lips, and Olivier, half crazy with sorrow, imprinted a chaste kiss upon it. "Farewell, my brother," she said once more, and then departed.

He watched her move away without being able to find a word to entreat her to reconsider her determination. Deciding to obey her, he prepared to leave the mansion, the doors of which had only been opened to him through a terrible misfortune; but he was unwilling to go away, perhaps, forever, without knowing at least a few of the details of the affliction which had just befallen his loved one.

Consequently, he decided to question one of the lackeys in the antechamber; but first of all he was desirous of thanking the Chevalier de Tancarvel, and setting him at liberty. He found him waiting faithfully at the same spot. I thank you for your loyal aid," he said to him, " but though I am in great trouble, I am at least certain of the safety of one I love better than my own life."

"Yes, I know," replied the chevalier, "it was poor Hanyvel—"

"What, you have heard?"

"I can even give you the particulars of the catastrophe."

"Pray do so."

"It will not take long; but I do not see that there is anything to detain you here."

"I only desired to learn the circumstances connected with this terrible event, and intended to question some servant."

"Thanks to me, that will be unnecessary. Allow me to accompany you home."

Olivier made a gesture of assent; his friend slipped an arm through his, and the two walked away. "You must know, my dear friend," began the chevalier, as they proceeded along, "that nothing more sudden could be imagined. The unfortunate man was giving a grand banquet; more than thirty guests were at table; the dessert had just been brought in, and everybody was in the gayest spirits. Suddenly, after proposing the health of his future son-in-law, Hanyvel raised his glass to his mouth, but he had scarcely moistened his lips when he fell—"

"Dead?"

"Struck down as if by lightning. A stroke of apoplexy, I fancy; the poor financier was exceedingly plethoric. Still, such may be the fate of us all," was the chevalier's philosophical conclusion.

'I suspected as much. But how about the guests?"

"They all lost their heads, of course; the men were terrified and the women shrieked: and when a surgeon, who had been summoned, arrived, it vas only to announce that there was no hope."

'I saw some physicians enter, nevertheless."

"Unnecessary zeal on their part, I assure you. Still, you know, one always cherishes a slight hope in such cases. This is one of those misfortunes which a person cannot believe in, as the marquise remarked to me."

"What marquise?" inquired Olivier in surprise.

"Why, the lady who took your arm on the staircase. She was one of the guests. Poor lady! the terrible scene affected her so much that she was unable to leave with the others. It was more than an hour before she recovered sufficiently to be able to take a step."

"Was it from her that you learned these details?"

"Certainly."

"And did she tell all this to you, a stranger?"

"But, my dear fellow, I was not a stranger. I have met her often enough at the house of my sister, Madame de Sarremont, and her husband is one of my best friends. She is a very charming and talented woman, and, in fact, she has but one fault in my opinion: she is a trifle too devout, and pays too much heed to the injunctions of her confessor. But don't you know her?"

"I met her this evening for the first time, and under such circumstances, alas! as I shall not forget while I live. But tell me, my friend, who is this lady?"

"She is called the Marquise de Brinvilliers."

X.

A DAY OF HAPPINESS.

ON reaching home, Olivier had the greatest possible difficulty in getting rid of his companion, for M. de Tancarvel seemed determined to remain with him. "You appear altogether too disconsolate for me to think of leaving you," remarked the light-hearted officer. "Believe me, solitude is a bad counsellor; and sorrow is a malady for which there is a remedy, as well as all others. Let me be your physician. What good will it do you to remain here to brood over your misfortunes? Won't you take my advice?"

Olivier maintained an obstinate silence. "Come, take my arm," insisted the chevalier, "and let us go out together. There is plenty of good wine left in Paris, so let us go and enjoy it. Wine is a sovereign balm for all wounds of the heart, believe me. If God allows the vine to flourish, it is because he knows that men will often have occasion to drown their sorrows in its fruit."

"Pray don't insist, chevalier. I need to be alone."

"So be it; if you refuse to listen to reason, I will go; but first let us talk the matter over a little. Why should you mourn for the death of Hanyvel, a man you did not even know? Two hours ago, your only desire was to rob him of his daughter. What was he to you?"

"Ah, he was Henriette's father; but, to tell you the truth, his death is not the cause of my grief. Henriette has sent me away, and refused to allow me to see her again."

" If that is all, my dear fellow, you can dry your tears. Before a week has elapsed, you will be recalled." And shaking hands with his friend, the chevalier departed, promising to return speedily.

" This Olivier is an excellent fellow," he said to himself, as he descended the stairs ; " but altogether too sentimental. Warm-hearted, but weak-headed. I am really sorry for him. My heart fairly ached at the sight of his tears ; his grief would have melted a rock, as Monsieur Quinault says."

Alone at last, and able to abandon himself unobserved to the thousand and one conflicting emotions that assailed him, Olivier could examine the situation more calmly. In his secret heart he speedily arrived at the conclusion announced by M. de Tancarvel a few hours before.

In fact, the financier's death, far from being a misfortune to him, might remove all obstacles, and pave the way for his happiness. Relieved of the terrible anxiety to which he had temporarily succumbed, he was obliged to admit that he did not feel as much grief on account of this demise as he had allowed his friend to suppose. That was no longer the principal cause of his anxiety and chagrin ; it was Henriette's resolve only to see him again with her mother's consent—that vow of blind obedience—that filial determination she had expressed to allow her heart to break, rather than cause her mother the slightest annoyance.

But, on reflection, these promises troubled him less. He himself felt ready to perjure himself a thousand times to win a single glance from the woman he loved. Would Henriette be less devoted and courageous? He did not think so. Consequently, he hoped that she would soon, in compliance with his entreaty, break a vow which had been extorted from her by such a cruel affliction. So he finally resolved to trust to time, that sovereign master of human destiny, and not to attempt to see his betrothed again, at least for the present.

His life resumed its accustomed course. He devoted himself once more to his legal duties, hoping to find in them both forgetfulness and the certainty of acquiring some claim, not only to the young girl's love, but to her hand. He spent his leisure hours in talking of her to Cosimo ; he could think of nothing else? He had constituted Cosimo his confidant, and the worthy fellow listened without as much as a frown of impatience to the never-ending rhapsodies of his young master. A faithful echo of Olivier's doubts, thoughts, and hopes, the old servant always replied as he was desired to reply, and the lover at least became resigned, in default of being happy.

So days, weeks, and even months went by without Olivier's receiving the slightest news from Henriette. His attempts to see her proved fruitless, and though he often went to wait for her under the church portico, as in former times, she did not come. And yet she was only a few steps from him ; a garden alone separated them, and from his window he could gaze upon hers, for winter had come, and the leaves which had formerly concealed the house from view, had fallen from the trees. It would have been an easy matter for him to effect an entrance into the garden, but he dared not disobey the commands of the queen of his heart.

As time wore on, a frightful doubt began to prey upon his mind. " What if she no longer loves me !" he said to himself.

In this extremity he decided to write to Henriette. Could she not allay all his fears with a single word? She replied as follows : "My dearest, to be deprived of the pleasure of seeing you is a cruel but just punishment for my past weakness, and for the crime which we so nearly committed. You are wretched, you say. Olivier, do you suppose there is any happiness for me separated from you ? In the name of your love and mine, I entreat you to have courage. The day that will unite us, is perhaps not far distant."

This letter was the most powerful restorative imaginable for Olivier ; and he kissed the dear words traced by Henriette's adored hand, over and over again. He did not understand how he could ever have doubted her, and he reproached himself, as if he had been guilty of a crime. "With such a letter," he said to himself, " ought I not to wait patiently through all eternity ? "

But the suspense was fortunately not of long duration. One day, less than a week after the receipt of this missive, a servant in mourning livery presented himself at Olivier's door. He had been sent by M. Hanyvel's widow, and came to request the young man to call at her house that same day. Olivier wished to start at once.

"She is waiting for me ! " he exclaimed. " To lose a moment, to delay my happiness, would be perfect folly, and a crime ! "

But Cosimo detained him. "Remember, monsieur," said he, " that the haste which would undoubtedly delight Mademoiselle Henriette might be disapproved of by her mother."

"Do you really think so ? "

"I am certain of it. The only daughter of such a rich financier must have an immense dowry, and at present your fortune does not correspond with hers. In your deep and disinterested love, envious and malicious folks would only see so much ambition and cupidity ; for now that you are about to be admitted into the house, those who were there in advance of you will become jealous, and will do everything in their power to ruin your prospects, and make you appear in the most unfavourable light."

The idea filled Olivier with consternation. In the innocence of his heart, and in his utter ignorance of the world, he had never suspected for a moment that his love might be considered mercenary ; and Cosimo's words opened something very like a new world before his wondering eyes. He hesitated, but only for a moment ; he was too deeply in love to be long deterred by such base considerations. "What does the opinion of the world matter to me ! " he exclaimed. "If her mother grants me her hand, I shall refuse her dowry. My earnings, to say nothing of the bounty bestowed upon me by the marquis, my second father, will more than suffice for our modest needs. Yes, I shall refuse every penny of it ; and in that case, no one can accuse me of having loved her for the sake of her fortune."

So without heeding Cosimo's protest, he went out after a hurried toilet, and a few moments later a servant ushered him into one of the magnificent reception-rooms of the Hanyvel mansion.

The financier's widow was half reclining on a sofa near the fire. Olivier recollected having seen her some months before, but he scarcely knew her now, so great was the change wrought in her appearance by sorrow. Her hair had become white and her cheeks wrinkled, while her eyes were red and swollen by sleepless nights spent in weeping. Henriette, more beautiful than ever in her mourning garments, was seated on a low ottoman at her mother's feet.

When the servant announced the young man, both ladies rose and bowed graciously as if to an expected guest. Then Madame Hanyvel pointed silently to an arm-chair, while Henriette walked to the window, and pretended to be looking attentively into the garden, doubtless to conceal the blushes that tinged her cheeks.

Cosimo's apprehensions were not realised. Olivier at once saw that his prompt response to the summons was not displeasing, but that it had been expected. This conviction gave him a little of the assurance he so sorely needed. He had never before found himself in such a trying position ; the happiness of his life was at stake and he realised it, but in spite of this fact, or rather on account of it, his emotion was so great that he was unable to utter a single word. He seated himself, blushing and confused, under the close scrutiny of Madame Hanyvel, who was studying his face as if desirous of reading his thoughts.

Olivier's embarrassment was greatly increased by a prolonged silence, but at last, Madame Hanyvel, probably satisfied with the result of her examination, took compassion on the poor lover's timidity, and came to his help. "A very important matter has led me to request your presence," she began—"a very imporant matter to a mother—her daughter's happiness."

Olivier attempted to reply, but the words died away on his lips. Henriette's interest in what was passing in the garden greatly increased, while a faint smile flitted over the sad face of the widow. "My daughter," she continued, "has at last confided in me. After the terrible misfortune which has recently befallen us, and from which I shall never recover, she has come to understand that the best friend a young girl can have in the world is her mother. She has told me everything."

Olivier had expected reproaches, and this quiet resignation surprised and touched him so deeply that a sob shook his breast, and the tears rose to his eyes.

"Poor children !" continued Madame Hanyvel. "Ah ! you were about to commit a sin that would have embittered your whole lives."

"My mother, my kind mother !" murmured Henriette who had drawn nearer.

"Yes, my daughter, a terrible fault, for sooner or later a child is always obliged to pay dearly for rebellion against a parent. Your father thought he was insuring your happiness when he chose a husband for you. You refused the man he selected, but you lacked courage, and when your father said to you, this man will make you happy, why, instead of resisting, did you not say to him the simple words that would have touched his heart as deeply as they touched mine, 'I love another?'"

Blushing and confused, Henriette hid her lovely head in her mother's bosom. Madame Hanyvel wiped away the tears aroused by the recollection of happier days ; and then, turning to Olivier, she added : "I believe my daughter, sir, when she assures me that you are worthy of her. I believe it too, because if it were otherwise, your face and your manner must both be very deceptive. But before coming to any decision, even before I ask myself if I shall confide my most precious treasure, or rather my only treasure to your keeping, there is another confession which my sense of honour compels me to make to you without delay."

Olivier bowed his assent.

"Perhaps," the mother continued slowly, with her eyes fixed upon Olivier's face, as if she were trying to read his most secret thoughts—"perhaps what I am about to tell you, may change your wishes, and you may discover that your love for my daughter is not so great as you suppose."

"Death alone, believe me—" began the young man.

"Know, then," said Madame Hanyvel, interrupting him, "that my daughter and myself are irretrievably ruined."

"Ruined !" exclaimed Olivier, springing up—" ruined ! "

And he gazed first at Henriette and then at Madame Hanyvel, as if seeking the confirmation necessary to convince him of the truth of such an astounding announcement.

"Yes, ruined."

"We are as poor as the poorest," added Henriette. "To-day, we are still living in a palace, but to-morrow we shall perhaps be without a shelter and even destitute of food."

"But this is impossible," repeated Olivier. "It is a dream—a delusion ! You poor ?—you reduced to poverty ? "

"You have said it, sir ; to poverty."

This time Madame Hanyvel's tone was one that made further doubt impossible.

"O, Heavenly Father ! " exclaimed Olivier, raising his clasped hands on high, " at last Thou hast vouchsafed me my share of this world's happiness —a share far greater than I had ever even dreamed of possessing, and which now leaves me nothing more to desire, but rather causes me to bless Thee, O God, for the rest of my days."

The mother and daughter listened in mute surprise, without the slightest idea of the young man's meaning. He perceived their astonishment. "Pardon me, madame," he continued, now venturing to take hold of Madame Hanyvel's hand and raise it to his lips—"pardon my want of self-control ; but it was my heart that spoke and I could not silence it. Pardon me for thus rejoicing on learning the misfortune which has befallen you, but has not this affliction insured my happiness and peace of mind forever ?'

"I do not understand you ? " faltered Henriette.

"Oh, my dearest, is it possible that you were as unmindful as myself of the abyss which separated us, and of which this calamity removes all traces ? Only this very morning, seeing you so rich, and myself so poor, I shuddered despairingly. ' Even if she deigns to cast her eyes upon me,' I said to myself, ' and even if her mother consents to honour me with the name of son, so sweet to every one, so unutterably precious to myself, who have never known a mother, should I dare to accept my good fortune ?' An old and faithful friend reminded me that when people saw me, a poor, friendless youth, aspiring to the hand of a rich heiress, they would believe that I only craved her dowry. This thought made me the most miserable of men, and I blushed with shame at my inferiority. But now—"

"It is for your wife that you will blush."

"Blush for her ! Madame, you are jesting. No king was ever prouder of his royal descent than I shall be of my love. Blush for her ! Will she not be the crowning glory of my life ? I had no ambition ; so far, wealth did not even seem to me worthy of being coveted ; but now, for her sake, I feel that I have courage to achieve anything. I long to give you a dozen fortunes, Henriette, in place of the one you have lost ; for I am indebted to you for the entire happiness of my life, and how can I ever repay all I owe you ? And you, madame," continued Olivier, falling on his knees before Madame Hanyvel, "will you not allow me to call you, from this day forth, ' my mother ?' I am worthy, believe me, to give you that name."

The widow pressed Olivier to her heart ; then taking her daughter's hand and that of the young man, she united them. "I have not long to live, my children," she said. " May I see you happy before I am called to join the father of my beloved Henriette."

Neither Olivier nor the young girl could believe in this great happiness; it seemed to them that the gates of Heaven had suddenly opened before them.

When Madame Hanyvel had sent for Olivier, in compliance with her daughter's request, and in order to study him with the keen eyes and instincts of a mother, she had certainly not anticipated such a speedy denouement, any more than she had expected to find such nobility of sentiment and purity of thought in the man her daughter had chosen. All the men she had so far met, affected that supreme contempt for money, which is the fashion in every age ; but she knew very well that not one of them was capable of putting his theories into practice, and above all, that none of them would have sufficient heroism to rejoice over the loss of an immense fortune. And thus Olivier's conduct had decided her. The day passed swiftly in long talks together and in the formation of delightful plans ; and it was with assurances of meeting again on the morrow, that they finally separated.

Cosimo had never seen Olivier so radiant with joy as on his return home. "She is poor," he exclaimed, seizing the old servant's hands ; "she is even poorer than I am. She will owe everything to me ! "

Four or five days after this interview, Madame Hanyvel informed Olivier that she was going to try to find some humble abode where she might conceal the poverty in which the two young people had found so much cause for rejoicing. Pitiless, grasping creditors had already begun to sack the house, for nothing in the costly mansion belonged to the two ladies now. They had scarcely been allowed to retain possession of the most necessary articles, and they were now obliged to wait upon themselves. All the servants had fled, like rats flying from a sinking ship. Of the army of servants which had formerly crowded the kitchens, halls, and stables, not one remained ; and in place of the sleepy, careless and insolent Swiss porter. that gloomy phantom of misfortune, a bailiffs' man summoned by the creditors, occupied the lodge.

Accustomed to opulence from her childhood, the financier's widow found this change in the habits of a lifetime to be a terible ordeal. Olivier vainly tried to console her, and to reassure her in regard to the future ; Henriette's efforts were likewise fruitless ; and the poor lady declared she should never recover from the shock she had sustained. Olivier placed at her disposal not only his own savings, but all the money his benefactor had given him ; but this little fortune seemed a mere trifle to a woman who had shared the wealth of one of the richest men of the time.

It was under such circumstances as these, that the idea of acquiring accurate knowledge of the deceased financier's affairs first occurred to Olivier. He thought it quite possible that the creditors had taken advantage of the ladies' want of experience in business matters, and that he might perhaps succeed in saving something from the wreck. The few details which Madame Hanyvel was able to give him, were calculated to confirm these suppositions, and after a mere superficial investigation he became satisfied that he was not mistaken.

Living, Hanyvel had been enormously rich ; dead, his fortune amounted to little or nothing. It did not take Olivier long to discover the cause of this. A sort of pioneer in his calling, the financier had embarked in enterprises which, though they would be considered mere child's play nowadays, appeared not only exceedingly complicated, but extremely hazardous at that time.

One of the first in France, which in money matters was two centuries behind England, he had realised the advantage of assisting national industry with the funds at his disposal. He had lent large sums to merchants and manufacturers whose concerns were destined to yield vast profit in the future, though for the time being, with French industry in its infancy, they barely paid their expenses. Now Hanyvel's creditors, less far-seeing and more narrow minded than himself, looked on these sums as lost. On the other hand, by the financier's death, large amounts had to be reimbursed at once, whereas, he living, they would not have been called in by investors who were then contented with receiving the interest of their money.

Among the most pressing creditors was M. Reich de Penautier, Hanyvel's former friend, who pretended to be in great financial distress personally, and who, to reimburse himself, claimed the position of treasurer to the clergy, left vacant by the death of his friend.

But Olivier did not relinquish all hope. He plunged courageously into the accounts, and carefully studied the books and papers, aided in his efforts by his employer, M. de Mondeluit. Everything was indeed managed so well that at the end of a fortnight he was able to inform Madame Hanyvel that he had succeeded in saving at least a quarter of the immense fortune. This, at least, meant an ample income.

Devoted to his betrothed and to her interests, the entire universe, so far as Olivier was concerned, was bound up in the house where Henriette still lived, and of which he fondly hoped to make her again the undisputed mistress. Consequently, his horizon was without a cloud, when one evening, while engaged in a conference with some business men at the Hanyvel mansion, Cosimo came to inform him that a woman desired to speak with him.

"I cannot leave at present," replied Olivier. "If she comes to ask some favour, try to act in my stead, my good Cosimo."

"Your presence is indispensable, monsieur."

"I cannot—"

"But, monsieur—"

"I tell you that it is impossible for me to leave now."

"Then, at least, allow me to speak to you a moment in private," insisted Cosimo, with unwonted obstinacy.

Though secretly annoyed by this strange persistence, Olivier followed his servant into the adjoining room.

"Once more, monsieur, I entreat you to make haste. The woman is impatient to see you and get away."

"What, do you still insist?" asked Olivier, angrily.

"My dear master, the message comes from the marquis," whispered Cosimo.

Olivier turned pale on hearing these words. A vague but frightful presentiment made his heart suddenly contract. But he hesitated no longer. "Run home," he said to Cosimo, "and tell the woman to wait. I will be there in a moment."

He returned to the room where the conference was progressing, excused himself, made an appointment for the following day, and then hastened home.

A woman, plainly but respectably dressed, rose as he entered his sitting-room.

"My good woman, this is my young master, Monsieur Olivier," remarked Cosimo. "You can now fulfil your mission."

The woman drew from her pocket a roll of paper and gave it to Olivier, saying as she did so : "I was told to deliver this into your hands, monsieur, and to inform you, as well as your servant, that it came from the marquis."

Olivier thanked the messenger, and after dismissing her with a gratuity, he carefully closed the door and unrolled the paper with feverish agitation. Inside the roll, he found a tiny phial filled with a crimson liquid.

On seeing it, Cosimo uttered an exclamation of dismay.

"What is the matter with you?" murmured Olivier. "You are pale—" "Nothing, monsieur, nothing," stammered Cosimo, making a fruitless effort to conceal his emotion. "Do not be alarmed about me; but read, I beg, the long letter that accompanies this phial."

Olivier said no more ; he too, was anxious to learn the contents of this letter from his adopted father. He read aloud as follows :

"My son :—Make yourself complete master of this letter. My life depends upon the prompt execution of the orders herein contained. To-morrow, Tuesday, one hour before sunset, repair to the Cemetery of the Bastille.

"Near the spot where paupers are buried promiscuously, you will find a freshly dug grave awaiting its occupant. Conceal yourself near it and wait.

"At nightfall, two jailers from the Bastille will appear, carrying a coffin. They will throw it hastily into the grave—Heaven grant that they do not pile too much earth upon it !—then they will go away.

"Await their departure from the cemetery; then, without losing a second, run to the grave, shovel away the earth, take out the coffin, and open it. Have no fears. As soon as the coffin is open, unclose the jaws of its occu-pant by inserting a knife between them, and pour into the mouth three drops of the crimson fluid contained in the phial I send you. Then after a few moments, repeat the same experiment. If after a quarter of an hour the body still remains apparently lifeless, do not hesitate to pour into the mouth the rest of the contents of the phial.

"In this way you will perhaps be able to restore me to life ; for it is I, Olivier, who, weary of my captivity, resort to this desperate and terrible means of regaining my freedom.

"One word more. At the same time as you arrive, you will perhaps see in the cemetery a cavalier of noble and dignified appearance ; in that case take good care that he does not see you. If he hastens to the grave after the jailers have departed, do not hinder him ; but if he departs with them, then act ; but note him well, for in this last case he will be my worst enemy. Be duly armed in case of need.

"You can confide in Cosimo and even take him with you. Courage and hope !"

When Olivier had finished the perusal of this strange letter he was paler than the corpse he was instructed to rescue from the grave on the morrow.

Cosimo's teeth chattered with terror. "Oh, monsieur," he exclaimed at last, "my blood runs cold at the thought of the terrible sufferings my poor master must have endured before resorting to such a frightful expedient."

"But what means will he employ to convince the jailers of his death?"

"Ah, monsieur," replied Cosimo, shuddering at some sinister recollec-tion, "the marquis is very powerful, very powerful."

The trembling voice of the old servant and his evident terror awakened the strangest suspicions in Olivier's mind ; his presentiments were becoming realities, but he was ashamed to ask any questions, and it was Cosimo who first broke the silence.

"Do you know, monsieur," said he, "that we shall to-morrow incur other dangers than the sword of the man who will be there? Violation of the laws of burial, sacrilege, a prisoner of state, etc., etc. But for all that we must execute my master's orders, no doubt ? "

" Can you doubt it ? " exclaimed Olivier. " It would be a crime even to hesitate. Even if he demanded the sacrifice of my life, I should give it without hesitation and without even a murmur. And yet my life is very dear to me now," he added, after a pause.

XI.

THE CEMETERY OF THE BASTILLE.

THE last rays of the setting sun were tinging the horizon with a brilliant crimson when Cosimo and Olivier, both armed to the teeth, passed by the ramparts of the Bastille, and proceeded towards the cemetery where the prisoners who died in the royal fortress were then interred.

The graveyard in which tyranny concealed its victims, sometimes after frightfully disfiguring them, in order that the grave as well as the prison might guard an eternal secret, was situated in a deserted corner of Paris, though not far from the Saint-Antoine gate, and to the right of the well frequented road which led to the Château de Vincennes.

From early morning Olivier had been impatient to start on this expedition. His slumbers had been troubled during the night by the most frightful dreams, which the strange letter he had received from the marquis sufficiently explained.

In order to excuse his impatience and persuade Cosimo, who wished to wait, the young man recounted the gloomy warnings he had heard in his dreams. "I heard a smothered voice which seemed to proceed from under the ground," he remarked. "'Olivier, Olivier,' said this voice, 'the weight of the earth is crushing me ; I am suffocating. In another moment you will only find a lifeless body, which all your attentions will fail to resuscitate.'"

"Merely the delusions of fever, monsieur," replied Cosimo, trying to conceal his own anxiety in order to reassure his master. "You would have acted more wisely if you had followed my example, and made no attempt to sleep."

"But remember the terrible responsibility which is resting upon us. The life of the man we love best in the world depends upon our zeal. What if the burial took place before the appointed hour? What if, while we are arguing here, they have already lowered him into the grave? My blood curdles at the thought."

"Impossible, monsieur. The prisoners from the Bastille are never buried in the daytime."

" You think so, my friend, but you may be mistaken. And what if to-day some event you have no knowledge of has led them to break one of their long-established rules? Ah ! I should never forgive myself · and you, Cosimo, would be a prey to the most terrible remorse to your dying day."

" No, for I should have done my duty."

"Your duty?"

"Yes, master, my duty. The marquis ordered us to follow his instructions to the letter; let us obey him. Punctuality does not consist in arriving before the appointed hour, but at the exact hour. I know the marquis; he leaves nothing to chance, be assured of that. He told us to go at nightfall, so let us wait. Besides, how do you know that our presence would not awaken suspicions? I have heard frightful stories of prisoners who were beheaded after death: the trunk alone being taken to the cemetery, and the head thrown into some *oubliette* in the fortress."

"Ah, my friend, how can you increase my suffering by relating legends which have not the slightest foundation, I am certain?"

"Alas! they are only too true."

"Then another and even more poignant fear is added to those which are already torturing me. Cosimo, what if we only found a mutilated corpse in the coffin?"

The old servant was silent for a moment. He could not control his emotion, and it was in a broken voice that he at last replied: "It would be a terrible calamity, monsieur; but the consciousness of having fulfilled our orders to the very letter would be our consolation. And this consolation would fail us, if we thought that our presence in the cemetery in the middle of the day had aroused suspicion, and perhaps caused this frightful catastrophe; how terrible would then be our remorse!"

Olivier was obliged to admit the justice of this reasoning; besides, Cosimo firmly declared that he would not accompany him before the appointed hour arrived.

So the young man waited, though with that breathless impatience only experienced by those who have counted the seconds, while awaiting some terrible and decisive event they can neither hasten nor retard. He waited with the mad anxiety of the gambler whose fortune and future are staked on a final card. Twenty times during the day he re-perused his benefactor's letter. He pondered over each word, striving to gain from it some indication of success or failure; but suddenly he paused, fancying he heard footsteps on the stairs. A strange fancy flitted through his mind. Could it be that the marquis had been buried, and that he had succeeded in breaking open the coffin and lifting the earth heaped upon it?

Then a fear closely akin to madness glittered in his eyes. "Listen," he said to Cosimo, "I was not mistaken. It is certainly his voice that I hear!"

Seeing the young man's excitement, poor Cosimo reproached himself bitterly. "What can I do to divert his mind? If this lasts, he will go mad before night-time. Ah! I ought to have opened the letter myself, and not to have informed him of its contents until the very last moment. You have been wanting in prudence, Cosimo, and you are being cruelly punished for it."

To divert Olivier's attention, the faithful fellow rehearsed their plan for saving the marquis, for the hundredth time. They reviewed all the chances, and devised all sorts of expedients in case of an emergency. They had everything that could possibly be necessary or useful—a spade, a chisel to open the coffin, and a hammer, besides some clothing for the man whom they hoped to rescue from the grave; and plenty of weapons, too, for they were resolved to fight to the last extremity, if need be. Their discussions were of great assistance in passing the time; and while they were still talking, the clock of a neighbouring church struck four.

"At last!" exclaimed Olivier, springing to his feet. "The hour has come at last; let us start."

"Not yet, master, I beg you."

"Yes," responded the young man, imperiously, "it is time to go. I will wait no longer. Don't you understand that it is impossible for me to remain shut up here? We will walk slowly, if you like; we will take the longest route, but we must start."

Cosimo offered no further opposition. So they hastily concluded their preparations for departure, concealing their weapons and their tools under their cloaks. It was exactly a quarter past four when they left the house.

As they stepped into the street, Cosimo remarked: "We have neglected to engage a coach, monsieur. Very likely the marquis will not be able to walk; besides, he will perhaps desire to leave Paris immediately. His safety may depend upon rapid flight."

The old servant had been thinking of taking this very necessary precaution ever since the morning, and if he had not spoken of it sooner it was because he had kept it as a last resource against Olivier's impatience.

"And we were very nearly forgetting this most essential precaution," said the young man. "Were we crazy?"

"A trifle so, perhaps."

"Speak for yourself, Cosimo. I was never more cool and collected. We must, at once, obtain a good carriage and a pair of strong horses which can take us fully fifteen leagues from Paris without requiring any rest. Let us make haste, for we have money enough to quicken the movements of the most dilatory grooms.

"But where shall we send the coach to wait for us?"

"On the little Place, just outside the Saint-Antoine gate. I know just the spot for the coach to wait; the driver will fancy a duel is on hand. If necessary—that is, if it is absolutely impossible for the marquis to walk—we will let the carriage drive to the wall of the cemetery, for I imagine we shall be compelled to get over the wall, as it is scarcely likely any one will be sufficiently obliging to leave the gate open for us. But let us make haste; we have no time to lose."

Despite their zeal, however, they did not immediately succeed in finding what they sought. In those days there were not fifteen thousand cabs rolling through the streets of Paris from morning until night. Still, at last, they secured suitable horses, but more than three quarters of an hour had been expended in the effort; however this was so much time gained for Cosimo.

But it was now really necessary they should start for the cemetery, and after they had seen the coach move off at a slow trot, Cosimo remarked to his master: "Now, I think, we can venture along."

They looked around them as they passed the gates of the cemetery; for at the decisive moment, a thorough acquaintance with the ground and its surroundings might prove of the greatest advantage. In this lonely and deserted spot it would have been easy for one to fancy oneself several leagues from Paris, in some quiet nook of the forest of Compiègne. Old trees shaded the spot, and as no gardener was intrusted with the task of checking the luxuriant vegetation, bushes of may and elderberries arose on all sides. The rustling of the leaves or the flight of some frightened bird was the only sound that broke the silence.

The graves were not very numerous; and it was only here and there that one perceived a mossy stone, half covered with ivy and weeds. The thick rank turf showed that the soil had not been disturbed for many years ; nor were there any of those undulations peculiar to cemeteries, so like the furrows one sees in wheat-fields after reaping time, and indicating that the earth has likewise garnered its harvest of death.

Olivier and Cosimo moved about stealthily, for they feared to disturb the melancholy quiet of the spot, or to attract attention. They spoke, moreover, in subdued tones.

"Do you notice the wall here, monsieur ? " inquired Cosimo.

"Yes ; it has almost crumbled away. It would be almost as easy to make one's way out through this breach as through the gateway."

"Certainly, and we will pass out this way."

"But I don't see the open grave," remarked Olivier anxiously. "Were it not for the two or three gravestones I see over there, I really should not fancy I was in a cemetery."

"Hush, monsieur," whispered Cosimo, "there is some one—"

Olivier paused. "Where ? " he inquired.

"There—a man ! He is digging a grave ; we need look no further."

In the part of the enclosure Cosimo designated, the trees had been cut down, the turf removed, and the surface levelled. The grave-diggers had acted as pioneers, and cleared the ground to give the defunct prisoners the six feet of earth to which we are each of us entitled after death.

"Doesn't it seem to you that we are rather far from the spot where we shall have business presently ? " asked Cosimo. "We can distinguish nothing from here."

"Yes, we must get nearer," replied Olivier, "but let us try to avoid attracting the man's attention."

"Yes, let us avoid doing so, if possible ; but if one of us attracted his notice by any unguarded movement, let us make no further attempt at concealment, for it would be almost certain to excite his suspicions. We will kneel, and pretend to pray, on the first grave we come to."

"Let us rather, my old friend, really pray to God to prosper us in our undertaking ; for, alas ! what we can do is valueless without His blessing."

They stole along behind the trees, taking advantage of the slightest in-equalities in the soil, creeping stealthily from tree to tree, and from bush to bush, until finally they succeeded in turning round the glade, and reach-ing the friendly shelter of a clump of elderberries, about twenty feet from the grave-digger. There they seated themselves, and concealed under the leaves the implements and clothing they had brought with them ; next, in order to be ready for any emergency, they prepared their weapons.

"Now we are ready," remarked Olivier, with a sigh of relief. "We can wait."

The grave-digger went on with his work in a quiet, leisurely manner, like a man who has plenty of time at his disposal ; and as he worked he cheerfully whistled a popular refrain. From their hiding-place, Olivier and Cosimo could distinctly see his slightest movement. In order to perform his task more easily, he had stepped down into the hole, which was now about two feet deep.

He rested a moment, after tossing out each spadeful of earth ; and if any peculiar pebble attracted his attention, he stooped, picked it up, carefully examined it, and then flung it aside again, leaving its course entirely to chance.

One stone of considerable size struck a branch a short distance from

Cosimo's head. "The fool came near hitting me," grumbled the old servant.

"You ought not to be angry with him for wasting his time," whispered Olivier. "It takes him as long to pick up and throw away a stone as it does to dig out two spadefuls of earth ; so we gain exactly that much by the proceeding."

The man had in the meantime stepped out of the grave, and was now leaning on his spade, and looking at something the two watchers could not see.

"Can it be that the jailers are already arriving with their grim burden?" inquired Cosimo, softly.

"No ; I can see now," replied Olivier. "It is the cavalier whom the marquis spoke of in his letter. He is approaching the grave-digger."

"I, too, can see him now," responded Cosimo ; "but I don't know him, and yet I have never forgotten the faces of any of my master's friends,"

"Nor of his enemies ?"

"No. This is the first time I have ever seen that face."

A cavalier, clad in the height of fashion, was crossing the cleared space, evidently with the intention of approaching the grave-digger. He was picking his way over the newly-made graves very cautiously, for fear of soiling his stockings and shoe-buckles ; and it seemed only natural that the grave-digger should uncover his head on beholding such an im-posing personage, and deferentially await his orders. Such was not the case, however. When the stranger had approached within a few feet of the labourer, the latter resumed his whistling, and set to work again with an extraordinary display of energy.

The cavalier paused, a trifle surprised by this reception. He was the first to speak, however. "You are engaged in a melancholy task, my friend," he remarked, pleasantly.

The man shrugged his shoulders, and, looking the speaker full in the face, replied by asking : "Why melancholy?"

"I believe it is generally conceded to be so," replied the cavalier, smiling.

"I know that, monsieur," answered the digger, resting upon the handle of his spade. "It is true that our profession is considered a lugubrious one, but what is yours? So far as I am able to judge from appearances, you are a soldier. In time of war, do you think your profession any more cheerful than mine? Is it such very delightful business to shoot and stab and mutilate one's fellow men. The thought of it is so distasteful to me that I have never been able to understand why the members of such a pro-fession should be so honoured. I have even asked myself how men could have the hardihood to admit that it was their business to kill their fellow-men. You make corpses, monsieur : I prepare their last resting-place ; and, take it all in all, I greatly prefer my vocation to yours."

These words seemed to plunge the cavalier into a fit of astonishment, so intense as to border on stupefaction ; but after a little, he recovered himself and began to laugh. "A philosophical grave-digger !" he muttered. "Upon my word ! this is marvellous. The fool deserves a sound drubbing. Still I have need of him just now, so I will allow him to go unpunished."

The grave-digger had resumed his work, and the cavalier had turned as if to retrace his steps ; but he paused, and was evidently hesitating to take a resolution. Cosimo and Olivier strained their ears but could hear nothing. However, the stranger turned again to the grave-digger, and remarked :

" My friend, I have just reflected on your words. and find them so sensible that I am almost of your opinion. So much sound judgment in a man of your position surprises me, and, upon my word, pleases me so much that I beg you will accept this louis in order to drink to my health."

The grave-digger scrutinised the face of the stranger who displayed such extraordinary generosity, but seemed undecided whether to accept the money or not. But the cold coin shone brilliantly, and, fascinated in spite of himself, the grave-digger extended his earth-stained hand.

" What, did you fear it was a counterfeit ? " cried the stranger. " But yours is a lugubrious task, after all," he continued, smiling.

" Not so lugubrious as you suppose, my good sir."

" Tell me frankly, why do you regard it in the light you do ?"

" It is because I am digging a grave for a prisoner, and as a prison—"

" Well ? "

" I should greatly prefer a grave to the Bastille."

The cavalier shuddered, and the grave-digger, perceiving it, remarked : " Upon this point, too, you seem to be of my opinion, and the name of the Bastille does not appear to be particularly agreeable to you."

" I confess it."

" Are you so familiar with its interior, then ?"

" Sufficiently so to prefer the prison you are preparing there."

" Ah, what did I tell you," retorted the grave-digger. " Am I not the deliverer of the unfortunate ? Ay, I am sure that the poor man who is to rest here will bless me from the quiet depths of his resting-place."

A cloud passed over the stranger's brow, and his lips contracted. " What, are they going to inter a prisoner here this evening ? " he inquired, in a somewhat husky voice.

" I am even now expecting the jailers who are to bring the body. It will not be long before they make their appearance."

" Ah, well, I will remain, then. I should like to witness the burial, and to learn what would have become of my body, had I died in my dungeon."

" And to say a prayer over the grave of the deceased, also, I suppose."

" Yes, I should like to do so."

" Then, monsieur, if such is your intention, it would be advisable for you to go off some little distance."

" And why ? "

" Because your presence here might excite the suspicions of the jailers. It has sometimes happened that persons have learned in some mysterious way of the death of one of their relatives imprisoned in the Bastille. These persons are desirous of gaining possession of their loved one's body, in order to inter it in their family burial-place, or if they have none, in some spot where they can have easy access, so as to go and pray at times beside the grave."

" But how do they manage to succeed in doing this ?"

" A friend, brother, or son, comes to watch the burial and note the spot where it occurs, then as soon as the jailers have retired, this son or friend, aided by a servant, hastily removes the earth, opens the coffin, and flees like a thief, taking with him the body which the king refused to restore to him."

" And do such things often occur ?"

" Yes, I have known of several cases, but I have always kept the secret. Besides, it is a very easy matter. After I leave, no one will enter the cemetery until to-morrow : all the people in the neighbourhood make a long détour rather than pass the spot, and over there in the wall there is an opening which answers all the purposes of a gate."

The stranger involuntarily quivered with emotion as he listened to these words, which seemed very like words of warning or advice ; indeed, it was very evident that the grave-digger thought he was conversing with one of the relatives to whom he had referred.

"So, take my advice, monsieur," said the man, "and conceal yourself. The jailers will soon be here, and if they see you, their suspicions will perhaps be aroused, and they may summon some of the guards to carry the body to another cemetery."

"Thank you, my friend," said the stranger, and taking another louis from his pocket and handing it to the man, he added : "This is for you. I am going to conceal myself."

"As you can see, the grave is not very deep," was the grave-digger's laughing response ; "and I am too tired to dig it much deeper before the arrival of the jailers."

The cavalier gave him a grateful nod, then hastened to the wooded portion of the cemetery, where he instantly vanished from sight, while the grave-digger resumed, or pretended to resume, his work.

This time the conversation had been conducted in loud tones ; and Olivier and Cosimo had not lost a syllable of it. "We know now that there will be nothing to endanger the success of our undertaking," remarked Olivier.

"Yes, but though I am reassured on that point, there is another that troubles me."

"And that, my friend ?"

"Is the presence of this cavalier."

"The marquis predicted that in his letter."

"But for all that, I do not like his behaviour."

"I must confess that I am delighted to find him here. He will be a valuable auxiliary in case of need."

Cosimo opened his lips to reply, but happening to glance at the open space, he stood as if petrified, and unable to speak, caught Olivier by the arm. The young man understood.

Two men, who were easily recognised by their costume as jailers from the Bastille, were advancing, bearing a litter covered with some tattered black cloth, under which the outlines of a coffin were plainly visible.

"Come on, my lambs !" cried the grave-digger.

"All right !" responded one of the jailers. "But we are tired."

"It is deucedly heavy," exclaimed the other.

When they reached the side of the grave, the cloth was removed, and then tilting the litter the jailers slid the coffin into the place prepared for it.

"Ouf !" they exclaimed with a gesture of relief.

The coffin fell into the trench with a heavy thud that re-echoed sadly in Olivier's heart. "Wretches !" he murmured angrily.

"Have a care, monsieur," entreated Cosimo.

Meanwhile the jailers had deposited the litter on the ground. "Come, we must make haste now," remarked one of them.

"The grave is not very deep," said the other, and addressing the grave-digger, he exclaimed : "Ah, lazybones, it is easy to see that you are working for the government ; the poorest citizen would have his grave at least three feet deeper."

"Are you afraid that he will get out of it?"

"No, but he is quite capable of complaining that his cell is too narrow."
Shouts of laughter greeted this pleasantry.

"It seems to me," said the grave-digger, when the hilarity had abated a
little, and he was assisting his comrades in lowering the coffin into the
grave, "that this was not a high-class prisoner."

"I fancy not," replied one of the jailers. "I did not know him."

"Now that is done, help me to fill up the grave."

We all know the lugubrious sound made by each spadeful of earth as it
falls on a coffin. Each of us has stood with bursting heart and tearful eyes
beside the grave of some relative or friend, and heard this gloomy sound
which rings out like the knell of hope. So the reader can easily imagine
the anguish that wrung Olivier's heart. He knew that the grave was closing not upon a dead but a living man. He could not endure the sight, and
burying his face in his hands he burst into tears. Cosimo, too, was paler
than a corpse, and like Olivier, averted his eyes. At last a cessation of
the sound warned him that the work was ended, and when he again glanced
at the spot there was a low mound over the spot where the hole had been but
a moment before.

The three men were standing beside it talking; but the honest grave-
digger, who had furtively glanced more than once towards the secluded
spot where the stranger had taken refuge a short time before, soon diverted
the attention of the jailers into a different channel by exclaiming:

"Comrades, let me offer you a drink."

"All right," was the quick response, and they thereupon all three left
the cemetery.

They had scarcely disappeared when Olivier was about to spring forth
from his hiding-place, but Cosimo detained him. "Have you forgotten
the stranger?" he inquired,

"He is of no consequence."

"But my master's orders were explicit."

"His life is the first consideration. Do not detain me, Cosimo. You
are murdering your master at this very moment."

"No, I am obeying him. But look, there is the gentleman. Let us see
what he is going to do."

The stranger approached the mound. He had removed his richly plumed
hat, not out of respect for the place, but to bare his forehead to the refreshing evening breeze. Had Olivier and Cosimo been nearer, they would have
read his evil thoughts on his brow. More isolated by his agitation and
remorse, than by the solitude of the spot, his agitation betrayed itself in
almost frenzied gestures.

Imprudent man! he was scattering his secret to the four winds of heaven,
without even asking himself if some indiscreet ear would not surprise it
and turn it into a formidable weapon at some future time. "You are here,
my master," he said, "lying here dead to every one but myself. You were
formerly so proud of your science, but what has become of it now? There,
in the ground, your heart is still beating, but who will hear its beatings
except myself. Rash man! how was it that you did not divine that your
pupil, the pupil of Exili, the poisoner, would betray his master as Judas
formerly did? You have taught me your art; you have given me the key
to your science. What further need have I of you now? You have not
told me all, you said; but have no fears, I will discover the rest for myself."

"Ah, ha!" he continued, with a burst of sinister laughter; "the master will never again humiliate his pupil. The master dead, the pupil will reign in his stead, and henceforth, I am the only master of the terrible secret of death!"

For one moment longer he remained motionless; then replacing his hat on his head, and scornfully spurning with his foot the fresh earth upon the mound, he sneeringly exclaimed : "If you could see me now, master, you would admire your work. If you were in my place, you would do exactly what I am doing. I desire neither master nor accomplice. I am worthy of you. Farewell, Exili, farewell ! Your pupil, Sainte-Croix, salutes you." And he walked away without once turning his head, striding hastily towards the gap in the wall which the grave-digger had pointed out to him.

It was time. Cosimo would have been powerless to restrain Olivier's fury much longer. Neither of them had been able to hear the stranger's soliloquy, but certain exclamations and gestures had convinced them that he was an enemy. Cosimo and Olivier were both perfectly satisfied that this man knew the terrible secret, and that he had decided to abandon the marquis to his fate. Twenty times already Olivier had attempted to rush out and kill him, but Cosimo had forcibly prevented him from doing so.

"Even admitting that you might come off conqueror," he said, "would not the moments spent in the conflict be so much time lost ?"

"The wretch !" exclaimed Olivier. "I will be even with him yet !"

At last the stranger disappeared among the trees, and then, with a single bound, Cosimo and Olivier reached the grave.

XII.

RESTORED TO LIFE.

"WHERE am I?"

This was the first thought that passed through Exili's confused brain on regaining consciousness.

Accustomed to living in comparative darkness, his eyes were dazzled by the bright light that streamed in through two large windows. He raised himself up, though not without considerable difficulty, and gazed with astonishment at the objects that surrrounded him.

The large and plainly furnished room in which he found himself, was almost monastic in its simplicity. The low bed upon which he was lying, an easy-chair, a desk, a wash-stand, a few leather-covered chairs, and a cedar coffer and some books on a small shelf fastened to the wall—such were the only appointments of the apartment.

This examination ended, he crossed the room with an uncertain step, and seating himself near the window, inhaled long draughts of the refreshing morning air. The sun was already high in the heavens, and the birds were singing loudly among the trees in a neighbouring garden. Opposite rose the slate roofs of a mansion which, to judge from the style of its architecture, must have been constructed during the reign of the late King, Louis XIII.

"Where am I?" Exili again asked himself, passing his hand across his forehead. "It seems to me that a veil has been spread over my memory, obscuring its clearness. Still, I am certainly not dreaming ; my brain is not under the morbid influence of an absurd illusion—a deceitful hallucination. Yes; I was a prisoner of state, living in the darkness and gloom of a cell in the Bastille. I remember now—I remember! I am not dreaming! Oliver came! This room must be his—I am free!

"Ah! how long it has been since I saw the blessed sunlight, breathed the fresh air balmy with the perfume of flowers, and heard the birds singing in the leafy branches. Long ago I was young, handsome, rich, and beloved—a dweller under the mild and sunny skies of Italy. The blue waves of the Tiber, the Bay of Naple sand the Adriatic, rippled below my palaces. The marble colonnades of my villas were mirrored in the waters of the Lakes of Como and Guarda. I was the king of those terrestrial paradises. Yet I sacrificed everything, youth, good looks, fortune, and even my name and my honour, as well as my strength and liberty, to a morose, jealous, and implacable divinity. Oh, Science, inexorable goddess! what hast thou done for me, who offered up at thy altar myriads of human victims? What hast thou given me in exchange? But a few secrets which a child will some day learn at school.

"And thou, Death, pale sister of Life, thou who hast never betrayed me, whose sinister colours I wear, thou who hast seen me pass from the gloom of my laboratory to the obscurity of a prison and the darkness of a tomb, why didst thou not keep me in thy arms where I was so lately sleeping? For here I am, decrepit, humiliated, vanquished, like a rebellious angel at the Master's feet.

"O God! it has only needed the joyful canticles of Thy feathered songsters to conquer the pride of one who was known as the Master of Poisons, and to draw tears from eyes which had never before been known to weep. Thou who knowest what I was, and what I have become, Thou who knowest my wasted and wretched life, grant me now quiet and repose. Permit me to forget the past, and to regain hope with freedom, since Thou hast restored me to life by sending the child of my adoption to rescue me."

"Yes, you are free, and here is your son!" cried a clear, joyous voice.

"Olivier!"

"My father!"

Exili tried to rise, but his limbs, still benumbed by the terrible ordeal through which he had passed, refused to obey his will; however, Olivier clasped him to his heart in a long embrace, then lifting him as if he had been a child, placed him gently upon the bed again. As he did so, Exili perceived Cosimo standing upon the threshold in a respectful attitude.

"And you, my old friend, are you not also coming to embrace me?" asked the alchemist.

"The marquis was always generous," replied Cosimo, kneeling to receive his old master's salute.

"The obligation is mine now," said Exili with a smile that brightened his austere countenance wonderfully.

"I owe everything to you, master, and you owe me nothing."

"Do not listen to him, father," interrupted Olivier gaily. "Had it not been for him, I should have ruined everything, by my lack of caution."

"That is a virtue in one of your years."

"My reckless imprudence came very near ruining everything, but I hope that this lesson will suffice, and that I shall know how to control myself better in the future."

"That is the secret of success," remarked Exili in his musical voice; "but do not imitate me, Olivier, I see only too plainly to-day that the man who attempts to do so would make a fatal mistake."

"If these words came from any other lips than yours," said Olivier, "I should feel inclined to pierce the tongue that uttered them with a red-hot iron, as one does that of a blasphemer."

"Tell me, Cosimo," asked Exili, in a more serious tone, "have you not somewhere a phial of that elixir which imparts strength to the arm, brightness to the eyes, and gladness to the heart?"

The old servant made a slightly deprecating gesture, which might be interpreted as a response.

"I understand you," said Exili, "I know that the reaction is equal to the action, and that the hours of artificial vitality are a frightful drain upon one's strength: but this elixir will help to dispel the clouds that now obscure my mental vision. I will drink to Olivier's health."

"As you please. You two must be humoured like spoiled children," remarked Cosimo, opening a casket.

He drew from it a flat bottle enclosed in a metallic case, and removed the glass stopper; then he poured out a glassful of the liquid, which strikingly resembled melted gold, glittering like a topaz, and silently presented it to his master. Exili drained it at a single draught. In a moment his stiff and benumbed limbs regained their suppleness and elasticity; a brilliant colour glowed upon his cheeks, a smile curved his lips, and his eyes sparkled with the wonderful brilliancy of a black diamond.

"What do you think of it, Cosimo?" the alchemist asked as he rose and laid his hand on his faithful servant's shoulder.

"I think you will be young until this evening."

"The next thing is to dress."

"There will be no difficulty about that; we have provided all that is necessary."

In the twinkling of an eye Cosimo arrayed his master in a fine linen shirt, with handsome lace ruffles at the wrists, then with knee-breeches, and a coat of black velvet, ornamented with rosettes of sky-blue satin ribbon; black silk stockings and high-heeled shoes completed this simple but elegant costume. When this part of his master's toilet was completed, Cosimo proceeded to cut the long hair which hung about his shoulders, and afterwards to shave off the heavy beard which reached to his waist, but he left the soft, silky moustache untouched. This task concluded, he placed a curled wig upon Exili's head, surmounted it with a plumed hat, handed him an ivory-handled ebony cane, and then retreated a step, like an artist contemplating his work.

Exili submitted to the scrutiny with a very good grace, and upon inspecting himself in turn, in the mirror, seemed well pleased with the transformation.

"I suppose you have destroyed my prison clothes," he remarked.

"Entirely: not even the ashes remain, marquis."

"The Marquis de Florenzi died three days ago, Cosimo. You are now in the service of the Count de Kronborg."

"There seems to be something grim and terrible about that name," remarked Olivier.

"It is the name of a Danish fortress as gloomy and grim as the mouths of its cannons. The name suits me; it harmonizes with my destiny, and will fulfill its promise."

"I have no fears in that respect," remarked Cosimo, with a smile.

"Now, Olivier," said Exili, "tell me all that occurred between the hour of my burial and that of my resurrection."

D

"I scarcely need assure you, father, that all the instructions in your letter were carefully studied and faithfully executed. We reached the cemetery an hour before sunset."

"Did you see the cavalier I mentioned?"

"Yes. He talked with the grave-digger, and then he concealed himself. Afterwards, when the grave-digger and the jailers had finished their task, he emerged from his hiding-place. At first I thought he intended to rescue you, but I was mistaken."

"Naturally."

"He stamped upon your grave as if he wished to bury you still deeper in the earth. Then he uttered words which I was unable to hear, on account of the distance between us; but his gestures and the sardonic expression upon his features admitted of no other interpretation than an insult or a curse."

"I anticipated as much That is why I did not hesitate to ask you to come to my aid with our faithful Cosimo. I knew that you would be exposed to some danger, but—"

"Father," interrupted Olivier, firmly, "you have too much good sense to attach any great importance to an act which only vulgar folks consider heroic without stopping to think that it would be natural to any animal."

"Well said, my son. A man, indeed, is only worthy of the name when he proves his superiority over the lower animals by his contempt of death and his determination to do his duty. But the mental power of which he is so proud is only the elder sister of instinct. But go on with your story. You were saying that the cavalier insulted my corpse and trampled it under foot."

"Yes, and it was then that I lost my head completely. I wanted to rush out and attack him on the spot, and should have done so if Cosimo had not held me with a strength which I did not suppose him to possess."

"Ah! ah!" said Exili, triumphantly, "I seems to me that is the effect of my elixir."

"Ah, master, I would have swallowed hell itself if you had distilled it, for I foresaw that Olivier would give me trouble."

"You should have given him some drug which would have lent him the years you have rid yourself off."

"The Count de Kronborg may if he pleases deride the Marquis de Florenzi's old servant, but Olivier will say whether I was right or wrong."

"Yes, no doubt. You must like myself admire the fiery power of youth we both regret. But what are you thinking of?"

"Of the supper, monsieur."

"Then leave us."

Cosimo at once went off to attend to the evening repast, and Exili turned to Olivier who resumed his narrative.

"After this person, whom I feel little inclined to call a gentleman, left the cemetery, we set to work to carry out the instructions you had given us. It did not take us long to open the grave, and then the coffin. My heart failed me for a moment; but a look from Cosimo restored my courage. I took the cold and rigid body upon my shoulders, made my escape from the cemetery through the opening in the wall, and succeeded in reaching the coach in which I deposited my burden. Once there, I unclosed your teeth with the blade of my poniard and allowed three drops of the liquid in the phial to trickle into your mouth; then, after a short interval, three more drops. In the meantime Cosimo had nailed up the coffin, replaced it in the grave and covered it with earth."

"Consequently," said Exili, "the grave-digger will find things in the same condition as when he left them ; and if my former companion should honour my resting-place with another visit, he will be satisfied that I am dead and safely out of the way. But he will have to make haste, for I propose to furnish him speedily euough with the materials for his own funeral oration. Supposing me dead, he will believe himself the sole and undisputed master of the universe. I might break the glass mask that protects his face while he is bending over his crucibles, imitating my experiments ; but, as Cosimo often says, 'A man who is born to be hanged will never be drowned.' At the appointed hour, however, an invisible hand will unmask the traitor, and he will perish by the poison he himself has distilled. Go on, Olivier."

"When Cosimo rejoined me he found me with my hand on your heart, father. It was beginning to beat again, though very faintly. Cosimo positively forbade me to administer the few drops of liquid remaining in the phial, and insisted upon a scrupulous observance of the directions, which only advised such a course, in case the first six drops failed to produce any effect at the end of a quarter of an hour."

"Well ? "

"The coach moved on very slowly, and it was dark when we reached this house, near the Place des Victoires."

"Then, as nearly as I am able to calculate," said Exili, "I must have spent forty hours in a leaden slumber, in addition to the thirty hours of lethargy."

"You are correct. Have you any appetite ? "

"Yes, I should be glad to eat something if Cosimo will allow it."

They sat down to table and, when the repast was over, Cosimo prepared some coffee with the utmost care.

"There's a famous slow poison," said Olivier, jokingly.

"Ay," replied Exili, "but it is the antidote for opium."

While the beverage was smoking in the cups, Cosimo brought two long pipes, the bowls of which, richly decorated with gilded hieroglyphics, were filled with Eastern tobacco of a pale tint.

"Now," said Exili, as he smoked with the impassibility of an Indian before the council fire—"now, Olivier, tell me how you have spent the years of your apprenticeship in life."

"To tell the truth, my life has been marked only by one event worthy of narration."

"And that is a love affair, of course ? " Exili murmured, with a sigh.

"Yes, father,"

"Ah, well, I will listen to your idyl, my dear child. It will rejuvenate me by reminding me of my own youth, O spring, the youth of the year, O youth, the spring of life."

"My history begins with an idyl but ends with a tragedy."

"You mean an elegy."

"I do not exaggerate. You shall judge for yourself."

"Proceed then ; I will not interrupt you again,"

XIII.

FATHER AND MOTHER.

OLIVIER related his romance with all the eloquence he was capable of, starting from the day when he first saw his beloved and proceeding to the catastrophe which had made the financier's only child a penniless orphan.

"This is a strange turn of fortune's wheel, upon my word!" remarked Exili with a peculiar smile.

"Father—"

"The dead do not hear their funeral orations, and it would be as well for you to know something about the family you are soon to form part of. It is said that Madame Hanyvel is a very excellent woman, and I am strongly inclined to believe it. But Hanyvel himself was a clever scoundrel, like many others. Your Henriette is an angel; but angels have wings, and if some one had not sent her father to his celestial home, you would have lost her."

"Her marriage was decided upon," said Olivier.

"But one event," resumed Exili, "has on my side marked our separation. As you are aware, walls have ears, even those of the Bastille. Even in the depths of my dungeon, I was in communication with the outside world, and I may truly say that my bitter heart was purified by the flame of your youthful passion. If Hanyvel had possessed a father's heart, if he had not been determined to sacrifice his daughter, I should not have allowed his name to be effaced from the book of the living."

"You?"

"Yes, I."

"Through whom?"

"Monsieur Reich de Penautier, Receiver-General of the Clergy."

"But why?"

"You shall soon know. Cosimo?"

"Monsieur!"

"I wish to see Monsieur de Penautier. You will propably find him at his house or at the Hôtel de la Ferme. Tell him that one of Exili's friends desires to see him. Go and bring him to me."

Cosimo bowed and left the room.

"One of Exili's friends?" said Olivier.

"Why not?" rejoined the poisoner.

Olivier appeared to be engaged in deep thought, but his eyes seemed inclined to avoid those of his adopted father.

"Exili," said the resuscitated marquis, "had for a companion in captivity the gentlemanly scoundrel who treated me with such impoliteness in the cemetery. He made him his disciple without initiating him into all his secrets, however. The man's name is Gaudin de Sainte-Croix. He pretends he is the illegitimate son of an illustrious family that has never acknowledged him. He is a mere pleasure seeker, destitute of principle and ability, and egregiously vain. He is an officer in a Normandy regiment, and a great friend of its colonel, the Marquis de Brinvilliers, and the lover of that nobleman's wife.

"It was this lovely marquise, whom you escorted half-way to her coach on the day of Hanyvel's death, and whom your friend the Chevalier de Tancarvel, lieutenant in the Guards, told you he had frequently met at the house of her sister, Madame de Sarremont. Penautier, who is a very crafty man, understanding that the Marquis de Brinvilliers would never make any open protest against his wife's scandalous conduct, secretly denounced her to her father, M. Dreux d'Aubray, lieutenant of police. He, jealous of the honour of his family, wrote the name of Sainte-Croix on a *lettre-de-cachet*, and sent him straight to the Bastille, where he remained a year. He left the prison only twenty-four hours in advance of myself.

"Penautier, wily as a fox, stealthy as a cat, as evil-disposed as an old monkey, visited Sainte-Croix while he was in prison, in order to make a cat's-paw of him. It was in this way that he obtained from Exili the poison that killed Hanyvel. M. Dreux d'Aubray, who believes that his daughter has repented, will be greatly astonished to learn that she smilingly poured the poison out with her own hand for a consideration of thirty thousand francs—a mere trifle to Penautier, who will make four millions by the operation, if I do not compel him to disgorge. To do him justice, I must admit that he manages such matters remarkably well."

"What! is it possible that such a crime can have been committed under the eyes of Heaven?"

"And of all the guests at the *fête?*" added Exili.

"It is impossible that the murderers can long remain unpunished. It would be doubting the justice of God to believe such a thing possible."

"That is nonsense. Penautier trembles like a child; Sainte-Croix is only a novice; and the marquise is ignorance personified. Still she has a positive genius for vice, and she will carry her crimes to any extent."

"Your smile makes me shudder," said Olivier. "I cannot doubt your word; and yet, when I think of that young and beautiful woman, my heart and my reason alike refuse to believe you."

"The *young woman* you speak of was married in 1651, at the age of twenty-one; consequently, she is now thirty-six years of age, and, moreover, she has children in every parish, and the marquis, her husband, winks at her goings on."

"I scorn the man."

"Ay, but one cannot afford to scorn his wife. She will justify the old saying, '*Adultera, venefica.*'"

"But her face is as sweet as that of a Madonna, her eyes as clear as those of a child. The day I met her, she had been weeping. There was a strange charm in her slightest movement, and it seems to me I still hear the musical notes of her silvery voice ringing in my ear."

"If you had studied natural history elsewhere than in books, you would recognise a strange resemblance to many of the inferior animals in the human face. The impression the marchioness produces upon me may be described in a few words. She has all the wonderful grace of a tiger, and all the fascinating power of a viper."

"Yes," exclaimed Olivier, as if struck by a sudden revelation. "Her eye is calm and cold. I touched her soft hand—it was supple and cold like the body of a serpent."

"Listen, Olivier," exclaimed the alchemist. "The words you are about to hear are one of Exili's predictions; and the Master of Poisons knows how to analyse human clay. This woman possesses an utterly depraved nature. She would put Messalina and Locusta to the blush. She is on the road to perdition, and no human hand can save her. She must have gold and absolute liberty. Her father is a morose censor; she will poison him while lavishing her deceitful caresses upon him. She will poison her two brothers in order to obtain possession of the entire fortune of her family. She will poison her daughter because she will be jealous of her beauty. She will poison her good-natured husband in order to marry her lover. She will poison her lover when she becomes weary of him. You will see her barefooted, her features concealed by a parricide's veil, and with a torch in her hand, standing outside the church of Notre Dame, ere her head falls by the hand of the executioner on the Place de Grêve."

"It is horrible!" exclaimed Olivier.

"The laws of nature are incomprehensible. It gives life to the serpent that crawls, as well as to the bird that soars. And yet, have you never seen a serpent fascinating the bird with its basilisk stare? It seems to say to it: 'Descend from heaven, and die.'"

"Yes."

"Henriette is as pure and gentle as a dove. Some day she will be at-tracted by the wonderful fascinations of the viper. She has seen you; she has smiled upon you. Beware, Olivier.'"

"But eagles destroy venomous reptiles. Punish Sainte-Croix as he deserves; but it is I who will place the Marquise de Brinvilliers in the hands of the executioner."

"He shall die by this hand, I swear it."

"And I swear by my love that *she*—"

"Hush Olivier. Remain silent in the presence of destiny."

"And why?"

"Would you know the truth?"

"Yes."

"The Marquise de Brinvilliers is your mother."

Olivier hid his face in his hands and wept.

Exili watched him some time in silence, then he said in a voice that made the heart of his adopted child thrill with emotion: "Yes, it is a hard thing for a son to despise his father, and to be unable to embrace his mother without horror and loathing. And I," he continued, after a pause, "have just accomplished the most difficult and dangerous of my experiments."

"You have poisoned my soul, father," Olivier groaned in his anguish.

Exili rose up as if the angel of darkness had set his hand on his shoulder; but overcoming his passing weakness, he said in a husky voice: "I have deserved this reproach; but nature is a kind mother, Olivier, and she shows me the balm that will heal your wound. I see a young girl walking about under the trees—your betrothed, undoubtedly, for she is gazing per-sistently at these windows. She is as beautiful as a lily, and the sight of her will prove an effectual antidote."

Just then the door opened, and Cosimo announced: "Monsieur de Pen-autier, Receiver-General of the Clergy."

XIV

HENRIETTE'S DOWRY.

ALTHOUGH he had certainly had plenty of time to prepare for this inter-view, the financier's face betrayed the vague uneasiness and instinctive terror that the redoubtable name of the great Exili had aroused in his troubled mind.

At Olivier's invitation he seated himself. "To whom have I the honour of speaking?" he asked, addressing Exili, who was standing before him with folded arms.

"Do you not recognise me?"

"It does seem to me, monsieur, that this is not the first time I have heard your voice ; but my recollections are too indistinct for me to speak with certainty."

"I am the Count de Kronborg, and your fancy is explained by a family resemblance. Exili was my elder brother."

"I regret to learn that he died in the Bastille. Your brother, monsieur, was a man of wonderful scientific attainments, and he has carried many secrets with him to the grave."

"Not all, monsieur," was the response, and after a moment's silence, Exili resumed : "I have come from England in obedience to his dying request, and shall leave the country almost immediately. All that concerns you can be explained very briefly. My brother desires that we should at once settle together all matters appertaining to the estate of Hanyvel, the deceased financier."

"I was his friend, monsieur," began Penautier, eagerly stretching out his hand, "and my knowledge of his affairs may enable me to aid you in saving something from the wreck ; but the estate is greatly embarrassed. Hanyvel's strength lay in his credit ; but unfortunately he is no longer at the helm, and his ship has virtually gone to pieces. His assets, which were formerly valued at four millions, will bring in scarcely one hundred thou sand francs."

"Why is that?"

"It can be explained in a few words : Hanyvel is dead !"

"And he died suddenly?"

"Who can be sure of the morrow? When a man's time comes, he must go."

"Yes, especially when a friendly hand hastens one's departure."

"That is a way of looking at Hanyvel's death, which might have been expected from your brother."

"And I am quite of his way of thinking, Monsieur de Penautier. Do you understand me fully? Hanyvel's entire fortune is invested in promising enterprises, and capital only is required for these investments to turn out most profitably. Will you share with me? The offices of the Farmers' General are two steps from here. Bring me four drafts of five hundred thousand francs each on Paris, London, Vienna, and Rome, and I will relinquish the other half of the property to you."

"Are you speaking seriously, count?"

"Do I appear to be jesting, Monsieur de Penautier?"

"Yes, in saying I could obtain two millions from the Farmers' General at once, on my mere signature."

"You may find them in your own cash-box."

"Yes, in money on deposit, but not money of my own."

"Let us understand each other. If you do not bring me within an hour, two millions in four drafts of five hundred thousand francs each, Exili will rise from his grave and present himself at your house."

"My servants are below, monsieur, and I have only to approach this window—"

"To see Hanyvel's deserted home."

"What do you mean, monsieur?"

"That you are his *executor*, and that his daughter Henriette's portion must be paid over to me, here in this room, and without delay."

"Is this a trap? I warn you that this scheme will result disastrously for you."

"You are at perfect liberty to leave this house, if you so decide, Monsieur de Penautier. I will add only a single word. I have told you that Exili would rise from his grave. Go to the cemetery of the Bastille, and open his coffin. It is empty."

"If Exili's corpse has disappeared, I will await its reappearance."

"Perhaps you would not recognise my brother in his new character. He has changed his name as well as his face. He resembles me. Look at me."

Penautier hesitated a second, and then in a faint tone, and with an entreating gesture, he slowly said : "I am ready to give my signature after explaining to you—"

"I know the story. Come, go into the adjoining room," interrupted Exili, "prepare the papers, and be grateful to me for permitting you to live."

Penautier, trembling like a leaf, hastily obeyed.

The door had scarcely closed behind him, when Cosimo reappeared, and said : "I have just admitted Madame Hanyvel and her daughter. They are in a terrible state of anxiety They have been in the habit of seeing Monsieur Olivier every day, and I neglected to warn them—"

"In one moment," said Exili rising.

But Cosimo had already disappeared.

XV.

REDEMPTION.

EXILI gloomily wrapped a cloak about his shoulders, and looking at Olivier, who stood before him as pale and motionless as a statue, he said : "In ancient times there were altars where the unhappy, and even criminals, found a safe refuge. Farewell !"

"If you are unhappy, father, tell me if it is not in my power to console you."

"O my beloved son, let me give you this name once more. The angel who bears those words to God will win the pardon of Exili the poisoner, for though he may have furnished food for the grave-worm, he has also reared a man like yourself, an honour to humanity."

"There is in my heart a deeper, more thoughtful and sacred love for you than the mere natural affection of a child for its parent."

"Whether the heart is overflowing with joy or with sorrow, how pleasant it is to hear the voice of a friend, the voice of a son ! Forgive me for having doubted you. If you had allowed me to depart unforgiven, I should have died of despair."

"'Judge not, lest ye be judged.' I know nothing, and I absolutely refuse to know anything about you. Exili may accuse himself, but his son will not believe him."

Exili sank upon his knees and lifted his trembling hands to heaven. "O God !" he faltered, "Thou knowest that I am not an assassin. Thou gavest me that vital spark men call genius, and I have preserved it as bright and luminous as the eternal lights of Thy Sanctuary. I have toiled to establish the supremacy of mind over matter, for death alone holds the secret of life. May others question her more successfully; my soul is too full of gloom to be able to find the light. The aged man is fast becoming a child again, and those who saw me ascending the hill will not recognise me as I descend it. Embrace me once more, my son."

A few moments later Penautier emerged from the adjoining room, placed the drafts in Exili's hand, and left the apartment, without another word having been exchanged between them.

A signal warned Cosimo, and he now ushered in the visitors.

Henriette entered first, and with an impulsive movement, she threw herself into Olivier's arms.

" Two hearts that love each other are united," Exili remarked to Madame Hanyvel, with a faint smile.

" Who is this handsome and melancholy stranger ? " Henriette confidentially inquired of her betrothed.

" It is my father. Will you love him, Henriette ? "

" I will be his daughter."

Exili now handed a small portfolio to Olivier.

" Here is your wife's dowry and my wedding present," he remarked. "Cosimo will accompany you to Venice. There nothing will trouble your love, and you will find the happiness that has been denied to me."

The marriage of Henriette and Olivier was quietly solemnised that same evening. As the newly married pair were about to leave the church, they glanced round for the Count de Kronborg, who had been present at the ceremony.

But Exili had disappeared.

END OF THE INTRIGUES OF A POISONER.

CAPTAIN COUTANCEAU.

ONE evening, in 1870, after the labours of the day were ended, we sat, a little group of us, all friends and neighbours, quietly chatting in the Coutan-ceaus' parlour—the windows of which were wide open on account of the excessive heat. Worthy people, these Coutanceaus, every one of them, from the grandfather—a man of iron, who seemed likely to outlast his hundredth birthday—down to the youngest of the children. They were folks of old-fashioned probity and honour, well known in our neighbour-hood, where father and son had lived for more than a century, and so loved and respected that it was a mark of distinction to be admitted to their house.

But that particular evening we were not as gay as usual. The news that had been rife for more than a week made us all thoughtful. It was affirmed that the King of Prussia, while on horseback at the head of his troops, in the full light of day, had dared, publicly, to spurn, with a disdainful gesture, our ambassador, the representative of France, who was advancing towards him.

"It is impossible," said M. Dohri, the wood-merchant. "Pride cannot have so utterly ruined the reason of those Germans."

At that moment a loud hubbub in the street below drowned his words, and we all rushed to the windows.

A number of young men were marching along carrying a flag, and shout-ing: "To Berlin! To Berlin! To Berlin!"

Quick as lightning, one of the Coutanceau boys darted from the room, and when he returned, an instant afterwards, he held an evening newspaper in his hand. He was slightly pale, and his lips quivered as lips are apt to do when one is under the influence of some powerful emotion, but his eyes burned with a dazzling brilliancy. "They have decided it!" he exclaimed. "War is declared. See, listen!"

He spoke truly. A deep, solemn silence pervaded the room, as if before each one of us there had risen a sudden vision of the grandeur, sacrifices, heroism, and suffering expressed by that terrible word *war!*

But it lasted only for an instant. Old Captain Coutanceau, whom we had fancied to be asleep in his arm-chair, sprang to his feet. Towering in the midst of us, he exclaimed, in that vibrating voice which in former days had fired the hearts of his soldiers: "Ah! they will have it so! So they taunt and defy us! Ah, well, so much the better. To Berlin then!"

But one must have known Captain Coutanceau to realise the emotion which his words and gesture roused within us. He was one of the few survivors of those heroic battalions who made their breasts a rampart for the defence of France when she was menaced by destruction in the days of the great Revolution. One after another he had seen all of his generation fall around him, until he alone remained, like one of those giant oaks, spared by the tempest, which here and there tower above the other trees of the forest. He must have been ninety-six or seven years old; but one would have scarcely believed him seventy when one met him in his daily walk, and noted his firm, quick step, and his tall form erect in a long frock-coat. At sight of him, one was struck with respect, so apparent in his noble face were all the unostentatious virtues with which he had adorned his life; so plainly visible upon his clear brow was the impress of honest pride and intelligence. A man whose conscience was not clear could scarcely have met unfalteringly the searching gaze of the aged captain, who never, I would swear it, had known a thought for which he had reason to blush. And yet, how good, how kind, how indulgent! Ah! his little grandchildren imposed upon him terribly at times.

Such then was the man who rose up among us, imposing and sublime, as if all the glories of our country shone in him incarnate. "Yes, so much the better," he continued. "Now I thank Heaven for having granted me so long a life. I shall now see our revenge before I die—revenge for 1815. Ah! if I were only thirty years younger! But you are here my grandsons: you are here, Louis and Henri."

With an enthusiastic movement both young men sprang forward to clasp their grandsire's hand. "We had resolved to ask your permission to enlist to-morrow," they cried, as with one voice.

A smile irradiated the old man's face. "That is well," said he, "that is well! It would be strange if there were fighting on the banks of the Rhine, and no Coutanceau in the French ranks." He paused, for he had detected a tear in the eyes of his daughter. "Why do you weep Marie-Louise?" he asked reproachfully. "This is a just war, our country's war. It is the duty of her children to serve her." Then more gently, he added: "Reflect, my dear child. The greater the number that go, the surer will be the victory; the less will be the danger. Reason and duty are in accord. Ah! if all who are able to shoulder a musket would but rise *en masse*, and rush upon the enemy, the war would be over to-morrow. Prussia, in her fright would retreat without striking a blow." He could not refrain from laughing at this idea, and added gaily, "Besides, Berlin is not so far away, not at the end of the world by any means. An army may reach it easily, and even visit it again and again."

We all knew that Captain Coutanceau had taken part in the wars of the Revolution and the First Empire, and we had always wondered how it happened that a man of his valour had remained in the lower ranks when so many of his old comrades had become generals and even marshals of France. It was owing, people said, to a terrible drama in which he had been involved, and which had shattered a career that promised most brilliantly; but no one had ever dared to question him on this subject. This evening, however, one of us was more courageous. "Ah! captain," insinuated his friend, the doctor, "if you would only—"

"I understand perfectly what you desire," replied the captain. "You want the story of my battles. Ah, well! I don't refuse. But by-and-bye. This evening I belong to these two boys, who, perhaps, before a month has passed, will stand face to face with the Prussians. Let me confine myself, for the present, to a part of my reminiscences. I should like to tell the lads who these enemies are with whom they have to deal."

The captain's favourite arm-chair was at once brought forward ; he seated himself comfortably and then began to tell us the following story :—

To give you, even in the slightest degree, a truthful picture of Paris in the early part of the month of June, 1792, would require an eloquence which I do not possess. No, I could never describe the terrible excitement, the exalted hopes, the fever that raged in the souls of us all, and raised us above ourselves. At that time people lived in the public squares, at the clubs, at the societies organised for the purpose of instructing citizens as to their rights. Public speakers harangued crowds at the street corners every evening, or read the daily papers aloud to the throng by the flickering light of a candle enclosed in oiled paper. The public gardens were always crowded with excited, enthusiastic people, and the *Café de la Régence*—the rendezvous of the officers of the National Guard—and the *Café de Choiseul*, whose landlord, a fiery patriot, always hustled any person who did not share his political opinions out of doors—were always full to overflowing. Bread was very dear, and all work and all business having ceased, there was a great deal of suffering and want.

My father, Jean Coutanceau, who was a baker, had his little shop in the Rue Saint Honoré, not far from the house of Duplay, a cabinet-maker, who was Robespierre's friend and landlord. But my father spent very little time at home. All night, bare to the waist, he worked at the kneading trough as industriously as any of his apprentices : but as soon as the bread was drawn from the oven he put on his coat and went off until dinner time ; and every evening, moreover, he repaired to the Jacobin Club and did not return until it was time for him to resume his labour. I often wondered what stuff he could be made of, to resist such fatigue and such constant deprivation of sleep. Ah, well ! there were many hundreds and thousands who were living the same life—men of steel tempered for their work and sustained by the invincible spirit of liberty. Under other circumstances, my mother would undoubtedly have been angry at my father's abandonment of his fireside. But she shared her husband's opinions, and if she was disturbed at times, she honourably concealed her disquietude. "Men must do their duty," she said. Every evening she awaited my father's coming with feverish impatience : and when he had returned, she made him relate all the news. She questioned him in regard to all that had taken place in the *faubourgs* and at the Tuileries, and was eager to know who had spoken in the Assembly and what had been said there.

On Sundays, however, my father always remained quietly at home. He reckoned up his accounts and made out his bills to be sent to those of our customers who did not pay cash. He had a good many such customers —so many, in fact, that, far from making money, we were almost every month obliged to draw something from our little capital. A baker's business in those days paid poorly indeed. On Sundays, M. Goguerau, a physician who had been elected a deputy for Paris in 1791, almost always came to partake of our modest dinner. He was a very old friend, my godfather, and almost a relative, since his sister had married my mother's nephew, a young man named Moisson, who was a cabinet-maker in the Faubourg Saint Antoine. When the dessert was placed upon the table, my father invariably went down into the cellar, in search of a bottle of old wine, and as he drank it with M. Goguerau they talked politics interminably. I did not altogether understand their theories, but what they said made it as clear as day in my mind that liberty is the most precious of all blessings and the most sacred of rights.

I was at that time seventeen, but unusually tall and strong for my age, and could easily have passed for twenty. My father had decided not to make me a baker like himself, or as his father had been before him. He was determined that I should have a better education than he had received, and he sent me regularly to a school kept by a priest behind the Church of Saint-Roch. Our teacher was a worthy old man who did not trouble himself about politics, and whose only aim in life was the rapid advancement of his pupils in Latin, history, and geography. I should tell an untruth if I said that I did not long to go out with my father instead of attending school, but he would not listen to that, and every day I was forced to stick to my books.

It was only through my mother's indulgence that I succeeded now and then in gaining a few hours of freedom. Sometimes, when crowds were gathering in the streets and we heard the quick beating of the drums, she took pity on me, seeing the tortures I was enduring from unsatisfied curiosity, and said : " There, run and see what it is, but don't be gone long." And how fast I did run !

So it chanced that I saw the great procession which visited the Assembly and then invaded the Tuileries on the 20th of June, 1792. It was the first great and ineffaceable event in my life ; for I had witnessed none of those glorious and memorable scenes that preceded it, neither the taking of the Bastille, the occurrences at the Hôtel de Ville, nor the catastrophe on the Champs de Mars. At the head of the first column in the procession marched Santerre and a man clad in the garb of a huckster, who was, some people told me, the Marquis de Saint-Huruge. A few paces behind them came some disabled soldiers dragging a car containing a tall, full-foliaged poplar. The people did not seem to be angry or threatening, but, on the contrary, quite gay and inclined to laugh ; and I noticed in the throng a good many women with children in their arms. I asked some of these people where they were going and what they intended to do. They replied that they did not know, but that Monsieur and Madame Veto—for so they had styled the king and queen—must be induced to listen to reason. For nearly four hours I was with the crowd, borne on by the current, when at last they burst open the gates of the Place du Carrousel ; but I did not enter the Tuileries. When I saw the cannon before the doors of the palace, I became afraid, I must confess, and I ran away.

My father was gloomy and despondent when he came home late that evening. " Everything is going wrong," he remarked. " What are our armies doing ? Nothing. And yet the enemy is at the frontier ! It is undoubtedly true that there are many Frenchmen unworthy of the name who welcome the invader with all their hearts. Woe to these scoundrels who would ally themselves with the enemy !"

My father was, naturally, an honest and kind-hearted man, but he uttered these words in such a menacing voice, and with such a ferocious expression of countenance, that I trembled. I have not yet told you that hostilities had commenced between France and Austria in the preceding month of April. And certainly no one could imagine a war begun under more unfavourable auspices. The campaign had scarcely opened, and already the want of discipline was seen. Indeed, the demoralisation of our army was at its height.

Luckner, Lafayette, and Rochambeau, the generals in command, had no confidence in their soldiers, who in their turn distrusted their leaders. Carried away by suspicion, our troops scented treason on every side. Two regiments had retreated without firing a single volley, and had thrown down their arms, crying, "We are betrayed!" Such a beginning might well fill the hearts of the enemy with exultation. The condition of affairs was terrible, and yet no one seemed trying to remedy it. In fact, in Paris folks said it was not the success of *our* armies that Monsieur and Madame Veto desired.

Such was the state of public feeling when the news spread through France that Prussia, openly violating her obligations of neutrality, was advancing upon our frontier with her army. It was my father who first told us this news on his return from the club, where he had read a letter from Coblenz, the head-quarters of the Prussian army. My mother was appalled. "Is it really possible?" she cried. "What cause can these men have for making war against us?"

"None whatever."

"Then why should they come?"

"Why? because they know our frontier is unprotected; because they believe that we are all at their mercy; because Prussia is a beast of prey and hopes to wrest something from us—a fortress, a city, a province, perhaps!"

For several days almost every one doubted the truth of this report; for, indeed, every one wished to disbelieve it. It would have greatly pleased us to find it untrue! And, besides, many persons, more honest than shrewd, thought the Prussians would hesitate or cease their advance entirely, as they could not possibly find any excuse to justify an aggression on their part. However, our anxiety was none the less intense. Paris seemed to rumble and tremble like some huge engine, the steam of which is seeking an outlet.

While we were in this state of uncertainty, I saw little of my father. He did not even take his meals at home, nor did he return at night until after I was asleep. Occasionally, however, some of his friends came to see him, and held a council in the little back shop; and, whenever I listened to their conversation, I heard them say again and again, in a tone of concentrated fury: "We must find some means of saving ourselves, for the king and queen are in league with the invader for our betrayal."

I heard such expressions of opinion everywhere. I had fallen insensibly into the habit of spending most of my own time away from home. Our old teacher had given up his school, and, as my mother no longer made me give an account of my movements, I had my time to myself. I was my own master, and I thoughtlessly took advantage of my freedom, like the child that I was. I roamed about the city, mingling with the excited crowds, following the processions which now constantly appeared in honour of everything and nothing, listening, questioning, and storing up all the rumours with which the air was filled. But before I returned home, I always visited the Palais Royal. There, under the same trees where Camille Desmoulins had given the first signal for the uprising of the people, an eager throng, breathless with curiosity, was always gathered around public readers and speakers. In those days, my friends, there were no railroads and no telegraph wires. Despatches were brought by couriers, and it required several days and many relays of horses to bring news from the frontier. You can understand our impatience and the fevered workings of our imaginations, and consequently the false rumours with which we were overwhelmed.

The fabrication of news became a mania. There were people who made themselves a name, and one might say with truth, a living, by it. The cleverest of these romancers were always to be found at the Palais Royal, and as soon as one of them appeared, people mounted him upon a bench, and listened to his discourse with wrapt attention. And according to what this fellow said, the crowd firmly believed everything lost or everything saved; and shouts of joy or still more absurd cries of fear filled the air.

One of these speakers I seem to see yet. He was a man called Mouchet, a dwarf about as high as my boot, humpbacked and bandylegged, with a dark, swarthy complexion, and a fiery-red nose. He was popularly known as the "lame Devil." His voice was so shrill and piercing that he could easily make himself heard through the wooden galleries, overpowering all the other speakers; nor did he lack a certain kind of rude eloquence, which had made him for a long time a power at political meetings. Mouchet's specialty was disastrous news. Every afternoon he announced that our soldiers had encountered the enemy, had been defeated, and were now flying in wild confusion; and if one of his hearers ventured to express a doubt, Mouchet would draw from his pocket a letter which he was willing to assert on oath he had just received from the army, and which he would read aloud to the panic-stricken crowd. He was in addition charged with daily denunciations of General La Fayette, who was now distrusted by the patriots. The time when they fought for the hairs of his white horse, to preserve them as relics, had long since passed by.

But, alas! Mouchet, the untiring talker, was not always obliged to invent his gloomy tidings. He only spoke the truth when he announced that the Grand Duke of Baden had welcomed the Austrians to Kehl, and when he said that a plot had been discovered to deliver Strasbourg up to the enemy. He spoke only the truth, moreover, when he pictured Alsace upon her knees, vainly imploring arms with which to defend herself. It was also from Mouchet that I heard of our misfortunes in Flanders, where the aged Luckner, the general of the Revolution, had not been equal to his reputation. Supported by Dumouriez, he had made an advance upon Courtrai, and taken it with two other important towns. But then suddenly, as if frightened by his own temerity or success, he had hastily retreated behind the guns of Lille, having done just enough to compromise his friends and the partisans of France. "Now," concluded Mouchet, in his rasping voice, "I would ask the brave *sans-culottes* who are listening to my words, what is the meaning of this retreat? It has taken place because Monsieur Veto has commanded it. Treason is evident; the court-party wishes to give the Prussians time to arrive."

But Mouchet did not say that, to hold his own against the entire Austrian army, Luckner had only a force of forty thousand men—burning with enthusiasm, it is true, but poorly disciplined and without provisions, almost without ammunition. I thought of this, and spoke of it to my father that evening; but purple with indignation, and with clenched fists, he responded: "And whose fault is it if our frontier is defenceless? if we are destitute of military stores? If our soldiers lack everything, if our generals are cowards or imbeciles, whose fault is it if not the king's, who has sworn to defend France, and who holds the means of defence in his own hands, but who will not use them."

This is true, I thought; my father is right. With increasing wrath he continued: "There was to be a camp established between Paris and the frontier. Where is this camp? Soldiers are not lacking."

Ah! it was only too evident; France was in peril. The most simple-minded could no longer deceive themselves. And this impending danger, how could one avert it? Alas! how were people to decide upon the means of prevention when they were not sure of the cause, each party accusing the other of treason?

At last, on the 30th of June, a deputy named Jean Debry presented to the Assembly a report upon the measures to be adopted in case of danger to the country. Received at first with almost unanimous applause, this report no sooner became the subject of debate than it caused an angry controversy which promised to be of long continuance. My father, I have since thought, was not sufficiently impressed by the real importance of these debates, and he was furious with these procrastinators. "Each day they lose in bickerings, the Prussians make a fresh march forward," he used to say.

Such was the condition of affairs when, on the evening of July 2nd, just as I was helping the boys to take some loaves into the shop, I saw our old friend, M. Goguerau come in.

"My dear Coutanceau," he said, addressing my father, "I know that you have been wishing for a long time to hear Vergniaud. He will speak to-morrow, and if you like, I will call and take you to hear him—and this young man too, if he wishes to go," he added, pointing to me.

It is unnecessary for me to say that my father was both delighted and grateful. By eight o'clock the next morning he was shaved and dressed in his Sunday clothing. I also was arrayed in my best apparel, wearing a shirt with a great frill according to the fashion of the time. At the appointed hour, M. Goguerau made his appearance, and we set forth. It was well for us that we were in the company of a deputy, for I have never seen a greater crowd than that which surrounded the Assembly hall that day. The preceding evening the report that Vergniaud was to speak had spread throughout the city, and every one was eager to hear the famous orator. However, at every door the throng found guards barring their entrance. But denial was not for us; M. Goguerau mentioned his name, and added, 'These citizens are with me,' whereupon the guards at once admitted us. Our friend then led us on along sundry long passages, opened a door leading up a narrow stairway, and finally left us in the galleries.

We found them already crowded with spectators, many of them women, and it was not without arousing a tempest of abuse and reproaches that we at last succeeded in securing two little seats at the end of one of the benches.

I was terribly ill at ease, and my discomfort was increased by a column at the back of the seat; but I soon forgot all about it, so deeply was I impressed by the grandeur of this scene, which I gazed upon for the first time. From my place I could command a view of the entire hall. I saw the Deputies of the Right or Court Party exchanging angry looks, venomous words, and threatening gestures with the members of the Left, or Radical Party; and I saw the Deputies of the Centre—the men of moderate views—trying to soothe and reconcile their implacable enemies. I could scarcely take my eyes from the president, who sat as motionless as a statue in his arm-chair, with his finger touching the ebony handle of his bell. Behind him there was a small space, perhaps twelve feet square, and surrounded by a grating. It was occupied by the reporters and shorthand writers, and it was there that Louis XVI., when driven from the Tuileries on the 10th of August, only a few weeks later, came to seek a refuge.

The tribune, whence members of the Assembly addressed their colleagues, and which was reached by some steep steps, was just then occupied by a short, slender man, who was talking loudly, and with convulsive gestures, about the public welfare, "the only and supreme law," he said. He received, however, but little consideration from his audience. He was frequently interrupted by the other members, while in the galleries the conversation was carried on aloud, as in the hall below. Near us some people were even eating and drinking as unconcernedly as if they had been at home. At last, however, the unappreciated orator ceased his efforts, and descended from the tribune. I then saw, advancing to take his place, a man who looked still young, and who had a mild, thoughtful face.

Around me I heard the spectators whisper: "Vergniaud! Vergniaud!"

What struck me first, in his appearance, was the careless ease of his movements, a certain graceful freedom of attitude, and an inexpressible charm of manner, which attracted you to him, made you love him and long to be his friend. But when his foot touched the floor of the tribune he became transfigured. The man was lost in the orator. He seemed almost a God upon the Sinai of liberty; and lightning seemed to play about his brow. The silence was profound, intense. Even outside the walls the noisy throng became suddenly hushed. Slightly pale at first, and deeply agitated by strong emotion, he surveyed his audience—and raised his arm with an imperious gesture. Then his lips parted—and he spoke. The words he uttered that day, my friends, mark a date in the annals of eloquence, mark a date in our revolution. You will find them in all our histories. But what these books will not acquaint you with is the inspiration he evinced, the deep and solemn tone of his voice, with its persuasive, almost caressing cadence, when he adjured his colleagues to unite for the salvation of their common country. Disdaining considerations of prudence, he went straight to the facts. What France was thinking and whispering he proclaimed that day in so strong a voice that the tottering throne of Louis XVI. was overthrown. After recapitulating the fearful calamities that had befallen France, he spoke of the immensity and the imminence of the danger that threatened us; he alluded to the criminal negligence of the king and his ministers. He showed us the enemy at our doors; the *émigrés* in arms at the frontier; the threatened invasion; the king paralysing by his veto all measures for the public safety—the king afraid to formally order defeat, but hypocritically denying our generals the means of conquering. "Call, oh, my colleagues!" said he, "call upon every Frenchman to come to the succour of his country. Show them the abyss yawning at their feet. It is only by a gigantic effort they can hope to escape it!"

An electric thrill sped through the whole assembly at these words. Each member seemed to have heard the knell of his agonizing fatherland. Then I saw for the first time the wondrous power of human eloquence. In that assembly a moment before so divided, so torn by conflicting opinions and passions, all hearts now beat in unison, animated by one thought, and one desire. From the benches of the Right, the Left, and the Centre, there came frantic applause. Pale, with set teeth and eyes swimming with tears, my father clutched hold of my arm, convulsively. "It is not a man who speaks," said he; "I hear the voice of France. Now I can hope."

And yet, three or four steps from me, I had observed a spectator whose expression contrasted strangely with the enthusiasm of those around him. He was a young man clad in the garb of a common labourer. He occupied one of the seats in the first row, and each time the speaker pronounced the name of the king I could see him angrily clutch hold of the wooden balustrade. Sometimes he scowled, half rose from his place and turned as if to cast defiance in the face of Vergniaud. Once he thrust his hand under his blouse with so violent a gesture that one might have supposed he was about to produce some concealed weapon. His manner was so peculiar that I could not refrain from watching him closely. The coarse garments that he wore were evidently not his ordinary apparel. The clear delicate tint of his hands, his carefully arranged light hair, the whiteness of his linen, all betrayed the aristocrat. But what had brought him there? What was the meaning of this disguise and these excited gestures? It was a time when the bitterest hatred and suspicion existed even between relatives, a time when conspiracy and treason was uppermost in the minds of every one, when folks only talked of enemies of the people, foreign spies and emissaries of the émigrés, and so this man's strange manner set my mind at work.

I was about to impart my suspicions to my father, when the young fellow turned towards me. His expressive face, full of daring and energy, was one never to be forgotten. Our eyes met, and I can still feel the strange shock which I experienced as we looked into each other's eyes. However, I could not speak to my father for the galleries were now rapidly emptying. Vergniaud had descended from the tribune, and was leaving the hall; every one was hurrying down to see him, and applaud him as he passed out, and my father dragged me away. But it was in vain that, with thousands of others, we stationed ourselves before the main entrance. Vergniaud had made his escape by a side door. To compensate for this disappointment everybody went that evening to the Comédie Française, where Mademoiselle Caudrille, Vergniaud's mistress, received a perfect ovation.

On the following day, July 4th, it was resolved: "That when the peril became extreme, the Assembly would itself declare the fact to the people by this solemn formula : ' The country is in danger.' Upon this announcement, all citizens would be required to place in the hands of the authorities all the weapons they possessed that a proper distribution might be made of them, and moreover, every man, young or old, who was able to bear arms would be enrolled.

This decree was greeted with enthusiastic acclamations. The news spread with the rapidity of a powder train to the furthest extremity of the faubourgs. That evening the crowds in the streets were even more than usually excited, and the newspaper vendors shouted : " Buy and read the decree that saves the country ! "

Was it indeed saved? There were some who really believed so, imagining that the Assembly had the power of changing the entire situation of affairs by the simple enunciation of its will. I saw with astonishment what not unfrequently happens in these great crises—a people suddenly pass from the wildest despair to the most boundless confidence. My father was most sanguine. " Have a good supper for four," he said to my mother, "I shall bring some good patriots home with me, and we will empty a bottle of wine in drinking to the prosperity of the nation."

That evening he returned accompanied by three friends, one of whom, a linen merchant named Fortier, was killed a month later at the storming of the Tuileries. They all felt sure that the Prussians, seeing the firm stand that had been taken by the people, and understanding how impossible it was for the king to favour the invasion, would pause before taking the de•

cisive step.　M. Goguerau, who was one of our guests, was the only member of the party who was not convinced of this.　"Let us wait until victory is certain before we boast of it," said he.

Still, all the news he told us was well calculated to increase our confidence.　He positively assured us that in every part of the country volunteers were ready equipped with arms and with caunon to form a camp near Soissons.　Five hundred were expected from Marseilles, and three hundred from Brest were already on the road.　They would pass through Paris, and were to participate in a grand patriotic fête which was to take place on the 14th of July, the anniversary of the storming of the Bastille.

"You see that everything will come right now," said my father.　"Business will be resumed and money will be plentiful again.　And I sha'n't be sorry, I confess, for I have some customers whose unpaid bills make me tremble."

However, from the way M. Goguerau shook his head I perceived that he did not say all that he had at heart.　He evidently felt that it would be worse than useless to disquiet these worthy people in advance.　My father's infatuation was so great that he announced his intention of going at once into the country to purchase grain according to his usual custom every year.

In spite of my mother's entreaties he indeed decided to leave the very next day, and I accompanied him to the Rue du Coq, the starting point of the diligence that ran between Paris and Chartres, my father's first stopping place.　I am certain you would laugh now, my friends, if I could show you this diligence which excited my intense admiration at that time; and no wonder, for people said, there could be nothing more beautiful, more comfortable, or more rapid.　It was a large, square-shaped coach, hanging high above the wheels, painted a bright blue, and having some little windows, about the size of my two hands, on each side.　It made the trip in fourteen hours, leaving the Rue du Coq at three in the afternoon and arriving at Chartres at five the next morning.

Remaining in Paris alone with my mother, and more than ever master of my own movements, I determined to be one of the most assiduous visitors to the National Assembly.　This would be comparatively easy for me, throught he kindness of M. Goguerau.　Alas! on the occasion of my first visit I saw plainly how chimerical had been the hopes of my father and his friends.　The question of deciding in what form the anuouncement of danger should be made had been settled it is true.　But whether it was advisable or not to issue the proclamation immediately remained to be decided.　And upon this subject, which really did not admit the shadow of a doubt, the debate recommenced with increased violence.

Public irritation was increasing when a message suddenly arrived from the king informiug the Assembly that hostilities with Prussia were imminent, and that an army of fifty-two thousand Prussian troops was advancing upon our frontier.　I can give you no idea of the storm of sneers and derisive laughter which greeted this announcement.　"It is another trap," said one deputy.　"The Prussian army numbers a hundred thousand men, and not fifty-two thousand."

"Without counting the twenty thousand émigrés," added another. "And it is only when they have reached Coblenz that the king deigns to inform the representatives of the nation!"

It is true that I could find no excuse in my own mind for this tardy notification of a fact which was known throughout Europe, which was the only topic of conversation in Paris, and which had been the subject of Vergniaud's powerful speech, and of the Assembly's decree which had immediately followed. The Assembly refused to receive the royal message, and the debates were about to continue, when a new orator appeared on the scene. He was an aged man with a noble face, and that benignant air which our imagination always bestows upon the Apostles. I asked his name, and was told that this deputy was none other than Lamourette, formerly grand vicar of Arras, and now constitutional bishop of Lyons. Revered by all his colleagues, irrespective of party, he was at once accorded a hearing, and, in a voice which shook with emotion, he began : "There have been proposed and there will yet be proposed various special measures to avert the dangers that threaten France. But of what avail will they be if you are unable to establish peace and harmony among yourselves ? I hear it said that a mutual understanding is impossible. Such words make me tremble ; they are an insult to this Assembly. Honest men may indeed be divided in opinion, but there is a common ground of honour and patriotism upon which they can always meet. Ah ! he who succeeds in uniting you will be the real conqueror of the Prussians and of Coblenz ! "

Nearly a century has passed, my friends, since I listened to the words of that good man, but I am sure that I repeat them exactly, so deeply are they graven upon my heart. He is indeed right, thought I, and he thinks of the interests of France, not of his own prejudices and ambition. And the emotion that his words had aroused in my own heart was, I could plainly see, shared by all who heard him.

In still more pleading tones he continued : "Let us swear to have but one aim—to be animated by but one desire ; let us swear to cast aside all personal prejudices and party spirit. The moment when our enemy sees that the will of one of our number is the will of all, that moment will Liberty triumph, and France be saved."

The words had scarcely escaped his lips before every member sprang to his feet and stood with hand uplifted to Heaven, ready to take the proposed oath. Envy and hatred were annihilated by the hot fire of patriotism which had been kindled in every breast. A cry of reconciliation and of fraternity resounded through the hall, and by a spontaneous movement all party bounds were obliterated. Men of the most extreme opinions threw themselves into the arms of their former enemies. Condorcet chanced to enter the hall at that moment, and Pastoret, who hated him, rushed forward and embraced him. There was no longer any Right, any Left, nor any Centre. They were all merged and lost in the National Assembly.

A deputation with Lamourette at its head was immediately despatched to the king, who came at once. I saw him enter the hall, preceded by his ministers, pale, agitated, and scarcely able to believe in this unexpected and sudden reconciliation. "I am one with you," he faltered ; "our union will save France—" And from the galleries and from the benches a wild shout of gladness responded, and tears of joy stood in every eye.

As I was wending my way homeward after the sitting was over, I was startled by hearing one man remark to another, "It was thus that Catholics and Huguenots embraced on the eve of Saint Bartholomew ! "

The words so angered me that I would gladly have sought a quarrel with the men. And truly how could I do other than rejoice after what I had just seen, and in presence of the spectacle that now greeted my eyes ? The king, upon returning to the Tuileries, had ordered the garden which had been kept closed since the scenes of the twentieth of June, to be opened. An immense crowd had gathered there, and pressed forward to the very windows of the château, everyone shouting, "Long live the king!" at the top of their voices. I ask you, my friends, what more could one desire?

My mother, when I told her what had occurred, said: "You must write immediately to your father. He will then understand that better times are at hand, and he will make more extensive purchases." I wrote as she bade me, addressing the letter as he had directed, to the National Hotel at Chartres, which was kept by a man named Serian, who always stayed at our house whenever he came to Paris to make purchases.

Fool that I was! Before my father received my letter all had changed. The condition of affairs was worse than before. This lovely dream of peace and concord lasted as dreams do, only for a night. Paris, on waking up the next morning, positively derided this plan of reconciliation, which was considered as much too good to be realised. At an early hour the streets were filled with men and boys offering the Great Sentimental Burlesque by the Gentlemen of the Assembly—a pamphlet far more injurious than witty, and written by the contributors to the *Journal du Diable*. Songs, ridiculing the scene, speedily appeared, for in those days everybody wrote verses. I can still see an old man, clad in rags, who stationed himself before the church of Saint-Roch, under an immense umbrella, and who sang a long plaint, of which the refrain was:—

> "One more kiss, Lamourette,
> One more kiss!"—

Then some of the very deputies whom I had seen with my own eyes clasped in each other's arms, sent communications to the newspapers denying the fact. Had this scene of reconciliation been merely a piece of premeditated hypocrisy, designed for the purpose of lulling suspicion? Had it indeed been, as some insinuated, a farce arranged between the king and the Bishop of Lyons to avert the attention of the Assembly from the important subject under consideration, and give the Prussians time to reach us? M. Goguerau, who permitted me to question him, replied that it was neither the one nor the other. "Why might we not have been sincere at the time?" he asked. "Hatred is not so pleasant! We were touched by emotion and lost our heads. Any Assembly is liable to sentimental attacks of this kind."

I give you the explanation which he gave me, but it did not prevent the scene, which had filled my eyes with tears, from becoming considered absurd and ridiculous in the extreme; and even up to the present time, the expression, "A Lamourette kiss," is a synonym for treachery and dissimulation. The kiss of the Bishop of Lyons, and the kiss of Judas, are considered to be one and the same. And parties were furious with themselves for having been duped by their better natures, and became more bitterly antagonistical than ever. I learned this from a workman who entered our shop one morning to buy bread. As he seemed intensely angry, I ventured to ask him what was the matter. He told me that the Directory of Paris had suspended Pétion from office, and meant to try him on the charge of instigating the manifestation of June 20th. This was so serious a matter that at first I did not believe the story, but thought it one of those groundless charges with which the very air seemed filled. To attack Pétion, the mayor of Paris, the most popular man at the time! Could this be possible?

It was indeed true. The next passer-by informed me that such was the fact, and also that the king, instead of annulling the decision as he had the power to do, had notified it to the Assembly and left it to take action on the matter. It is another piece of treason!" cried the *sans-culottes*, furious with rage.

"What a terrible mistake!" sighed all right-minded patriots.

But it was the general impression that the court would not have ventured to take this step had it not been sure of the speedy arrival of the Prussians. However this might have been, it was in the midst of universal excitement that Hérault de Séchelles presented to the Assembly a resolution declaring the country to be in danger. It was the 11th of July, 1792.

The report was read, the resolution immediately adopted, and a moment later the president rose, and in a voice full of emotion pronounced the solemn formula: "Citizens, the country is in danger!"

The silence was frightful. There was not a sound from the crowded galleries, not a word, not a gesture. And when the sitting was raised, the usually turbulent throng which filled the corridors with the buzz of noisy discussions, vanished in mute consternation. Still the patriots were well pleased. "This is an act," they said, "which is worth more than all that embracing of the other day. . We shall have to be up and doing; and Monsieur Veto will have to walk straight!"

But it was in vain that we looked for the adoption of immediate measures to insure the public safety. The resolution proposed to the Assembly on the 30th of June, agreed to upon July 4th, and finally passed July 11th, would not come into force until the 22nd; this delay being necessary to procure the necessary approval from the executive power. You can under-stand how the excitement was intensified by those eleven days' anxious waiting. I could see the blaze burn fiercer hour by hour. All the ministers had tendered their resignations and had been replaced by others. But no one cared a straw for that. It was not to them that we looked for help.

I purchased a map of the frontier, and all our neighbours flocked to see it. I had to show them Coblenz, or, as they said, the Prussian army, and we calculated again and again the number of days that would be required to move a large body of troops from the frontier to Paris.

People repeated as solemnly as if it were holy writ, a passage from Robespierre's speech to the Jacobins. Under circumstances like these, ordinary methods are not to be thought of. Frenchmen, save yourselves!

But the threatened invasion did not cause us to forget Pétion. M. Goguerau, who had promised my father to come and see us every day during his absence, was obliged to break his promise on account of our neighbours, who assailed him with the most indiscreet questions. All Paris signed petitions in favour of the mayor, and one was circulated in our neighbourhood. I signed my name, and our three apprentices, who could not write, affixed their crosses. Not for a kingdom would I have failed to attend the sitting of the Assembly when Pétion appeared at the bar. He came forward with his head proudly raised. Never was there a man who appeared less like a criminal seeking to exculpate himself. "My crime," he began, "is that of having prevented the flow of innocent blood—"

But the representatives would not allow him to continue. He had been disgraced by the Court, while the Assembly accorded him every possible mark of honour and distinction, and decreed that he should be at once reinstated in office as mayor of Paris, and that the executive power should be required to give effect to the decree that same day.

This was on the 13th July, 1792. The morrow was appointed for the *fête* of the Federation, which, instituted in commemoration of the taking of the Bastille, caused the gravest apprehensions to all thoughtful patriots. Paris then resembled a powder magazine; and every one felt that the least spark might cause a fearful explosion. And then, what would be the result? No one was able to say with any degree of certainty. Who could feel sure that the excitement would not turn into frenzy, and that our precious patrimony of conquered liberty might not be fatally compromised by the rash deeds of a single day?

This anxiety was increased by the presence of a large number of volunteers from the provinces, who had just arrived in Paris. The five hundred men expected from Marseilles had not yet arrived, but many from Brittany and from Lyons had already reached the city. Most of them were young men, and their enthusiasm had been fanned to a white heat by the patriotic demonstrations they had witnessed all along their route. Some of them were lodged in the houses of the citizens, but most of them were installed in the old barracks formerly occupied by the guards. Bands of them had been seen in the streets for several days; they haunted the clubs, and were met so frequently that one might easily have believed there were thousands of them in Paris.

There had already been several disturbances. On the evening of July 13th, eight of these volunteers had tried to break everything in Cerni's restaurant, at the corner of the Rue des Moulins. It is only just to admit, however, that they had met with considerable provocation. A party of them were dining there, and finding the wine that was served them to be of very inferior quality, they asked for something better; whereupon the landlord contemptuously responded that he had better wine no doubt, but he was keeping it for the Prussians. The grocer in our street, who had witnessed the scene, came running to tell us of it. He found five or six of the neighbouring shopkeepers assembled at our house, and the question of closing shops on the next day was under discussion.

"I sha'n't close, whatever happens," said my mother. "A baker ought never to close."

For a long time I tried in vain to obtain her permission to go and witness the *fête*. She could not forget that the Champ de Mars had been the scene of a bloody conflict on the 27th of July the previous year. "Why do you wish to go?" she asked. "You are still too young. It is no place for you."

But I begged so hard, that she finally gave a reluctant consent on condition I went with our head journeyman, and would promise not to leave his side. This journeyman's name was Fougeroux, and he was about forty. He had been in our employ for many years, and had come to be regarded as a member of our family. He ate at our table and lodged in our house, and my mother always took care of his clothes. He was a Hercules, with shoulders as broad as that table over there, and arms which had grown to truly colossal proportions from constantly kneading dough. His mind was not particularly developed, however, and he was as obstinate as a mule, though honest and kind-hearted. To say that he was devoted to our family is stating the case very mildly. His affection for my father, for my mother, and especially for me, whom he had fondled when an infant, verged upon positive fanaticism. He always spoke of his little "master," as he called me, in the most extravagant terms, and woe to any of his hearers who did not share his opinion. Fougeroux was a fervent *sans-culotte*, and the intense interest he took in public affairs was the more remarkable as he had only a vague idea of the revolution that was going on. His great affliction now was that he had never learned to read ; but he resorted to all kinds of bribes and cajoleries to induce me to read the daily papers to him, I often did so, amply repaid for my trouble by the amusement it gave me to see him, with mouth wide-open and staring eyes, listening to the flow of words of which he understood absolutely nothing, but which nevertheless delighted him.

The idea of accompanying me to the *fête* could not fail to suit Fougeroux. " I will be responsible for him," he said to my mother, rolling up his sleeves in order to show his brawny arms, a gesture he was very prone to. So the next morning at six o'clock we sallied forth, in too much haste to eat more than a mouthful.

We expected to find the streets full of people, but no one was yet stirring. Never had I seen Paris so deserted. No sound broke the stillness, no milkmen, no hucksters, not even a shop-boy cleaning his employer's windows, could be seen. At last, however, we perceived a little group going in the same direction as ourselves. After a long interval we saw another and another, but when we reached the Champ de Mars, or Champ de la Fédération, as it was then called, we found it absolutely deserted.

Fougeroux was amazed. " And folks say," he remarked, "that two years ago, by four o'clock in the morning, the crowd here was so dense that if any one had thrown a pin in the air it could not have fallen on the ground."

For the first time in my life, my friends, I was to witness a great public solemnity, and I was very much excited. Everything appeared marvellous in my eyes that day. Seventy-eight years have gone by since then, but there is not a detail of that *fête* that I do not remember as plainly as if it had occurred yesterday. On some tiny sand hills stood eighty-three little tents, arranged in a circle, and each shaded by a poplar. They were intended to represent the eighty-three departments into which the country was divided. It was France camping in the presence of the enemy. Two persons who, like ourselves, were walking about examining everything, did not understand this symbolical meaning, or else did not approve of it, for one of them said, loud enough for us to hear : " While they were about it, they ought to have planted forty-five thousand poplars to represent the forty-five thousand municipalities."

Thereupon the pair laughed, and the sneer was so apparent that Fougeroux began to roll up his sleeves, and I deemed it prudent to get him away.

In the centre of the Champ de Mars four catafalques had been erected, emblematical of the sepulchres of the volunteers who had died in the defence of their country, and each of these catafalques bore the inscription : " We will avenge them."

The altar of the country, surmounted by a broken column, was reached by the steps constructed in 1790. Upon four smaller altars stood some funeral urns and vessels of burning incense. A hundred paces from the altar, in the direction of the river, rose a large tree—the tree of feudality. All the branches were hung with crowns, tiaras, cardinals' hats, bishops' mitres, ermine mantles, suits of armour and scrolls of parchment. This tree was to be burned in the presence of the people. A statue representing Law, and another symbolising Liberty, both of colossal size, and mounted on wheels, stood near the tree. To the right and left there were two immense tents, one intended for the king and the National Assembly, and the other for the Municipality of Paris. Fifty-four cannons bordered the

Champ de Mars on the river side, and all the trees were surmounted by the *bonnet rouge*.

We had walked about and examined everything, and still the immense plain remained deserted. It was not until nine o'clock that any considerable number of people made their appearance, and among the new-comers there was a friend of Fougeroux's, a *sans-culotte*, who told us that everybody had gone to the Bastille, where sixty deputies were to lay the corner-stone of a monument, which was to be erected on the ruins of that accursed prison. My first impulse made me exclaim : " Let us hasten to the Bastille ! Let us run and see it ! "

But Fougeroux stopped me. "It is too late now," he said, evidently angry at having missed seeing that ceremony, "and since we are here among the first we may as well profit by it, and choose a good place where we can see everything."

An immense quantity of building material had been piled up near the Ecole Militaire, to be used in the erection of some new stables, the foundations of which had already been commenced. Here, to the great detriment of our hands and clothing, Fougeroux and I stationed ourselves on a huge pile of bricks, which raised us to the level of a first floor. We had scarcely installed ourselves comfortably when a short, meagre man, clad in black, whom I at first took for a lawyer's clerk, came and politely requested a place by our side. My only response was to hold out my hand, which he caught hold of, and then clambered up to a place beside us.

From our point of vantage we commanded such a view of the entire plain that I could even distinguish the cannon that bordered the river bank. It had been announced that the ceremony of administering the oath at the altar of the country would take place at twelve o'clock precisely. Eleven was sounding when the salvoes of artillery and the rolling of drums announced the approach of the king. He soon appeared seated in an huge gilded coach of state, and accompanied by the queen, his children, and the Princess de Lamballe.

On either side of his carriage marched his ministers, which seemed to revolt our little shrivelled-up companion. "Is it not a shame," he asked, "to see the ministers of a nation on foot, in the dust, with nothing to distinguish them from the herd of footmen and lackeys ? It is etiquette, it is true."

I made no reply, for in those days one was not disposed to be too communicative with strangers. But I own that I myself was shocked, and I understood for the first time how the most trifling question of ceremony may engender the most intense hatred. Our companion seemed to have the whole Court at his fingers' ends. He mentioned by name all the persons who followed the royal family in two superb carriages. He pointed out the Prince de Poix and M. de Brézé, Madame de la Roche-Aymon, Madame de Maillé, and Madame de Tarente. The men all wore richly decorated court costumes, and the ladies were in gala-dress, with very high coiffures.

The cortege, which was most imposing, was composed of cavalry and troops of the line. Some grenadiers, and national volunteers, did escort duty for the carriages, and the procession closed with four companies of the Swiss Guard. The king seemed languid and depressed. He leaned back in the carriage, his face was very bloated, and one might easily have supposed him to be asleep. But the queen, who was superbly dressed, held her head proudly erect, and her eyes closely surveyed the crowd, as if to count her enemies and her friends. One could see, however, that she had been weeping.

A portion of the procession passed through the central portico of the Military School, and formed in the court beyond. The king and queen then descended from their carriage, and a moment later appeared upon the balcony of the Ecole Militaire, which had been hung with rich velvet embroidered with gold. From this spot they were to witness a review of the troops.

" We can see as plainly as they can," said Fougeroux, delighted.

But already the cannon began to thunder again, and the drums resumed their beating. The troops were approaching. Almost at the same instant a flood of people poured on to the plain from every side by every approach. Only a sea breaking its bonds could produce the effect of such a spectacle. In the twinkling of an eye the immense space which had previously been comparatively empty was filled by a compact mass of pushing, crowding, struggling people, while from every throat issued one incessant, determined, furious cry : " Long live Pétion ! "

Fougeroux rubbed his hands in high glee ; and our companion said: " This is the mayor's revenge."

But I did not listen to them. I was too much engrossed in watching the scene before me. The volunteers entered by the Rue de Grenelle, filed past the balcony, and drew up in a line before the altar. The National Gendarmes came first, followed by two or three hundred musicians who were playing the *Ça ira*, with a sort of frenzy. Then came a battalion of infantry, then two companies of cavalry from the provinces then—then nothing but a shouting delirious throng in which people of both sexes and of every age and condition were mingled in indescribable confusion.

" All these people won't find room," said Fougeroux, but still they came pouring in—crowds of red-capped *sans-culottes*, brandishing loaves of bread on the tips of their pikes, groups of young girls crowned with flowers, and bands of women bearing banners with the inscription : " Honour to the brave who fell at the taking of the Bastille," or " To arms. Avenge those who have died at the frontier."

And the drums beat madly on, and the wind instruments shrieked, and the cannon incessantly thundered, and filled the air with a dense cloud of smoke ; but above all, rising higher and higher, resounded the same hoarse, terrible roar : " Long live Pétion ! " It was upon all the flags, and thousands of men had written in chalk upon their hats and their caps the words, "Pétion or death ! "

From my elevated position I could see the king distinctly. He stood as motionless as a statue, looking sadly upon the ever-increasing sea of human faces. Then the delegations appeared ; the 140th regiment marched past, preceded by some of the Fédérés, bearing the tables of the law and a plaster model of the Bastille. Then came the delegation from Saint Marceau, with a band playing the air, " Où peut-on être mieux qu'au sein de sa famille." Finally the hero of the day, Pétion himself, at the head of the city officers. His garments were disordered, his hair was dishevelled, and he was pale as death. He seemed literally crushed by the magnitude of his triumph. He was leaning upon the arm of a friend, and he made from time to time an appealing gesture as if to say, " Thanks ! enough ! " But this gesture, instead of calming the clamour, only increased it.

As he passed us, Fougeroux sprang up, and, madly waving his hat, thundered out, "Pétion or death !" Then, turning to me, he exclaimed, "Ah ! there is a man for whom one would gladly die."

I was mad with enthusiasm myself, but I could not refrain from smiling as I asked him, "Why ?"

He was embarrassed for a moment, then shrugging his shoulders, he replied : "I don't know, but no matter : Long live Pétion !"

It was now the turn of the National Assembly to advance. It came forward a compact body of eight hundred men, with its president, Aubert-Dulayer, at its head. The representatives paused before the balcony of the Military School, and the king descended in order to advance with them to the national altar. As the deputies resumed their line of march, the queen left the balcony, but she reappeared an instant later with a field-glass in her hand, by the aid of which she closely watched the movements of the king. From our mountain of bricks we could easily distinguish him by his richly decorated court costume. He advanced slowly, pushed from one side to the other by the throng, just like a cockle-shell is tossed backwards and forwards by the surging of the waves. Twice I lost sight of him in the crowd, then at last I saw him standing at the altar. I saw him lift his hand to take the solemn oath. Again the air was rent atwain by the thunder of the cannon, accompanied by the quick rolling of drums, and a burst of acclamations rose to the very sky. An instant afterwards the king disappeared, but I noticed something like a disturbance at the foot of the steps leading up to the altar.

I heard, that evening, what it was that had caused the confusion. The president of the Assembly had requested the king to set fire to the tree that represented the feudal system, but Louis XVI. had refused, saying : "It is unnecessary. There is no longer any feudalism in France."

No matter ! The programme had been carried out, or nearly so. A squad of cavalry was passing at the time, and their passage enabled the king to regain the Military School without difficulty. He appeared upon the balcony, and was greeted by a few faint shouts of "Long live the king !" which were instantly drowned in the cries of "Long live Pétion !" which resounded more furiously than ever. A moment afterwards we saw Louis XVI. re-enter his carriage and drive away.

We were now quite ready to get away ourselves, but we found that it would be no easy matter to cross the Champ de Mars and reach one of the gates. The departure of the king had not diminished the excitement in the least ; on the contrary, it seemed to have increased it. Instead of the king, four deputies, Jean Debry, Gensonné, Antonette, and Ganeau, applied torches to the inflammable matter piled up around the tree of feudalism, and the people crowded forward to see it burn, clapping their hands whenever the flames reached one of the emblems with which its branches were hung. From our point of vantage we could only distinguish a cloud of smoke and sparks, but this was enough to delight Fougeroux, who cried, "Good ! good ! Ça ira, ça ira !"

However, our companion was more difficult to please. "The fools !" he growled, "they believe they annihilate the reality by destroying the symbols !"

For my part, knowing how scarce saltpetre was, and how the municipality were organizing expeditions in search of it through the cellars of Paris, I thought they had better reserve the powder they were wasting, for the Prussians. Heaven only knows how much of it they wasted. The heavy booming of cannon was constantly accompanied by the sharp rattle of musketry. Every man, either soldier or citizen who was armed with a gun, fired it into the air, and the noise was so deafening that one might have supposed oneself in the midst of an actual battle. The smell of powder filled our nostrils, and over the Champ de Mars there hung a heavy cloud of smoke and dust, amid which the white paper of the cartridges floated about like butterflies. Twenty paces from us there stood a waggon containing a printing press, at which some men, busily at work in their shirt-sleeves, were striking off and distributing a profusion of patriotic songs. Opposite the Military School some of the volunteers had cleared a space, I know not how, and were now dancing wildly to the sound of maddening music. I had never, and I have never since that time, witnessed such a scene. All Paris was there—Paris seized with vertigo, drunk, delirious. Now I understood the contagious character of the intense passions that sway the masses. I felt the fever beginning to rage in my own veins; my thoughts became confused; I felt a vague but powerful longing to imitate the people I saw about me, and dance and shout with them.

But, unfortunately, I was suddenly overcome by a sensation of weakness, and feared for a moment that I might faint. It was now four o'clock, and I had taken no sustenance all day, save a crust of bread and a thimbleful of wine. Fougeroux noticed my increasing pallor, and became alarmed. "We must go, cost what it may," he exclaimed, resolutely. "Your mother will be very anxious."

I was of the same opinion, but surveying the distance we had to traverse before reaching any of the gates, and noting the appalling density of the throng I felt discouraged. "If we once get into that crowd," I replied, "it will, perhaps, be hours before we can get out again."

"Let us try at all events," growled Fougeroux, rolling up his sleeves and preparing to descend from his lofty perch.

But the man by my side stopped us, saying, "Allow me, citizens. One good turn deserves another. Thanks to you, I have had a good opportunity to witness this grand spectacle; and now, in payment, I will pass you through the crowd. Those people know me, and will make room for me. Just allow me to precede you."

He slid to the ground, and we followed his example, but without feeling much confidence in his promises. In fact, Fougeroux said to me, in a muttered aside, "That man is an idiot. You will find that he is depending upon my elbows."

But he was deceived, for we had scarcely entered the crowd, which quickly closed behind us, when we were amazed by the strange power of this man whom I had mistaken for some poor clerk. He slid through the throng as easily as an eel slides through the mire, exchanging greetings with almost every one he met on his way. Fougeroux, in whose footsteps I closely followed, was astonished; and, turning to me, whispered, "Who the devil is this man?"

We did not remain long in ignorance. As we passed a company of volunteers, eight or ten of them, shouted, on seeing our companion, "Long live Goudril!" and all the others took up the cry.

Everything was now explained. I knew this Goudril well by reputation. I had seen his name mentioned in the papers many a time; and often had I heard my father denounce him as a dangerous rascal. He had formerly been a clerk of Danton's; had afterwards been employed by Marat, and was now the editor of a paper that outdid in scurrility even the famous *Père Duchêne*, that foul sheet conducted by Hébert. He was also an extempore speaker, and had acquired considerable notoriety by reason of the virulence of his language and the eccentricity of his ideas. Just now he seemed to be actually revelling in his notoriety, and I was greatly amused to see the patronising air with which he greeted his acquaintances. After a little, some of his friends begged him to make a speech, and he immediately climbed upon the shoulders of a Herculean patriot, hoisted his sails, as it were, and began his discourse. In spite of the noise and confusion he actually succeeded in making himself heard, and even in commanding the attention of those around him, his shrill and penetrating voice piercing the air like the notes of a fife. But he was not the only orator in the crowd. By standing on tiptoe, I could see, in the throng around us, five or six other speakers who were mounted upon similar pedestals—upon "the true patriotic tribune," as we said in those days. But we did not stay long listening to Goudril. Seeing that he had entirely forgotten our existence, Fougeroux turned to me and said : "Get behind and keep a tight hold on me. We will try once more."

For awhile all went well, thanks to the broad shoulders of my guide ; but when we neared the gate, we saw such a frantic multitude pressing against it, that I feared we should be forced to beat a retreat. The struggling crowd was so dense that people were literally smothering, and on all sides there arose cries of fear and suffering. At last a vigorous push freed us from the crush and we found ourselves in the Rue de Grenelle, safe, but scarcely sound, since Fougeroux's clothing was badly torn and I had lost my hat in the meléc.

We walked on hurriedly for a short distance in order to escape from the throng, and then seated ourselves on the steps of a house to draw breath. We had been sitting there perhaps five minutes, when I noticed a young woman—a young girl rather—clad in the garb of a servant, running at the top of her speed down a narrow street, directly in front of us. Ten or a dozen men, in ragged clothing and with hang-dog faces, most of them armed with pikes, were pursuing her. The poor girl was a few steps in advance, but blinded or bewildered by fright, instead of turning the corner she dashed blindly on, precipitating herself against the wall of the very house upon the steps of which we were seated. She righted herself in a moment, but it was too late; the men instantly surrounded her, pouring forth a flood of frightful oaths and invectives. I am forced to admit, my friends, that during the heroic but strangely troubled period in our history, of which I am trying to give you some idea, not a day elapsed without a scene of disorder or violence in the streets. They were of such frequent occurrence, that the people who were returning from the Champ de Mars did not even stop to ascertain the cause of the present difficulty.

More curious or less blasé, however, I at once approached the group. The girl stood against the wall and confronted her enemies unflinchingly, although she was deadly pale and her hair was hanging in wild disorder from under her white cap. I was struck by her marvellous beauty ; and as her large, dark eyes met mine, my heart throbbed wildly. To the insults heaped upon her by her persecutors, she made no reply. One of them brandished his pike above her head, but not a muscle of her face moved. But I could bear it no longer, and exclaimed, indignantly: "Have you no shame, that ten of you unite to insult and outrage one weak, defenceless woman ? "

They all turned and looked at me in surprise ; and one whom I took to be their leader, perhaps because he had a worse face than the others, replied with a contemptuous sneer, "Allow me to give you some advice, my soft-hearted youth. Go home and mind your own business."

I was not, naturally, very patient, and all the excitement of the day had brought my nerves to a state bordering on frenzy. Springing upon the man, I caught him by the throat and shook him roughly, as I replied : "And I—I warn you that the first man who is wanting in respect to that young lady there, will have to answer to me."

Their fury was now directed upon myself. "And who are you?" one of them asked, sneeringly. "What fine aristocrat is this who dares to insult honest patriots?"

"Don't you see," cried another, "that he has just arrived from Coblentz? He is evidently an emissary of the Prussians."

Such accusations as these were quite sufficient at that time to send a man to the bottom of the Seine with a stone about his neck. But I did not think of that. Darting between the men, I placed myself in front of the girl, crying : "Here, Fougeroux."

But he had not waited for me to call. He had dashed upon the group, separating it by his powerful shoulders, while a couple of blows from his ponderous fists had caused two of the most offensive of the band to measure their lengths upon the pavement. "Now, come on, if you want to touch my young master !" he shouted in a voice of thunder.

His assailants were stupefied for an instant, and it was not without awe and amazement that they surveyed the gigantic form of this champion of mine, who seemed to drop from Heaven in response to my call for aid. He, as calm as if he had been standing before the kneading trough, put the young girl's hand in mine, and pushing us gently forward, said : "Go and wait for me at the corner of the Rue du Bac. I must have a moment to settle our account with these fellows."

They were recovering a little from their surprise, and two of them darted forward and caught Fougeroux by his clothing, but he shook them off as easily as a lion shakes off a dog, and as I was returning to his help, he cried angrily : "Go on, you fool ! don't you see that you are in the way of these citizens and myself?"

By the appearance of our opponents, I judged that they were quite weary of fighting, and disposed to descend from blows to bickering, so taking the girl's arm, I led her rapidly down the Rue de Grenelle. It had amazed me to see her remain mute and impassive during the whole scene. Was this courage, or stupefaction? I did not know. As we walked on, I watched her stealthily. The colour had returned to her cheeks, and she moved forward with an easy, swift tread. Seeing her so cool and self-possessed, one would never have suspected the terrible ordeal through which she had just passed. Naturally a thousand questions were in my mind ? Who was she and who were her pursuers ? What had she done? How had she aroused their anger, and what were they trying to do? But I dared not question her, for I was the one who trembled now.

In all my life I had never seen so beautiful a young woman. The daughter of M. Despois, the gunsmith, one of our neighbours, was celebrated for her beauty. But I could have lived ages near Mademoiselle Despois without once feeling my heart throb the faster ; while near this girl— Then there seemed to me something surprisingly imposing about her in spite of her more than simple attire. There was so much nobility and grace in her every movement that, beside her, Mademoiselle Despois, who, people said, had the bearing of a queen, would have looked like a scullery maid.

If I can describe my sensations so exactly now, you can imagine, perhaps, what must have been my feelings then. I longed to speak to her, and still I dared not. I felt that I ought to say something, but my tongue seemed to cleave to the roof of my mouth. And the more keenly I realised the absurdity of my situation, the more embarrassed I became. We should certainly have walked to the Rue du Bac without exchanging a word if she had not broken the silence.

She laid her hand gently upon my arm, as if to suggest that we should slacken our rapid pace, and in a voice which seemed to me as sweet as celestial music, she said, " I owe you my life, monsieur—perhaps even more. How can I ever repay you ? "

I felt my face grow red as fire, and it was in a voice husky with emotion that I stammered out something like this, "I am too much rewarded already, mademoiselle, by the pleasure of having been of any service to you. What I did was nothing."

"How nothing? It was at the risk of your life."

"Don't believe that, mademoiselle."

"Excuse me. Those wretches would certainly have killed you had it not been for that gigantic citizen who came to your aid."

"No, mademoiselle, no. Those men were very much excited, it is true, but at heart they are not actually wicked."

She stopped short and looked at me attentively. "Do you really believe what you say?" she asked.

"Certainly."

To tell the truth, I only half believed what I had said, and I suppose my voice lacked assurance. She, however, seemed to believe me, and walked on. "At least," she continued in a half-jesting, half-earnest manner, "at least, I hope you will tell me the name of my preserver, so that I may remember him in my prayers. What is your name, monsieur? "

"Justin Coutanceau, mademoiselle." And urged on by a feeling of vanity, I continued. "The name of Justin is that of my godfather, M. Goguerau, the deputy."

I felt her arm tremble as she rejoined, with strange earnestness. "What, you are Goguerau's godson ! He is a great friend of Vergniaud, is he not, and of Gensonné, and Minister Roland, and of all the Girondins?"

"Yes, mademoiselle," I replied, amazed at hearing a young girl, dressed like a servant, speak of these men as if she had known them well. Until then my companion had not deigned to look me in the face, but now she bestowed upon me a glance of keen but rapid scrutiny. She must have been deceived by my clothing, which was of better quality than that generally worn by people of my own station, and also by my height and build, which gave me the appearance of being four or five years older than I really was. "And you, citizen," she resumed, "you are doubtless studying to become a famous lawyer, like those gentlemen in the Assembly."

She no longer said, "Monsieur;" she said "Citizen." The irony was evident, she was sneering at the National Assembly and at Justin Coutanceau in the same breath.

"My ambition is not so lofty, mademoiselle," I responded, nettled by her tone rather than by her words.

She curled her lip disdainfully and murmured : "Oh ! so lofty ! so very lofty !"

"I live with my father," I continued, "and as yet I have no profession."

With a burst of laughter, my companion thereupon rejoined : "Astonishing ! I see I have had the rare good fortune of being rescued by a philosopher. But I very much doubt if your fine sentiments would have sufficed to release me from the hands of those patriots, who would gladly have torn me in pieces. The brawny fists of that friend of yours inspired me with far more confidence. You know that giant intimately ?".

" He is one of our—I mean one of my father's workmen."

" And he is devoted to you ? "

" Blindly devoted."

" What is your father's business ? "

" He is a baker, mademoiselle."

" And a patriot as well—is he not ? That is to say, an ardent supporter of these new ideas, and a frequenter of political clubs ? "

This seemed to afford me an excellent opportunity to take my revenge for her sarcasms, so assuming all the dignity I was capable of, I replied : " You have said it, mademoiselle—my father is a patriot. My father is one of those who consider all citizens as equals ; and if there is to be any distinction between them it should be by reason of goodness and not by reason of birth. My father believes that every man has his individual rights, and that he ought to die rather than relinquish them."

She became thoughtful, and I tried to gather together my scattered wits. I was so unsophisticated that I never for a moment suspected this young girl to be anything else but a servant : and I admired her *sang froid*, her courage, even her easy mockery of myself, all the more.

We had now reached the corner of the Rue du Bac, and I looked about for some suitable place where my companion could arrange her disordered toilette, which, although she was quite unconscious of it, was attracting the attention of the passers-by. I had about decided to take her to a little restaurant in the vicinity, when I perceived Fougeroux in the distance, advancing with his usual heavy-swinging gait. I experienced a feeling of joy and relief at the sight of him, for in spite of my confidence in his great strength, I had felt some anxiety for his safety, when I thought of the number of his adversaries. I hurried, with my companion, to meet him, and as soon as he came within reach of my voice, I shouted out, " Well, what luck ? "

He replied with a disdainful shrug of his shoulders, and a broad smile which stretched his mouth from ear to ear, " They found I had the best of them," he said, "and rewarded me with a bottle of wine." Then turning to my companion, he asked, rather brusquely : " Now will you be pleased to tell me what those brave patriots wanted with you ? "

She blushed a little, but replied indifferently : " That is something they quite forgot to tell me."

By the doubting air with which Fougeroux shook his head, I was convinced that the men had been talking to him of the girl, and had made him believe that they were justified in threatening her with violence. " Impossible ! " he growled. " Good patriots are quite incapable of maltreating a young girl like you without good cause. I questioned them, and they declare you are an aristocrat in disguise, an emissary from Coblenz and the Prussians."

" Ah ! they pretend that ? "

" Yes ; and they say that just as the queen was leaving the Champ

E

de la Fédération, they saw you run up to the carriage and throw a note to her."

I presumed she would deny this, but she did not do so. "And what if I did," she answered, boldly; "is there any law preventing a person from giving a note to the queen of France?"

I saw very plainly that she was becoming angry, and I felt her hold on my arm relax. I trembled at the thought that she might leave us there; that I might learn nothing more concerning her, and never see her again. Fougeroux's blunt speaking had irritated me, and silencing him by an imperious look, I said very humbly: "Pray believe, mademoiselle, that this citizen has no intention of offending you. And the proof of it is that he, as well as myself, will only be too happy to escort you home."

She evidently hesitated. "Really, citizen," she replied at last, "I am not sure that I ought to accept your offer. I have caused you trouble enough already."

"I beg you will allow us to accompany you."

"As you please, then," she rejoined, and taking my arm again, she led me on so rapidly that one might have thought her desirous of separating me from Fougeroux, who, with his hands in his pockets, and whistling the "Carmagnole," was following closely in our footsteps. However, you may rest assured that this suspicion did not occur to me at the time. My mind was far too much engrossed with the idea that I should soon have to separate from this charming girl, and my misery at the thought gave me courage to say: "May I not know, mademoiselle, to whom I have had the good fortune of rendering a slight service?"

"You have been told," she answered, smiling, "to an aristocrat in disguise."

"Then you do not even allow me the hope of seeing you again?"

"What would be the use of that?"

"Who knows? I might, perhaps, be of further service to you."

She paused, giving me an earnest, searching look that brought all my blood to my face. "Very true, Monsieur Justin," she murmured in a voice of infinite sweetness, "very true; and if I should ever ask a favour of you, would you grant it?"

Ah! she no longer called me "citizen." "I would give my life for you, mademoiselle," I cried, passionately.

She reflected a moment, and then asked, hurriedly, "Where do you live?"

"In the Rue Saint Honoré, directly opposite Doniol's, the queen's glovemaker."

"Doniol's! oh, yes, I know where it is; and in case I should wish to see you, how could I send you a note?"

"Address it to Fougeroux. He is devoted to me, and will deliver it safely into my hands. Fougeroux, you will remember the name?"

"Very easily. So it is understood; if you receive a note signed Marie Thérèse, you will come to me at the appointed place?"

"I swear it."

We had now crossed the Seine, and were standing opposite the entrance of the Tuileries. The girl abruptly dropped my arm, and turning to Fougeroux and myself, said, hastily: "Then it only remains for me to thank you. I have reached my place of destination. According to circumstances, then, adieu—or *au revoir*." Like a bird, she thereupon darted through the gateway of the palace and vanished.

Really I cannot tell how long I should have stood rooted before the

Tuileries, had not Fougeroux aroused me from the ecstatic dream in which I was lost. "Come, come," he said, pulling me by the sleeve, "it is time to go home. I must attend to my fire."

"Yes, go, I am following," I responded, mechanically. But I could not tear myself away from the spot where this young girl, who had changed the current of my whole life, had disappeared. Why did I wait? Was it from a hope that she would reappear? I knew there was not the slightest chance of that. But I tarried there, trying to picture to myself the interior of the palace, aided by the descriptions that had been given me by some of the participants in the scenes that occurred within its walls on the 20th of June. What was she doing there now? Doubtless she was engaged in narrating the danger through which she had passed. In that case, she must be thinking of me. What a beautiful thing youth is, my friends, and how I pity those who have known no years of radiant illusions and generous follies! However, although I was completely dazed, Fougeroux, fortunately, retained his senses; and as he dragged me up the Rue Saint Nicaise, which leads from the Seine to the Rue Saint Honoré, he exclaimed, "Well, wasn't I right in saying that the girl we rescued from the hands of those patriots was an aristocrat in disguise?"

"There is nothing to prove it," I replied.

This assertion was so audacious that Fougeroux was, at first, dumb with amazement. "What! there is nothing to prove it?" he exclaimed, after a pause. "A shameless jade who disguises herself in order to throw notes into the queen's carriage, who sneers at the National Assembly, and who lives at the Tuileries! And I haven't told you all, either. When Madame Veto had read the note she tore it into scraps, and then gave an order to an officer on horseback, who started off like the wind. What was that note, then? Another conspiracy against the patriots, of course."

"What of that?" I interrupted; "it is no business of ours. Some scoundrels were ill-treating a woman, and it was our duty to protect her."

Fougeroux did not question the soundness of my reasoning, but after another pause he exclaimed, in the tone of a man amazed by some sudden discovery; "Oh! oh! it's true that she is confoundedly pretty."

Never had the honest fellow appeared to me so coarse and stupid. I could have beaten him. "I beg that you will keep your opinions to yourself," I retorted, angrily.

It was the first time in my whole life that I had ever spoken to him unkindly, and he must have been deeply hurt. "But, is it really true," he insisted, "that you will go to a rendezvous with her if she appoints one?"

It was my turn to be surprised. "How do you know she might write to me?" I asked.

"The pretty rogue! I was close behind you, though she tried to keep you out of hearing, and none of your conversation escaped me."

Denial was useless since I had to secure Fougeroux's co-operation, being otherwise unable to conceal a clandestine correspondence from my parents. "If she would grant me the favour of another interview, I would go through fire to meet her!" I said.

The worthy fellow lifted his hands to heaven with a gesture of intense dismay. "What can you be thinking of, Monsieur Justin?" he exclaimed. "Go to meet an enemy of France, a Prussian emissary, a friend of Madame Veto!"

There were few patriots who would not have shared Fougeroux's horror, so odious was the reputation of Marie Antoinette and her female friends.

It has often been asserted that it was the Revolution—in other words, the people—who invented the atrocious calumnies which were current in 1792, concerning the queen. This is false, however, for the pamphlets that flooded Paris, describing her supposed orgies, her boundless extravagance, her disreputable acquaintances, and her pretended adventures at the masked balls of the Opera, were written at Versailles, at her very court. Was it strange that the people should have given credence to these stories told by the nobility? I believed them so firmly myself that I could find no response to Fougeroux's words, and he continued : "Besides, what can you hope for? That the girl loves *you?* this young aristocrat love you ! you, the son of Jean Coutanceau, the baker! You know that is quite impossible. So, if she ever grants you an interview, it will only be for the purpose of amusing herself at your expense, or else to obtain some favour of you. I know them, the worthless set! It would not surprise me in the least to find her trying to corrupt you; to induce you to take up arms against your country, and become an agent of the Prussians." And maddened by the thought, as men were maddened in those feverish days, he exclaimed, "You, a foreign emissary, you! Ah! I would kill you with my own hands !"

If Fougeroux's fears were exaggerated, his suspicions, I must admit, were not unreasonable. But Passion always has Sophistry at its command ; and I not only reassured the kind-hearted fellow, but I succeeded, though not without considerable difficulty, in making him promise to keep my secret.

It was time, for we were approaching the house, and I could see my mother standing near the shop-door talking with two of our neighbours, one of them M. Doniol, the glove merchant, and the other, M. Laloi, a grocer, who kept a shop at the corner. By the way in which my poor dear mother came to meet and embrace me, I knew how terribly she must have been frightened by my long absence. Nor was it to be wondered at, considering all the sinister reports which were rife in Paris that day. Had it not been rumoured everywhere that the Swiss Guard had fired on the people, and that hundreds of dead bodies were strewing the ground? I did not need to be told that it was M. Laloi who had repeated these terrible stories to my mother. He was one of those mischief-makers who are never so happy as when they have bad news to communicate. He was a sneak and a coward as well—poorly concealing his cowardice beneath his pretensions as a bully. Until January, 1792, he had been known by the name of Leroi, as his father had been before him, but a riot occurring about that time on account of the high price of sugar, a band of angry women sacked his shop. Imagining that his name had something to do with his ill fate, he made all possible haste to transform Leroi into Laloi.*

This idiot had not attended the *fête* at the Champ de Mars, but he had been present at the laying of the foundation stone of the monument which was to be erected on the former site of the Bastille. While there, he had purchased a snuff-box made from the wood of the prison, and was proudly displaying it. A certain Palloy, who styled himself Palloy the Patriot, had secured the contract for demolishing the captured fortress. The idea of manufacturing relics out of the ruins and selling them occurred to him, and enabled him to make his fortune. He had miniature Bastilles made out of the stones; canes, snuff-boxes, and even fans made out of the woodwork; and he transformed the old iron into buckles for shoes and hats.

* For the benefit of the reader, unacquainted with the French language it may be mentioned that "Leroi" literally means "the king," and "Laloi," the law."—*Trans.*

M. Laloi gave us a lengthy account of the laying of the foundation stone. He told us that a cedar box containing a brass tablet on which the declaration of the rights of mankind was inscribed together with a copy of the Constitution, and some coins and deeds, had been placed under the corner-stone. But what struck him as most marvellous, was that ashes from burnt title-deeds and papers belonging to members of the old nobility had been mingled with the cement employed to secure the stone in position.

"All that," sighed M. Doniol, "won't enable me to sell a pair of gloves." I was young at the time, and could not help laughing at the lamentations of our neighbour, and still it was not strange that he should complain. When the very existence of a nation is threatened, people do not think about buying gloves. And it was very evident that our peril was increasing every hour. The newspapers began to give us definite information respecting the enemy. We knew that their army numbered ninety thousand men, all old and tried soldiers, commanded by the Duke of Brunswick, who was considered the greatest general in Europe, having won his laurels under Frederick the Great, in the Seven Years' War. But what exasperated us beyond endurance was the certainty that several thousand *emigres*, among whom were the brothers and friends of the king, were united with these invaders. When we heard this, how could we believe in the king's sincerity even admitting that he had been sincere before? "He is obliged to side with us," said the patriots, "but it is only too evident that his heart is with the Prussians and the nobles who formerly composed his court; and it is their triumph that he longs for with all his heart."

It must be confessed that the king and the queen took no trouble to convince the people, either by word or by act, that this opinion was unfounded. While the leading nobility had left the court to repair to Coblenz, their majesties had remained at the Tuileries, surrounded on every side by ambitious schemers, who, while pretending to serve the royal cause, really did it the greatest harm.

Some of these conspirators had established in the Rue Saint Nicaise a kind of recruiting office, where they enlisted men to serve in the invading army, or in the 'army of the king,' as they were pleased to call it. They collected all the idlers they could find in the streets, with such poor devils as were dying of hunger. Then, while waiting to send these recruits to the enemy's head-quarters, they quartered them to a miserable little inn near the Tuileries. I often saw a crowd of them sitting in the shade by the inn door, smoking their pipes, and doubtless sneering among themselves at the credulity of the intriguers, who thought they had succeeded in purchasing their devotion. In fact did one of these recruits ever reach Coblenz? I am strongly inclined to doubt it. Passing them over the frontier would have been attended by many difficulties, and besides, those who were sent deserted before they reached their destination.

It was only by hearsay that I knew of this recruiting office; but I became aware of the existence of the famous National Club by personal observation. I must confess that it was chance alone that sent me on the track of it; and in a very simple way. Recollections of the mysterious unknown girl I had met so engrossed my mind that I could not sleep. I bitterly reproached myself for my timidity, and for not having insisted upon knowing who she really was, for there was nothing to prove that the name of Marie-Thérèse which she had given me was really hers. Still, I thought it a beautiful name! Never had any combination of syllables sounded so melodiously in my ears. Of course, an empire would not have tempted me from the shop on the day following the *fête* of the Federation. I expected a note, but it did not come. I was both disappointed and angry; and the satisfaction of my confidant, Fougeroux, exasperated me beyond endurance. "The pretty aristocrat was decidedly better than I supposed," he said, in response to my lamentations. "She was simply making fun of you, Monsieur Justin; and this promised interview was only an excuse for getting rid of you politely. Believe me, you are very lucky."

This was so far from being my opinion, that I swore I would find the ungrateful girl, even if I was compelled to search every house in Paris. A man makes many such vows at that age. But there was no need of such extreme measures, since I knew, or I thought I knew, that she lived at the Tuileries. So, from that time forward, I spent most of my time in hanging about the palace, standing on guard for hours at the gate, peering into the faces of all the ladies who came out and went in, and giving myself a stiff neck by trying to watch the forms that appeared now and then at the windows. I said to myself that, by dint of time and patience, I should finally succeed in seeing this young girl whose memory had become my torment.

All my efforts were in vain, however; but one morning, on crossing the Rue du Carrousel, I was rudely jostled by an officer in uniform, who was walking in the same direction, and who passed me. I opened my lips to reproach him for his awkwardness, but he turned at the same moment, and on catching a glimpse of his face, I was struck dumb with amazement. I had seen this face somewhere; I was sure of that, but where? An effort of memory gave me the clue. The officer was none other than the pretended labourer whose excitement had attracted my attention in the Legislative Assembly on the day of Vergniaud's speech. Astonishment literally rooted me to the spot, but I followed him with my eyes, and saw him enter a house some twenty paces from me. Involuntarily I approached the house to examine it; and in less than five minutes I counted more than sixty well-dressed persons who entered it, after saying a few words to an old man stationed at the door.

At a time when every newspaper had its own special conspiracy to denounce every morning, it was quite natural that I should be assailed by the most sinister suspicions. Instead of passing on, I waited; and at the end of half-an-hour, I had seen all the persons who entered the house emerge from it again, having exchanged their handsome clothes for ragged apparel, and wearing the *bonnet rouge*. Once outside, they pretended not to know one another, but went off in little groups of three or four.

Dogging the steps of two of these spurious *sans-culottes*, I saw them pause on the Terrasse des Feuillants, where they were soon joined by all the others. Then they presented themselves at the doors of the National Assembly and were admitted. I had gone too far not to pursue the adventure to the end; besides, my curiosity was so intense as to make me forget even Marie-Thérèse. I followed these men into the debating hall, and discovered them scattered about the public galleries with such art as to make their number appear much larger than it really was. One would almost have supposed that their places had been reserved for them. Soon an orator mounted the tribune. He was one of the Girondist deputies, and the spurious *sans-culottes* would not allow him to speak ten words. He attempted to struggle against the storm, but his efforts were fruitless. The president of the Assembly sounded his bell furiously, but all in vain. Various deputies rose to demand silence; but their voices were drowned in hisses.

I rushed downstairs and sent an usher in search of my godfather, M. Goguerau. As soon as he made his appearance, and before he could ask the cause of my agitation, I drew him into a corner and told him what I had just discovered. He listened, and tears gathered in his eyes. When I had finished, he said : " I know this, Justin, and all my colleagues know it. Yes, these men are trying to kill Liberty by the excesses they commit in her name. If they succeed, the Revolution and France are alike doomed. But we are watching : and the hour when their wicked hopes will be disappointed is near at hand, I trust. And you, my boy, mustn't talk of what you have discovered. There are only too many reasons for distrust and dissension already."

I had too much respect for my godfather not to obey him when he recommended silence. But my confidence in Fougeroux was so complete and absolute, that I saw nothing wrong in telling him of my discovery. I half regretted it, however, so terrible was the anger aroused by my confession. The episode gave me an opportunity to judge of the effect produced upon the uncultured patriots of the faubourgs by the stories of treason which were circulating everywhere, and which increased in magnitude as they passed from lip to lip. This honest and good-hearted fellow, who would not have harmed a mouse, became frantic with passion on hearing my tale ; his face turned livid, his eyes flashed fire, and shaking his clenched fist threateningly, he exclaimed : "We must make a finish of all these conspirators—of Monsieur Veto and these cursed aristocrats ! They look on us as cattle that belong to them ; and rather than acknowledge our rights, they seek the aid of foreigners, like as a man might summon the police to bring his rebellious servants to order ! Remember what I tell you, Monsieur Justin, this treason will cost them dear."

I could calm him, for my influence over him was unbounded ; but I said to myself : "Who will calm others who are equally incensed ? After they are once started, who can hope to control them ?"

Fougeroux solemnly promised to be discreet ; but it was not long before I recognised the fact that my secret was like that of a drama—everyone knew it. The newspapers were filled with denunciations of the National Club of the Rue du Carrousel ; and *The Friend of Truth*—a paper generally moderate in its tone—published a list of the club's prominent members, and a long article on its constitution and its object. The list included several military men and journalists, a former minister of state, some public singers, in short, men of every condition in life, who adopted any disguise, so as to effect an entrance into the debating halls of the National Assembly, and the patriotic societies, including even that of the Jacobins. This club had in its employ several public speakers who glibly repeated speeches they had learned by heart, readers who were liberally paid to read the journals of the day in the public squares, distributors of pamphlets, and a legion of reporters and spies—in short, a whole army of spurious *sans-culottes*. *The Friend of Truth* added that this National Club cost the court one hundred and sixty-four thousand francs a month. The same day that these revelations were printed, there was a quarrel between these false *sans-culottes* and some of the soldiers from the provinces in the public galleries of the Assembly, and in the altercation two men were severely wounded.

Paris was full of soldiers, and more were arriving each day. It had been asserted that they only came to take part in the *fête* of the Federation, and that they would leave the city immediately afterwards ; but they had received no orders to that effect. According to their opinions and sympathies, they either declared that they were detained by the court to prevent them from checking the Prussian invasion, or that one or another of the parties which were then struggling for supremacy in the National Assembly kept them in Paris so as to use them for its cause. Meanwhile, they received thirty sous a day, and spent their afternoons at the National Assembly and their evenings at the clubs. I had several conversations with these men ; and I must admit that they were very violent in their sentiments. But were they wrong? No ; at least not in my opinion. Inspired with the purest patriotism, they had left everything, home, family, friends, and business interests, to march upon the enemy, and they were not allowed to leave Paris. The government had declared the country to be in danger, and yet refused to utilize the strength of the nation !

The provinces were scarcely less agitated than Paris. My father wrote word that it was becoming more and more difficult to purchase grain. Although the crop had been unusually large, there was none in the market. Those who had any wheat concealed it—some through fear, some from a desire to speculate. Those who ventured to show a few sacks required gold in exchange for them. Gold ! one might have thought that it had emigrated, for all debts were paid in paper money, or *assignats*, which were the more depreciated in value on account of the many counterfeits in circulation. The high price of food increased the sufferings of the people and exasperated them still more. In a small town near Chartres, my father said a band of armed men entered the market, set a price on the grain, and took it away forcibly at their valuation. A similar scene had occurred at Etampes during the preceding year, and the mayor of the town—Simoneau, by name—had been killed in trying to prevent this iniquitous violation of the freedom of commerce. The National Assembly had decreed, that in remembrance of his devotion to the law, a monument should be erected on one of the public squares of Etampes, and that his sash and sword should be hung on the walls of the Panthéon. But there was no Simoneau near Chartres, and my father saw the wheat he had just purchased wrested from him at two-thirds of the price he had paid for it. His letter evinced profound despondency and the gloomiest apprehensions. " I am not as much troubled by the loss of the money," he said in conclusion, "and I pity, rather than blame, the poor wretches who injured me; but if this is the state of affairs now in July, what will it be this winter?"

The dread of a future which appeared darker and darker, haunted all sensible men and destroyed business—there was no more industry, no more traffic, no more work—nothing. To run after news, to read the papers, to attend the meetings of the Assembly, to argue, discuss, and distrust the acts of the court even more than those of the enemy, and to watch, upon the maps, the progress of the Prussian army ; these were the sole occupations of Paris. To see the idle crowd that thronged the streets and filled the public squares and promenades to overflowing, one would have supposed that one was in a city of people living on their incomes, and that each man's fortune was made. But never had there been such frightful poverty. More than once, while seated behind the counter of our shop, I saw the haggard and emaciated face of some poor patriot pressed closely against the window-pane. And an instant after the man would enter timidly, his cheeks crimson with shame, and falter in an almost inaudible voice : " Citizen ! I have eaten nothing since the day before yesterday."

Never did my mother or myself have the frightful courage to deny a loaf of bread to those who asked it of us; neither would my father have allowed it. And God knows that the name of those who implored our aid was legion. Some days there was an actual procession of beggars ; and I saw whole bakings go in this way, loaf by loaf. Fougeroux was often angry. "You are too generous, Madame Coutanceau," he said sometimes. "They abuse your kindness."

My mother did not reply ; she wept. "What a terrible calling to follow in such a time of destitution. My God, we cannot feed all who are hungry !" she sometimes sighed.

No, we could not. The little that we could do was a terrible drain upon us, and the small capital that my parents had amassed with such painstaking was gradually dwindling away. However, my father did not complain. He was not a person to see only an opportunity for self-aggrandizement in the Revolution. An ardent and sincere patriot, he was ready and willing—as I often heard him declare—to sacrifice his fortune and his life for the main-tenance of the rights of man. Believe me, the generous ideas of my father were those of a large proportion of the Parisians ; and though brokers and contractors made a great display of lavish expenditure, honest citizens bore their privations proudly and without a murmur. One was not ashamed of being poor.

Momentous events were approaching. It was now the 22nd of July, 1792. This, my friends, is an heroic date in our history, and no true Frenchman can ever forget it. France, on that day, for the first time, gave proof of her invincible energy ; and sure of her power regained her self-possession and shook off her fears. It was not six o'clock in the morn-ing when I was awakened by a loud noise which I could not explain. I listened. The sound was heard again, and the windows of my bedroom rattled. There was no mistaking it ; it was a salvo of artillery ! I bounded out of bed, flung on my clothes, and rushed into the shop, which was crowded with our workmen, who had just completed their tasks, and with our neighbours—all talking excitedly. "What is it ? what has hap-pened ?" I cried.

Fougeroux advanced towards me, and in a voice vibrating with patriotism, replied : "Monsieur Veto has been compelled to yield. The decree which proclaims the country in danger will be promulgated to-day."

Fool that I was ! Absorbed in thoughts of Marie-Thérèse, I had for-gotten this. Furious with myself, I was going to rush out, when hon-est Fougeroux detained me. "Wait for me, Monsieur Justin," said he ; "I will accompany you."

In a few moments he had made arrangements so that the bakery would not suffer in his absence, and we went out together. The Rue Saint Honoré was already thronged with people, and street-hawkers were selling pro-grammes of the ceremony to the crowd. The municipality desired the promulgation to be made with a dignity and austere solemnity befitting the terrible gravity of the occasion ; and had intrusted the charge of the ceremonies to Sergent. Sergent, not feeling equal to the emergency, had gone to Danton for inspiration ; and the latter had surpassed himself. There was not a single detail in the arrangements that was not admirably calculated to impress the imagination and arouse the patriotism of the masses.

David, who was afterwards Robespierre's master of ceremonies, might have planned something grander, but not more appropriate. The cannon on the Pont Neuf had announced the solemn event by the three discharges

of artillery which had awakened me. And the guns belched forth their thunder each hour until seven o'clock in the evening, finding an answering response
in the roar of the artillery at the arsenal. Six legions of the National Guard had
been ordered to the Place de Gêrve, and there Fougeroux and myself found them
awaiting orders. At eight o'clock precisely they were divided into two
columns, each of which started at the same time, but in different directions,
to carry the proclamation throughout Paris. Each cortege was headed by
a squad of cavalry, with drums and trumpets and six pieces of Artillery.
Four mounted hussars, in full uniform, bearing flags upon which were inscribed: *Liberty, Equality, Constitution, Paris,* came next. Then twelve
municipal officers, wearing their sashes, followed clustering round a
mounted National Guard, who bore an immense tri-coloured banner, upon
which was written in large letters, these terrifying but saving words:
"THE COUNTRY IS IN DANGER." Then came six more pieces of artillery,
rolling over the pavement with a sinister rumble, and then fresh detachments of the National Guard, a troop of cavalry closing the procession.

At all the cross-roads, the bridges, and public squares, the cortege
paused. The hussars waved their flags, and a prolonged roll of drums commanded silence. Then a municipal officer separated himself from the group,
and rising in his stirrups, in order to be heard at a greater distance, read
the decree of the Assembly. Finally he twice repeated: "*The country is
in danger!—The country is in danger!*"

It seemed to all of us to be the voice of threatened France, making a
supreme appeal to the devotion of her children. So, at each repetition a
shudder ran through the crowd, like wind rustling through fields of grain.
With the thought that the country was in danger there came to each
listener the recollection that it was his own existence which was threatened
—his honour, his family, his liberty. And amid the salvos of artillery and
the calls of the trumpets, arose a loud cry, the cry of the people replying:
"To the frontier !—To the frontier !"

Ah ! one never forgets these poignant emotions when one has experienced
them ! My teeth chattered, my ears tingled, and it seemed to me that fiery
flames were mounting to my brain. That day I understood the exaltation
of martyrs, the holy delirium of sacrifice—I understood the joy a man
would feel in shedding his last drop of blood for the sacred soil of his country. Swayed by an emotion no less profound than my own, Fougeroux
caught hold of my hand, almost crushing it in his grasp. He was very
pale, great tears were rolling down his cheeks, and it was in a scarcely
audible voice that he faltered: "Now the Prussians can come. France is
ready to receive them !"

But it was not this spectacle alone that excited our patriotism to a pitch
bordering on madness. On every side enlistment offices had been opened.
There was one on the Place Royale, another on the Parvis Notre Dame, on
the Estrapade, and on the Square of Saint Martin. Each consisted of a
roughly constructed platform, covered with canvas, hung with tri-coloured
streamers, and flags, and ornamented with branches and garlands of oak
leaves. Five or six steps led up to it. A broad plank, supported by
drums, formed the table, at which three municipal officers and six well
known citizens were seated. They recorded the name of each volunteer,
and gave him his certificate of enlistment. A triple row of National Guards
surrounded the platform and kept back the crowd.

And this was certainly a wise precaution. The throng was so wild with
enthusiasm that the municipal officers had great difficulty in moderating

and restraining it. I heard one old lady near me say, "They could not crowd more if they were trying to enter the gates of Paradise."

She was right. Each man longed to be the first to leap up the narrow staircase, obtain his certificate and wave it in the air, shouting, "*Vive la Nation!*" Every few moments a municipal officer was obliged to rise to calm the tumult. "Patience! patience!" he repeated. "We cannot take the names of everybody at once!"

But this did not appease the eager throng. On every side men were shouting: "Take my name, I am such or such a one, and of such an age, living in such a street, and at such a number." Others wrote their addresses in pencil, upon slips of paper thrown them by the municipal officers.

Men of every rank, profession, and age, shared the same frenzy. There was absolute equality in the presence of this peril that threatened their common country. There was no longer any high or low, rich or poor, all were citizens, claiming the same right: that of defending their fatherland. There were many very young fellows, mere children, who tried their best to prove that they were sixteen—the extreme limit of age fixed by the Assembly—and who retired in despair, because they were not accepted. And old men presented themselves, brandishing guns in their withered hands, swearing that the sight of the enemy would restore all their former vigour, and that they were yet strong enough to fight, or at least to die. The recruits departed singing, when the municipal officers conducted them to the Hôtel de Ville that evening. There were nearly five thousand enrollments the first day. It had been impossible to take the names of more. And what had been done in Paris, had been done on the same day, and at the same hour, in every commune of France. Wherever the country's cry of distress was heard, similar devotion responded to it. The department of the Gironde declared that it would not send detachments, but would march *en masse*, to the Rhine. At Argenteuil, every man enlisted.

This was the news brought us by the papers: which added that there was but one difficulty—that of overwhelming numbers. A letter from my father, whose business had taken him to Vendôme, gave us an accurate idea of the enthusiasm in the provinces. "Everyone is up, and on the march!" he wrote. "The people of each village draw lots as to who shall go. Those upon whom this honour falls repair at once to the nearest town, where they are provided with powder, ammunition, and means of transport. There is no question of uniform. France has none to give, nor is it indispensable. There is no need of a uniform to march to battle, to conquer or to die!" And my father added: "It is a great satisfaction to me to find that parties have forgotten their differences. I have seen men of the most contrary opinions reconciled to each other before the altar of their common country. I have seen them embrace, and depart arm in arm for the field of battle! They remembered but one thing—that they were Frenchmen, and that France was in danger."

M. Goguerau could not conceal his emotion when he read this letter. "God grant that your father is not deceived!" he exclaimed. "In such great peril only union can save us! To waste our energy in internal dissensions now would be to open our frontier to the enemy; and in less than a month the Prussians would water their horses in the Seine."

Any one must have been destitute of reason not to feel that my godfather was a thousand times right: and all the neighbours assembled at our house that evening, and who were listening religiously, applauded his words most

heartily. "Nothing could be more true," chimed in Fougeroux. "If we
are not united now, we can settle our differences by-and-bye; but first of
all we must crush the enemy."

M. Goguerau, with an air of a prophet, continued: "We must not allow
ourselves to be deceived, my friends. It is not a political war that we are
waging with Prussia—it is a war of races. The inhabitants of the North
arc sure to encroach upon the South. It is the immutable law of invasions.
What has aroused the covetousness of our enemy is our milder climate, our
fertile soil, our sunny hillsides upon which the grape ripens. It is not an
army that we must send against them, nor two armies, nor three, but the
whole nation. It will not be sufficient to vanquish them; they would only
return in greater numbers. They must be crushed, annihilated. So, up
and to the frontier!"

The whole nation arose. The excitement was so intense, that there were
many people foolish enough to say and to believe that those who had
planned this rising were appalled by it. It seems to me I can still see that
harbinger of evil, M. Laloi, the grocer, enter our shop, draw Fougeroux
and me aside, and whisper, with an air of profound secrecy: "Have you
heard what has happened? All the deputies are leaving Paris. Vergniaud,
Guadé, Gensonné, and Brissot have already procured passports for England."

But Fougeroux would not allow him to continue. "It was certainly not
worth while for you to leave your shop to come and tell us such a parcel of
lies," he said, curtly.

And Fougeroux was right to listen to his own good sense rather than to
the ridiculous hoaxes which M. Laloi took such delight in relating. The
following day, indeed, Brissot published in his paper, the *French Patriot*,
this spirited and noble reply to the accusation: "The enemy's agents—and
there are too many of these wretches in Paris—are the only persons who
have circulated the report of our intended flight. We despise these
cowards too much to desire to share their ignominy."

But the persons most surprised by the great enthusiasm of the volunteers and by the large number of enlistments were the old recruiting
officers on the Quai des Ferailleurs, whose occupation was now gone. These
men were old soldiers, known by the strangest possible names. One styled
himself Beautiful Rose; another, Tulip; another, the Cross-bar; and still
another, the Key of Hearts. Charged with the task of gathering recruits
for the king, they roamed about the city, haunting the vilest dens, and
jingling bounty-money in their pockets. When they found a man that
suited their purpose, they scraped acquaintance with him under some pretext or other, invited him to drink, and plied him with wine until he was
sufficiently intoxicated to drink the health of the king and affix his signature or his cross—if he did not know how to write—to his indenture. And
the next day, the man awoke from his drunken sleep a soldier; extremely
fortunate too, if he did not find himself robbed of the money which had
tempted him.

But in spite of these shameful manœuvres, in spite of the traps set to
catch the unwary, recruits had been scarce; and it was only with the
greatest difficulty that these officers had succeeded in collecting each year
a few hundred half-witted men and boys—poor devils dying of hunger, or
rascals who had exhausted their resources and expedients. Now, however,
at the sound of the drum, whole armies began to arise. "How the people
have changed," said the officers. "Formerly there was nothing they dis-
liked so much as military service, but now they seem in love with it."

They were mistaken. It was not the people who had changed, but the conditions of military service. The soldier of the *ancien régime* was what? A pariah. The slave of his king, or rather colonel, what did the cause he fought for matter to him? How could it affect him? He had not even a flag to defend; for the flag, the ensign of our country, is one of the products of the Revolution. Until then, the soldier had fought under a banner bearing the arms of the owner of his regiment. In exchange for his liberty and his blood, what had he to expect? Nothing. The army of the monarchy was the exclusive apanage of the nobility. No common soldier could hope for promotion, as each post of honour was reserved for the sons of noblemen, whose expenses ate up more than one-half of the funds set aside for the army. A common soldier remained a common soldier. There was no amount of application, courage, or genius that could bridge the abyss which separated the sergeant from the officer. And yet it was among the non-commissioned that the Revolution found some of its greatest generals.

Jourdan, Joubert, and Kléber had first served as common soldiers; but had left the army, regarding it as a blind alley—as a hopeless career. Augereau had been a sub-officer of infantry; Hoche a sergeant in the Guards; Marceau a common soldier. Hoche had struggled hard to obtain an education, as if he had a presentiment of his destiny; and, as the pittance he received was not sufficient to enable him to purchase indispensable books, he embroidered waistcoats for officers and sold them in a *café*. People knew of this. So was it strange that they had a horror of military service?

But everything was changed when the soldier of the king became the soldier of the nation. Proud of his rights, and feeling that the cause for which he was about to struggle was his own, he sprang to arms without an instant's hesitation. Nor was this all. A generous emulation and a most laudable ambition inflamed the courage of the army of '92. The volunteers knew it would be necessary to choose the officers, that were to command them, from their own ranks. They understood that posts of command were not the prerogative of noble birth, but the reward of the most worthy. How could such an army fail to be invincible?

But in 1792, my friends, France was as yet ignorant of the heroic qualities of the troops to whom she was about to confide her destinies. She was anxiously asking how these volunteers, who had so willingly forsaken studio, workshop, and fireside, in order to defend her, would stand fire. Could they resist the old Prussian soldiers who were considered irresistible? Certainly the courage of these volunteers was equal to the danger, and their souls were on fire with enthusiasm; but there is a wide difference between wishing and doing. It is one thing to say : "I will go, and obscure though I am, I shall know how to die for my country;" but it is quite another thing to do it.

As the young fellows marched through the streets on the evening of their enrollment, singing,

"Petits comme grands, tous sont soldats dans l'âme!"

one might have wished to see them display more of that gravity and thoughtfulness which nerves a man to make great sacrifices. Hence, I must confess it, France was feverish and anxious. There was not a patriot who did not feel ill at heart when, on passing the Hôtel de Ville, he saw the great tri-coloured banner upon which was written : "The country is in danger." There was not a single citizen worthy of the name, who would not have shed his last drop of blood for the joy of seeing the peril exorcised and the banner furled.

Anxiety and suspense paralyzed everything. Strangers addressed one another, each hoping that the other knew something respecting the movements around Sierk and near Longwy, where our soldiers were defending the country. "And where is the Prussian army?" asked every one. Some said it was at its old quarters, or that it had retreated ; others declared that it was advancing by forced marches. And as each person insisted that he had his information from the most reliable sources, no one knew what to believe, what to fear, or what to hope.

It had been decreed that relays should be established between Paris and the frontier, and that every morning and evening a courier should bring the Assembly a bulletin from the army, which should be published immediately. But frequently some accident happened to the courier ; horses could not be found, or the general in command was so overwhelmed with care and fatigue that he had not found time to write a report. Often the despatches contained only these words : "Nothing new !" And then the fever of excitement increased. "How could it be possible that there was nothing new?" people asked.

The shameless speculators of the Palais Royal were the only folks who did not share this feeling of despondency. If they paid any heed to the sorrowful anxiety that filled the hearts of the Parisians, it was only to increase it as much as possible. As long as the value of gold and assignats constantly varied, they were satisfied ; and they shrunk from no trickery to bring about such a result when it was not produced naturally. This fact was so well known that "news from the exchange" became the synonymous term for "shameless falsehood."

Yet the number of volunteers constantly increased ; and, though some were not conscious of the responsibility and duties devolving upon them, many were fully prepared to act their part nobly in the terrible struggle for the preservation of France. These felt that it was not enough to bare their breasts to the enemy's balls, but that they must learn to use the weapons which would be intrusted to them skilfully and effectively. Resolved to die bravely if need be, they wished that their deaths might at least be profitable, and were determined to sell their lives as dearly as possible.

Among the volunteers were many of my boyish acquaintances, and I drilled with them. Every day we went to the house of an old fencing-master named Sylvain, who had been a sergeant in the Guards ; and he taught us what conscripts are taught when they first enter a regiment. It was he who first made me stand erect with my heels on a straight line, and my shoulders squared : who initiated me into the mysteries of Right !— Left !—About face ! and made me march counting: "One, two !—One, two !" He had not enough guns for us all ; but members of the National Guard, residing in the neighbourhood, were glad to lend us theirs, which we carefully returned after each lesson. Hour after hour Sergeant Sylvain drilled us in the practice of arms, with unwavering patience and interest. He taught us how to repair our guns, how to load and unload them ; how to shoulder, adjust, and fire them. He also instructed us in the use of the bayonet—the weapon *par excellence* with the volunteers of 1792. One day, one of our comrades, weary of the long and rather tedious drill, threw his gun into a corner, and exclaimed : "I have had enough of shouldering and presenting arms. I know more than one needs to know in order to die for one's country." On hearing this, Sergeant Sylvain crimsoned to the roots of his hair, and exclaimed in a voice of thunder : "To die, citizen, to die? that is an easy matter ! It is not a question of dying, but of conquering !"

I was becoming quite a proficient in military exercises when, one Saturday evening, just as we were sitting down to supper, my father came in. His last letter, dated from Blois, had made no mention of his intended return, and we were so much surprised to see him that we could not restrain a cry of astonishment. And as my mother sprang up to welcome him, he embraced her with a tenderness that seemed to presage some misfortune. The same thought must have occurred to her, for she inquired quickly : "What has happened, Jean ?"

"Nothing," he replied ; "at least, nothing that I have not foreseen for a long time. I have simply returned because it is sheer waste of time to run after grain when there is none to be had."

My mother had already prepared a place for him at the table ; so he seated himself, and while he was eating he said in the simplest and most natural way in the world : "Ah, our affairs are not in a very prosperous condition. My poor dear wife, and son, do you know that of the thirty thousand francs I possessed a year ago, scarcely twenty thousand remain. Of course this means ruin in a given time." And as my mother sighed heavily, he continued : "I tell you this to prepare you for what is inevitable, not by way of complaint. A man who would think of his own interests while the foot of the invader is upon the sacred soil of France is not worthy to be a Frenchman. Our country has a right to our blood ; and we owe her all we possess."

I had never doubted my father's ardent patriotism ; and yet his last words made my heart thrill with joy. For they were equivalent to a promise, a certainty that he would not oppose a resolution I had long since made. So, as soon as our frugal repast was concluded, and my mother had left the room to give some order, I said : "Father, while you were absent, it was my duty to remain here ; but now that you have returned, what ought I to do ?"

My father instantly understood what I wished to say, for he turned very pale. Ah ! my friends, the agony he experienced then, I have since experienced myself. My heart has been rent by the same terrible sorrow which only those who have known what it is to part with a son can understand. A tear glittered in his eye, but it was in a firm voice that he asked, "Do you wish to enlist ?"

"Yes, father."

"You would leave your father and mother to go to the frontier ?"

"Yes."

I feared some objection ; but it did not come. "It is indeed your duty, my son," said my father, quietly. "The country is in danger ; you offer her your life. This is only right. I have already promised her my fortune; to-day I give her my son—Almighty God ! in exchange for so many sacrifices, for a just and holy cause, grant us victory !"

These were my father's words, but I can give you no idea of the deep feeling in his voice, or of the look of passionate tenderness which he bestowed upon me. I wished to reply, to speak, to tell him what I really felt ; that my sacrifice was nothing, absolutely nothing in comparison with his ; but I could not utter a word; my tongue seemed paralyzed. However, he began to walk hurriedly about the room in order to conceal his emotion. After a little, he poured out a brimming glass of water which he drank, and then turning to me, he said : " I should never have advised you to enlist, Justin ; but yet, I feel here "—striking his breast—" that if you had not done so, I should, perhaps, have loved you less. You are young ; you are healthy and strong ; you will make a good soldier. Ah ! if you only knew how to handle a gun ! "

"I do know, father, not very well, perhaps, but sufficiently well to sell my life dearly. I have been drilling every day."

My father's face brightened, and pressing my hand he cried, approvingly, "Well done ! well done ! Ah ! if all our young men had done that. If they had only employed the time they have wasted in discussing the news in the *cafés* in learning the use of arms, France, to-day, could laugh at the threats of these barbarians who are threatening her with destruction." He reflected for a moment ; and then, as if in response to some objections which had risen in his own mind, he remarked. "No matter ; the masses are a force, and an irresistible force ! Those who do not know how to fight, will know how to die, how to exhaust the ammunition of the enemy and to form a rampart of their dead bodies."

Yes ; it was to me, his only son, on the eve of my enlistment that he said this ; and an instant after, he added : " To-morrow, Justin, I will accompany you to the enrollment office."

He said no more just then, for M. Goguerau, who had come to pay us his daily visit, was entering the room. He was both surprised and pleased by my father's unexpected return ; but his features did not lose the expression of profound sadness which I had observed when he first came in. "Are we threatened with some fresh disaster ? " I inquired, anxiously.

He shook his head gravely, as he seated himself. "Possibly," he replied. "I have just left the Palais-Royal and the excitement is at fever-heat. The crowd is so great that one cannot move about. Every few moments there are violent altercations and broils, apparently without the slightest reason. The stands of the trades-people in the galleries have been overturned repeatedly ; the people in the *cafés* are quarrelsome and disorderly ; and bands of young men are roving about, shouting no one knows what, but apparently with the intention of increasing the tumult." He sighed, and in a still graver voice, he added : "One would suppose that we were divided in opinion—divided in opinion, when the Prussians are at the gates of Sierk. Can this be possible ? Ah ! we have been too generous ; we should have guarded against the friends and agents of our enemies. In Prussia, they know all that is going on in Paris ; but we know nothing of their movements. This very evening, I have heard people say that we were not strong enough to struggle against our enemies, and that we had better throw ourselves upon their generosity. Were those who said this Frenchmen ? No ! that is impossible ! " He dealt the table a terrible blow with his clenched fist, and becoming more and more excited, he cried : "The generosity of the Prussians ! what a mockery. Generous !—these barbarians who have long vainly sought a pretext for invading our country, and crushing us with the armies they have been silently gathering together for years ! It is the old contest between German and French blood for power and supremacy. Their hypocritical protestations of disinterestedness are heard all over Europe. Do you believe them ? I have already told you what they desire of us. It is two or three provinces. They might as well ask one of us to cut off a hand as to ask France for one of her provinces. To enter Paris as conquerors—this is their dream ; but believe me, if that day ever comes, the glory of victory will not satisfy them. They will regard Paris as a rich prize to be despoiled. 'There,' they say to themselves, 'we shall find enough to appease every covetous desire—sumptuous fare, wines such as we have never tasted, and trembling women on their knees before us.' And so they come with the hope of returning home laden with booty."

As I listened my hair seemed to rise on my head, and I trembled with such anger as I had never felt before. Then, for the first time, I understood the hatred, the revengeful spirit, the blind fury which makes a soldier throw himself upon his enemy without a thought of his own life, provided he can take that of his foe. "No, they shall never enter Paris!" I exclaimed; "no, never! for she will have a million defenders—a million. Sons, who in default of guns will fight with clubs, scythes, pitchforks, and the very stones in the road."

"Good!" cried my godfather: "good! That is the way any man of spirit should talk: and in France, thank God, there is no lack of such men!"

He was right. A man deserved no praise for sacrificing his life in such a cause; any one who seemed to hesitate, deserved only scorn and contempt. In one small village, the name of which I have forgotten, twenty young men having refused to enlist, the village maidens sent a distaff to each of them. Often in Paris, when bands of young men were marching through the streets bareheaded, and singing patriotic songs, the tradespeople left their shops, and, barring their passage, asked: "Are you enlisted men? In that case, show us your certificates." If they could show them, that was sufficient: the shop-keepers shook hands with them, and let them pass on; but if, on the contrary, they replied that they were not enrolled, or had no certificates to show, "Then we forbid you to sing!" said the trades-people. "Only those who are resolved to go to the frontier and die for their country have a right to sing patriotic songs."

If the young fellows resisted, the shop-keepers compelled them to obey, certain that all the passers-by would side with them. But nine times out of ten the singers replied: "Ah! so we must enlist to be able to do as we please. Very well! we will do so at once." And they did.

Whatever people might do, nothing seemed strange—so many minds were driven to the verge of madness by the thought of all the misery, sorrow and humiliation expressed in those five terrible words, "The country is in danger!" It would require days to tell you of all the chimerical projects and ridiculous ideas which resulted from this excited condition of the public mind. And yet, since I am attempting to give you some idea of this glorious time, there are certain peculiarities which I must not pass over in silence. One evening I went with my father and Fougeroux to one of the clubs. In the middle of the sitting, the president rose and said: "Citizens: I ask you to give a hearing to a letter from a patriot at Landrecies, which has just been handed to me."

"Read! read!" was the response from all sides of the hall.

He placed the letter on his desk, and then began as follows: "Citizen President—It is with very great surprise that I learn through the public press, notably through the *Friend of Liberty*, that you Parisians admit the possibility of the advance of a Prussian army to the walls of the capital. It is because you have not reflected, Citizen President; and I will prove it. How many trees, and thickets, and ditches, and rocks, capable of concealing a man, do you think there are, between the eastern frontier and Paris? At least four million. Very well! behind each ditch, each thicket, each tree, must be there a man ready to fire, to kill, or to be killed. For this sort of warfare, no uniform nor artillery are necessary. A gun, some powder and shot, with a few loaves of bread, will be a sufficient equipment. It is thus that I shall begin the campaign this evening with my eldest son and my cousin Fichet. And if the Prussians advance, so much the worse for them. We are in our own country, are we not? Let two millions, or only a million, of those patriots who are either too young or too old to join the army, follow our example, and if a single Prussian returns home to tell his wife what he has seen in this country, I will forswear the name I sign.

"Liberty and Fraternity. SATURNIN VAROT, Patriot of Landrecies."

Immense applause greeted this letter. "He is right! he is perfectly right!" resounded from every part of the hall. And it was voted that a complimentary letter should be sent to Citizen Varot; and that his name should be placed upon the roll of honour.

But no one was as enthusiastic as Fougeroux. Of all the plans of defence which had been proposed, none suited his fancy like this. "This patriot has a deal of good sense," he remarked to my father as we were returning home. "Yes, I understand his idea. A man needs only a gun and knap-sack; that is as plain as daylight. The cannon of the Prussians would not be of much use to them against him."

God be thanked! it was not necessary to adopt this last resort of a people whose liberty and independence are threatened, and whose resources are exhausted; but I have often wondered if Citizen Varot's letter did not inspire the organization of those roaming bands of sharp-shooters, which afterwards defended the passes of the Vosges against these same Prussians with such wonderful intrepidity.

Every day, my friends, we heard of similar cases of heroic devotion to the country. Even antiquity furnishes none more magnificent. Never shall I forget a letter from Citizen Lanthoine, which drew a cry of admira-tion from all Paris, indeed from all France. This citizen, who was very rich, and who had always led one of those luxurious existences which so often enervate the character, wrote the following letter to one of the news-papers of the time: "Citizen Editor—Three of my friends and myself have enlisted, equipped, armed and mounted, at our own expense, a regiment of cavalry, numbering five hundred men, who have elected us officers. We start to-morrow for the frontier, where we shall place ourselves at the orders of the commander-in-chief; and, as long as the war lasts, the regiment will pay its own expenses. As our number will probably be lessened by the first battle, we call upon patriotic citizens to fill the vacancies. For admission to the places in the ranks left vacant by death, it is only necessary to be healthy, to be a good rider, and to know how to handle a sabre. Still it is requisite to take the following oath, ' I swear not to return to my fireside until the country has freed her territory of the enemies who are polluting it; and if fortune deserts our armies, rather than survive the humiliation of France, I will die by my own hand!'"

Such, my friends, was the condition of the public mind, when on the 20th of July, 1792, a rumour reached us that the Prussians were advancing in a single but interminable column—marching straight upon us like one of those terrible armies of red ants which destroy everything along the route. It was reported, moreover, that their commander-in-chief, the Duke of Brunswick, had issued a manifesto to the French people.

As it was our neighbour Laloi who told us this with an air of the greatest consternation and mystery, we at first thought it one of those false reports which he was so fond of disseminating. We were all the more inclined to this opinion, since the details he gave us seemed beyond all credence ; so much so, indeed, that my father turned his back upon him, saying : "Hold, Laloi, once for all, come to me with no more such stories. You people who circulate such ridiculous reports ought to be flogged in the public streets."

And yet, for once in a way, our neighbour was right. I procured one of the copies of this manifesto, which some men who came from no one knew where, and who were paid by nobody knew whom, were distributing with a lavish hand. The proclamation declared that his majesty, the King of Prussia, far from coveting our provinces or desiring to enrich himself by conquest, had only the good of the French people at heart in thus making war upon them. It added that the Prussian army invaded France solely for the purpose of re-establishing law and order. That until the arrival of the King of Prussia in Paris, the National Guard and the authorities would be held responsible for any disorders, and that such inhabitants as DARED TO DEFEND THEMSELVES would be punished as REBELS, and their houses demolished or burned.

Ah ! even now, after the lapse of nearly a century, my heart swells with wrath and indignation whenever I think of this manifestation of foolish insolence. How it was possible to find a king to sanction such a monstrous manifesto, and a general to sign it, is something difficult to understand. However, this proclamation was like a spark falling upon a barrel of gunpowder. All France sprang to arms, trembling with unappeasable rage. It was as if each citizen had received a buffet on the cheek. What ! a foreigner dared propose that France should surrender her capital without a struggle ? Millions of voices responded. "Our capital ! Come and take it."

And Vergniaud expressed the thought of each Frenchman into his own grand and beautiful language when he exclaimed ! "May every nook and corner of the empire resound with the sublime cry : 'We will live as free-men, or die !' till the words reach the thrones that have united against us. Let them learn that they were wofully mistaken, when they counted upon our internal dissensions ; let them discover to their own confusion that when our country is in danger, we are animated by one desire alone : to save her or die for her ; and, finally, if fortune deserts so just a cause as ours, let our enemies know that they may insult our dead bodies, but that they will never hold a single Frenchman in their chains."

It was amid this excitement that I went to enroll my name as a soldier. It was one of those dates that one never forgets : July 29th, 1792. Faithful to his promise, my father accompanied me, and no sign of emotion appeared upon his determined face. It had been decided between us that we would say nothing to my mother until the last minute—until the time came for me to leave my paternal home, with my knapsack on my back and my gun upon my shoulder. Not that she was a woman who would endeavour to detain me. Her soul was too noble not to rise to the sublime heights of duty and self-sacrifice ; but we wished to spare her the agony of suspense and the difficult task of hiding her tears.

It was only nine o'clock when we reached the recruiting office. Groups of patriots were standing about the building, talking with great animation ; while others were straining their eyes to read the bulletins which were affixed to the walls night and morning, and which gave the latest news from the army, the provinces, and the National Assembly. Before the door a dozen National Guards were clustered around two of their comrades, who sat astride a bench, playing cards and smoking their pipes. Upon a large placard, nailed to the wall, I read : " The enrollment office is to the left." Following this direction, we reached a large room, with a very lofty ceiling, and as cold and bare as a dismantled church, where about thirty young men stood waiting their turn. In the centre of the room, behind a table so small that the register covered it entirely, there sat a solitary clerk. There was none of the imposing and theatrical display which had characterised the first days. No one could be less martial in appearance than this clerk, a short, podgy man, whose nose was surmounted by spectacles, and who was shabbily dressed, with black serge office sleeves on his arms. I can see him yet ; and I still smile when I think of the air of importance with which he inscribed the names of the volunteers who presented themselves one after another at the little table. One would have supposed that he saved the country by each stroke of his pen.

We were obliged to wait a long time, for he performed his task very slowly and methodically, in perfect conformity with clerical traditions. My turn having come at last, he measured me with his eyes from head to foot, and asked in an imperious tone : " Your name and residence ? "

" Justin Coutanceau, residing in the Rue Saint Honoré."

" How old are you ? "

" Seventeen and a half."

"Indeed ! you are tall for your age. One would think you at least twenty-two."

He asked me several other questions, taking notes of my answers, and finally gave me a pen and told me to sign my name. I obeyed, whereupon he gave me my papers, and my father and I were just turning away, when a loud and familiar voice beside us exclaimed : " It is my turn, now."

It was Fougeroux. I had never spoken to him of my plans, but the worthy fellow knew me ; he had noticed certain glances which my father and I had exchanged in my mother's presence, and having divined my intentions, he had watched and followed intending to surprise us. " What ! do you wish to enlist ? " inquired my father.

" That is exactly what I do wish to do, master. You see it made me mad to think that the Prussians should dare to talk of coming here and laying down the law to us ; and when I found that Monsieur Justin was going, I couldn't stand it any longer, and here I am. We will go together. He is very young, you know, and it would never do to let him go alone to fight, and march long days in the sun or rain and sleep on the damp ground, often with nothing in his stomach. But if I am there with him 'twill be different." And addressing the clerk : " Come," said he, " write Pierre Fougeroux, aged thirty-six—a journeyman baker by profession—"

Then when he had received his papers : " Now, what shall we do next ? " he inquired. " When shall we start ? When shall we receive our equipments ? Where shall we go to drill ? "

" You will be informed ? "

" When ? "

I saw that these vague responses did not suit Fougeroux. His broad face turned scarlet, and he was beginning to talk very loud and to take this poor devil of a clerk severely to task, when a door in the rear of the room opened and a man hastily entered. He was rather below then above the medium height ; but his form was powerfully developed, his shoulders were as broad as those of Fougeroux, and his turn-down collar and loosely knotted cravat revealed an enormous neck and a brawny chest. He was ugly, but his ugliness was of a strange and rather attractive type. Small-pox had disfigured his face, and discoloured his skin; his nose looked as if it had been flattened by a powerful blow of the fist—but his features wore an expression of mingled audacity and disdain, his full lips seemed formed to emit seething torrents of sarcasm and vituperation, and an ominous light flashed from his eyes. He must have overheard Fougeroux, for turning to him, he said brusquely: "What do you wish? A uniform? The country has none to give her volunteers. She has not even shoes for their feet, nor bread to keep them from starving. She will have these things, however, when citizens learn to understand the full meaning of the word in which lies our only salvation : ' patriotism.'"

I still remember his exact words. They were not remarkable, you may think. Possibly not; but he spoke them in such a tone and with such a manner that I was thunderstruck. And not I alone, for Fougeroux stood in silent but open-mouthed astonishment, and my father stepped forward and said : "I understand you, citizen. I am not rich—but no matter ! I pledge myself to arm and equip my son and this man here, as well as two other poor volunteers. In less than a fortnight they shall be on their way to the front."

The stranger bestowed upon my father a look of marvellous sweetness and gratitude, and grasping his hand : " Ah ! you are a true patriot ! " he exclaimed, " and if you should ever have need of me—"

A loud clamour wafted from the street interrupted him, whereupon the clerk turned to him quickly and remarked : " More of those cursed volunteers ! Every day they come and howl about the door, and not un-frequently some of them find their way in and abuse me. They declare that as they have enlisted, they ought to be furnished with equipments at once."

" I will speak to them," the other replied.

He went out, and we followed him. At least four or five hundred men had congregated in front of the building, and were singing the *Ca ira* in a sort of frenzy. However, when this man appeared, the tumult ceased. He sprang upon one of the stone benches stationed on either side of the door, and in a voice which thundered forth like the notes of a great organ, he began : " It is not by your songs that you will vanquish the Prussians ! What do you desire ? "

One and the same cry rose from the throng : " Arms ! "

With a gesture so despairing and so terrible that a shudder ran through the crowd, and with a violence that held his hearers spellbound, he replied : "Ah ! if I could make them from my own flesh, you should have them forthwith. But the country has none. Let those who desire them rush to the front, and there, when the dying soldier drops his gun, seize it, and use it to avenge his death ! "

You will find these words in all our histories. This was the occasion on which they were spoken. "Long live Danton ! " shouted the excited crowd. For it was he ! I turned quickly to look at him again, but he had disappeared.

When my father had once given his promise, nothing on earth could have induced him to break it except a strength superior to his own. He had promised to arm and equip four volunteers. How he should accomplish it was now his only thought. Unfortunately, there were no arms nor military equipments to be had in Paris. And when I say this, my friends, I do not

mean arms or equipments of one particular kind. Literally and actually,
it was impossible to procure the articles which are absolutely indispensable
to a soldier. The gunsmiths' shops were empty ; and as for finding an
artisan who was willing to work at his trade—that was an impossibility.
The workshops were deserted for the public squares, for the *cafés* and
wine shops, and for the hall of the National Assembly. The Terrasse
des Feuillants was too small for the crowd which assembled there, and
which the National Guard tried in vain to disperse.

You ask what all the inhabitants of Paris were doing? Nothing, absolutely nothing. Stirred to the depths of their inmost souls, breathless
with anxiety and suspense, tortured by suspicion, they were fighting
against the empty air, triumphant or terrified according as any idiot cried :
"Victory !" or "Fly who can !" Above all, they were waiting for news.
News from whom? Of what? From where? This was a question no one could
answer. Nothing had happened in the past ; no matter ! Every one
wished to read the bulletins that told one nothing. And at every corner
an orator was holding forth, asking what had been done, telling what ought
to be done, declaring all the measures that had been proposed absurd in
the extreme, and offering to save the country if people would only have
confidence in him.

So, towards the end of August, we were still in Paris, Fougeroux and
myself, and the two volunteers with whose outfit my father had charged
himself. One of these men was a locksmith, and the other the clerk of an
attorney in our neighbourhood. During this month which seemed to us
impatient ones an eternity, how many important events occurred ! The
Marseillais had arrived in Paris. The tenth of August had come and gone,
and Danton, to use his own expression, had been blown from the mouth of
a cannon into the ministry—Danton, the man who advised the infuriated recruits to rush to the field of battle and arm themselves with the guns belonging to the dead. The Marseillais, of whom I speak, were five hundred
volunteers who had crossed France in response to the appeals of Barbaroux
and Rebecqui the deputies of the department of the Bouches-du-Rhône.
These men reached Paris on the 30th of July, and it seems to me that I can
see them yet at the barrière de Charenton, where they were received by
two battalions of volunteers from the provinces, and by a deputation of
Jacobins, with Héron, of Brittany, and Fournier, the American, at their
head.

I was then too inexperienced to clearly understand the *rôle* they were to
play in Paris. But I did see that these Southerners, elated by the ovations
which they had received at every step of a journey of more than two hundred leagues, were guilty of many unfortunate excesses. They tore off the
hats of the passers-by, all cockades of tri-coloured silk, and compelled them
to substitute cockades of woollen stuff. And one evening, after a banquet
which had been given them in the Champs Elysées, they drew their swords
and attacked a party of grenadiers who were carousing in a neighbouring
restaurant.

But this requires an explanation. While the Marseillais were drinking
to the salvation of the country and to the victory of our soldiers at a
restaurant which rejoiced in the high-sounding title of the Grand Saloon of
the Coronation of the Constitution, they heard mocking laughter, and cries
of "Long live the king," proceeding from a neighbouring establishment,
known as the Royal Garden. Their patriotism was cruelly wounded ; and
thinking themselves insulted and defied, they tore down the trellis-work

that separated the two establishments, and a fratricidal struggle ensued. I was in the Champs Elysées that evening with my father and godfather, and it was not without a shudder that I saw the latter plunge into the thickest of the fight, in his attempt to separate the combatants. They did not know who he was, and men of both parties pointed their pistols at his head and threatened him with their naked swords. But what did this deputy care for death ! Who knows but it was his ardent wish thus to die upon the field of honour and of duty ! Ah ! it was a terrible sight to see this white-haired man, with his head bare, and his clothes wildly disordered, tossed violently to and fro between these furious, antagonists—a living rampart between such wild hatred and fury. In his case, the expression, " to bare one's breast to the sword," was no mere figure of speech.

He was determined to speak, and he did speak. He knew how to command the attention of men who seemed utterly incapable of listening to anything. " Fools ! " he cried, " do you not understand that our quarrels rejoice the hearts of our enemies, that they are the source from which they derive their audacity. What ! while our volunteers are weeping with rage because they have no weapons, you, who are fortunate enough to possess arms, turn them against one another ! The tide of invasion is rising, and for a ' *vivat* ' you lift your hands against one another. Must I read Brunswick's insulting manifesto to you again ? France should have but one thought, one cry ? 'Out with the barbarians.' The wretched man who sheds a drop of French blood, while the foot of the Prussian defiles our soil, will be doomed to the execration of generations yet unborn."

I render the words of my godfather very imperfectly. They were reported in the journals of the day ; perhaps you can still find them there. But I did see the swords creep back to their scabbards, as if thoroughly ashamed of having left them. And the Marseillais, wishing to do homage to the courageous man who had recalled them to a sense of duty, escorted him to his house, singing the sublime hymn which they were the first to chant in the streets of Paris.

That hymn, my friends, was the " Marseillaise ! " How this sacred chant of the patriot army originated at Strasburg, only a few steps from the enemy, almost in the very smoke of battle, every one knows. The volunteers were to leave the next morning, to attack the enemy. The Mayor of Strasburg, Dietrich, invited them to a grand banquet, which was attended by the officers of the garrison, who came to bid them God-speed. The Demoiselles Dietrich and a number of the maidens of Alsace were present at this farewell banquet. Their hearts were heavy, and they could scarcely hide their tears. Towards the end of the repast, while the brimming glasses were clashing noisily, they all wished to sing some patriotic song—but what ? The savage *Carmagnole* and the angry *Ça ira !* were out of place. They did not express the emotions of these patriots, who were uniting in one fraternal communion service, as it were, before facing the bullets of the enemy in defence of the sacred cause of liberty. They tried to find even a refrain, and one of the volunteers exclaimed, " To arms ! "

" To arms ! " These words furnished the key-note. Rouget de l'Isle, a young officer, sprang up, rushed from the room, and a few moments afterwards, with a face inspired with the genius of liberty, he reappeared, singing :

> " Allons enfants de la patrie,
> Le jour de gloire est arrivé—"

It was a revelation—this song which they heard for the first time, they seemed to recognise it. Before leaving the table they all knew it ; and they spread it through all France, through the entire world. And certainly it was time to find a battle hymn for our threatened country—to find a song that would electrify her battalions and lead her soldiers on to victory.

The Prussians had kept up a steady advance through the whole month of August. On the 27th the Parisians heard that the enemy had crossed the frontier, that they had pitilessly hanged some poor peasants, who had been guilty of the crime of defending their country, and finally that they had taken possession of Longwy. Paris was stupefied for an instant. Longwy taken ! Longwy in the hands of the Prussians ! Impossible ! No one would believe it. The very persons who had predicted disaster only the evening before, were the most obstinate of sceptics when misfortune really came. " Longwy was garrisoned by French troops," they said ; " so the Prussians could not have captured it. It was out of the question."

Those who had loudly proclaimed the country's peril, doubted it now ; for in proclaiming it, they had scarcely believed it, or at least they had thought the danger still far off. They thought it advisable to be prepared for the improbable ; but what they had regarded as an act of prudence and foresight had become their only means of salvation. For, at last, they were obliged to yield to evidence. The news brought by the first courier, was soon confirmed by others. The Prussians were at Longwy.

Oh ! my friends, I witnessed a sublime uprising of the people that day ! No sooner had the foot of the invader touched the soil of France than a convulsive shudder shook the land from end to end ; and each citizen sprang from his house, his weapons in his hands, crying : " Where are they ? Show me the foe ! "

Then people began to ask the cause of this strange defeat ; and a frightful word flew from mouth to mouth, whispered at first, then loudly proclaimed : " Treason ! Treason ! " And each man looked distrustfully at his neighbour.

But how could we ascertain the truth ? Where could we obtain trustworthy information ? How could we procure the details ? By reason of the education which my father had given me, I was better able to furnish information respecting Longwy, its situation and its importance, than the majority of our neighbours. One evening I was engaged in searching my books for particulars which would satisfy everybody's curiosity, when M. Goguerau came in, accompanied by a young man—I am sure he was not more than twenty—wearing the uniform of the artillery. He wore long, heavy boots, and was spattered with mud from head to foot. It was one of the couriers who had been despatched to the National Assembly from Longwy ; and my godfather, knowing it would be agreeable to me, had invited him to dine at our house.

Through this young officer we learned all that had happened. It was on the 19th of August, 1792, that the Prussian army crossed the frontier and advanced in the direction of Longwy. This fortress was a hexagon, with five half moons, and a horn-work, which means, in military parlance, an outwork composed of two demi-bastions united by a curtain. The casemates were in excellent condition ; seventy-two cannon were mounted on the ramparts, and the magazines were abundantly provided with food and ammunition. With such means of defence, not one of the eighteen hundred soldiers comprising the garrison doubted but what the commander of Longwy would make a long and glorious resistance. On the very day that the enemy's troops took up their positions, the King of Prussia made a formal demand for surrender, but the commander Lavergne replied in the presence of the garrison that he would hold out as long as he had a crust, a bullet, and an able bodied man. The second demand was made the following day, and it met with the same proud response.

The Prussians then announced that they should proceed to bombard the city ; and at nightfall on the 21st, they opened fire, having stationed two batteries of four howitzers each on the heights around. But they did little damage. The profound darkness of the night prevented a close calculation of the distance ; and a heavy rain entirely destroyed the effect of the shells. The garrison of Longwy responded by a lively fire, but it was so badly directed on account of the youth and inexperience of the gunners, that the Prussians suffered very little. The bombardment was suspended about three o'clock in the morning, but was resumed at daybreak. At eight o'clock it was raging violently, but the defenders of the place were undaunted. They had acquired a certain amount of skill, the officers directed the cannon, and the fire began to be effective.

This was the condition of affairs when, a little before nine o'clock, eight or ten bombshells exploding simultaneously in different quarters of the city, killed a dozen of the inhabitants, both men and women, and set fire to two houses and a forage store. Appalled by these disasters, the populace assembled, and loudly demanded that the gates should be opened to the Prussians, declaring surrender preferable to the destruction of the city by incendiaries. Threatened with death by these cowards, the municipal authorities who formed part of the council of defence became alarmed in their turn, and asked the commander to capitulate without delay. Lavergne resisted at first, trying to convince them that they were already under the ban, since, according to the Duke of Burnswick's manifesto, resistance, be it little or great, was to be punished with equal severity. But the municipal authorities were sure that they could make favourable terms with the Prussians, so Lavergne asked time to confer with his officers, and this request being granted, he summoned them from their posts of duty on the ramparts, and laid the case before them. With one voice, they replied that it would be arrant cowardice to surrender the fortress. Persuaded that their commander shared this opinion, they retired ; but after returning to the magistrates he allowed himself to be converted to their way of thinking. He then sent an envoy to the enemy's outposts, and finally signed the capitulation. The only favour granted him was that the garrison should march out of the city with the honours of war on the following day, the 23rd. Only one of the municipal counsellors refused to affix his name to this infamous agreement, whereupon the inhabitants set fire to his house, and the Prussian commander condemned him to be hanged. The fatal rope was already about his neck, when the knot suddenly slipped, and he was precipitated to the ground. He sprang up uninjured, and made his escape before his murderers had recovered from their astonishment. The next day, this courageous man succeeded in reaching the French army, safe and sound, and was made a captain as a reward for his gallant conduct.

Such, my friends, was the doleful story of the surrender of Longwy, as related by my father's guest—one of the intrepid soldiers who had been compelled to lay down their arms before striking a blow. I can still see the young officer as he appeared that evening. The tears of rage which his humiliation had drawn from him were not yet dry ; and one could tell by his voice that he had only one hope, one ambition in the world : to have his revenge.

"Nothing can convince me," he said, "that the whole affair of the surrender was not agreed upon, and a stipulated price paid in advance. That six hours' bombardment, which did not injure the town in the least, was a mere farce ! This disturbance among the populace, this meeting of the Council of Defence, the pretended resistance of the governor of the city— were again, only a mockery. It was necessary to deceive the garrison since it was impossible to corrupt them. And while we poor, simple soldiers thought we were to do our duty, and were resolving to die at our posts if need be, these traitors were opening the gates to the enemy, and betraying us."

We had gradually become as grieved and as indignant as our guest. My mother wept. Fougeroux, seated in his accustomed corner, swore lustily, and shook his ponderous fists in an ominous manner. As for my godfather, whom I was watching anxiously, I saw that his face grew more and more gloomy. "Perhaps you are right, young man," he remarked to the officer, "perhaps there was treason."

My father interrupted him. "What! can you doubt it, my old friend?" he cried, vehemently. "Resolved upon an invasion of our territory in the hope of gaining a part of it, the Prussians scattered gold with a lavish hand before they dared to draw the sword. An invasion of traitors has preceded and prepared the way for this armed invasion. Too honest to suspect such treachery, we have welcomed their spies as friends—we have granted them our confidence, and they live in our midst, listening to all our talk, watching our every movement, and trying to discover our most secret plans in order to disclose them to the enemy. Ah ! such wretches deserve no mercy. Do you owe any clemency to a scoundrel who, after he has sought a shelter under your roof and a place at your table, repays your hospitality by creeping stealthily down to open your door to a band of assassins at night-time, while you are sleeping ?"

Anger carried my father beyond the bounds of reason, perhaps ; but he was not altogether wrong. Three days later Paris received ample proof of the treason which had placed Lougwy in the power of the Prussians. On the 31st of August, 1792, Guadet, the Girondist deputy, who was charged with investigating this shameful affair, ascended the tribune and said : "Among the private papers of M. Lavergne, there has been found a letter written in the enemy's camp the evening before the town was invested. This letter contains the following infamous proposals : 'You will not hesitate, certainly, between the opportunity of serving our cause, and of remaining the poorly-paid subordinate of Pétion. You know that your wife is anxious for your return as she has written you to that effect several times. I am requested by His Majesty, the King of Prussia, and by the Duke of Brunswick, to assure you that your zeal for our interests will not remain unrewarded.'"

But the indignation of the National Assembly had displayed itself before this accusing document was discovered. In fact this brief proclamation had been issued : "Citizens, the fortress of Longwy has just been surrendered or betrayed. The Prussians are advancing. Perhaps they flatter themselves that they will only meet with cowards and traitors elsewhere. If so, they will find themselves mistaken. Your country calls you—Go !" And this decree was passed the same day : "Any citizen who, in a besieged city, shall speak of surrender, shall be punished with death !" Moreover, the Assembly decided that the town of Longwy should be razed to the ground ; that the inhabitants should be deprived of their civil rights for ten years ; and that the citizens who refused to join the army should be condemned to relinquish their weapons to those who were ready to start for the frontier.

Still there were men whom nothing could reassure ; neither the energy of the Assembly, nor the great number of volunteers, nor the grand spectacle of a nation in arms. M. Laloi was one of those cowards, of course. He shook his head at every measure of relief that was proposed, and repeated : "I have no confidence ; no, I have no confidence."

One evening he came into our shop brandishing a dozen leaves of a book. "Read this, and then we will see if you will continue to call me an alarmist," he said to me.

"This" was a dozen pages from an old history of Frederick the Great which M. Laloi had found in a package of old paper which he had purchased from a bookseller to wrap up his groceries. When I had finished their perusal. "Ah, well ?" he said, inquiringly. "Do you understand what is printed there ? Doesn't it say that Prussia is an immense camp ? That each city is a barracks, and each house a military post ? Every Prussian is a soldier from the time he is weaned, and they all spend their lives in acquiring proficiency in their profession. It was one of their kings, Frederick the Great, who organized his kingdom after this fashion, so that he might be able to conquer the whole world. Have you never read how this monarch spent enormous sums of money in gathering all the tallest and strongest men from every nook and corner of Europe, to fill his corps of grenadiers ? And he compelled these men to marry giantesses in order to obtain from these unions soldiers of exceptional height and strength. Ah, well ! my dear Monsieur Justin, these are the very troops that are coming to attack us ! How can you hope that we shall repulse them ?"

Although I did my best to repress a smile, I was not entirely successful. "In that case, what do you think we ought to do, my dear M. Laloi?" I inquired.

He blushed, and it was with visible embarrassment that he stammered : "Really—I don't know. It seems to me that—if the Prussians are not too exacting—"

"Silence !" cried a threatening voice. "Do you propose surrender ? Remember the decree. The penalty is death !"

But M. Laloi had already rushed from the shop. He had not waited to discover that my father was only laughing at him. Unfortunately, all the alarmists were not so easily silenced. And it is really wonderful how great an influence was wielded by these pusillanimous, weak-minded individuals. They multiplied the enemy's battalions beyond all reason, and at the same time, diminished the number of our troops to almost nothing. According to their estimates there were not ninety thousand Prussians, but five hundred thousand, a million, several millions. And judging from their accounts, the Prussians were here, there, everywhere. They held not only Longwy but several other strongly fortified towns—in short, all our most formidable fortresses.

Alas ! appearances seemed to indicate that these gloomy forebodings would prove only too true. Early one morning, Paris received intelligence of the capitulation of Verdun. This news, brought by a courier who, in twenty-three hours, had covered the sixty-five leagues lying between Paris and Verdun, had been printed during the night, and by seven o'clock in

the morning the papers were in the hands of the news-vendors, who ran
through the streets, shouting at the top of their voices : "Buy the latest
edition, with news of the surrender of the town and citadel of Verdun.
Full accounts of the siege and of the heroism of the commander of the troops."
So we were doomed to no torturing suspense as in the case of Longwy.
France knew the misfortune that had befallen her, with all the circumstances capable of alleviating her regret or of rendering it more poignant.
This account of the affair was furnished by an experienced soldier, and gave
us an accurate idea of the operations, the intentions and the hopes of the
enemy. Master of Longwy, instead of profiting by the advantage he had
gained, the Duke of Brunswick had wasted several days in the camp where
he had entrenched himself; and though strongly urged by the king and by
the *émigrés* who thronged his head-quarters to continue his offensive movement, and march immediately upon Mouzon or Sedan, the duke refused to
do so with invincible obstinacy. He declared that before he made a further
advance he must make sure that nothing would interfere with his communications between Longwy and Luxemburg, that he must wait for
the various army corps charged with the protection of his line of march,
establish provision and forage dépôts, construct pontoon bridges, etc., etc.
The four days which he wasted in this way saved France.

The Prussian army did not take up its line of march again until August
28th. And it was only on the 30th that it encamped on the heights of
Saint Michel, barely more than a quarter of a mile from Verdun. The
fortifications of Verdun were poorly calculated to resist such an army,
besides, they were greatly out of repair ; but Beaurepaire, the commander
of the garrison, was a brave man. He had been a cavalry officer under the
old *regime* ; nevertheless in 1789, he had organised, and had since commanded, the battalion of Maine and Loire. On hearing of the threatened
invasion, these intrepid patriots did not waste a single hour in fruitless
discussion, but crossed France with the speed of race-horses, and dashed
into Verdun. They were so certain that the treason which threatened the
Revolution on every hand would doom them to certain death, that each
man had entrusted his will and a farewell message for his family to the
keeping of some friend. Though Beaurepaire had been married but a few
days, and though his hands were still wet with the tears of his beautiful
young wife, he at once determined upon one of those desperate struggles
which render a city and its defenders illustrious. His three thousand five
hundred soldiers were eager for the fray, and the mere names of the officers
under his command speak more eloquently than any commentary. These
names were Lemoine, Dufour, and Marceau.

Unfortunately, the inhabitants of Verdun were not in the least inclined
to second the heroic efforts of the garrison. Many were longing for the
arrival of the Prussian army. Many had already left the city, and gone
to meet the approaching army, and on the very first day the populace
attempted to pillage the store-houses and wet the powder, crying all the
while—"No siege ! No siege ! Long live the Prussians ! "

On the 31st of August, by means of a pontoon bridge thrown over the
Meuse, the Duke of Brunswick completely surrounded the place ; and the
King of Prussia then made a formal demand for its surrender. " There is
no such word as ' surrender ' in the French language," replied Beaurepaire,
on dismissing the envoys.

A few moments later, at six o'clock in the evening, the bombardment
commenced. It was kept up until one o'clock in the morning, resumed

again at three o'clock, and lasted until seven. Was it a real or a pretended bombardment? The fire was so badly directed that there can be little doubt on the subject. The shot and shell only struck five or six houses. And yet the people assembled as at Longwy, clamouring for capitulation, and declaring that they would not consent to be buried—they and their families—under the ruins of their native town. As at Longwy, the Council of Defence met, deliberated, and decided that a longer resistance would be only a useless shedding of blood.

Beaurepaire and his officers strenuously opposed this détermination, but in vain. Vainly did Marceau insist upon the necessity of defence, and assured the inhabitants of ultimate success. A second summons to sur-render, accompanied by the threat of an immediate assault, redoubled the fears of cowards, and excited the audacity of traitors to such a degree that the council decided to capitulate at once. Trembling with indignation, Beaurepaire once more attempted to make these unworthy Frenchmen listen to the voice of honour. They would scarcely grant him a hearing. Then, turning upon them with a look of withering contempt, he said : "Gentlemen, I have sworn to die rather than surrender. Survive your disgrace since you have the courage to do so. As for me, I die." And he blew his brains out in their presence. This, my friends, was the act that gained Beaurepaire an immortal name, and the passionate admiration of France—but it had no effect upon the Council of Defence. They dared to step over his dead body to carry the keys of Verdun to the King of Prussia.

Lemoine had scarcely time to shut himself up in the citadel with a few brave followers; but they had neither bread, water, nor powder ; so naturally they were obliged to capitulate. And the next day, when the King of Prussia entered Verdun in triumph, twenty young girls dressed in white advanced to meet him, and to strew flowers beneath his horse's feet. Lieutenant-Colonel de Noyon, who had been made commander-in-chief by the death of Beaurepaire, had succeeded in obtaining honourable condi-tions of surrender for his soldiers. The garrison marched out with all the honours of war—drums beating and flags flying. They also took with them all their arms and munitions of war, two four pounders with their caissons, and a bier upon which reposed the lifeless body of the heroic Beaurepaire. Standing at one of the gates of the city, surrounded by his staff, the King of Prussia was watching these brave soldiers as they filed by, when he observed an officer walking at the head of his men, clad in a torn uniform, without a cloak, and without a weapon of any kind. On making a few inquiries and learning that this officer had lost all his bag-gage—that he had been robbed of everything, the king approached him, and inquired : "What do you wish returned to you?"

But the other looking at him with flashing eyes, simply replied : "My sword."

The officer was Marceau.

However, this blow was so terrible that people could think only of the result. The treason of Longwy had been a calamity, an accident. The capitulation of Verdun seemed an irreparable misfortune. "How far is Verdun from Paris?" was the question one heard on every side. And when you replied : "Sixty-five leagues," people tottered away in utter consternation.

Paris was terrified—Paris was seized by a frightful vertigo—Paris beheld the Prussians at her very gates. Then all the gloomy prophecies sown by the alarmists sprang up and bore fruit. Seven or eight hundred persons fled from the city that same day, carrying their valuables with them. The price of carriages rose each hour. At noon one of our neighbours paid one thousand livres in *assignats* for a miserable vehicle drawn by two emaciated horses which was to convey him and his family to Orleans.

The accounts of the proceedings at the meetings of the cabinet, and of certain deputies, considerably increased the fears of the populace. It was rumoured that the Girondins, on hearing of the disaster, had exclaimed : " Let us abandon Paris to the Prussians ! Let us carry the ark of liberty to the South."

People declared that Roland, the Minister of the Interior, had said : "The news is alarming. The Ministers and the Assembly must leave Paris !"

" To go where ? " Danton had asked.

" To Blois, and we must take the king and all the money left in the Treasury with us."

Clavières and Servan had supported Roland's proposition, as well as Deputy Kersaint, who was admitted to the conference as he had just returned from Sedan, where he had been sent on an important mission. "Yes, we must go," Kersaint had exclaimed ; "for the Duke of Brunswick will certainly be in Paris in less than a fortnight."

One heard on every side : " In less than a week—in less than three days —to-morrow, the Prussians will be in Paris, and God only knows what will be our fate ! "

The threats contained in the Duke of Brunswick's manifesto alarmed every one. Had he not declared that he would regard as a rebel, and summarily condemn and execute, every Frenchman who dared to defend himself—every Frenchman who had espoused the cause of the Revolution ? In other words, he would destroy Paris—annihilate it ! " And that is what he will do," said the pallid tremblers. " All the populace will be driven out upon the plain of Saint Denis, like a flock of sheep, and slaughtered, without regard to age, sex, or rank."

You see, my friends, in whatever age we may live, the same calamities always produce the same wild, unreasoning terror. However, Danton remained calm, and on leaving the conference he went straight to the Hôtel de Ville, where he assembled the city authorities. Manuel, the *procureur syndic*, acting at his dictation, then rose and proposed that " All citizens who were able to bear arms should assemble on the Champ de Mars, encamp there, and the next day start for Verdun to free the soil of France of the barbarians, or perish in the attempt." The municipality also decreed : " That all suspicious houses should be placed at the disposal of the volunteers who were starting for the frontier. That an estimate of the number of men ready to start should be made at once. That a cannon should be fired at regular intervals, the bells rung, and a general alarm sounded."

The Assembly applauded the measures that the Commune had taken to produce a general uprising of the people ; and Vergniaud, the great Girondin orator, sprang to the tribune, and said : " It now seems to be the plan of the Prussians to march straight upon Paris, leaving the strongly fortified towns unmolested. Ah, well ! this plan will be our salvation and their ruin. Our armies, which are yet too weak to oppose them successfully, will be strong enough to harass them in the rear ; and when they arrive here, pursued by our battalions, they will find themselves confronted by the presence of the Parisian army ; and, surrounded on every side, they will be swallowed up by the earth they have profaned. Still, while we have every reason to hope, there is one danger which we must not overlook—the danger of panic.

Our enemies rely upon it. They have scattered money with a lavish hand, in the hope of producing it. And, as you are well aware, there are some men so constituted that they are completely unnerved by the mere thought of danger. I wish we could confine all those soul-less creatures in a single city—in Longwy, for instance, which will ever be known as a city of cowards. There, regarded with contempt by the whole human race, they could no longer demoralise their fellow-citizens. You must no longer take pigmies for giants, nor, deceived by the dust raised by a single squad of Uhlans, mistake them for an innumerable army. Parisians ! now is the time to show your energy ! Why are not your entrenchments under way ? Where are the spades and pickaxes which prepared the Champ de Mars for our great *fête* two years ago ? On such occasions you have displayed great enthusiasm. Will you evince less ardour for the fight ? You have celebrated, lauded, and chanted the praises of liberty. You must now defend her. It is no longer a question of overturning a lifeless statue, but a monarch of flesh and bone, the King of Prussia, armed with all his power. Hence I suggest that the National Assembly should set the example by sending twelve of its members, not to incite others to work, but to work themselves, with pickaxe in hand, in the sight of all the citizens."

Frantic applause greeted Vergniaud's last words. His proposition was enthusiastically adopted, and Danton took his place at the tribune. He briefly recounted the measures adopted by the Commune ; then, with that imperious gesture that bent the masses to his will : "Some of the people must hasten to the front," he continued, " others must dig in the entrenchments, and the remainder must protect our arsenals and public buildings. But this is not enough ; we must send commissioners and couriers everywhere, to persuade all France to follow the example of Paris ; we must issue a decree by which every citizen will be obliged, under penalty of death, to serve in person or to give up his weapons."

It was then just two o'clock. The cannon was beginning to thunder ; all the bells were flinging the wild notes of the tocsin to the wind ; the drums were beating the assembly in the streets. Danton paused, lifting his hand as if to say : " Listen ! " And for more than two minutes the whole Assembly, including the public galleries, was wrapt in solemn silence like that around the death-bed of a departing soul. Then in tones of indomitable energy, Danton exclaimed : " The cannon you hear is not an alarm-gun. It sounds the charge upon the enemies of your country. To conquer them, to crush them, is the duty that lies before you. Audacity, more audacity, still ever audacity, and France will be saved ! "

Ah ! my friends, the cry of the great orator of the Revolution, was the cry of the entire country. Recovering from her previous terror, the great city rose in her might, more formidable and dangerous than ever before. We each felt that we were striving for something more precious than life. It was the patrimony of our rights, our liberty, which was endangered— the precious patrimony acquired by so many great sacrifices. To think that one must not merely fall beneath the sword of the invader, but that the first, faint light of the new civilisation which was dawning from Paris upon the world, was to be crushed out beneath the feet of the Prussian war horse !

The intense excitement which had followed the proclamation declaring the country in danger, was re-awakened. The zeal of many recruits had flagged. Some were even disputing the validity of their contracts, others who were constantly clamouring for arms with frantic shouts of " Ça ira ! "

certainly had no intention of rushing to the front. But the news of the surrender of Verdun fell like oil upon a partially extinguished fire. The flames of patriotism revived again. And from that day, dates the real great effort.

Paris instantly assumed the appearance of a strongly fortified city in a stage of siege. Soldiers, cannon, muskets, and munitions of war were seen on every side. Regiments of volunteers were constantly drilling on the Champ de Mars. On the Plaine des Sablons, a regiment of cavalry was organized with the carriage horses which had been requisitioned by the Government. The amount of work accomplished was really wonderful; the activity unceasing. The flames of the gunsmiths' forges blazed day and night. Churches had been transformed into workshops, where hundreds of women toiled incessantly in the manufacture of tents, clothing, knapsacks and equipments. Every man turned recruiting officer, and preached elegant sermons on the righteousness of this war; and old men went about from door to door, offering the young men an old uniform, a sword, a gun, or some cartridges. For all who could not offer their country their blood, wished to render her such service as was in their power.

Patriotic gifts flowed in in quantities which would seem to you inconceivable. Two men, unaided, armed, mounted and equipped three regiments of cavalry. Lemoine, a manufacturer, gave his entire fortune, about eight hundred thousand livres, reserving only an annuity of about two hundred louis, not for himself, but for "his aged and infirm wife." Gerson, a landed proprietor of Burgundy, sold his vineyards by auction— "the proceeds to be turned over to the National Treasury;" and he found a wealthy financier who was glad to purchase them at twice their value. Some of the villages assessed themselves, and sent the Assembly fabulous sums, at least for those times—thirty, forty, and a hundred thousand livres and in gold, not in *assignats*. It costs a poor peasant a terrible struggle to part with his hard-earned and slowly acquired gold. It is the greatest sacrifice he can make. When the peasant has given his money, what does he care for his blood? He spends that lavishly.

And in this long list of patriotic gifts there were many touching offerings! Some poor huckster women who had stood in the markets for years, brought one day four thousand francs, the proceeds of the sale of their ear-rings, and wedding rings. A woman who kept a little haberdashery shop in the Rue Saint-Denis, gave her gold cross. One poor widow gave a silver cup, fork and spoon, precious relics of a child she had lost years before. One young girl, to swell the fund, sold the gold thimble which her lover had given her.

Five hundred, a thousand, and sometimes fifteen hundred volunteers left Paris for the front every day for some time. Twenty thousand men departed in quick succession; and many more stood ready. But it became necessary to decree that certain workmen, locksmiths, for instance, should remain in Paris, since they could serve their country far better by manufacturing weapons for her defence than by fighting her enemies on the frontier. The earth fairly trembled beneath the tread of gathering armies —for all France had sprung up to confront the Prussians, determined to conquer though it cost her rivers of blood and millions of lives.

But these immense sacrifices would have been useless, had it not been for the as yet unknown heroes who marched in the ranks and whose genius was only awaiting a suitable opportunity to reveal itself. To lead to victory and glory these volunteers who departed with feet and hearts keeping time to the strains of the Marseillaise, Providence provided leaders, any one of whom would have sufficed to render a country illustrious in less troubled times. There were Kellermann, Macdonald, Massena, Desaix, Hoche, Marceau, Ney, Bernadotte, Jourdan, Augereau, Joubert, Victor, Lefebvre, Kleber, Oudinot, Mortier—all that crowd of famous soldiers who were resolved to conquer or perish.

I see your surprise, my friends. You are wondering how we could fear defeat with such resources at our command; but in 1792 France could only be compared to a giant who, unconscious of his strength, never having tested it, is frightened by the threats of a mere child. Besides everything was in disorder. We were fighting in the midst of ruins.

Of the former Government, what remained? Nothing. Or rather, it had bequeathed us all its encumbrances and all its difficulties. And while everything was to be done, there was no time in which to do it. We could not devote weeks or days, but only minutes to work that required months of patient labour. And, alas! many of our noblest minds had not recovered from the intoxication produced by their newly acquired liberty.

The volunteers who were arriving by hundreds and thousands were willing to sacrifice their interests, their home-ties, their lives—everything but their own wills. They were willing to obey no one but themselves; that is to say, officers elected by themselves. And these officers, though they might be remarkable for personal valour and patriotism, were almost entirely ignorant of the first elements of military science. The discipline to which the volunteers were unnecessarily subjected made them sullen and dissatisfied. Any attempt to assimilate them to the regular troops wounded their pride. They took offence if any one told them that an undisciplined army could never conquer its enemies. The idea of subordination could not be separated from the idea of despotism in their distrustful minds. One of my relatives named Léfort—a manly fellow about twenty years of age, a tanner, by trade—had been chosen captain by a company of volunteers. In a conversation with my father I once heard him say: "The *sans-culottes* I command will never submit to the orders of any general, nor would I submit myself."

"But," objected my father, "in conducting a campaign, or in a battle, how—"

"There is not the slightest need of a general," interrupted the young man. "I shall lead my men to the enemy—that is not a very difficult task, is it?—I shall order them to charge, and we shall rush upon the foe and conquer them or die."

My father and I wasted an entire day in trying to teach him that there are no efforts so efficacious as those which are made in concert. In vain we tried to impress it upon his mind, that a battle is a concerted action, each detail of which should be regulated by a commander who understands how to utilize all his resources. He listened to us attentively, and even nodded his head approvingly; but just as we were flattering ourselves that we had convinced him, he said: "All this is very fine no doubt, but my theory and the theory of my men is to attack the enemy whenever and wheresoever we can find them."

I did not see Léfort again for two years. He was still a captain of grenadiers. We spent a day together, and when I saw him tyrannizing over his men a trifle after the approved military fashion, I reminded him of his former opinions. Never in all my life have I seen a man laugh more heartily. "Yes it is true, quite true that I did say all these absurd

F

things," he replied; "and what was still worse, I believed them. It is useless to reason with people on subjects they know nothing about. But the most absurd follies are always the shortest lived. Mine did not last long. We had not been with the army three days before my opinions changed entirely. So I called my men together, and after forming them into a circle around me, I said, 'My boys, why have you made me your commander? because I am an honest man, a popular fellow, and a soldier who will not dodge the Prussian bullets. I thank you for the honour, but unfortunately I am not capable of commanding you; as the first corporal passing this way could prove to you; and in case I took you into action, I should probably get you all massacred and the country would not profit in the least by the operation. For this reason I am going to find the commander-in-chief and ask him to give you a leader who knows his business, which is to kill the greatest possible number of enemies and to have the least possible number of his own men killed. If this suits you, so much the better; if it doesn't, I can't help it. Now *Vive la Nation!* and break ranks!' And it was no sooner said than done. Kellermann sent us a thorough soldier who knew the drill as well as a priest knows his *pater nosters;* and I became a common soldier like my comrades. In a month I was a sergeant; now I am captain; and in five years, if a bullet does not carry me off, I shall be a general, and I shall know my business."

But all the volunteers had not so much honesty and good sense. There were only too many who did not, or would not; acknowledge that courage without discipline would be of little service. And Kellermann, Beurnonville, and Custine, had only too much cause to complain of the insubordination of the volunteers who joined the camp at Châlons. There were others who had not counted the cost of the sacrifice they had promised to make for their country—who had started for the front as they would have started on a pleasure excursion, and who were irritated and astonished to such a degree by the privations of a soldier's life that they openly revolted. If I had at hand the newspapers of the month of September, 1792, I would read you a petition which was addressed to the National Assembly by a company from one of the little towns in the west. But I am sure that I can repeat it for you *verbatim.* "Citizen legislators," wrote these soldiers, "we come to you to complain of our general, who is either a traitor and the paid tool of the Prussians, or an aristocrat. For four nights we have slept in the open field, upon the bare ground, without covering, and this in a heavy fog that has wet us and chilled us to the bone. So almost all of us are afflicted with throat distempers and severe colds. This traitor only last night pushed his perfidy to such an extent as to prevent us from lighting our fires, on the plea that their light might reveal our position to the Prussians—as if to conceal oneself from the enemy was not an act unworthy of a patriot. For the past two days we have had no food but flour. Of this we make a sort of porridge, which is all the more detestable as we are entirely destitute of salt. We have no wine, no meat, no brandy. Nothing, in fact. It is quite evident, citizen legislators, that the aristocrat who commands us has infamously resolved to enfeeble and debilitate us in order to deliver us into the power of the enemy more easily. We ask you to take the case into consideration."

Ah, well! there was a member of the Assembly who was simple enough to support this strange petition. He demanded an investigation, and who knows what else he would have demanded, if his voice had not been drowned in shouts of laughter.

About the same time several conscripts belonging to a battalion from Saint-Laurent requested an interview with Kellermann. They were in a state of intense excitement. "Citizen general," began the orator of the party, "the shoes that have been given us fit us so badly, and are made of such coarse leather, that we shall suffer with our feet."

Kellermann gazed at his visitors with the astonishing phlegm that never deserted him; and then calling the attention of some grenadiers who were standing by near to the crowd of malcontents, he said: "Boys, did you ever see such aristocrats? The country gives them shoes, and still they are not contented."

However, these conscripts, who were alarmed because they had taken cold, and who were indignant because their shoes did not fit them, became, after their baptism of fire at Valmy and Jemmapes, the indomitable grenadiers who for twenty years bore the principles of enfranchisement and liberty through Europe in the folds of our tri-coloured flag.

In 1792, we had other causes of anxiety. The municipal authorities of the various localities, in their eagerness to welcome whomsoever presented himself as a defender of the country, had forgotten that a soldier should be in a condition to bear the arms intrusted to him, and to use them effectively. Means of transport had been furnished to an incredible number of half-grown boys and aged and infirm men, who were not only useless themselves, but paralyzed the efforts of those who were conducting the campaign. On the 20th of August, 1792, exactly one month before the battle of Valmy Kellermann, in a report to the Assembly, said: "If patriotism were the only thing needed to make the enemy bite the dust, I might tell you that we could defy all Europe; but, unfortunately, no enthusiasm can survive two days of starvation, and we are starving here. Provisions are scarce, and there are so many useless soldiers to be fed." Two days later, the same general despatched a courier to Servan, the Minister of War, with this letter: "Stop the movement of volunteers to the camp without delay. The majority of these men come without weapons of any sort, and are clad in rags. They are not of the slightest use. When all other resources fail, I will take them into action, but not until then. Now it would be simply barbarous to expose these poor wretches to a fire which they are in no condition to return. If they are left to themselves, or rather to their chosen leaders, these volunteers will never be of the slightest assistance to me, so I have decided to send them to the rear with instructors who will make them good soldiers in less than a month. In the meantime, I will incorporate the best and most reliable of the new comers in the troops of the line, where they will be invaluable."

Biron also wrote to this same Servan: "The National Guards make admirable soldiers—calm and firm. The volunteers are called upon to perform a great work, and they will save the country, perhaps, if they can only be persuaded that they are soldiers, and that the first duty of a soldier is unquestioning obedience. Unfortunately, this is not the case now. The officers whom they themselves have chosen, up to the grade of lieutenant-colonel inclusive, have not the slightest influence over them. While we are in camp, everything goes along smoothly; but during our marches, the lack of discipline becomes apparent. The men linger by the way, many remain in the taverns, and some have deserted during the two or three marches I have made."

Nor was this all. The wild flood that rushed towards our frontier swept along with it not a little of the scum and dregs of our large cities. These men, who were unworthy of the name of soldiers, left their regiments, deserted their flag, and roamed about the country, robbing and murdering and making requisitions upon the terrified inhabitants of the little villages through which they chanced to pass. "These scoundrels," wrote emphatic Beurnouville, in a report to Pache, "are no longer the honoured children of France, but the companions of crime and debauchery. I have a number of these wretches in prison now, and I have found it very difficult to prevent the indignant army from punishing them as they deserve."

If I enter into these details, my friends, it is only that you may understand the truth. For it is annoying to see legendary stories substituted for history, and to hear the merits of all other generations depreciated for the benefit of one alone. People never seem weary of saying, "Ah! the men of '92." The men of '92 were only men after all, and in every age, and in every clime, human nature is the same strange mixture of all that is best, and all that is worst.

Alas! if we had our splendour, we also had our miseries—if we had our virtues, we also had our faults. To-day one only sees the virtues; the faults are not discernible at a distance of a century. However, I can swear to you, that in the beginning of the month of September, 1792, France almost despaired. After the general uprising, after this terrible explosion of anger, came a period of despondency and inaction. All that France could do, she had done. Henceforth her destiny was in the hands of Providence. Her fate depended upon the result of a battle. The Prussians were only six days' march from Paris; would the army of the Revolution be able to stay their progress? So you can judge what intolerable anxiety and torture we endured when we thought how feeble our chances of success were in comparison with those of our enemy. The Prussians had so much; we had so little.

All social amusements were suspended. People scarcely ate or slept. Everybody was waiting for news—for tidings of life or death. Any man who was seen on horseback was taken for a courier; and everybody stopped him and questioned him. Many listened constantly, fancying—in their intense anxiety—that they heard the sullen roar of cannon in the distance. Only the grand voice of Vergniaud could have aroused France from the stupor into which she had fallen. One day he appeared at the tribune. "I hear you say on every side," he began, "that we must be prepared for a defeat. In such a case, what will the Prussians do? Will they come to Paris? No, not if Paris is in a state of respectable defence—not if you will erect fortifications at every point that offers facilities for strong resistance; for then the enemy will fear lest they should be pursued and surrounded by the remnant of the army they had just vanquished—lest they should be crushed like Samson beneath the ruins of the temple he had overturned. To work, then, citizens, to work! What! when your fellow-citizens—your brothers, have heroically abandoned all that nature makes them cherish most fondly—their wives, their children, their firesides—you would stand by idle? Is there no other way of showing your patriotism than by hanging about the streets asking, as did the Athenians: 'What is the news to day?' To the camp, citizens! To the camp! While your brothers are, perhaps, drenching the plains of Champagne with their blood, you refuse to water with your sweat the plain of Saint Denis, in order to provide a safe retreat for them in case of need."

Every true patriot heartily applauded Vergniaud's eloquent and energetic exhortation. The most obtuse citizen could not fail to understand that the

Prussians would inevitably be annihilated, if dazzled by their recent victories they ventured between a strongly fortified city such as Paris was fast becoming, and the nation which had risen up in arms against them. "The Prussians," wrote Camille Desmoulins, at the time, "will be like a flock of wolves which has ventured down from the mountain only to be caught between the waves of the rising tide and an impassable marsh."

Yes, Paris must be made impregnable; but people were not sufficiently impressed with the necessity of this. There was a great deal of talk. Engineers drew plans and measured off the ground, but each had his own particular theory, which he explained and discussed with great vehemence. So no progress was made; nothing was done. At last, Vergniaud, seeing what little effect his speech had had, resolved to set the people an example. One morning, the idlers who strolled out every day to watch the progress of the fortifications were greatly surprised to see the famous orator appear, accompanied by two of his colleagues from the National Assembly. They doffed their coats, and each armed himself with a pickaxe and began work upon a ditch which had been traced out long before by one of the engineers. And all day they toiled as diligently as the poorest of the workmen.

When this incident was reported in Paris, it created a great excitement, and between noon and six o'clock in the evening, more than thirty thousand people came to see with their own eyes if the story were true. My father, Fougeroux, and myself were, I must confess, among the idle, curious throng. But when we saw Vergniaud and his friends hard at work, their faces wet with perspiration, shame seized us, and catching up some spades, we began to dig beside them. Hundreds of patriots did the same. The impetus was given.

After that, to lend a helping hand at the fortifications became a *furore*, the rage, the fashion, in short! People made up parties to dig in the trenches, to roll wheel-barrows, or to work on the palisades, just as they had formerly made up pleasure parties. It became as much the fashion as it had formerly been to show oneself in a carriage at Longchamps. Now all Paris was eager to work on the entrenchments. One day all the actors of the *Comédie Française* came, with Fleury and Louise Contat at their head. Tools were all that was wanting now, and they were not lacking long. Some dealers erected a number of booths where people could purchase shovels and pickaxes. Several restaurants were also established where people could obtain refreshments, and even breakfast or dine quite sumptuously after playing the labourer.

But all this did not prevent the public anxiety from becoming more intense, in proportion as the decisive moment drew nearer. Ah! if we had only had the Prussians to fear! But in 1792, my friends, France had all Europe against her, for the kings who did not make open war upon her, were secretly plotting her ruin. The revolution which had just overthrown the throne of Louis XVI. had shaken all the thrones of Europe so terribly, that every ruler formed part of a coalition to stifle popular emancipation in its infancy. Our northern frontier had been invaded, our eastern frontier was threatened; the enemy was everywhere, on every side. The Prussians, intoxicated by their success at Longwy and Verdun, were advancing rapidly into the Champagne. The English fleets prowled round our coasts. The Austrians had entered France, and Luckner, one of our generals, had been obliged to abandon his position at Longueville, near Metz, to try and arrest their progress. Never was any nation in any age nearer destruction than ours was then, for, if the Austrians and Prussians had triumphed, they would have treated us as they soon after treated unhappy Poland. Before entering France they had drawn lots between them for their prospective spoils : Alsace-Lorraine and Franche-Comté.

However, the Prussians were the principal cause of our anxiety. They were, as we well knew, our bitterest and most rapacious enemies. Their army was the most numerous. Besides, they were in the Champagne, at the gates of Paris. Every day came letters from officers belonging to our army which were copied in the papers. Each told us of some new outrage on the part of the invaders.

Frederick William II., their king, and the successor of the great Frederick, was then forty-eight years of age. This implacable adversary of the French Revolution was all the more dangerous, owing to the weakness of his character, his immoderate fondness of pleasure, his superstition, and his greed for glory, which made him the ready victim of unworthy favourites and audacious courtesans. The confidant whose opinion had most weight with him was Rietz, his *valet de chambre*, the complaisant husband of one of his mistresses, Wilhelmine Encke, who afterwards received the title of Countess of Lichtenau. Another intimate friend and adviser was Rudolf von Bischofswerder, who owed his influence solely to his skill as a necromancer. After Frederick William had supped, Bischofswerder was in the habit of conjuring up phantoms—the ghost of Cæsar for instance—who predicted that the king of Prussia was to rule over the ancient empire of Charlemagne. On the other hand as regards the king's relations with the fairer sex, I may mention that without repudiating the queen, his wife, and without parting from Wilhelmine Encke, he had morganatically married the Countess von Enhof. It is true that at the time of this outrageous scandal, he favoured his subjects with the famous "Edict of Conscience," which was intended to effect a salutary reform in moral and religious matters.

Such was the sovereign who was advancing into the heart of France, impelled by the hope of reaping a magnificent reward. Certainly, he had not the slightest doubt of a speedy and glorious success. His journey from Berlin to our frontier had been one triumphal march. Everywhere, he was greeted as conqueror even before the conflict began. Houses were decorated with flags in his honour, and his path was strewn with flowers and laurel-branches. At Erfurth, where he spent one night, his arrival was celebrated by illuminations and fireworks ; and over the gateway by which he entered the city, the inhabitants erected a triumphal arch bearing this inscription, the work of an ingenious courtier :

ALL HAIL TO

FREDERICK WILLIAM II.

Who will annihilate the French.

To annihilate the French people and to wrest their eastern provinces from them ! What a delightful dream, and besides, Frederick William's friends and advisers did their best to convince him that this glorious dream was to become a reality. Rietz, his *valet de chambre* and confidant, guaranteed that he would be successful ; and had he not heard the inspired Bischofswerder remark to the generals after a review, "Do not purchase too many horses, gentlemen. The farce will not last long. The army of clerks and cobblers will soon be destroyed, and we shall return home before autumn."

And his majesty's generalissimo, the Duke of Brunswick, shared this belief. Yet he was reputed to be a sage, a shrewd politician, and a philosopher. He had been victorious in many battles ; and he had done much to put an end to the disorders of the dissolute court in which he had been reared. He had gained his opinions of matters in general from personal observation. A sovereign, he had travelled as a private individual, and had visited France and spent several months in Paris. Mirabeau, who had studied the Duke of Brunswick in his own capital, has left us this portrait of him : "His face evinces great shrewdness and penetration. He speaks with elegance and precision. He is exceedingly industrious, well-educated, and clear-sighted. Really desirous of fulfilling his duties as a sovereign, he understands that economy is his first duty—and his mistress, Fraulein von Hartfeld, is the most sensible and prudent woman in the whole court. A veritable Alcibiades, he loves pleasure ; but he never allows it to make him forget his work, his duties, or even the rules of propriety. When he acts in the capacity of a Prussian general no person could be more industrious, more energetic, or more prudent. This prince is only fifty, and his active imagination and his ambition make him eager for any new enterprise ; but his distrust of mankind, and a jealous regard for his reputation, cause him to act with extreme caution and deliberation." In a private letter, Mirabeau moreover speaks of the duke as being under an extraordinary fear of losing, or compromising the great reputation as a military commander which he gained during the seven years' war. So, if the king of Prussia had any doubts left, they were dissipated by the assurances of this cautious generalissimo, who, no less sanguine than Bischofswerder, said to his officers on the eve of departure : "Above all, gentlemen, no encumbrances, no expense. It is not a campaign that we are undertaking, only a simple military promenade."

It is true that the duke also had been surfeited even to disgust—this is the expression he uses in one of his own letters—by the servile adulation he had received. He had not left Coblenz before he was hailed as the "Right arm of kings, and the hero of the Rhine."

I must also add that the king was surrounded by a crowd of *émigrés*, so troublesome, so exacting, and boastful that the Emperor of Austria had been compelled to drive them from his head-quarters. These nobles, who left the king and queen at the Tuileries to run and implore foreign aid in putting down the revolution, did not understand the *rôle* they were playing. They did not ask themselves what a foreign power would demand from France after a victorious invasion. Perhaps they had really been deceived by the hypocritical protestations of disinterestedness under which invaders always conceal their covetousness. They promised Frederick William great things. They insured him a civil war in Paris, which would make an invasion an easy matter. If one could believe them, France was longing for their return ; there was a powerful party there awaiting their orders—a party which would rise at the first signal, overthrowing the government of the cities and the discipline of the army, and ready to betray the country for the sake of the enemy. The French forces did not cause them the slightest anxiety. They could not find sneer and jibes enough for this "unruly mob of tailors and cobblers," as they styled the Revolutionary army. And they solicited the honour of a place in the advance guard of the Prussian army—the honour of guiding it through France, in order to open the way for it and to provoke treason.

But Frederick William could discover what was going on in our midst without their assistance ; and though he accepted their aid, and was very willing to profit by it, he depended chiefly upon his paid emissaries. For in obedience to the traditions of his country, he had sent an advance guard, more formidable than any artillery, before his invading army. From the frontier to Paris, Prussian spies were as thick as swallows. Our arsenals and storehouses held no secrets from them, and they assumed every conceivable disguise in their efforts to obtain plans of our strongholds, or to discover the condition of our fortifications. They were even on the public highways, busily engaged in counting our volunteers on their way to the front. In the fortifications about Paris, there was not a crown-work or a ditch of which Frederick William did not possess a plan. This was true to such an extent that Lanverdale, in his "Memoirs," declares that between Paris and the Prussian head-quarters, the communication was much more rapid and certain than that which existed between our own army and the National Assembly.

As you may suppose, these circumstances vastly increased the confidence of these Prussians who were invading our territory in open defiance of all the laws of justice. From the monarch down to the humblest soldier, every man in the invading army was convinced that he would sleep in Paris in less than a fortnight.

All the histories of the time—and they are many—are unanimous on this point. At Coblenz, the *émigrés* amused themselves by making wagers of dinner parties and entertainments payable in Paris ; and on their side, the Prussian officers—men renowned for their prudence and economy—industriously obtained information in regard to the mode of living in France, and especially in Paris. They tried to ascertain the price of everything, the fashions that prevailed, and the most desirable neighbourhoods to live in. Some provided themselves with a sort of guide-book, which mentioned the best hotels in the localities through which the army was likely to pass, and the wines peculiar to each province of the country. I once saw one of these books ; I found it in the pocket of a Prussian officer, killed at the battle of Valmy. In it the poor devil had jotted down the address of a restaurant in the Rue Saint-Honoré, and that of a lodging-house in the Rue du Roule. After these came a long list of toilette and fancy articles which his sister or his sweetheart desired him to purchase for her. Indeed, many of the principal officers had written to Paris to engage lodgings ; and so strong was their conviction that they should occupy the city, that some had paid in advance.

Goethe, whom the King of Prussia brought in his suite, in order that he might act as the historian of his victories, has recounted, in his private correspondence, his sovereign's transports of pride. It was the eve of the invasion, and the entire Prussian army was encamped upon our frontier. As far as the eye could reach, one could see glittering lines of bayonets, helmets, and breastplates. In the centre was massed the artillery, while on either side, straight, and as firm as solid walls, stretched long lines of the famous grenadiers of Frederick the Great—each man six feet high—the remnants of the old army which had conquered Silesia—men who had been hardened into bronze by heat and cold, long marches, want of food, and nights spent on the damp ground. These were considered invincible soldiers, the first in Europe for discipline, and for their utter contempt of death which they had so often braved.

Frederick William made his appearance on horseback, followed by the Duke of Brunswick, and escorted by a crowd of plumed and decorated officers. He paused upon a hillock, and, surveying the swarm of men and horses that stretched to the horizon, he became intoxicated with pride, and exclaimed : " France is at my mercy !—I shall be generous ! "

On the day following this review, the Prussian army entered France. Unfortunately, the generosity which the king had been so ready to boast of, did not extend to the hearts of his soldiers. They had accepted literally the shameful order which made the Duke of Brunswick's manifesto seem more like the declaration of war of a savage chief, than that of a civilised prince. " All inhabitants of towns, or villages, who dare to oppose the troops of his Majesty, the King of Prussia, and fire upon them through either the doors or the windows of their houses, shall be instantly punished with death, and their dwellings burned or demolished."

Sierck was the first French village visited by the Uhlans—and the first scene of their bloody exploits ; and its inhabitants were the first to learn the distance which separated the hypocrisy of the leaders from the cruelty of the soldiers. At Sierck, a company of volunteers from Seine-et-Oise had been placed on guard with orders to retreat to Thionville as soon as the enemy appeared. But the poor fellows were not on the alert. Perhaps they considered prudence beneath their dignity, or perhaps they were ignorant of the marvellous way in which Prussian cavalry were wont to appear where they were least expected, and where they would meet with little or no resistance. The volunteers were preparing their soup when suddenly they found themselves attacked, surrounded, walled in. It was impossible for them to defend themselves. The very weapons of most of them were beyond their reach. They surrendered. But what did the sacred laws of civilization, which declare an unarmed foe safe from attack, matter to the Uhlans ? From the prisoners they had taken they selected two, the captain and a lieutenant, and the whole party sprang upon these two defenceless men, and killed them. This was the signal for a general massacre, and as murder did not satisfy their ferocity, they stripped the lifeless bodies of their clothing, and after placing red caps upon their heads, they hung them on trees near the entrance of the village.

Did the dying moans of these poor wretches ever reach the ears of his magnanimous majesty, Frederick William II. ? No, certainly not. And, besides, what would it have mattered to him ? Fortune was smiling upon his arms ; his spies and traitors had just delivered Longwy into his hands.

He had triumphed, but he complained that the victory had been too easily won. He did not wish too much resistance, but he desired a little, that he might not seem ridiculous, as the eyes of Europe were fixed upon him. Hence his resolve—which, by the way, was executed—to throw a few shells into Verdun. Three hundred were fired at the town. Wasted ammunition ! since treason was already within, awaiting the enemy's approach with her finger on the latch of the door. Another triumph for the King of Prussia ! a victory fragrant with the roses which the young maidens of Verdun strewed in his path. Alas, poor girls ! Poor virgins of Verdun ! They were soon afterwards condemned to atone with their lives for their parents' crime.

Verdun captured, the King of Prussia occupied it during a few days. He reigned supreme there—he administered justice as he would have done at Berlin. He appointed a governor, mayor, and judges—all Prussians. This made even the *émigrés* open their eyes in surprise. Perhaps they realised at last that if this disinterested monarch did conquer France, it would be extremely difficult to make him release his hold on what he had conquered. They made some complaints; but the king replied that he had not time then to listen to their remonstrances—that he would grant them a hearing when he reached Paris.

Emboldened by the intelligence which they had received from Thionville, and by the aid which they had reason to expect from some of its disloyal inhabitants, the king and the Duke of Brunswick flattered themselves that this stronghold, which had closed its gates against them, would not resist for long. This was their first disappointment, however. Longwy and Verdun had surrendered, but Thionville absolutely refused todo so; and the besieged responded to a second demand by placing on the ramparts a wooden horse with a wisp of hay tied about its neck. Beneath it they had written, "When this horse eats this hay, Thionville will surrender."

However, this resistance did not disturb the plans of the Duke of Brunswick, who had decided not to attack any more fortified strongholds, but to march straight on Paris. So a division of Austrian troops was told off to blockade Thionville. And the King of Prussia advanced with but one fear: that our army would not wait for him, but scatter at his approach, as dry leaves are scattered by the breath of the approaching storm.

And to confront this horde of barbarians, to resist these legions of angry *émigrés*, what had we at our disposal? Ah, my friends, as you know the want of unity that prevailed among the ministers, the stupor of the Assembly, the discouragement of Kersaint, the panic in Paris, you can answer this question; remembering all the gratitude we owe to those who did not despair of the salvation of the country even when she was in such a desperate strait. The army with which we had to confront the invader, the National army, as yet existed only on paper, on the enlistment registers. Its uniforms were not yet completed, its weapons were still in the hands of the workmen. Many who had received their equipments began their military education without delay in the camps and on the public squares; but not a few dispersed in little squads, taking different roads in ignorance of the halting-places, in order to join the enemy more quickly. So our only available force was composed of a few regulars, a few hundred companies of the *Federés* of '91, and National Guards.

And even if this feeble army had only been united, well disciplined, manageable, and animated with equal enthusiasm! But two-thirds of the officers of the regular forces were among the *émigrés*, and the army itself was completely demoralised. It was torn by dissensions, tainted by gross licentiousness, preyed upon by suspicion and distrust, and constantly subjected to the tempting proposals of the Prussian spies. "I have, among my troops," wrote the despairing Kellermann, "at least a thousand scoundrels, who are only awaiting a shot to disband and raise a panic by shouting, 'Save himself who can! we are betrayed!'"

And if this small army, our only recourse, our only hope, had been compact! But no! Ignorance, favouritism, the desire of furnishing several officers with an opportunity to distinguish themselves, the hope of insuring their devotion by distributing the commands as much as possible, and more than all, perhaps, the fear of giving too much power to a single general, had caused an unwise scattering of our forces. At Lille, Mauberge, and Maulde, we had thirty thousand men whose impossible mission was to protect our northern frontier. Twenty-three thousand were camped at Sedan. Twenty thousand were at Longueville, and thirty or thirty-five thousand more were distributed through Alsace.

These made in all one hundred thousand men, scattered over a vast extent of country, cut off from any communication with one another, destitute of orders or plans, and whose presence on the frontier had proved utterly useless since Brunswick had forced their lines, was already beyond the reach of most of them, and was boldly advancing into the heart of France. And among all the generals, there was not one with sufficient authority, sufficiently recognised superiority, or the necessary devotion or audacity, to withdraw from his perilous position upon his own responsibility.

I should add that the troops at Sedan had no commander. Their general, the man on the white horse, whom Mirabeau had dubbed Cromwell Grandison—Lafayette in short—had gone over to the enemy. When he discovered that he would never succeed in constructing for himself a dictator's chair out of the remnants of the throne he had helped to overturn, the Revolution filled him with horror ; and on the 21st of August he deserted his troops, crossed the frontier, and placed himself in the hands of the Austrians. But some men have a lucky star which protects them against themselves. The Austrians, who ought to have welcomed Lafayette warmly, cast him into prison, and kept him for several years in the dungeons of Magdeburg and Olmutz. And this persecution excited so much sympathy and interest that his odious crime was forgotten.

Lafayette, having gone over to the enemy, it was hard to find a suitable person to oppose the Duke of Brunswick. Beurnonville, Moreton, and Duval, the commanders at Maulde, Mauberge, and Lille, though they were excellent officers, did not possess the qualities requisite in a commander-in-chief. Kellermann's genius had not been revealed. Custine, then in Alsace, was regarded with suspicion. Marshal Luckner, the commander of Metz, certainly had one advantage : he was a foreigner, a native of Hanover, and belonged to neither of the parties then struggling for ascendency in France. Luckner was not without talent ; but his soul was petty and sordid. He was inordinately avaricious, and he had little or no education. He was a *parvenu par excellence ;* and in spite of his exalted rank, his habits and tastes were those of the lowest subaltern, and invariably reduced him to that *rôle.* He had all the bodily activity of a hussar, but his ideas were vague and confused, and his mind slow to act. Of the whole plan of campaign in the Netherlands, which had been confided to him, he could remember nothing save a few unimportant details ; and in response to the directions of the Minister of War, he could only repeat : "Yes, yes ; I am to turn to the right, to the left, and make all possible haste."

Thus the expedition to the Netherlands which might have arrested the tide of invasion, had it been properly conducted, proved a complete *fiasco.* The strength of the marshal's army, and his supplies of stores and equipments, embarrassed him, and he gave them as objections to all the movements which were proposed to him. No doubt, he was brave, and had he merely been the commander of an advance-guard, he would have led his men to the ends of the earth. On political questions as on military matters, his opinions fluctuated strangely. In the morning he was all devotion to the nation ; but when evening came he was the earnest champion of the king. He did not understand the Revolution in the least. He confounded all objects and all parties, and always complained that he was surrounded by fault-finders. As a final touch to his portrait, I should say that after the death of Frederick the Great, he considered himself the greatest of living military leaders, and he was sustained in this belief by the chief of his staff, Berthier, the future major-general of the empire, and prince of Neufchâtel.

Was it really necessary for us to intrust the destinies of our imperilled country to this foreign soldier? Ah! it would have been profanation! And so Dumouriez was appointed commander-in-chief. Dumouriez had his faults, and died in exile, pensioned by the king of England, but this much is sure, positive, indisputable: he saved France. The men of his time—his intimate friends and associates—who possessed his confidence, have declared that he was deeply impressed with the conviction that he had some great mission to fulfil. And those who knew him were as fully convinced that his genius was equal to the greatest emergencies. Endowed with varied talents, well educated, energetic, keen-sighted, ambitious, and thirsting for renown, Dumouriez seemed well-fitted to overcome all obstacles, and to reach any goal, no matter how remote, at a single bound.

But such had not been the case. Until the Revolution he had languished in the lower ranks of the army, or in the diplomatic service, with duties not much above those of a common spy. Between his dreams and their realization there had arisen an obstacle, which seemed almost insurmountable at the time—his birth. Dumouriez was of noble descent, but his parents belonged to the petty nobility, and previous to 1789, rank, decorations, and royal favour were the patrimony of the court aristocracy exclusively. Born at Cambrai, in January, 1739, of an old Provençal family, Charles François Dumouriez was indebted to his father, the most honest, but the most peculiar of men, for a superior education. His infancy was clouded with sorrow and suffering. Until he was seven years old he was well nigh paralyzed, and he was drawn about almost encased in iron, in a rolling chair. He would have died in this barbarous armour, in which the ignorance of a country physician had imprisoned him, had it not been for a worthy precentor of the cathedral of Cambrai, who pitying the boy, took him to his own house, delivered him from his bondage, cared for him, and made the puny, wretched urchin, a robust lad capable of enduring the greatest fatigue.

At seventeen, after three years spent at the college of Louis-le-Grand, he had so far forgotten the infirmites of his early childhood as to enter the order of Jesuits, and become a missionary, in order to have an opportunity to work off some of his superfluous energy in travel and in braving unknown dangers. But he did not persist in this resolution. The seven years' war having been declared, he followed his father, who had just been appointed to a commissaryship in the army which was to operate in Hanover under the command of Marshal d'Estrées. Dumouriez profited by this opportunity to initiate himself into all the mysteries and details connected with the commissariat, a modest department, certainly, but one on which armies and victories depend. In his leisure hours he received most valuable instruction from a talented staff-officer, M. de Montazet, who took a great fancy to the youth, and often asked his assistance in the performance of his own important and delicate duties.

But it was not long before the battle of Bremen took place. Dumouriez took part in it, and the smell of the powder seemed to rise to his brain. He relinquished the pen for the musket, and taking his place in a company of Grenadiers, he charged the enemy and received his first wound, and a half dozen bullets in his uniform. The battle taught him his true calling. He was so convinced of this, that without saying a word to his father in regard to his intentions, he enlisted one fine morning in the regiment of Escars—the same which had inscribed upon its standard this motto, "Do your duty, come what may." After this bold stroke, he returned to his father somewhat dismayed, for he feared a paternal lecture. But no. "You have done well to follow your tastes," said his father, quietly ; whereupon Dumouriez, radiant with delight, exclaimed : "I am late in entering the service, but I shall lose no time. I swear that in less than four years I will be a Knight of the Order of Saint-Louis or dead." And he started for Normandy with the regiment which he had entered as a common soldier.

He did not forget his promise to his father, and by his conduct it was easy to see that he intended to keep it. After an engagement in Germany, which was lost through the blind folly of the Chevalier de Muy, he rallied the decimated and disordered companies around the regimental standard, saved a battery of five guns, and covered the retreat of a whole brigade across the river. His horse was shot under him, and he received two severe wounds. Can you guess, my friends, what reward he received for such abundant evidence of courage and coolness? I will tell you, and then you will better understand the difficulties with which he was obliged to contend in his struggle to achieve fame. He received a gratuity of fifty crowns which he divided among the members of the company to which he belonged. But destiny in a capricious moment was planning a strange re-venge for him. She was about to introduce him to the Duke of Brunswick. It was just before the battle of Klosterkampen ; Dumouriez, who was then in the ordnance division, was sent to the left wing of the army with order from his general. On his way he was attacked by twenty hussars, defended himself in spite of the terrible odds against him, and soon two of his assailants ; but his horse fell dead under him, and in such an fortunate position that Dumouriez could not extricate his foot from the stirrup. Even then he fought valiantly for several minutes. Finally he succeeded in sheltering himself between a hedge and the body of his horse, and wounded three more men. His assailants at last overpowered him One of them disabled his right arm by a sabre stroke, another wounded him in the left arm, another shot him in the thigh, and the others disfigured his face and burned off his eyebrows, eyelashes and hair by discharging their pistols in his face.

He was evidently about to succumb when a German officer who chanced to be passing that way—Baron Behr—rescued him and ordered the men to carry him to his own tent, where a physician rendered him the attention he so much needed. Dumouriez had received thirteen wounds, without counting a large number of scratches and bruises, and the grains of powder in his face, which also caused him great suffering. But what distressed him most was his inability to use his arms, and the knowledge that he was completely at the mercy of those around him, though they treated him with the greatest kindness, it must be admitted.

The next day, however, he was presented to the Duke of Brunswick, who received him most graciously, and complimented him upon his bravery in the most flattering manner, but who kept him a prisoner. He was detained several weeks, and as a compensation, probably, the duke, on restoring him to liberty, wrote to the Duke de Castries, lauding Dumouriez's courage to the skies. Certainly, the Duke of Brunswick little thought that this letter would be the turning point in the military career of his young prisoner, or that he would meet him again opposing his passage to Paris in the capacity of commander-in-chief of the French army.

However, the four years that Dumouriez had accorded himself had not elapsed when he received the cross of Saint Louis. Moreover, he was promoted to a captaincy in the regiment which he had entered as a common soldier. He was not twenty-three at the time. The captain of a company in the regiment of Escars, and a Knight of Saint Louis, at an age when other young men were just entering the army, one might reasonably suppose that Dumouriez could safely count upon a brilliant career. But this proved a delusion, at least for many years. After the peace of 1763, he, in common with many other gallant officers, suddenly found himself out of employment. What compensation did he receive for the genius he had displayed, for his acts of bravery, and his twenty-two wounds? Merely a pension of six hundred livres.

Any other man would have been discouraged, but not he. "Through the clouds of adversity, I see my star still shining brightly," he wrote to one of his friends. Still it was then that the necessities of daily life, even more than the unwavering activity of his imagination, forced him into the rather crooked paths of secret diplomacy. "There are some who accuse me of having been unscrupulous in regard to my method of elevating myself," he said in a letter to his friend Favier. "But I should like to see my censors in my place. As if I could choose my means!"

After his return from a journey to Italy, which he had undertaken and accomplished on foot, and almost without money, he sent the Duke de Choiseul, then prime minister of France, a memorial on "the ways and means of closely uniting the island of Corsica to France." This memorial was very unfavourably received by the minister, who was opposed to Dumouriez's views, and not at all conversant with the subject. During an interview with M. de Choiseul, moreover, Dumouriez became so angry and forgot himself so completely, that he deemed it advisable to put the frontier between himself and a *lettre de cachet* as soon as possible after the conclusion of the audience. But M. de Choiseul changed his mind. It was not long before he sent for Dumouriez, and appointed him assistant quartermaster-general of the expedition which France had sent to Corsica, thus granting him the much-longed for privilege of re-entering military life.

His self-respect satisfied, he became as zealous as he had been daring. And the talent, the valour and the activity which he displayed in the Corsican war would have more than sufficed to assure the reputation of any other man. But he was—as one of his bitterest enemies openly avowed—one of those instruments which are so valuable that those who use them have no desire to bring them into public notice. Indeed, the fact is, he was fated to receive no reward for his achievements in Corsica. On returning to Paris with the Duke de Lauzun to give the king the details of the conquest of the island, he was received like a servant of whom his employer would gladly rid himself if he had the shadow of a pretext for doing so.

He was too keen-sighted not to detect the danger that lurked in a courteous smile, so he retired to seclusion, living upon the three thousand livres a year which he had recently inherited from his father, and upon a pension which the Duke de Choiseul allowed him. His circle of acquaintances was composed almost exclusively of artists and men of letters. He spent his evenings pleasantly in their society; and then, as his ceaseless activity must needs have some outlet, he passed his nights in planning campaigns.

He believed himself forgotten, and it must be confessed that the thought made him almost inconsolable, when suddenly M. de Choiseul again sent for him. The minister was thinking of sending an agent to Poland to organise a party sufficiently strong to resist the encroachments of Russia, which was already preparing to efface that unfortunate country from the map of Europe. A man of expedients and decision was needed for such a mission, and at the same time a devoted man, ready for anything, even to be censured and punished in case of need ; for the expedition must be kept secret from the ambassadors and official agents of the French government. Dumouriez accepted all these risks and departed on his mission. The amount of work he accomplished in six months was almost incredible. From nothing, he wrought wonders. He made a few roving soldiers the nucleus of a really fine army. He improvised artillery from the old cannon of every sort which he disinterred here and there. He even fortified two towns—one of which successfully resisted a formidable attack by the Russians. He did even more. Effectually aided by an intriguing, witty, and beautiful woman, the Countess of Mniszeck, he almost succeeded in putting an end to the unfortunate but ancient feuds between the Poles themselves—lamentable divisions, which had caused the decline of the country, and eventually brought about its ruin. If Dumouriez had succeeded in this, Poland would have been, to-day, the ruling power of northern Europe. And he was on the eve of success, when the Duke de Choiseul was removed from office.

The policy of the government had changed. Dumouriez received orders to return to Paris, which he did, again lamenting his baffled schemes, but by no means discouraged. It was a time when all the European courts were united by a thread of intrigue, and a man like Dumouriez was not allowed to remain inactive. He had not unlocked his trunks when he was ordered to Sweden—still in the capacity of a secret agent. But this time, he was unfortunate. Compelled to deny him, those who had employed him ordered his arrest in Hamburg where he was raising troops ; and he was thrown into the Bastille. He remained there six months. He was well treated, but was subjected to a constant and rigorous examination by the judges who would have been delighted to wrest his secret from him. He defended it so bravely, however, that one of his examiners said : " Upon my word ! if, as we are told, this is a chicken, it is a confoundedly tough one ! "

His firmness was at last rewarded, for on his release, he was appointed to a post more worthy of him. He was made commandant of Cherbourg, and was charged with erecting fortifications at this great military port. Promoted to the rank of a lieutenaut-general, or " maréchal-de-camp," in 1788, he was in 1791 attached to the 12th division, and sent to La Vendée, where, as his letters prove, he had expected a general insurrection for some time already.

Recalled to Paris in 1792, by the Minister of War, he found himself reduced to such pecuniary straits, that after selling his silver and even his books, he was compelled to accept the assistance of a faithful and devoted friend, none other than the sister of Rivarol. But undismayed by poverty and the uncertainty that shrouded his future, he toiled more diligently than ever upon his scheme for the reorganisation of the army, and finally succeeded in submitting it to the examination of the king, through the intervention of his friend Laporte. All this labour did not prevent him from appearing at the Jacobin clubs, and from attending the meetings of the Assembly. He also allied himself with the most influential people among the Girondins, especially with Gensonné. And this explains how it happened that Dumouriez was made Minister of Foreign Affairs on the 15th of March, 1972.

If there was in all France a man capable of saving the almost lost cause
of the monarchy, that man was most assuredly Dumonriez. But if the
weak-minded Louis XVI. had any vague presentiment of approaching misfortune, the wily and ambitious friends who surrounded him were less
discerning. There were cries of anger and astonishment in the ante-
chambers of the Tuileries, when the names of the members of the new
cabinet were announced. The few courtiers who had remained with the
king wandered through the corridors, their faces a yard long, shaking their
heads and repeating : "There is no denying it. We have a ministry of
sans-culottes."

This was said so openly that Dumouriez heard it. "*Sans-culottes*, yes,
certainly," he replied ; "but people will have an opportunity of seeing
that the so-called *sans-culottes* are men."

He, himself, was known as Minister "Bonnet Rouge," because one
evening at a Jacobin meeting, he had been seen in the tribune with the
famous red cap on his head. Perhaps he put it on no more willingly than
Louis XVI. did, on the 20th of June. At least, he declares in his
Memoirs that this was the case, but he was not above such a conces-
sion when expediency dictated it. Did he not say, himself, on the subject :
"If I were the king, I should be a Jacobin, and such a fierce Jacobin that
the most violent members of the party could be no more compared with
me than with these rascally aristocrats."

But he could not impose silence on his enemies by such venomous remarks
as these, so when he came to attend the cabinet meetings at the Tuileries,
everybody shunned him as they would the pestilence. The courtiers
sneered as he passed by, and even the members of the body-guard glanced
at him contemptuously. Very frequently they attempted to embarrass
and annoy him about questions of etiquette. For the etiquette of the court
was still observed at the Tuileries : the ceremonials of power survived the
power itself ; the semblance outlasted the reality. The first time that
Dumonriez appeared at court accompanied by his colleague, Roland, the
newly-appointed Minister of the Interior, the simplicity of the latter's
costume—he looked like a pedagogue arrayed in his Sunday clothes—his
round hat, and shoes tied with a bit of ribbon, excited the astonishment
and contempt of the valets. The master of the ceremonies even approached
Dumouriez in great distress, and pointing to Roland, whispered frowning
darkly : "What, sir, no buckles on his shoes—no buckles ?" Whereupon
Dumouriez coolly replied : "That is true, sir—all is lost."

Dumouriez was then on the best of terms with Roland, and this friendship lasted until he offended Madame Roland, and consequently all the
Girondin deputies. The cause of the quarrel which resulted in the breaking
up of the cabinet is worthy of relation. After their appointment, the six
ministers agreed to dine at each other's houses three days each week. Each
minister was to bring his portfolio, and they were to decide upon the matters
that should be referred to the king, discuss them, and form a common
opinion. This arrangement lasted about a month, at the end of which
Roland asked that his wife should be admitted to their conferences. This
request excited the wrath of Dumouriez, who, with military brusquerie, replied that Madame Roland's place was in the drawing-room, where she did
the honours with unequalled grace.

No remark could have inflicted a deeper wound upon this woman, who
was the incarnation of vanity, the absolute ruler of her husband, and the
oracle of a strong political party. She revenged herself by telling every-

body that Dumouriez was a talented but exceedingly untrustworthy man, and that it was unwise to place any confidence in him ; that he was undoubtedly a great general, and capable of the most gigantic undertakings, but that he was absolutely destitute of moral character. She said that, though he was invariably courteous and affable to his friends, he was always trying to deceive them. She accused him of being too apt in intrigue, and declared that he had degraded himself to the level of a buffoon in order to win the king's favour. Madame Roland, when once she attacked an enemy, showed him no mercy. But she was wrong. It could not have been by buffoonery that Dumouriez had become a favourite with the king, for no monarch ever had less taste for it. His attraction, so far as Louis XVI. was concerned, lay rather in a sort of brutal frankness, which was certainly assumed, for Dumouriez was naturally politeness itself. During their first interview, the newly-appointed minister spoke his mind so freely, that the king, unaccustomed to such plain speaking, was actually stupefied with amazement, and after his departure repeated, again and again, " Never have I heard the like ! Never have I heard the like ! "

Dumouriez conducted himself in the same way during an audience with the queen ; and Marie Antoinette, crimson with anger, exclaimed : " Take care, sir ; take care ! You may be all powerful just now, but this state of things will not last for ever ! " The explosion of wrath which he had provoked did not cause the minister to lose his *sang-froid*, and he conducted the rest of the interview so skilfully, that he flattered himself on retiring that he had won the entire confidence of the queen.

Of course, Dumouriez entered the ministry with all sorts of plans and theories of reform in his head. Naturally, a man who had studied diplomacy, military organization, and government for thirty years, saw the necessity of introducing ameliorations everywhere ; for he judged, and judged wisely, that the people would not allow the political machine to continue its workings, unless its institutions were modified to suit the spirit of the times. At last, he was to forsake the domain of theory for that of reality. Need I tell you that he began work with the feverish activity that was one of the essential traits of his character, and actually frightened his employés, who were not at all inclined to follow his example. Rising at four in the morning, by five o'clock he was in his study, and at six o'clock his secretary, Bonne-Carrière, came to work with him. At eleven o'clock began the appointments and audiences which were torture to him on account of the time he lost by them. At four o'clock he sat down to dinner ; at half-past four he returned to his study, and did not leave it until twelve or one o'clock in the morning, when he took supper or went to bed. It is true that his burden of care and anxiety was greatly increased by the fact that he had to discharge the duties of the Secretary of War in addition to his own ; for Degrave, who was then acting in that capacity, had no practical knowledge of military matters. It is a well-known fact that it was Dumouriez who regulated the movements of the troops and the promotion of the officers, and who planned the campaign.

But the task which he had undertaken required more than human power. He had hoped to reconcile the interests of the revolution, with what Louis XVI. called his rights. He failed. On the 14th June, 1792, the cabinet was dissolved—three ministers having resigned. Dumouriez then became Minister of War—but just one month later, the 14th July, he too was compelled to tender his resignation.

His political opponents then tried to impugn his honesty ; but he

answered the charge so conclusively, that the attack resulted in their dis-
comfiture and his complete justification. He had again retired to obscurity,
and in a half jesting, half melancholy tone, he remarked to his friend Ber-
neron : "I certainly enriched myself in the ministry with an inexhaustible
supply of enemies."

How could it have been otherwise? He had retained his composure
when all his companions had lost theirs ; he had endeavoured to act as a
moderator when every passion was unchained. Appointed to office through
the influence and by the efforts of the Girondins, his course in the cabinet
had transformed his former friends into his bitterest enemies. When he
was only an obscure lieutenant-general, he had been a favourite with the
Jacobins ; but as soon as he became a minister they vented all their wrath
and spite upon him. If the army had only remained faithful to him ! But
while he held the portfolio of war, he had pursued the chimerical plan of
rendering honour where honour is due, and had succeeded in making as
many enemies as there were commanding officers and marshals.

He was obliged to live, however, so he was forced to resume his old rank
of lieutenant-general, which afforded him a bare subsistence. After much
reflection, he decided to re-enter the service, under the command of
Marshal Luckner, who had just evacuated Courtrai and retreated to
Valenciennes. So it was to Valenciennes that Dumouriez repaired.

He was not very cordially received by the old marshal, and he was even
less civilly treated by the officers of the staff. There were persons in Paris
who had declared that he would not dare to join this army ; while others
had asserted that he would not be received. Berthier, the chief of the
staff, issued no orders on Dumouriez's arrival, though by right of seniority,
the latter should at once have received command of the left division. But
they sent him no message, no orders, neither did they assign him any
quarters nor furnish him with a guard. Indeed, he remained several days
at Valenciennes entirely unnoticed.

He waited patiently, and discovered the lack of discipline and military
spirit in the army, and the incompetence of its leader. At the end of a
week, he forced the marshal to grant him an audience, hoping to induce
him to abandon the camp where he had concentrated his army, and which
was undesirable in every respect. But Luckner, angered by this interference, promptly replied that he would listen to advice from nobody, and
that he was fully resolved to send the first officer who ventured to oppose
him to the citadel, be the officer even Minister of Foreign Affairs or Minister
of War.

The camp, which was afterwards taken by the Austrians, was exceedingly
ill-chosen. Its close proximity to Valenciennes kept the troops in an
intolerable condition of insubordination and debauchery. The officers and
soldiers spent most of their time in the town, drinking and gambling.

In the rear of the camp there was the Scheldt ; but in case of a defeat,
this afforded no protection to a retreating army, since it could be crossed
only at three points, two of which would inevitably fall into the
hands of the enemy. In front of the camp there was another river, it is
true ; but this was only a small stream, fordable anywhere, and as both
banks had an equal elevation, the site offered no facilities for defence. All
these disadvantages struck Dumouriez so forcibly, that at the risk of
another rebuff, he presented himself a second time at the marshal's door,
determined to make him listen to reason. Luckner, convinced at last,
cursed the officers who had recommended the position, accused them of being

traitors or fools, and swore that there should be a different state of things in the future. And during the dinner to which he had begged Dumouriez to remain, he openly insulted his aides-de-camp, Lameth and Montmorency.

The result of all this was that Berthier, the following day, paid his first visit to the general to whom he was indebted for his promotion, and Dumouriez told him seriously, but kindly, that it was time to end this farce, and to think of making war in earnest. Unfortunately, Luckner was never of the same mind during seven successive days. His aides-de-camp soon regained their former ascendency over him ; and Dumouriez, after another stormy interview, received orders to start within twenty-four hours to assume command of the camp at Maulde.

This camp, which has since become famous, was intended to protect the rich plains and pasture lands lying between Lille, Douai, Valenciennes and Condé. But it was ill-fited for the importaut service expected of it. It would have been an excellent position for an army of ten or twelve thousand men ; but for the little body of troops quartered there, it was a most dangerous post, for there was a constant risk of their being surrounded and their retreat cut off. The general whom Dumouriez had superseded had crowned the neighbouring heights with seven redoubts and had thrown up a few earthworks in front of Maulde, but there was not a sufficient number of troops to defend these fortifications, which were so weak that they could easily have been carried by a bayonet charge. At the first glance, Dumouriez saw that Luckner's principal object in sending him here had been to free himself of a troublesome censor. Quite possibly, too, he hoped that Dumouriez would meet with some reverse that would cost him his military reputation. Indeed, the marshal went so far as to write to some influential persons in Paris, so that no blame might fall upon him personally, in case any misfortune occurred. Dumouriez wrote several times to the marshal for reinforcements, and ended by sending an accurate report of the condition of the camp. But the marshal did not grant him the reinforcements he asked, nor did he condescend to make any answer to his communications.

Seeing that he was not likely to recive any help, Dumouriez left Saint Amand and took up his abode in the camp, where he won the affection of his soldiers by sharing their hardships and privations. He established regular communications with the generals commanding Douai and Lille, and arranged for a combined movement in case of need. He made provision, so far as it was in his power, for protecting the frontier ; stationed some batteries near the village of Saint Amand, and carried on a petty warfare against the towns of Tournay, Bury, and Leuze, in order to make the enemy suppose that he had a large force under his command. He also fortified Orchies, and stationed there a battalion borrowed from the garrison at Douai.

Of course he reported these movements to Luckner, who approved of them. Meanwhile, he continued his system of petty warfare, in which he was so successful that even his enemies were forced to confess that the region he commanded was the only point at which the foe had not penetrated our territory, the only point where we were still acting on the offensive. Everywhere else, even in the immediate neighbourhood of our armies, bands of Uhlans were ravaging the country, sacking villages, setting fire to isolated farm-houses, and murdering the defenceless inmates ; conducting themselves, in short, rather like highway robbers than as the soldiers of a nation that prided itself on its eivilization.

By this warfare, which required constant vigilance, and by daily engage-
ments, Dumouriez's troops speedily arrived at the perfection of discipline.
It was thus they acquired that eagerness for the fray, and that solidity under
fire which characterized them through the entire campaign. His enemies
imagined they had buried him; but, on the contrary, they had simply
furnished him with an opportunity to display a patience and perseverance
which no one had suspected to exist in his impulsive nature. It is true,
however, that he was constantly at work upon a plan of invasion. To carry
the war into the enemy's country, and thus force them to evacuate our
territory, had become a fixed idea with him. "The more I study the
question upon the scene of action itself," he wrote to a friend in Paris, "the
more thoroughly I am convinced that the plan of campaign which I recommended at the beginning of the war is the best one possible under the circumstances. Either through ignorance or wilfulness, the generals have not
followed it, declaring it impracticable. We must return to this plan, however, and I have sent some notes on the subject to the Minister of War."

Later on, he did resume this plan of campaign, and proved its excellence
by its success. But at that time he was in disgrace and without influence;
and he was compelled to stand by and see his superiors neglect the opportunity which he would have been so quick to profit by. As usual, his indignation found vent in plans and notes. "In the great hereafter, rather
than write no memorials at all, you will address them to the Almighty on
the art of governing Paradise," his friend Beurnonville once jestingly remarked to him.

However, in his days of adversity, Dumouriez still preserved the secret
of making everything contribute to the success of his plans. There was
quite a romantic example of this at the camp of Maulde. In the village of
Mortagne lived a retired officer named Fernig. This man, who then held
the office of recorder, had five children—a son, an officer in one of Dumouriez's regiments, and four daughters. Two of these girls—one aged twenty-
two, and the other seventeen, delicate, well educated, and modest—had
several times followed the detachments that were sent out on reconnoitering
expeditions, and had stood fire bravely. One of them, the youngest, was
said to be the mistress of Dumouriez. The rumour spread through the
camp, and the soldiers always called her " La Générale." But Dumouriez
constantly denied the story. Still, this much is certain : the courage of
these two heroines were of no little help to him in exalting the valour of his
troops. How could a grenadier think of flinching, when he saw two young
girls face a fusilade with utter indifference ? The Demoiselles Fernig became
so celebrated that the Convention granted them a pension, and one of the members of the legislature, who had been sent to the head-quarters of the army
on some mission, said of them in his report: "They have distinguished
themselves in every action; and are as remarkable for their modesty and
virtue as for their courage. The soldiers respect them as much as they love
them ; and it would be well for all our young volunteers to follow the example of these beautiful patriots."

Unfortunately, our other generals did not possess Dumouriez's genius, or,
possessing it, did not know how to use it. At the very moment when each
commander should have been at his post to defend the portion of the
frontier intrusted to his charge, with troops familiar with the country, the
Minister of War and Marshal Luckner decided on a most extraordinary
and dangerous movement. This was to transfer Marshal Luckner to Metz,
and to bring the army now quartered at Metz to Valenciennes. This move-

ment left the frontier unprotected for several days, and enfeebled both armies by a march of forty-five leagues in the middle of July. Some political combination could alone explain this manœuvre.

However this may have been, on the 10th of July, while Dumouriez was engaged in planning the fortifications of Orchies, a courier arrived from Luckner, who ordered him to report immediately at Valenciennes. He started at once. The marshal received him cordially, and not without some embarrassment acquainted him with the movement, which was to begin the next morning at daybreak. Then, without giving Dumouriez time to open his lips, he added: "I shall leave here all my rear guard, composed of six battalions of infantry and five companies of cavalry. Nor shall I take any of the men from Maulde, Mauberge, or Dunkirk. Those who are left will constitute a sufficiently strong force to guard against any accident during the week or ten days required for the transit of the troops. You will be in command of these men, and of the department of the North until the arrival of General Dillon, to whom you will resign your charge."

There were several good reasons why Dumouriez should dislike to serve under Dillon, who was certainly a brave, talented and loyal officer, but terribly ambitious, and the possessor of a most ungovernable temper. Still, he displayed no discontent, but simply said to Marshal Luckner that he would obey him, although he considered the movement extremely injudicious and very likely to prove disastrous.

The events that followed proved that he was right in this opinion. The Austrians, encamped at Tournay, no sooner heard of Luckner's departure through their spies, than they organised a corps of five thousand men, and attacked Orchies, which was garrisoned by a battalion of volunteers, two field pieces and thirty dragoons.

The Austrians attacked the town fiercely upon two sides. There had not been time to complete the fortifications ordered and planned by Dumouriez. Still the little band defended themselves with great courage, but overpowered by numbers, they were finally obliged to retreat to Saint Amand, leaving one of their cannon in the hands of the enemy. One captain, named Thory, covered himself with glory in this affair ; and it was to his bravery and *sang-froid* that the remnant of the battalion owed its salvation.

That same evening, Dumouriez heard of the disaster. He started at once with all the men that Luckner had left him, and the next morning, at daybreak, he reached Saint Amand. In obedience to his orders, Beurnonville had already assembled the troops encamped at Maulde, and was advancing by forced marches to cut off the enemy's retreat. On another side, the commander of Douai was advancing with eight hundred men. The Austrians would certainly have been entrapped had they not executed a hasty retreat during the night, and regained their previous positions. However, this attack taught Dumouriez a lesson. He saw plainly that if he allowed the small force which Luckner had left him to remain scattered, it would gradually be fritted away, while, at the same time, it was impossible for the troops to render the frontier any efficient protection. He then decided, upon his own responsibility, to combine these scattered detachments into a single corps, capable of strong resistance, and even able, in case of need, to inflict serious injury upon the enemy. The camp at Maulde seemed to him the best position. So he installed himself there with his entire forces, threw up new earthworks, and did his best to harass and annoy the enemy while awaiting the arrival of Dillon, for which he was eagerly longing.

Dumouriez afterwards confessed that never in his whole life had he been so deeply discouraged. There seemed to be no hope for him in the future. His enemies had a majority in the ministry, and he knew that he was equally hated by the two parties who were struggling for ascendency. Conscious of his own valour and military talent, he saw himself condemned to spend his life in a subordinate position, at the orders of factions and incompetent generals, whose minds were engrossed with politics instead of war. "There is only one course for me to pursue," he wrote to a trusted friend; "that is to sink into oblivion. I am going to perform my duty mechanically hereafter—after the manner of oxen, which follow a beaten path without a thought of the purpose they serve, or the object for which they are labouring. And, however valuable my ideas may be, I will keep them to myself. The *rôle* of counsellor is a thankless one, and one that wins a man nothing but enemies, whether he be right or wrong."

This was a wise resolution, but it was far more difficult for a man of his temperament to follow it than to take it. And so when General Dillon arrived, Dumouriez's first care, after resigning his command, was to communicate his views and to try and induce his successor to assume the offensive. But General Dillon was not disposed to listen to Dumouriez's advice. It had always been his opinion that a man must be a fool to think of making an attack when he had already proved that he was unable to defend himself. Moreover, he witnessed with jealousy Dumouriez's influence over the troops, and the extent of their affection for him. Besides the sycophants on his staff had always told him that Dumouriez, merely because he had been a Minister of State, put on airs of superiority, scoffed at his brother officers, and opposed their plans whenever it was possible to do so.

Still, in spite of all this, Dillon was too honest a man, and too true a patriot, to abuse his power and injure an officer whose merit he could not fail to recognise. So he contented himself with thanking Dumouriez very coldly for his advice, and telling him that he would think of it. He reinstated him in command of the camp at Maulde, augmenting the force stationed there to a corps composed of twenty-three regiments of regulars, as many volunteers, and five companies of dragoons.

With twelve or thirteen thousand men under his orders, Dumouriez was himself again, and plucked up fresh courage. Knowing the laxity of discipline that generally prevailed in the army, he felt that the day was not far distant when France would find herself almost without defence against her foes. Convinced of this, he conceived the project of forming a corps of superior soldiers, which could be made the nucleus of an effective army in the hour of extreme peril. This plan once formed he devoted all his time to it. From morning until night, in fair weather and foul, he might have been seen on horseback, hurrying here and there, clad in an old and ragged uniform. There was not a single detail that escaped his vigilant eyes. The provisions, the ammunition, the equipments—he examined everything. Ah! he would never have given his soldiers those famous paper shoes that created such a scandal in '93. With indefatigable patience he taught, or rather prepared, the instructors who were afterwards to form his troops. And when evening came he convened the officers in his tent, and the lessons were begun again. Wrapped in his cloak he slept on the ground like the common soldiers, and it was to their mess-pot that he usually sent for his dinner.

Their close promixity to the enemy, and the consequent danger that threatened them at any moment. dispelled the *ennui* of camp life, and to lend it a tinge of romance there were the Demoiselles Fernig, in hussar costume, acting in the capacity of aides-de-camp. Dumouriez began by organizing two corps, each numbering four or five hundred men, who were despatched every day on a reconnoitering expedition. The officers and men of these corps relinquished their places to others at the expiration of a week ; so that each soldier, in his turn, became accustomed to the enemy, and to fatigue. The commander of each detachment received written orders from the general, and at the same time a sketch map upon which the roads, bridges, villages, and forests through which he was to pass, with the points to attack, and the places to station outposts, were all care-fully indicated.

These expeditions were generally successful, and brought many horses, cattle, and prisoners into camp. There was no bickering nor idleness in that army. Nor was there a Jacobin, a Girondin, or a Feuillant among the men. Each man was a soldier. General Dillon, whose troops were al-ways on the eve of a revolt, was positively astonished.

Though Dumouriez had achieved these wonderful results, his mind was so completely engrossed in purely military matters that, at the time the news of the Prussian invasion reached Paris, he really believed himself for-gotten. I have described, my friends, the anger of France. I have told you how the very earth shook beneath the feet of the gathering legions. But these champions of a holy cause required a leader.

They needed a commander who would know how to make effective use of the noble blood which was ready and eager to be shed for the country's salvation. Then it was that the National Assembly and the Ministry gave the world a sublime example of patriotism. They fixed their choice on Dumouriez, and yet God knows that they had no love for him.

The ministers then in power were the very men who had been set aside when Dumouriez was minister of Foreign Affairs. The Girondins and the Jacobins of the National Assembly hated him equally. One party had ac-cused him of duplicity and ingratitude ; the other had suspected him of betraying the revolutionary cause.

But that made no difference. From the moment that invaded France was in danger party feuds were forgotten, or rather a laudable spirit of self-abnegation and sacrifice took possession of all parties. Every man gloried in the renunciation of his most firmly rooted predjudices ; every man repeated the saying of Gensonné : "There is no rancour in a patriot's heart which is not effaced by hatred of the foreigner."

One timid voice was heard to say : "Dumouriez is ambitious, Dumouriez is an intriguant of the *ancien regime!*" But twenty deputies sprang up to exclaim : "What does that matter, if he is the only man who can arrest the progress of Brunswick?" And then Danton, at that time Minister of Justice, rose to add : "Dumouriez loves glory too much not to wish to conquer at any cost."

So it was by almost unanimous consent that they selected Dumouriez to confide the destinies of the nation into his keeping. They dismissed, or subor-dinated to him, all the marshals and officers who could have ventured to aspire to the position of commander-in-chief. Luckner was sent to Châlons to organize the recruits. Dillon and Kellermann received orders to yield im-plicit obedience. Force and power —everything was concentrated in the hand of the man from whom everything was expected.

Dumouriez, as a general rule, was promptly informed of all the doings of the National Assembly, but this time he was in complete ignorance of what had occurred. Standing near the outskirts of the camp, with the youngest of the Demoiselles Fernig by his side, he was watching some soldiers erecting palisades, when a carriage drew up ten paces from him. It was a rickety old equipage, drawn by two superannuated horses with dilapidated artillery harness. Three men, clad in the costume of deputies of the National Assembly, alighted, while a fourth, who was still young, remained in the vehicle. The three deputies were Delmas, Dubois, Dubaye, and Bellegarde. The young man half reclining in the carriage, with his limbs enveloped in furs, was none other than Couthon, to whom the Revolution was destined to lend a tragical renown, and who had taken up his abode a short time before at Saint Amand, near the camp, in the hope that the medicinal waters of the village would cure the paralysis he was suffering from.

Dumouriez knew them all, and yet he did not stir from his place. Such was his situation, indeed, that he really believed they had been sent to arrest him. However, they came forward, and the eldest, Bellegarde, drawing a paper from his pocket, began to read to Dumouriez the decree constituting him commander-in-chief.

Many years later the youngest of the Demoiselles Fernig, in requesting a licence for a tobacco shop, described the whole scene in her petition to the Government. Dumouriez became extremely pale, and in a husky voice, and with the wondering air of a man who doubts the evidence of his own senses, he repeated : " Commander-in-chief !—Commander-in-chief ! "

Bellegarde continued : " The entire army is intrusted to you. From this moment you have absolute authority."

The man to whom he spoke was, of course, thunderstruck. He had suddenly attained heights to which his fancy in its most audacious moods had never soared ; and that at the moment when he believed himself about to sink into the lowest depths of obscurity. But he quickly recovered his composure, thanks to his wonderful self-control ; and it was in the coldest possible tone that he said : " At least, citizen representatives, you will grant me twenty-four hours for deliberation."

They interrupted him : " There is no time for reflection."

Never had Dumouriez been subjected to so severe a test. With a brusque gesture he pulled his hat down over his eyes, and began to walk aimlessly to and fro, terribly perplexed. Then, suddenly returning to the deputies, in a tone that betrayed all his distrust he asked : " Who will be my security ? "

" What ? " asked his visitors, as if they had not understood him.

" I may be—unsuccessful."

" Well."

" In that case, I may be accused of treachery—treason."

Not one of the three deputies responded. But from the interior of the carriage came the voice of the paralytic Couthon, who had heard the entire conversation, and who cried : " What ! Your country calls you, and you hesitate ! The country is in danger, and you think of self."

Dumouriez stood silent and thoughtful for a moment—then he who usually had all the readiness of speech, and all the vivacity peculiar to the children of the South, replied slowly, weighing each word with the greatest care : " It is more than life that you ask of me, citizen representatives : it is, perhaps, honour. I am not blind ; and I know the weight of responsibility which will devolve on me. If I am vanquished—and I probably shall be—my name will be handed down to posterity branded with the foul epithet of traitor."

" What does that matter ? " interrupted Couthon.

" Well, yes, what does it matter ? Vergniaud traced my line of conduct for me the day he exclaimed at the tribune—' Perish our memories, so that France be saved.' Citizens, I shall do my duty—I accept."

Meanwhile the rumour that three deputies had arrived on a mission from the National Assembly had spread through the camp. The soldiers had viewed, at first with astonishment and afterwards with anxiety, this carriage which had passed through their lines. And the same idea entered every brain : " They have come to take away our general ! " "Ah ! that is something we will not permit," was the universal cry. And seizing their arms, they hurried to the scene of the interview. Soon several hundred soldiers were gathered around Dumouriez and the envoys of the National Assembly. But when they understood what was going on, when they realised that the dignity of commander-in-chief had been offered to their general, and when they heard Dumouriez reply : " I accept," then their joy overflowed in loud shouts of : " Vive la nation ! Vive Dumouriez ! "

In fact, there was not a single soldier who did not feel flattered by the Assembly's choice—not one who was not persuaded that some of his general's glory would reflect upon himself ; for these men worshipped their leader. But their joy was soon dimmed by the thought that they would lose their idolized commander. " Now that he commands all the armies he will leave us ! " So this is why, after the deputies had retired, all the troops gathered around Dumouriez's tent and entreated him to remain at their head.

How could he fail to be touched by these proofs of attachment on the part of these volunteers whom he had subjected to the severest discipline ? He promised them that he would not desert them. He was now in a position to carry out his former plan. Absolute master, henceforth, he could institute an offensive warfare, the project he had cherished so long and so hopelessly. Dumouriez believed that it would be impossible to defeat Brunswick in France, and drive him from our territory ; but he was persuaded that a strong blow struck in the Netherlands would inevitably cause the Prussians to return to their own country. And in the event of carrying this project into execution, it was upon his own soldiers that he depended for the boldness and rapidity of action necessary to disconcert the enemy. The very night following the visit of the deputies, Dumouriez's plan of campaign was clearly arranged in his mind, carefully drawn up, and despatched to the Assembly in the form of a memorial. And the very next day, he began to organize his army of invasion and to select his leaders.

Unfortunately, this last undertaking presented enormous difficulties. Would the generals obey him ? And even if they dared not revolt openly, would they not follow his instructions with that artful awkwardness which makes the cleverest schemes abortive? But Dumouriez was a shrewd diplomatist, as well as a talented military leader. To interest a dozen or more generals in the success of his plans, to flatter their self love, to utilize their distrust of one another, to arouse a spirt of emulation among them, and still hold their ambition in check —this was only child's play for a man who had once been the chosen agent of M. de Choiseul, for a man who had almost succeeded in reuniting Poland. His first effort in this direction was a master-stroke. He persuaded Dillon, who believed himself entitled to the position of commander-in-chief—Dillion, with whom he had always been at odds, and whose subordinate he had been only the evening before—

he persuaded Dillon to embrace his (Dumouriez's) views, and to take a prominent part in a plan which he had openly sneered at a short time before.

However, many unforeseen circumstances conspired to defeat Dumouriez's long-cherished project. He had completed his arrangements for an attack on the Netherlands; his officers had received orders to march, even the rations for the campaign had been distributed. The confidence of the troops was absolute, the enthusiasm intense, and the movement was to begin on the day but one following, when another emissary from the Assembly arrived at the camp; not in an official capacity, it is true, but none the less the bearer of the last decision of the Ministry. This emissary was Westermann. An Alsatian by birth, concealing the most consummate shrewdness beneath the brusque good-nature of a peasant, Westermann was the friend of Danton, then Minister of Justice and all powerful, and he remained his faithful and devoted friend until death. Appointed a lieutenant-colonel after the 10th of August, Westermann had retained his coolness at a time when delirium had seized every brain. He understood the situation, and was courageous enough to say that discipline alone—and an iron discipline—could render the army in which lay our only hope of salvation, effective. He held that the soldier who received an order must execute it, and that he was not a slave because he obeyed. And he declared that the dismissal of a talented general merely because he was of noble birth, was a piece of arrant stupidity; and it made him indignant to hear every officer who happened to be unfortunate, vilified by the name of traitor.

Such a man could not fail to sympathize with Dumouriez. The soldiers saw them walking about arm-in-arm for more than an hour. What were they talking about? Every one in camp was wondering. It was impossible to catch a sentence, or even to seize a single word of the conversation. The sentries kept the curious at a distance, and even the Demoiselles Fernig were forbidden to approach.

Sent by Danton, Westermann had come to inform Dumouriez of the first successes of the Duke of Brunswick, and the treachery at Longwy and Verdun. He came to tell him that the time for offensive warfare had passed, and that the Prussians were almost in the heart of France, that they were threatening Paris, and that they must be driven back at any price. Hesitation was out of the question. So Dumouriez replied that he would leave the camp at once, and hasten to Sedan to assume command of the army which Lafayette had recently abandoned. He spent the night in countermanding previous orders, and in dictating new instructions; promising—what no one believed—that he would return in six weeks, and that there would certainly be an expedition into Belgium before the close of the year.

But there was a great disturbance in the camp as soon as the soldiers heard that their general was going away. However, he quieted his men, who were loudly begging to be allowed to follow him, by explaining the necessity of their presence at Maulde, and by telling them how much they would embarrass and retard him on his journey. And the next morning, at daybreak, he set off on horseback, accompanied by Westermann, a single aide-de-camp, the youngest of the Demoiselles Fernig, and Baptiste, his faithful valet.

On arriving at Sedan, he found the condition of things much worse than had been represented. The army was divided into two corps. The advance-guard, numbering six thousand men, occupied on the right bank of the Meuse, a position, for the defence of which at least forty thousand men would have been required. The second corps, scarcely eighteen thousand strong, was encamped three leagues farther back on some hills overlooking Sedan. Never was a position worse chosen. Everybody saw this so plainly that the consternation was universal. The soldiers regarded their officers as traitors ; and considered this to be a sufficient excuse for their indiscipline and disobedience. And the officers were in such fear of their soldiers, that they did not dare to insist upon obedience. No one gave any orders ; provisions were no longer brought to the camp ; ammunition was lacking ; and entire regiments went off to plunder and pillage the country for leagues around. Certainly if the Duke of Brunswick had advanced upon Sedan with only ten thousand men, the French army would have disbanded, have taken refuge in the nearest fortress, or have fled to Paris.

On arriving at Sedan, Dumouriez began operations by ordering a fresh horse and reviewing his new troops. The appearance of everything was extremely discouraging. The cavalry, especially, was in a deplorable condition. While inspecting a company of grenadiers, Dumouriez heard one of them remark, pointing to him : "That is the rascal who declared war." This was a report which had been circulated among the soldiers in order to make Dumouriez unpopular. He knew it ; so pausing and confronting the soldier, he asked : "Is there anyone here sufficiently cowardly to wish for peace ? Do you expect to gain your liberty without fighting for it ?"

These words had a good effect, and seemed to revive the spirits of everybody. But the situation was none the less desperate. The army had no superior officers ; it was rent by factions, and ready to revolt. The troops were not acquainted with their new commander ; and they were the more distrustful of him as he had never held any active military position of importance, and was known as a writer rather than a soldier.

He did not know a single regiment, nor a single officer, in this division ; nor had he ever studied the region of country he was now called upon to defend.

On whichever side he turned he found fear, distrust, treachery, or aversion. The fate of Longwy and Verdun taught him how little dependence he could place on the resistance of fortresses. Moreover, Sedan was not in a condition to stand a week's siege, and Mezières was in no better plight. And last, but not least, he had only twenty-three thousand demoralised soldiers to oppose one hundred thousand of the best disciplined troops in Europe, under the leadership of an illustrious general.

And yet he was compelled to abandon the mountains, where the enemy's magnificent cavalry would be useless, first, for the broad plains of Champagne, and afterwards for the open country that stretches between the Marne and the Seine. And what aid could he expect ? None. The army he had just left was too far away to be of any service. The army at Metz had enough to do to protect that city, which, by some deplorable oversight, had not been put in a condition to withstand a siege. Paris remained : but what could Paris send him ? Only a few hastily enrolled battalions of volunteers, burning with enthusiasm, no doubt, but undisciplined, destitute of officers, and barely knowing how to fire a gun.

Dumouriez faced this gloomy prospect with indomitable firmness. Officers and men regained confidence when they saw the imperturbable assurance and even cheerfulness of their commander-in-chief, who only took the deputies from the Assembly into his confidence, respecting the formidable strength of the enemy's resources, the weakness of his own,

and our correspondingly poor chance of success. He confessed, indeed, to
the representatives, that he did not entertain the slightest hope of defeat-
ing Brunswick and his army of one hundred thousand men, elated by
their recent victories. He only hoped to check their progress, or to retard
their advance. But to check their progress for a month, or even for a fortnight, was to vanquish them. For this would give France time to organise
a second army which would protect Paris, and take the place of the first
one in case that were worsted. "But to succeed in this, citizen representatives," added Dumouriez, "the National Assembly and the army
must have but a single thought—to repulse the enemy. We, who are
here, are ready to sacrifice the last drop of our blood ; you, iu Paris, must
sacrifice your animosity and rivalry. For every lover of his country there
must henceforth be but one cry, 'Out with the Prussians ! and long live
France !' "

On the evening preceding the departure of the deputies, Dumouriez held
a council of war at the miserable inn where he had established his head-
quarters. Lieutenant-general Dillon, Adjutant-Generals Vouillers, Chazot,
and Thouvenot, and Petiot, the chief of the commissariat service, a man of
great merit, were among those present at the conference. After showing
them a map of the Champagne aud informing them that the Prussians had
captured Longwy and Verdun, and were now threatening Metz, so that a
union with Marshal Luckner's forces was quite out of the question ; after
stating that turn which way they would, they could not hope for reinforcements under two or three weeks, and that the country was therefore
dependent upon the little army encamped about Sedan for her salvation,
Dumouriez continued : " Our forces are only one-fourth as large as those
of the Prussians, it is true ; but our cavalry is the best that France possesses, and our infantry has been disciplined and hardened by more than a
year of camp-life, by long marches and incessant skirmishing. Moreover,
our artillery is excellent, and numbers more than sixty field-pieces, besides
the regimental cannon. Passing from this statement of our condition to an
examination of the enemy's situation, I may be allowed to say that the
Prussians will naturally be delayed, and their number diminished, by the
necessity of besieging fortresses, and assuring their communications as well
as by the difficulty of procuring supplies, by the length of their baggage-
trains, by the very magnitude of their army, and, above all, by the
enormous quantity of artillery they possess. And last, but not least, the
presence of the king and the numerous princes of his suite, all provided
with gorgeous equipages and hosts of servants, must contribute not a little
to retard the progress of the invaders."

The conclusion Dumouriez drew from all this, was that it would be an
irreparable blunder to remain any longer at Sedan, and that it was by all
means advisable to take the field at once. It was the first council of war
that he had ever convened ; and it was the last while he was in command
of the army. It was his opinion that the decision should come from the
person who was to bear the responsibility ; and that to communicate one's
plans to one's subordinates would only suit a weak and undecided leader
who was endeavouring to provide the means of excusing himself in case of
failure. But, on this occasiou, Dumouriez wished to test the characters
and dispositions of his generals, and to discover which one of them could
be depended upon.

Lieutenant-General Dillon thought it advisable to retreat across the
Marne, and reach Châlons in advance of the enemy. He said, with great

truth, that if the Prussians forestalled us, they would be between Paris and our army; and that the salvation of the capital was of greater importance than the preservation of a province which we were not sure of defending effectually. Dillon concluded by advising Dumouriez to leave General Chazot at Sedan with a small force, and to transfer the rest of the army with all possible rapidity, by way of Sainte Ménéhould, to Châlons or even to Rheims, if Châlons were already occupied by the enemy. They would thus be able to shelter themselves behind the Marne, and, by closely guarding the river, and preventing the passage of the enemy's troops, they could await the arrival of reinforcements, and afterwards assume the offensive. This advice was supported by such strong arguments that it was adopted by the Council. Dumouriez then rose, said that he would reflect, and ordered Dillon to take command of the advance-guard, and to cross over to the left bank of the Marne and encamp at Mouzon.

The party separated, Dumouriez keeping with him only Adjutant-General Thouvenot. He had studied this officer attentively while the conference was going on, and he believed that he could detect in him a superior mind, and opinions in harmony with his own. He was not mistaken in this, and from that evening, Thouvenot became his faithful friend—his right arm. Thoroughly acquainted with his profession, versed in all the details of camp-life, reconnaissances and marches, endowed with great courage, indefatigable activity, and an extraordinary fecundity of invention in trying moments, Thouvenot was the best assistant that a general-in-chief could possibly desire. As soon as they were alone, Dumouriez told him that he did not approve of this proposed retreat to Châlons. It simply meant to abandon Lorraine and the Ardennes, and to recapture them after the enemy had fortified his positions. The Prussians, too, would soon be upon the heels of the retreating army, and in that case, the retreat would speedily degenerate into a rout. And if they retreated across the Marne, Châlons, Soissons and Rheims would inevitably be sacrificed. The enemy would also be in a position to cut off all communications between Luckner's army and the troops stationed at Maulde.

To station the French army at Châlons was to open for the King of Prussia and his generalissimo a road to Paris, either by way of Rheims, Epernay, Vitry, or Troyes. Moreover, if the Prussians once became masters of the Ardennes and Lorraine, it was more than likely that they would go into winter-quarters there and wait for reinforcements. Besides, was there any certainty that the French army could defend the passage of the Marne at Châlons? Assuredly not. And this much was positive : the river once crossed, the Prussians could drive the French army back to Paris, or destroy it *en route* by means of their numerous and efficient cavalry.

Convinced by this clear statement of the case, Thouvenot held his peace. And then Dumouriez, pointing to the forest of Argonne upon the map, exclaimed : " There are the Thermopylæ of France ! If I am fortunate enough to reach that point before the Prussians, they are lost ! "

His country's imminent danger had elevated Dumouriez's military talent to positive genius. Thouvenot was so deeply impressed with this fact, that, overcome with emotion, he threw himself on Dumouriez's neck, exclaiming : " Now, indeed, France is saved ! " And then they decided upon the new plan of campaign together.

This plan had many great advantages. First, our line of defence was not strictly confined to the Marne ; secondly, it compelled the Prussians to lose a great deal of valuable time, and to remain in Champagne Pouilleuse, where the barren soil did not furnish adequate supplies for an army of one hundred thousand men. However, if the march through the forest of Argonne was opposed, would not the Prussians endeavour to circumvent the French by passing round it? That was possible, and even probable. But if the enemy tried to proceed in the direction of Sedan, that fortress would offer a vigorous opposition to their passage; if, on the contrary, they attempted to advance by way of Metz, the French, under Kellermann, could meet them and give Dumouriez time to hasten up and attack them in the rear, thus bringing them between two fires.

But I must give you some idea of the ground which Dumouriez had selected for this conflict which was to decide the destinies of France. The forest of Argonne is a stretch of woods extending from Sedan to Passavant, more than a league beyond Sainte Menéhould. Even from that point, patches of forest, intersected by plains, extend towards Bar-le-Duc; but Argonne, properly speaking, only reaches as far as Passavant; that is to say, a distance of thirteen leagues. It is extremely unequal in width. In some parts, the forest is three or four leagues wide : in others, scarcely half a league. It separates the rich and fertile province of the Trois-Evêchés from Champagne Pouilleuse, or "lousy Champagne," the most sterile district in France; a district where the soil is a tenacious clay, and where one finds hardly any trees, streams, or pasturage: only a few insignificant villages being scattered at wide intervals over the desolate region, whose inhabitants find it a difficult task to wrest a meagre subsistence from the ungrateful soil.

Intersected by mountains, rivers and marshes, the forest of Argonne presents but five passes through which an enemy could advance : the Chêne-Populeux, the Croix-aux-Bois, the Grand-Pré, the Chalade and the Islettes. Now these passages had to be occupied, and the Prussian advance by any one of them arrested. Dumouriez decided that General Dillon, with five thousand men, should defend the pass of the Islettes, and send a strong detachment to guard the Chalade route. He intrusted the defence of the Croix-aux-Bois to a detachment under the command of General Chazot; and reserved for himself the Grand-Pré pass. As for the defile known as the Chêne-Populeux, he was for want of a sufficient force obliged to leave it unguarded for a time. But he expected reinforcements. General Duval was coming to his aid with four thousand men, and Beurnonville had been ordered to hasten the advance of the well-disciplined troops from Maulde, as much as possible, while Rheims stood ready to send four cannon and eighteen hundred men, fully armed and equipped.

The plan was bold and in execution it was an extremely difficult one. The merest trifle might awaken the suspicion of the Prussians;—the slightest indiscretion—a report from one of the spies who had spread over the country—a single blunder in the movements of the French army. If the enemy were informed of our plans, they would hasten to take possession of the very passes in which we hoped to arrest them, and it would be all over with us. But Dumouriez surpassed himself in the skilful arrangement and execution of his plans. His courage, discernment and promptitude were really marvellous.

From Sedan, the position he then held, to Grand-Pré, the position he wished to occupy, there was either twelve or twenty leagues, according as he took the road in front or in the rear of the forest of Argonne. If he took the first route, there was great danger that the Prussians would discover his plans. If he chose the second one, there was great danger that he would be attacked while on the march, and lose his camp-train, and artillery. After profound reflection, he decided upon another and far more audacious plan, which proved successful. He concluded, since the enemy made no offensive movements on the west bank of the Meuse, that the force stationed there must be very small, merely a picket-guard, which would beat a hasty retreat across the river if it discovered any movement on the part of the French army. Acting upon this conviction, he resorted to strategy. Behind Stenay there was an excellent position known as the Camp de Brouenne. Dumouriez had not the slightest doubt but what the enemy would hasten to take possession of it, as soon as they discovered that the French were advancing. So he divided his force into three corps. The first was ordered to attack Stenay, while he assumed command of the second division, consisting of twelve thousand men without baggage. This corps he intended to use as a support for the advance-guard; while at the same time, General Chazot, with five thousand men, removed the camp equipage by way of Tannay.

If you suppose that Dumouriez's subordinates were pleased at the turn which affairs had taken, you are greatly mistaken. Some officers, less intelligent than Thouvenot, did not understand the plan they were executing; others were indignant because their advice had not been followed. Dillon obeyed orders, mindful of the promise he had made, but as his vow did not forbid him to grumble, he did grumble, and that so loudly that the officers and even the men heard him. "The fool is walking us straight into a trap," said he. "We shall be in a nice fix when he gets us shut up in the defiles of the Argonne."

The language of the other officers was not much more complimentary; and their discontent increased to such a degree that one fine morning, while the army was on the move, five or six of them came to ask an audience of Dumouriez. He complied with their request at once, and the most eloquent of the party proceeded to air his grievances and those of his friends. It was a long story, but Dumouriez patiently heard him to the end; but when he had concluded. "Comrades," he replied, "this is very like a council of war, and councils of war are only held at my orders. When I ask for your advice, it is the duty of each of you to give me the best you have to offer. But I alone am responsible: and I know what I am doing. Return, each of you to his post, and merely think of carrying out my orders faithfully."

Dumouriez's firm attitude was worth almost as much to him as a victory, in the sense that it brought over to his side all the officers who had no personal grievance against him. General Chazot said: "This young man would not be so arrogant if he was not sure of the success of his plans. Let us hold our peace, and help him as far as lies in our power."

The others, who were now compelled to conceal their dissatisfaction, decided to write to Paris and complain of the commander-in-chief, painting the situation in colours even more gloomy than the reality, and trying to convince their friends in the National Assembly that this forest of Argonne was to become the tomb of the French army. Though he was aware of their manœuvres, Dumouriez treated them all with equal courtesy. "They are obstinate," he remarked to Thouvenot, "and there is only one way to convince them—that is to succeed."

Almost any other general would have been compelled to yield to the murmurers, or at least to modify his plan; but Dumouriez, fortunately, had near him, and for him—always ready to sustain him and vouch for him—Westermann, who represented the thought and the will of Danton, now Minister of War and all-powerful in the Assembly as well as in the Cabinet. Now Westermann, having enthusiastically adopted the plans of the commander-in-chief, would listen to no objection. When Dillon essayed, in covert words, to predict an approaching defeat, Westermann looked him straight in the eyes and replied in words the significance of which, at that epoch, was terrible enough to make the bravest men turn pale : "Do you really wish it ? One would almost suppose so."

For the hero of the 10th of August never trifled when discipline was in question. Many volunteers, when he arrived at head-quarters, imagined that he would listen patiently, even sympathetically, to their complaints. They were quickly undeceived. If you could only have seen the air with which he listened to their murmurs, and the tone in which he shouted: "Are these sacrifices worthy of mention when they are made for your country ? To the right about, and back to the ranks ! "

He was even more determined than Dumouriez in his refusal to restore Laveneur to his former rank. The latter was an impulsive man who had been misled by friendly feeling. An intimate friend of Lafayette, whose aide-de-camp he had been, he thought it his duty to follow that general when, after the 10th of August, he deserted his army and went over to the enemy. But with Laveneur it was only a momentary madness. He no sooner felt the enemy's soil beneath his feet than despair seized hold of him, and he returned to France even more quickly than he had left it. Holding the rank of lieutenant-general when he left France, he thought they would be only too glad to give him back his epaulettes and his old position in an army which stood greatly in need of commanding officers. But neither Dumouriez nor Westermann would listen to this for a moment. "You lost your rank the day you crossed the frontier," they declared.

Tears sprang to Laveneur's eyes. "What! you reject me, when the country has need of all her children ? " he exclaimed. And as the others made no reply, "I *will* fight ! " he insisted, passionately.

Then Dumouriez coldly responded : "One of our hussars died last night, I am told. I authorise you to take his horse, his weapons, and his place in the ranks."

Laveneur asked nothing more. "I thank you," he answered, promptly. "I shall not remain a private long."

He kept his word ; and his name is linked with one of the most audacious exploits of the campaign of '92. It occurred after the battle of Jemmapes. General Valence had entered Namur after the capitulation of the city ; but six thousand of the enemy's soldiers had shut themselves up in the castle, and now undertook to dictate terms to the French army. Orders were immediately given to storm the castle ; but it was first necessary to obtain possession of Fort Vilatte which guarded the entrance ; and an attack upon this was extremely dangerous on account of a network of mines placed beneath the *glacis* by the defenders of the position.

It was Laveneur who planned the capture of the garrison, proposing to take the enemy by surprise. To the left of the castle there was an almost inaccessible path, defended by parapets and palisades. This path led to the fort. At midnight, under the guidance of a deserter, Laveneur sallied forth at the head of two hundred men. The little band marched on through the darkness in profound silence, and at last they reached the line of parapets. These were not guarded, or the sentinels were asleep ; for Laveneur and his men leaped the barrier unchallenged and unmolested. But when they reached the palisades, the sentinels there gave the alarm and fired. The danger was so terrible that Laveneur's men hesitated ; he sprang forward, but found that he was too small of stature to leap over the palisades. "Throw me over," he exclaimed, imperiously, addressing a very tall and robust officer who chanced to be standing beside him. The officer obeyed, and then followed his chief, while several grenadiers, inspired by such an heroic example, imitated it in spite of a murderous fusillade.

Laveneur had escaped uninjured. He sprang up and ran to the commander of the position, who was trying to rally his men, seized him by the collar, and pointing his sword at his breast, said : "Lead me to the mines." The astonished officer hesitated. "Lead me to the mines," repeated Laveneur in a terrible voice ; "and instantly, or you are a dead man !" At the same time he pressed the point of his sword still closer to his enemy's breast.

The frightened commander, losing his presence of mind, hastened to obey, and Laveneur, following his directions, tore away the matches with his own hands. An hour later, the garrison surrendered, and the next day the castle, with its six thousand defenders, was in Laveneur's power.

Ah, well ! this was the man who was compelled to assume the jacket of a simple hussar. The surprise of the soldiers was great, it must be confessed ; but the effect was admirable, and perhaps decisive. It is so often true that trifling circumstances produce great results. This fact really decided the discipline of the troops ; and the mutinous volunteers said to one another : "There is no foolishness about the general." And seeing a man of Laveneur's temper obey Dumouriez uncomplainingly, they added : "We may as well obey him too."

Everything promised well at the outset of this campaign which was to decide the fate of France, and circumstances seemed to unite in rewarding Dumouriez for his promptness and shrewdness. At each step of the difficult movements which he was making with a view to reaching the defiles of the Argonne in advance of the Prussians, some bit of good news awaited him. The advance-guard of the Prussian army had] fallen into the snare he had set for it, and had retreated before Dillon's threatening demonstrations. Several new pieces of artillery had been received at Châlons. The troops from Maulde, delighted with the prospect of rejoining their adored general, were making forced marches each day. And Kellermann sent one of his aides-de-camp with promises of faithful aid.

On the 4th of September, Dumouriez felt that he could at last pause to take breath. He held the defiles of the Argonne, and was himself in command at Grand-Pré. It was at this time he wrote to the National Assembly that celebrated letter in which he said : "Now I await the Prussians—I am at Thermopylæ, but, more fortunate than Leonidas, I shall not perish there."

Then, my friends, the soldiers began to share the hopes of their commander. Faith illumined their pathway through the forest with her gleaming torch. Anyone who despaired of success would have been considered a coward—a traitor. Among all these volunteers, torn only a few evenings before from their workshops or from their counters, there was not one who would not have sacrificed his life for his country cheerfully, even joyfully. And when an army has no fear of death, it is invincible.

At night, when the men gathered around the camp fires heedless of the falling rain, hunger, and privations, they said, one to another : "Let the Prussians come. They shall see how hard we Frenchmen die !" And the men of culture—for there were many such in the army of liberty—and the philosophically inclined, added : "Éven though the Prussians kill us, the idea that animates us—the idea of liberty—will escape from our gaping wounds and avenge us ! "

I was there, my friends—and with a soul inspired with the most ardent enthusiasm, I said to myself : " O France, sacred and adored mother for whom we are ready to shed our last drop of blood—if ever in the future similar danger threatens thee, God grant that thy children—our children—may be worthy of us, and that they may be willing to die to save thee from the slightest taint of dishonour ! "

It was now the 13th of September. The rainy reason had made the roads almost impassable. The Prussians having consumed all the provisions at Longwy and Verdun, and eaten up the country already exhausted by the French army, were obliged to send to Trèves or Luxemburg for their supplies. The garrisons of Montmedy, Thionville, and even Metz, were beginning to wage an implacable war with the invaders, threatening their communications and capturing their provision trains. On the 14th, Beurnonville was to arrive with reinforcements at Réthel, ten miles from Grand-Pré. Kellermann was to be at Bar, on the 18th and after that, a junction with him would require only a little dexterous management and address.

The attacks upon the Prussians had greatly increased the courage of the French army, while on the other hand the king of Prussia and his generalissimo were becoming alarmed. The popular movement upon which they had counted had not taken place. On the contrary, the peasants, who had been terrified at first by the duke's threatening manifesto, were regaining courage and beginning to bring out their old muskets from their hiding-places. The Prussian soldiers began to suffer from hunger, and when these robust Northerners do not eat heartily, they soon fall ill. They could be seen wandering along the roads, their cheeks pale and hollow, and their eyes glittering with fever, in quest of unripe fruit, which was actual poison to their disordered stomachs, and which predisposed them to attacks of dysentery.

Then, the men who had slandered Dumouriez became his champions and flatterers. By extravagant praise they endeavoured to make him forget their former abuse ; and they urged him to give the foe battle. " With an army like yours, victory is certain," they said to him.

But he, cool and unmoved in the midst of all this tumult and excitement, tranquilly responded : " Leave it to the weather ; leave it ⁓o the rains. I give battle ? No ; I am not such a fool ! I might lose it. Let us shut ourselves up in our fortified positions, beyond the reach of the Prussians, convert the surrounding country into a desolate waste, cut off their supplies, harass them, tire them out, and teach them that France is a desert in which they must wander about like famished wolves. Thus we shall conquer without a battle."

Fortune seemed to be steadily favouring us, when a blunder committed by Dumouriez changed the entire aspect of affairs, and placed the country in a more critical and dangerous position than before. At the pass known as the Croix-aux-Bois, the general had stationed a colonel of dragoons with his regiment, two battalions of grenadiers, and four field-pieces. This force seemed to him quite sufficient to defend this difficult pass. Moreover, the colonel assured him that he had carefully obeyed orders ; that his entrenchments were impregnable, and that he had rendered the road impassable by means of trenches and pits. The colonel added that there was a well-drilled battalion of volunteers from the Ardennes at Vouziers, and that if these men were provided with guns and ammunition, and united with one of the regiments previously belonging to the garrison at Longwy, the force would be more than sufficient for the defence of this defile. Such being the case, he asked permission to rejoin Dumouriez, bringing with him one of the battalions under his command, as well as three companies from his own regiment. Dumouriez, without further inquiry, and with unpardonable carelessness in a commander-in-chief, acted upon the suggestion of this colonel, who had taken part in the American war, was of mature age, and seemed to be a person of excellent judgment.

The colonel's letter was dated September 11th. On the 12th Dumouriez sent him orders to leave two hundred men in the entrenchments, and to rejoin him with the remainder of his troops. At the same time he gave orders for six hundred muskets to be sent at once to the battalion from the Ardennes, with one hundred cartridges for each gun. He also ordered the leader of the Ardennes battalion to proceed at once to the Croix-aux-Bois, with his own men and three hundred of the National Gendarmes stationed at Vouziers.

Although the Croix-aux-Bois was near Grand-Pré, Dumouriez had never found time to visit this important post. He trusted entirely to his maps when he gave orders concerning the fortifications there ; but he should have known that maps, in France, at least, seem to have been made for the express purpose of deceiving those who consult them. It was his first mistake. He had not even sent Thouvenot, who would have done admirably in his stead. He had not even stationed a battery there, though he had plenty of cannon. But worst of all, he had relied upon the judgment of a subordinate of whom he knew little or nothing, although the man passed for a clever officer. As if he ought not to have known what to expect from a person who had never done anything to merit the reputation he had gained, but had won merely by his assurance, the honours which should be reserved for worth alone. A second mistake—which came near causing the complete failure of the admirable plan Dumouriez had conceived, and which, until now, had been so well conducted.

So on the morning of the 13th, the Croix-aux-Bois was abandoned by the colonel and the greater part of his troops ; and as if this were not misfortune enough, the chief of the ordnance department entirely forgot the order he had received, and sent no ammunition to the Ardennes battalion. Warned by their spies, the Prussians lost no time in trying to profit by these blunders, and by noon, on the second day following, they appeared in the defile in force. The abattis works had been so badly constructed, that they were scarcely an obstacle. And the road had been cut up so little that it was soon repaired sufficiently to give passage to the artillery. The men, about one hundred in number, who had been left at the post, endeavoured for a time to defend it ; but soon recognising the futility of their efforts, they disbanded, and made their way back to Dumouriez's camp as best they could.

The general was filled with consternation. He saw the Argonne, the rampart of France, in the power of the Prussians. Without losing a second, he gave General Chazot two brigades and twelve eight-pounders, ordering him to repair to the Croix-aux-Bois with all possible speed, and to recapture the position at any cost. "And no hesitation," he said, imperiously. "Don't give the Prussians time to strengthen their position. Charge them with the bayonet."

Unfortunately, Chazot did hesitate. He wasted one entire day, though on the morrow he succeeded in recapturing the position, but not without herculean efforts and a terrible conflict. If he had only known how to keep it. But no! He was scarcely master of it before he allowed his troops to rest, instead of setting them to work to erect new fortifications. The Prussians soon returned with reinforcements, attacked Chazot with irresistible fury, and forced him to retreat to Vouziers with the loss of his cannon. At the same time, another division of the Prussian army took possession of the pass known as the Chêne-Populeux.

But Dumouriez did not lose courage in spite of these reverses. The situation which had seemed so favourable only a day or two before had become desperate. He saw himself surrounded, hemmed in, caught in the very snare that he had laid for the enemy. No matter. He was so firmly resolved to die rather than surrender, that he retained all the presence of mind and apparent confidence which are indispensable in a commander-in-chief. He called his aides-de-camp together, and issued his orders with the promptitude and decision which are the characteristics of all great leaders. Beurnonville was to leave Réthel at once, and hasten to Sainte Menéhould, where Dumouriez would join him. Kellermann was to repair to the same spot with all possible speed. The defence of the defiles known as the Islettes and the Chalade was left to Dillon, with orders to stand firm as a rock.

These arrangements made, Dumouriez gave his undivided attention to the withdrawal of the division which he commanded in person, from Grand-Pré, where he was likely to be attacked at any moment by the whole Prussian army. Still he dared not make any visible preparations for departure, nor above all, any change in the position of his advance-guard, while daylight lasted. His embarrassment was greatly increased by the receipt of a message from the Prussian general, Prince Hohenlohe, requesting an interview with him. This proved conclusively that the enemy distrusted him, and desired to penetrate his lines.

It was impossible for him to repair to the rendezvous himself; but knowing that a refusal would excite suspicion, he sent General Duval in his stead. The prince kept his appointment; there was an interchange of civilities, and the visitor did not attempt to conceal his surprise at the order that everywhere prevailed, and at the sight of so many polite and gentlemanly officers. The *émigrés* had told the Prussians that the French army was commanded only by jewellers, shoemakers, and tailors, who did not even know how to load a cannon. Duval, who was a highly educated officer, undeceived the Prussian emissary, and explained that all the French generals had taken part in several campaigns, and that the commander-in-chief, Dumouriez, had held a high rank under the *ancien regime*. The prince certainly saw no signs of a retreat of which the officers were as yet ignorant, and Duval—who prevaricated all the more skilfully because he really supposed he was speaking the truth—announced that Beurnonville and Kellermann would reach Grand-Pré in a couple of days.

But when night came on, the advance-guard received orders to divide into three columns, and without noise, and without increasing or extinguishing its camp-fires, to take up its line of march. The right division was to pass through Marque, the central one through Chevières, and the left through Grand-Pré. They destroyed the bridges behind them. Stengel and Duval were in command. After marching a certain distance, they halted, in order to give the main body of troops time to come up;

for this advance-guard was to be converted into the rear-guard of the retreating army. At midnight, Dumouriez left the Château de Grand-Pré, which had been his head-quarters, and went to the camp. The roads were so bad, and the night was so dark, that several cannon which had been sent on in advance were lost. Dumouriez forbade the sounding of the reveille, and the order to break up the camp was passed from mouth to mouth. Less than an hour afterwards, at about two o'clock in the morning, the whole army silently marched off.

On gaining the heights of Autry, the general ordered a halt and formed his division in order of battle. By eight o'clock, the last company of soldiers had passed the bridges of Senucque and Grandchamp.

Thanks to this bold and skilful manœuvre, Dumouriez had saved his army, and placed it in a position to offer a successful resistance. Re-assured, he wrote to Danton : "I have been obliged to abandon the camp at Grand-Pré. The retreat has been made with a success that I dared not hope for. I am willing to assume the whole responsibility."

He was right to assume it. On the 20th of September, 1792, a date for-ever memorable in our history, at about three o'clock in the morning, the Prussians advanced to attack the little French army which they saw perched audaciously on the heights overlooking Valmy. A ravine separated the two armies, whose positions were extraordinary in this respect, that the French troops were facing France, while the backs of the Prussians were turned upon the country they had just invaded.

The Duke of Brunswick began the attack with a furious cannonade, thinking, as he afterwards avowed, that a dozen discharges of artillery, the whistling of cannon balls, the noise and smoke, would suffice to frighten and disperse these volunteers who were foolish enough to oppose his veterans. But he was mistaken. The Army of the Revolution maintained such an heroic attitude under fire that the duke, overcome with astonish-ment, turned to his officers and said : "See, gentlemen, see with what troops we have to deal ! Who the devil would have believed it ! "

Yes ; who would have believed that the old grenadiers of Frederick the Great, stimulated by the presence and the exhortations of their king, would have failed to capture the position occupied by Dumouriez ! Such was the case, however ; after a cannonade of more than twelve hours, after seeing his long attacking columns five times repulsed, Brunswick decided to give the order for retreat. Twice the King of Prussia, trembling with anger, ordered his generalissimo to make one last effort. "It is of no use. We shall not succeed here," replied Brunswick, despondently.

The Army of the Revolution had received its baptism of fire and won its first battle. In less than a month, the Prussians were in full retreat. Dumouriez had kept his promise ; he had saved France !

THE END.

VIZETELLY'S ONE-VOLUME NOVELS.

By English and Foreign Authors of Repute. ⊛

"The idea of publishing one-volume novels is a good one, and we wish the series every success."—*Saturday Review.*

CRIME AND PUNISHMENT.
By FEDOR DOSTOIEFFSKY.
Pronounced by the *Athenæum* to be "the most moving of all modern novels."

THE TRIALS OF JETTA MALAUBRET (Noirs et Rouges).
By VICTOR CHERBULIEZ, of the French Academy.
Translated by the Countess GASTON DE LA ROCHEFOUCAULD.

ROLAND ; or, The Expiation of a Sin.
By ARY ECILAW.
" A novel entitled 'Roland' is creating an immense sensation in Paris. The first, second, and third editions were swept away in as many days. The work is charmingly written."—*The World.*

PRINCE ZILAH.
By JULES CLARETIE.
" M. Jules Claretie has of late taken a conspicuous place as a novelist."—*Times.*

THE IRONMASTER ; or, Love and Pride.
By GEORGES OHNET. From the 146th French Edition. Sixth Edition.

A MUMMER'S WIFE.
By GEORGE MOORE. Author of "A Modern Lover." Sixth Edition.

MR. BUTLER'S WARD.
By F. MABEL ROBINSON. Third Edition.

NUMA ROUMESTAN ; or, Joy Abroad and Grief at Home.
By ALPHONSE DAUDET. Third Edition.

COUNTESS SARAH.
By GEORGES OHNET. Author of "The Ironmaster." From the 110th French Edition.

THE CORSARS ; or, Love and Lucre.
By JOHN HILL, Author of "The Waters of Marah." Second Edition.

THE THREATENING EYE.
By E. F. KNIGHT. Author of "The Cruise of the Falcon."

BETWEEN MIDNIGHT AND DAWN.
By INA L. CASSILIS. Author of "Society's Queen."

PRINCE SERGE PANINE.
By GEORGES OHNET. Author of "The Ironmaster." From the 110th French Edition.

THE FORKED TONGUE.
By R. LANGSTAFF DE HAVILLAND, M.A. Author of "Enslaved."

A MODERN LOVER.
By GEORGE MOORE. Author of "A Mummer's Wife." Second Edition.

(A.)

WAYWARD DOSIA, & THE GENEROUS DIPLOMATIST
By HENRY GRÉVILLE.
"As epigrammatic as anything Lord Beaconsfield has ever written."—*Hampshire Telegraph.*

A NEW LEASE OF LIFE, & SAVING A DAUGHTER'S
DOWRY. By E. ABOUT.
"'A New Lease of Life' is an absorbing story, the interest of which is kept up to the very end."—*Dublin Evening Mail.*
"The story, as a flight of brilliant and eccentric imagination, is unequalled in its peculiar way."—*The Graphic.*

COLOMBA, & CARMEN. By P. MÉRIMÉE.
"The freshness and raciness of 'Colomba' is quite cheering after the stereotyped three-volume novels with which our circulating libraries are crammed."—*Halifax Times.*
"'Carmen' will be welcomed by the lovers of the sprightly and tuneful opera the heroine of which Minnie Hauk made so popular. It is a bright and vivacious story."—*Life.*

A WOMAN'S DIARY, & THE LITTLE COUNTESS. By
O. FEUILLET.
"Is wrought out with masterly skill and affords reading, which although of a slightly sensational kind, cannot be said to be hurtful either mentally or morally."—*Dumbarton Herald.*

BLUE-EYED META HOLDENIS, & A STROKE OF DIPLO-
MACY. By V. CHERBULIEZ.
"'Blue-eyed Meta Holdenis' is a delightful tale."—*Civil Service Gazette.*
"'A Stroke of Diplomacy' is a bright vivacious story pleasantly told."—*Hampshire Advertiser.*

THE GODSON OF A MARQUIS. By A. THEURIET.
"The rustic personages, the rural scenery and life in the forest country of Argonne, are painted with the hand of a master. From the beginning to the close the interest of the story never flags."—*Life.*

THE TOWER OF PERCEMONT & MARIANNE. By GEORGE
SAND.
"George Sand has a great name, and the 'Tower of Percemont' is not unworthy of it."—*Illustrated London News.*

THE LOW-BORN LOVER'S REVENGE. By V. CHERBULIEZ.
"'The Low-born Lover's Revenge' is one of M. Cherbuliez's many exquisitely written productions. The studies of human nature under various influences, especially in the cases of the unhappy heroine and her low-born lover, are wonderfully effective."—*Illustrated London News.*

THE NOTARY'S NOSE, AND OTHER AMUSING STORIES.
By E. ABOUT.
"Crisp and bright, full of movement and interest."—*Brighton Herald.*

DOCTOR CLAUDE, OR, LOVE RENDERED DESPERATE.
By H. MALOT. Two vols.
"We have to appeal to our very first flight of novelists to find anything so artistic in English romance as these books."—*Dublin Evening Mail.*

THE THREE RED KNIGHTS, OR, THE BROTHERS'
VENGEANCE. By P. FÉVAL.
"The one thing that strikes us in these stories is the marvellous dramatic skill of the writers."—*Sheffield Independent.*

www.ingramcontent.com/pod-product-compliance
Lightning Source LLC
Chambersburg PA
CBHW030539040726
47497CB00008B/2509